# THORN

A novel by Chris Drnaso

Edited by: Lourdes Aguirre
Cover Photo: Ean Adams

ISBN-13: 978-1542722902 (CreateSpace-Assigned)
ISBN-10: 154272290X
Library of Congress Control Number: 2017901472
CreateSpace Independent Publishing Platform,
North Charleston, South Carolina

*Disclaimer:*

*This is a work of fiction. Names, characters, businesses, events and incidents are the products of the author's imagination. Any resemblance to actual persons, living or dead, or actual events is purely coincidental.*

*That being said, Prohibition and the Great Depression were very real. These events are essential to the telling of this story. Certain characters existed in real life. Herbert Hoover and Eliot Ness, along with other historical figures, and a plethora of real gangsters are mentioned in the book. None of these real people are major characters in this work. Every effort has been made to portray them as historically accurate as possible.*

*Author's Note:*

*You first met Reilly Thorn in CLEARING. THORN is a self-contained story. In other words, you do not need to read CLEARING first in order to appreciate THORN*

Also by Chris Drnaso

**CLEARING**

To:

# Pat Koche

My sister and my friend...

Thank you for your encouragement, your help, and your belief in your little brother as a writer.

# Thorn-1967

Prologue...

The sky mourned, as did much of the city, as the day dawned donning a heavy grey veil. This backdrop, both ominous and portentous, was moved to even greater sadness as the morning wore on. The universe struggled to hold back its tears. At times, the effort became too great, and fat droplets of rain would fall on, '....him that gives and him that takes' as Portia, according to the Bard, had told Shylock. The line of mourners started around the corner from the small chapel and ended, where much in life ends, at a casket. It was a curiously diverse crowd for 1967, as black and white faces were interspersed somewhat evenly throughout the line. Few spoke, some wept; all had their reasons to be there. A water logged edition of the Chicago Sun-Herald lay unnoticed in the gutter. The headline proclaiming, *City Mourns Hero*, lay face down in the gutter as if it too was so grieved it was trying to drown in its own lament. Below the banner is a second line reading, 'Wil and Shar-The Final Chapter'.

It is early summer in Chicago, and the article is making a reference to a series of stories that ran in the Sun-Herald since the previous Christmas. It all started innocently enough ...boy meets girl. Doesn't seem like the story of two sixteen year old kids meeting and falling in love would even merit a mention in a major metropolitan newspaper, let alone fuel a whole series of articles. The newspaper, along with radio and even some television, conspired to bring the story of these young lovers into every home in the city. The story began to take on a life of its own and eventually broke free of the city-limits and expanded nationally. The two kids were young and attractive; nothing noteworthy there. They were coworkers who had started working together the previous summer in the restaurants at the Marshall Field's State Street store. Their first jobs but, again, who would care?

Together, the two had met and made friends from throughout the city. Some afternoons, small groups of coworkers, diverse in composition, would go out after work. They might go to an arcade on Randolph Street or perhaps bowling at Marina City. The two got to know one another and then to like each other as more than just friends. Some would have called it 'puppy-love', but puppy love is still powerful mojo that is not to be taken lightly. The story is timeless and, truthfully, more than a bit pedestrian.

Somehow these two not only generated multiple newspaper articles; they also galvanized the city. Some people loved Wil and Shar while others hated them. Hate, by the way, is not an exaggeration. They, along with Barbara Ferguson who authored of the articles, received death threats. What could these two young people have done to generate this kind of reaction? They didn't kill anyone or sell state secrets to the Communists. They were God fearing Christians who both did well in school and worked towards what they hoped would be a bright future. The only noteworthy characteristic about the two was that Wil, who was in reality Billy Bellamy, was white, and Shar, more commonly known as Sharisse Sullivan, was black. Tragically, the two discovered that 1967 was the wrong time, and Chicago was the wrong place, for a young interracial couple to cultivate their seed of love in such unforgiving soil.

Allison Bentley, one of their coworkers that summer, became a friend and confidant to Sharisse. The two would talk sometimes for hours, and Sharisse would describe what she and Billy would need to do in order to create some semblance of a normal relationship. Allison, the editor of her school's literary magazine, wrote a chronicle of their trials for the magazine. The school felt it was too 'uncomfortable' of a subject for a high school publication and asked Allison to withdraw the submittal. Allison was angry and upset over the rejection and sought consolation from her father, David Bentley. Mr. Bentley, who worked in the marketing department of the Chicago Sun-Herald, read the rejected article and saw the potential of the paper picking up the story. The idea worked too well as Chicago became enchanted, enthralled, appalled, angry, and captivated with the story. Allison unwittingly became an informant. Sharisse would confide in her about the struggles she and Billy would need to endure just to be able to spend a little time together, and Allison would share those stories with her father. A recurring theme in the series was how Wil and Shar fantasized about going to a free summer concert in Grant Park.

As events leading up to the concert spun out of control, Sharisse reached out to Reilly Thorn. Reilly was a kindly character from her past who had known Sharisse as a small child. Mrs. Sullivan cleaned offices in a Chicago high rise at night and would bring Sharisse with her when she couldn't find a sitter. Reilly, a security guard in the building, grew to love the small child and became fiercely protective of her. When the building hired a new cleaning service, Sharisse's mother lost her job. Reilly was heartbroken when he never even had a chance to say goodbye to his small charge.

Billy and Sharisse were constantly challenged on where they could spend time together. Sharisse remembered a small seating area on the fourteenth floor of the high rise where, as a child, she would color or watch the ever changing street scene below while waiting for her mother to finish her shift. The unlikely couple adopted the guise of students working on a project and would enter the building late in the afternoon. The building would start to empty out at that time, and those left were more interested in getting home than in the two young people doing homework. The young couple fell in love with the small seating area and laughed that they were, 'hiding in plain sight'. Evidently, they did not hide well enough as a security guard by the name of Nick Abramowitz discerned their pattern of arrivals, always separately, and departures, again separately. When Nick finally confronted them, Sharisse mentioned Reilly's name and discovered he still worked in the building.

Sharisse and Reilly rekindled their friendship with Reilly being the one who connected the dots between Wil and Shar from the newspaper articles being in reality Billy and Sharisse. Billy and Sharisse were shocked to discover their story was widely known. They were shocked a second time to find out Nick was a bit star struck by their celebrity. He, like many followers of the articles, thought the stories were a fabrication and Wil and Shar simply a figment of someone's imagination.

As the concert approached, Sharisse became more and more concerned about the fervor their story had created. When they make the decision to attend the concert, Reilly offers to make his services available and with the help of Nick create an ad hoc security force. The police are on alert as thousands will be attending the concert and many hundreds more are expected to be on site. Many will be Wil and Shar fans but just as many are not.

The night of the concert is magical. Billy and Sharisse arrive in a limousine provided by the Sun- Herald newspaper. They are greeted by Ben 'The Old Man' Rhodes, the aging patriarch of the newspaper. Their first surprise is Jackie Bellamy and his very pregnant girlfriend Janie. Jackie is in a wheelchair, the result of injuries sustained in Viet Nam. During the course of the evening they meet celebrities and Chicago icons including Mayor Richard

J Daley and his wife Sis. The biggest surprise of the evening has been arranged by Allison Bentley. Sharisse is still angry with Allison for her part in making their relationship so public. Allison has convinced the Sun-Herald to let Sharisse sing at the concert. Simply stated, she stuns the crowd. Sharisse is approached by a record promoter after the concert who tells her the world needs to hear her voice, and he can make that happen.

The whole time, Reilly, who is across the street from the entrance, is keenly focused on the crowd. He spots a suspicious loner who he suspects of carrying a weapon. As Billy and Sharisse's limo arrives, the perpetrator makes his move. Reilly is ready. The two become entangled, a shot is fired and...

The serpentine path that steered them to a concert under the stars on that fateful night has ultimately led them, and hundreds of others, to the plain wooden coffin, in a small overcrowded chapel. Lying in state, looking peaceful with almost a hint of a smile, is the lifeless form of Reilly Thorn.

# Chapter One -1905

Reilly Thorn was born poor, dirt poor, in 1905, in a predominately agricultural area of rural Mississippi. His parents were the children of slaves. His grandfather, who also lives in the small share cropper bungalow, was a slave. The same was true of his deceased grandmother. Following the Civil War, his grandfather opted to stay in the south. He acquired a few cruel acres and began a life where he worked harder than he ever did as a slave, under worse conditions, and for less reward.

When Reilly was seven, the family had scratched out enough from the sale of most of their earthly possessions and, against the protestations of the grandfather, moved north. Reilly's father ciphered that the money in hand would get the family as far as Chicago. After that, they prayed the Good Lord would provide. The family found themselves south of the City proper, where they lived in and witnessed worse poverty than they had ever seen in Mississippi. Reilly's father found a factory job working 11 hours a day, six days a week. His mother worked in a laundry for a posh south Loop hotel. Reilly and his grandfather were always close, but they became even closer as he took on the role of parent as his folks spent so much time at work. The Thorns enrolled Reilly in a public school not far from the house. Grandfather would escort him there in the morning and be waiting for him at the end of the day. Daily they would pass a small store, which regardless of the time of day never failed to have a collection of young tough looking black youths loitering in the doorway. This group at first ignored the two until one day one of the youth stepped in front of them, effectively blocking the sidewalk. His four compatriots circled in around Reilly and his grandfather, blocking any thought of retreat. They didn't need to bother as the old man was not the retreating type.

"You boys want something?"

"Do we want something?" began the boy who was apparently the spokesperson for the group, "Well, that depends on what you got. What you got, old man?" As he said this, the door to the shop closed quietly. The unmistakable sound of a lock being engaged could be heard. As Reilly chanced a glance at the door, he could see the window blind slowly descending.

To Reilly's amazement, his grandfather threw his head back and laughed. "Shit, I ain't got shit," said the old man. "What you think? You think

1

that if I had a pocket full of money I'd be living in this shithole ghetto. What are you stupid, boy? You must be goddam stupid to be trying to hustle people in this neighborhood."

"You ought to be careful how you talk to people, old man," said the boy. He looked uncomfortable as he wasn't accustomed to anyone standing up to him. The old man had hit a nerve with him as he and his gang would be out daily trying to hustle people in this neighborhood. They often got very little for their trouble. The shop owner, who had so little to begin with, gave them a few bucks for protection. On most days, all they got from the proprietor were Cokes and maybe some candy bars. They talked about hitting the big-time and maybe robbing a downtown department store. Their talk included starting a numbers racket or dealing drugs, but they knew they had to be careful as bigger gangs operating in the neighborhood already had those markets sewn up. They would never tolerate these small-timers cutting into their action. One of the five, Luther, a lanky pencil-necked kid, had a very attractive sister, and the group got it into their collective heads that she could do well hooking on the street. They could be her protection. They were enticed by the roll of being pimps and convinced Luther to approach his sister. They followed Luther home and waited several houses away as their emissary went in with the proposition. They spent the time talking about how this could be the first pony in a whole stable full of fillies that they could put out on the street. There are now cars on the road, and the conversation had progressed to when they would buy their first automobile. Suddenly, there is a commotion from down the block. Sprinting diagonally across the street was Luther with his sister, brandishing a baseball bat, in hot pursuit.

"Well, seeing as how I ain't got shit, get the hell out of my way," said the old man, "The boy's got to get to school so he don't turn out stupid like you."

Several of the gang laughed at the old man's comment with one hulking character saying to the leader, "Let him go Jackson, why we wasting our time on this old coot for anyway?"

Jackson, not sure what to do with the old man and seeing this as the best opportunity to de-escalate the situation, stepped to the side. Inside, he was seething. He wanted to knock the old man to the ground and beat him until he showed him the respect he deserved.

2

Reilly was awed that his grandfather would talk to these hoodlums like this, and as they walked away, he said, "Grandpa, weren't you scared?"

Even though he knew they'd be late for school, the old man stopped and turned Reilly towards him. He took his small shoulders into his large gnarled hands and fixed him with an intense but kindly look. "People like that are thieves, Reilly, and you got to be careful what they steal from you. Today, they would have stolen any money we had, but I didn't care about that, mostly because I ain't got but two-dollars in my pocket. I know two-dollars don't seem like much, so why didn't I just give it to them?"

Reilly said nothing as his grandfather continued.

"Let me ask you Reilly, what do you think would happen tomorrow if I would have given them that two-dollars today?"

Reilly thought about the question. He answered with a sense of revelation, "They probably would have wanted another two-dollars tomorrow."

The old man smiled at the intuitiveness of his young charge and told him he was right. He then asked, "How do you think you'd feel after giving those punks money every day?" The question was rhetorical, and the old man continued, "You'd feel bad, and do you know why? Because every time you handed them two-dollars, they would be taking a hell of a lot more than just a couple of bucks."

Reilly nodded slowly as he let the words sink in. He didn't say anything.

The old man knew the message was received, and said, "We better get you to school or we're both going to be in trouble with your Momma, and that does scare me." Reilly laughed and took his grandfather's hand.

When they got to school, he hugged his young grandson and whispered in his ear, "Just so you know Reilly, I was scared back there. Sometimes it's smart to be scared because it makes you careful. Fear ain't a bad thing unless you let it knot you up inside."

The grandfather watched with a mixture of love and pride as Reilly ran up the stairs and disappeared into the building. He knew even at this young age that his grandson had potential, but he also knew that without the right guidance good kids could go bad in this world. He saw some of it in the South, but this hopeless neighborhood had even more potential to make that happen. He'd be damned if he'd ever let that boy end up as a street punk hanging out like the youth he saw that morning. The old-timer, nobody's fool, decided like the wise men to go home by another route, navigating himself away from the store front.

The old man had a lot to think about as he walked. Growing up in the south as a slave his universe was relatively small. He rarely left the plantation except on occasions when supplies needed to be brought from town. Under the watchful eye of an overseer, they would load sundries onto the back of a horse drawn wagon and offload the same supplies when they returned to the plantation. He considered himself fortunate as the plantation owner was a good God-fearing man. He treated the slaves well, not from any sense of altruism but more from a sound business perspective. Healthy slaves were stronger; stronger slaves were more productive. He fed them well and rested them because it made good business sense. He didn't think about whether they were happy or not as that did not concern him; the same way he would have given little thought to whether a cow in his pasture was happy. The owner didn't have a problem with runaways only in part because they were treated humanely, but mostly because they knew it was worse on other plantations. Most of the slaves believed that any of them breaking free of their bonds and escaping to the north was laughable. Occasionally, a slave would make their break for freedom and invariably be tracked down and returned. Plantation owners would herd their slaves into town where the runaway would be shackled and beaten before being dragged back to his plantation. The slaves didn't consider the runaway a hero or an inspiration. They considered him a fool.

There was one slave on a neighboring plantation whose thirst for freedom was so strong that he attempted escape not once but three times. Each time the beatings he took for his indiscretions got worse. As the slaves gathered for his third punishment, they were not led to the town pillory. Instead, they gathered around a dead tree at the edge of town. The chronic offender had been beaten so badly he needed to be half carried to the base of the tree. He was thrown to the ground while the rope was being prepared. In most hangings, the recipient is dropped quickly and is more likely to die of a broken neck as compared to asphyxiation. This slave's owner was not a man prone to violent outbursts or unnecessary cruelty, but he took this slave's actions as a personal affront to his authority. That was unacceptable. This was the opportunity to teach a lesson, and he wanted to make sure the lesson left an impression on all the slaves present. The noose end of the rope was thrown over a branch. The other end attached to a horse's saddle. The runaway was hauled to his feet. The slave's name was Samson, which was in stark contrast to the offender as he was a small man with a slight build. Reilly's grandfather looked closely at the man in the hopes of understanding why he had brought this upon himself. Blood trickled from the man's nose and ears. One eye was completely swollen shut, so Reilly's kin focused on the open eye. Within that eye, he saw a flicker of something that he didn't fully understand. There was no doubt in his mind that this man, given the opportunity, would run away a fourth time and then a fifth and a sixth. The noose was affixed, and the horse slowly began to walk, and as the old nag moved, the runaway was brought to his full height. For a brief second he attained a sort of majesty; a royal bearing. The horse took another step, and the hanging man was no longer in contact with earth. When the slave's feet were mere inches off the ground, the slave owner shouted for the horse to halt. The slave stoically hung, determined to not give his owners the satisfaction of seeing him suffer. The ballet began mere seconds later. His legs began to twitch as his body began to scream for the sweet air that was being denied. His feet desperately sought solid ground; ground that was tantalizing close and yet so far away. Following that, his entire body convulsed involuntarily. If the assembly had understood electricity, it would have looked as if the man's body was being violated with mass amounts of voltage. That was not the case. What they were seeing was the body demanding life as life was being stripped away. Soon, the dance was winding down, the song almost over. The convulsions still came but less often and less violently. The eye that Reilly's grandfather was so focused on now bulged comically as if the dying man was privy to something surprising that only he could see. The body, now completely still, swings slowly. The only sound is a mournful creaking from where the rope is in contact with the branch.

Years later this scene would be disturbingly described in the song 'Strange Fruit,' hauntingly sung by the legendary Billie Holiday.

He wasn't sure why that ancient memory came creeping back in, but it did, and it troubled him. He stopped and sat on a bench and wiped sweat from his brow.

He thought about the talk that night around the cooking fires when the slaves knew the bosses weren't within earshot. Opinions varied on whether Samson was a martyr, who should be honored and remembered as a hero, or a fool too stupid to understand the consequences of his actions. Reilly's grandfather knew the man wasn't a fool but couldn't comprehend what would compel a man to surrender sweet life itself in exchange for a slim shot at freedom. He thought now of the fire he saw in the doomed man's undamaged eye.

In his short time in the north, he witnessed something that troubled him mightily. Blacks, all confined to this impoverished ghetto, were all too often victims of crimes committed by other blacks. In all his time in the south, he rarely saw that happen. Down south the majority of blacks had nothing of value, so it was unlikely that anyone was going to steal from another man. Booze, which can lead to trouble, was forbidden in the slave quarters even though some with a taste for it would mix up batches of 'jack' out of raisins or other fruits. His owner would preach scripture to the slaves, and many fearing eternal damnation and not wanting to risk the promised rewards of heaven, willingly lived by the Commandments.

Reilly's grandfather as a young man, knew of a beautiful young Nubian who had caught the eye of the plantation owner. The master knew the longing he felt was wrong, and he prayed for strength, but the urges became stronger. He took to watching her work and became entranced by her supple movements. The tattered shift she wore was both tight and threadbare. As she walked, her buttocks swayed in a most pleasing manner. Her bosoms stretched against the thin fabric. In the hopes it would cool his passions, the owner presented the girl with a new dress. He made sure it was too big and made of a heavier material. It achieved the opposite effect as the owner found her even more desirable.

One late afternoon, the overseer appeared at the shack she shared with her husband. He ordered the girl to bathe and put on the house dress he had slung over his arm, and left with the simple order, "The boss needs you up at the house."

Crying, she ran to her husband, a powerfully built young man as he folded his massive arms around her. "Go on now," is all he said. Her husband knew what was happening but also knew that when these things occurred he was better off choking back his anger and frustration. Anything he did would only bring heartbreak to him and perhaps all the slaves. Still crying, she undressed and began washing herself with a bucket they kept for this purpose. She dutifully put on the dress and left for the night. The husband, angry and distraught, left the meager little shack, eventually finding his way to the cooking fires where slaves gathered in the evening to talk or sing. Most knew what was going on, and all but one said nothing. The offender, a slim troublesome slave named Alphonse, began taunting the big man. The more the other slaves told him to back down, the more the taunts came. The big man sat with his head hung, his shoulders slumped. He knew Alphonse had designs on his wife as she would tell him how he would cautiously approach her at times he felt it was safe to do so. The husband would let these indiscretions pass as he trusted his wife and knew that Alphonse was prone to stir up trouble in the quarters. Slaves were good at letting things roll off their backs as every day held the potential for both mental and physical abuse. The rule for survival was understood to be, *'you got to go along to get along'*.

Alphonse took a perverse pleasure in seeing the pain he was inflicting on the big man. This emboldened him to escalate the abuse. When things happened, they happen quickly. Afterwards, those present would agree that it looked as if the big man had been shot out of a cannon as he flew across the fire and landed with his full weight on the slight man. He pummeled his face several times with his powerful fists before wrapping his massive hands around the man's thin neck. Now all the slaves were gathered around with one shouting, "He's gonna kill him. Someone go get the boss." Two or three men were on each side of the big man tugging on his huge arms and begging him to let go. Then, as quickly as it started, it was over. The tension went out of the big man's back and shoulders. He released the grip on the thin neck as the man gulped in huge mouthfuls of air. The hulking man wept openly as others led him away.

"What's going on here!" asked the overseer, a rifle at the ready.

Collectively, the slaves said all the things they knew would placate the supervisor. "Nothin' to worry about here, boss", and "They was just a little misunderstanding, boss; everybody be OK now."

The overseer saw the big man still choking back tears and the impish Alphonse slowly righting himself into a sitting position. He knew what was going on with the buck's wife, and he knew Alphonse was a troublemaker. It wasn't difficult to puzzle together what had happened.

"Alright, I don't want any more trouble tonight. Get to bed, it's late", and on that note he went back to the edge of a small copse of trees and stood in the shadows until he was sure the incident had passed.

As the grandfather sat on the bench, there was no question about why that memory resurfaced after so many years. It was one of the few examples of black on black violence he had witnessed in all of his years living as both a freeman and a slave in the south.

## Chapter Two

Grandfather continued to walk Reilly to and from school. On the first day after the encounter with the delinquents, Reilly asked the old man if they could take a different route. His grandfather laughed and said there was no need for that even though that is exactly what he would have liked to do. The two groups settled into an uneasy truce for the next week with the gang of young toughs adopting an apathetic air towards the duo. Almost as if they couldn't be bothered with anything as inconsequential as Reilly and the old man. As they would pass, the old man would sneak a glance at Jackson, the leader of the group, and he knew the boy hadn't forgotten the incident or forgiven the old man's impertinence. The old man continued walking past the storefront on the way to school as he felt it taught the boy a valuable life lesson but took a more circumspect route home. The alternate route took him through a less populous but every bit as impoverished part of the neighborhood. He walked with his thoughts in the clouds, his guard down. As he passed an alleyway, he was grabbed roughly and pulled into the midst of the small gang.

"What you got now old man?" asked Jackson.

The old man, trying to muster a courage he did not feel, said, "Shit, I ain't got...."

He never got the last word out as Jackson sent a roundhouse punch into the side of the old man's head. Within seconds, like wolves the pack was on him. Swinging and kicking wildly as the old man crumpled to the ground. He tried to protect his head as the blows violated every part of his body.

One of the attackers said, "Let's get the hell out here."

Jackson sends one more kick into the old man's side, splintering two ribs. Before fleeing, he breathlessly said, "You got shit now old man?" and just that quickly they were gone.

The old man lay perfectly still trying to control his breathing as he took inventory of his wounds. Every breath hurt like hellfire, and he correctly deduced his ribs were broken. One eye was swollen shut, and for the second time in a week he thought about the slave lynching he had seen as a young boy in the south. That man had been beaten in a quest for freedom. Reilly's grandfather wasn't sure why he had been beaten so badly. He knew he might die in this alley if he didn't get some help. Out of his one good eye he could see the entrance to the alley an impossibly long ways away. In reality, it was but fifty-feet. Standing wasn't an option, so instead, he tried to get to his knees. The pain was incredible, but he managed to move a few feet and then a few more. Within feet of the street, his will and his strength gave out, and he collapsed. He lay unconscious. At one point, he sensed somebody rifling through his pockets and then heard this unknown person running off. He slipped back over the edge of consciousness.

"Hey, hey old timer, are you OK?" he was asked as he felt the gentle shaking of his shoulders. Slowly, he made the climb back towards consciousness. As his vision comes into focus, he sees a police officer on one knee bending over him. The grandfather tries to get up on one elbow but immediately slumps back down. His next recollection is jostling over an uneven road; every bump sends ripples of pain through his fragile frame.

Later, he has no idea of how much later, he awakens in a strange bed in what he correctly assumes to be a hospital. He can feel bandages tightly wrapped around his head. The same is true of his chest. He remembers the indignity of the final kick and the sickening sound of frail bones breaking. A woman in white, a nurse, is busy with things that are out of the sight of his one good eye. No, he sees more of the habit. She is not a nurse. She is a nun. She, in reality, is both.

"Oh good, you're awake," she says with a warm smile. She gently caresses the side of his face and tells him he is too old to be getting into street fights. "The doctor will want to see you now that you're once again back amongst the living. I can let you have a sip of water if you'd like."

In a raspy voice he says, "Yes, please."

A short time later the doctor is waking him. His manner is brusquer than the nun as he says little while he examines the old man. He peers into his unbandaged eye and asks the patient to follow his finger back and forth. The exam is a short one. The doctor stops on his way out and talks to the nurse at the doorway. He's a good doctor but didn't like the idea that a Negro had been brought to this hospital. He knows there are black-only options for him in his own neighborhood, and he should have been brought there instead. He was relieved that he wasn't the doctor on staff when he was brought in as he didn't like to touch black people. There are more and more times that he has been forced to examine blacks during the course of his day, and it is upsetting to him. On those days, he would scrub extra hard before returning home to his wife and children.

The grandfather recognized the doctor's uneasiness as he had been around enough whites that shared the doctor's attitude.

"So, am I going to live?" he asks as the nun approaches. She assures him he will and lets him have some more water.

"Do you feel strong enough to receive some visitors? There are several people waiting who are very concerned about you."

The family; his son, daughter-in-law, and Reilly, fairly fly into the room. They surround the bed and all begin talking at once. The nun quickly restores order. She tells them in a no-nonsense voice that this is going to be a short visit, and following that, she's throwing them all out so her patient can get his rest.

"Is that understood?" she asks. Even though she is delivering a harsh message, there is a kindness in her eyes. They quickly nod in agreement. She tells them they have ten minutes and then visiting hours are over. One reason the nun wants to hustle them out is because the police officer who found him in the alley has returned and also wants to ask him a few questions. Curiously, the family's questions will closely align with the cop's questions.

His son starts gently, "Dad, what happened? Reilly told us about some street gang you're having trouble with. Did they do this?"

The old man is able to see Reilly who appears embarrassed about telling his father these details. Reilly looks away. The grandfather says nothing. Further prodding from the son yields no additional information. His wife asks him to drop the subject. She knows her father-in-law can be a stubborn old goat, and when he sets his mind to a thing, it stays set. They spend the remainder of the time saying little. Instead, they busy themselves making sure their patriarch is comfortable. Water is offered, pillows are fluffed, and lips are sealed tight.

The nun reappears with a police officer in tow. The cop can see and feel the entire family tense at his arrival. It is almost as if the room temperature has dropped dramatically. He recognizes this reaction from his work in predominately black neighborhoods. It's not an assignment any in his precinct volunteer for, but as he has more tolerance or empathy for the plight of the blacks, he finds himself assigned to the black ghetto often. He introduces himself to the family and asks them to wait outside while he talks to the injured man.

After they exit, he approaches the bed. He's a big man with a ruddy face and red hair. The polished name plate pinned to his chest reads, *McMahon*. "Well, I must say you look a bit better than when first we met," he begins, "I'm the one what found you taking a wee-nap in the alley." There is no reaction from the old man. "Tis a shame too as you missed a lovely day today. The sky was as blue as Robin's eggs, and the air had a sweetness to it that you could almost taste. T'was lovely. Surely it t'was."

The old man, caught off guard, chances a look at the inquisitor. He is treated to a warm smile. The police officer continues, "So, do you have any plans for the evening, or do you believe you'll remain here a bit longer? You may want to leave before dinner. I hear the cuisine is not good. Tis a hospital dedicated to healing the sick, but as I understand it, the meatloaf kills off its share of patients."

The old man smiles in spite of his best efforts to remain disinterested.

The big cop feigned not to notice and went right on, "They serve something called 'shit on a shingle' that was responsible for the deaths of no less than two-hundred people last year." The old man laughed out loud and immediately winced in pain. "Oh, careful there old timer, my bad jokes have killed off more than a few people as well." The cop placed a beefy hand on the frail shoulder and asked with warm sincerity, "Would you like to tell me what happened today?"

"I must have fallen down," said the old man, looking away.

"Hmmm, I thought that might have been the case. Had a fella just last week that, according to witnesses, took a nasty fall. He died right on the spot. It had nothing to do with the three bullets they dug out of him, mind you. Yes sir, those falls can be a nasty business." The police officer continued, "I don't like my citizens getting beaten up on my watch. Those are my streets out there, and I like to keep my streets clean. If you tell me who did this, you can help me in my job. If you don't, then how am I going to help you or others?"

The old man wasn't used to being this familiar with white people. Most of his life whites had simply ordered him around. Here was a white man, in a position of power, who was treating him with respect. He asked himself why he was being so resistant. Why not just tell the cop what he knew and be done with it. Instead, he turned towards the wall, and with that, the interrogation was over.

The nun led the officer to a small seating area where the Thorns were waiting. He introduced himself and was greeted in turn by mumbled hellos and virtually no eye contact. No surprise there. Reilly's father told the cop what his son had told him; that they had run afoul of some street toughs they encountered on their way to school. The young boy was mostly hidden behind his mother while his father spoke.

When his father finished the retelling of the little he knew, Officer McMahon smiled warmly at the young boy, saying, "Your grandfather is a brave man, but somehow feels he has to protect these hoodlums. I hope you don't feel the same way young man." Reilly said nothing. The officer continued, "Reilly, do you know who did this to your grandfather?"

Reilly thought back to the look his grandfather had given him moments ago at his bedside. The look unquestionably told Reilly to say nothing. He wanted to tell the cop the whole story but didn't want to disappoint his grandfather. He mumbled something about not knowing anything about what might have happened.

Before saying his goodbyes, he took a knee by the young boy so they could talk eye to eye. "Reilly, if you should happen to remember anything, you come on down to the station and ask for me. Would you do that for me?" He thanked them for their time and left.

# Chapter Three

The next morning was a school day as well as a work day. His parents couldn't jeopardize their jobs by not showing up, so they asked Reilly if he could walk to school by himself. He assured them that he could even though he feared another encounter with the street thugs.

As he turned the corner, which would take him past the storefront, he saw the gang milling around. As he got closer, Jackson stepped in front of the boy. Reilly felt his knees go weak. He suddenly needed to urinate.

"Hey boy," asked Jackson, "Where's the old coot this morning?" When Reilly said nothing, Jackson continued, "I hope he learned a lesson. I own this street and ain't nobody going to disrespect me or my boys here. Isn't that right, boys?" Jackson's crew nodded their agreement.

Reilly thought of his grandfather and knew that he would be disappointed if he showed fear. The smug look on Jackson's face infuriated the young boy. He thought of his grandfather still busted up in a hospital bed and these losers crowing about it like beating up an old man somehow made them big shots.

"What are you gonna do? Are you gonna cry little man?" asked the leader derisively even though he saw more hatred in those eyes than tears.

The young boy took a step forward and fixed the much larger boy with a menacing stare. "You're going to get yours, Jackson. You can't go around beating up people and acting like a tough guy."

Everyone, including Jackson, laughed at this inconsequential threat. They now surround Reilly. One of the gang shoved Reilly from behind, asking, "What you gonna do, little man? Teach us a lesson." Reilly is spun around and sent flying into another boy as the taunts rain down upon him. They are too caught up in their little game of ping-ponging him back and forth to notice Officer McMahon sidle up behind them.

"Good morning Reilly," he announces in a rich lyrical voice. With his arrival all activity stops immediately. Reilly looks at the big uniformed man with a combination of love, respect, and thankfulness and understands at this moment in his young life what he wants to dedicate his life to.

"Reilly, why don't you get on to school and let me talk to your friends here?"

Reilly never knew what the police officer told those punks that day, but he must have put the fear of God into them as they never said another word to Reilly or his grandfather again. Reilly anxiously waited for his parents to get home that evening and, over a sparse meal, told them both what had happened on the way to school. His mother said a silent prayer of thanksgiving for the policeman's intervention. His father chastised him for not saying something the day before about the troubles he and his grandfather were having. Before they got up from the table, Reilly told both of them that he was going to be a policeman. It's not unusual for a child to announce to his parents what they want to be when they grow up. Often the choices change weekly from cowboy, to nurse, to President of the United States. Both his mother and father took pause when he made the announcement as he said it with such conviction, they could almost believe that Reilly would be a police officer someday.

They cleaned up quickly before heading to the hospital where grandfather would need to stay one more day. When they arrived they were surprised to find Officer McMahon at his bedside. He greeted them warmly, explaining that he had other business in the hospital and decided to stop in and say hello. His real agenda had been to see if the old man could be convinced to press charges against Jackson and his gang. He was not surprised when the victim resolutely refused to do any such thing. The family thanked the big man repeatedly for helping Reilly that morning. When McMahon left the room, he was surprised that Reilly had followed him out into the hallway. He turned and smiled warmly at the young man.

"And what can I do for you today, Reilly?"

Without hesitation, Reilly answered, "I want to be a policeman when I grow up."

The big man looked to the ceiling and rubbed his chin reflectively before bending at the waist, looking Reilly directly in the eye, and replied, "After the way I saw you stand up to those hooligans today Reilly, I think you would make a very good police officer. The force could use a man like you. Someone who's bright and brave."

Reilly beamed at the endorsement.

"Now keep in mind policing is hard work. You've got to stay in school and study hard. You've got to stay out of trouble because they would never allow a trouble maker to join the force."

The boy struggled to continue, and when he did, he said hesitantly, "I'm a Negro."

The big officer studied the boy closely, and answered, "Hmmm, so you are. It's funny, I hadn't noticed that before."

The boy understood he was being teased, "I mean, would they let a Negro become a policeman?"

"I'm told there have been police officers of your ilk on the force since shortly after the Civil War. There are not many as near as I can tell, but I've served with a few of them, and I can tell you they were fine men and good officers."

"May I tell you a story, lad? Have you heard of a place called Ireland?" Without waiting for an answer, McMahon continued, "Ireland is a beautiful and enchanted island on the other side of a great sea. My family came from Ireland around fifty years ago. They didn't want to leave their beloved island, but hard times were the only thing they had too much of. They were forced to look for a new home. They came to America because they thought it was a land of great hope and opportunity, but when they arrived they found something much different. My people came to places like New York and Boston where, instead of the good life they hoped for, they found hatred and resentment. Well, about this same time a lot of black people were coming to these same places from their life of slavery in the south. At first they were runaways, but later on they were emancipated, but no matter how they ended up in these places, they were not welcome and weren't treated any better than the Irish. My grandfather was the first of my family to come to this great land. He would tell of how he was not even allowed to apply for work as at the bottom of help wanted signs would be written, *'Positively no Irish need apply'*. My grandfather found himself begging for jobs that no one else wanted and competing for those jobs with the Negros who had come up from the southern states. It was an ugly time for both our people. The saddest thing my grandfather told us was that some of the Irish who met them as their boats landed treated them worse than anyone else. These scoundrels were called 'runners' and cheated their own people terribly. Grandfather said it broke his heart to hear someone telling lies and making empty promises in his beloved Gaelic tongue."

Reilly thought about Jackson and his gang.

"But the strong and the clever are always going to figure out a way to survive," said the big man. He finished by saying, "There are going to be times in your life where being a Negro is going to be a problem for you or someone else, but never let that keep you from being who and what you want to be."

Reilly politely thanked him and headed back to his grandfather's bedside. Officer McMahon watched as he walked away, and like the boy's parents, believed that Reilly might indeed don the uniform one day.

# Chapter Four

The more Reilly saw of his neighborhood, the more he knew he wanted to dedicate his life to law enforcement. He grew strong and tall as he ventured into his teen years. Everything Reilly did from the moment he decided to join the force, until the day he applied for the Academy, was done to better his chances of becoming a police officer. He studied hard at school and consistently finished at the top of his class. Given the curriculum, he didn't consider this a great accomplishment as he rarely felt challenged by the day's lesson plans. He read voraciously to help round out the education he felt was lacking in school. He discovered a gym in the neighborhood and convinced the owner to let him help around the place in exchange for membership. It was a boxing gym and would be Reilly's first introduction to the sport. There was a ring in the back of the gym. A common fixture at ringside was an ancient relic of a black man who went by the name of Uppercut most of the time, but Reilly heard many refer to him as UC. Occasionally, Reilly would watch UC train a member.

One day Uppercut saw the boy observing from a safe distance. "What you lookin' at, boy?"

Looking embarrassed, Reilly mumbled an apology and went back to sweeping.

"Come here, boy," said Uppercut. As Reilly approached, UC pointed to the trainee who was currently skipping rope. He whispered conspiratorially, "You see that guy? He could be a good boxer, but he don't like to work hard enough to get there."

Reilly looked at the trainee and thought the guy looked fit enough to punch a hole in a brick wall. He was jumping rope like a mad man and sweating profusely. "He looks to be working pretty hard right now, sir," answered Reilly.

"Ahhh," Uppercut said dismissively, and asked, "Are you a hard worker Reilly?"

"Yes," replied Reilly simply, surprised that Uppercut knew his name.

"I knew you was," said UC, with a smile lacking several teeth, "I see you hustling around here. You don't never wait to be told what to do. You just do it. I like that."

Reilly thanked him. He thought back to what he had heard about Uppercut from the gym owner; that he was an accomplished fighter in his day. Reilly had a hard time picturing it as he looked at the old man.

When UC asked him if he ever thought about putting on the gloves, Reilly replied that he had never given it much thought. The truth was that he had thought about it. The men he saw training looked to be in great shape. He also thought that the ability to throw and take a punch might be a useful skill for a policeman to have.

"I'll tell you what," said UC, "If you do give it some thought, you come see me and we'll get you started."

"I don't have much money,"

"The first thing I'm gonna do is train your heart. If you got the heart for this and I think you're worth training, then we'll talk about money."

When Reilly told him his next scheduled shift in the gym was the following afternoon, Uppercut told him to run a mile and a half before then. Reilly completed the run, and that was the way their relationship started. Every day that Reilly worked, UC would ask if he had done what he was told and then give him a new set of tasks to complete before his next shift. His instructions always included running. In addition, he skipped rope, much to his grandfather's disdain.

"You look like a damn sissy skipping rope like that. Why don't you do that in the alley so you don't embarrass your family?" the old man would ask.

Reilly didn't fully understand everything Uppercut asked him to do, but he liked the old man, and he liked working out. Several weeks into his training, he thought back to the mile and a half that had left him winded on his first day. That seemed like a joke now.

On the days he trained at the gym, UC had him working his core with hundreds of sit ups and intense work with a medicine ball. When Uppercut would catch Reilly looking at the heavy bag and the speed bag, he would chasten him with, "You ain't near enough ready for that yet." Following that, there would be more sit ups and more wind sprints. Oddly enough they hardly ever touched weights. This surprised Reilly and he asked about it one day. Uppercut told him it was a stupid question. Next, he told him to go run two-miles and think about it.

He met several of Uppercut's other trainees who were all much older, which meant they were in their late teens or early twenties. They all told Reilly the same thing, 'Hang in there and Uppercut would turn him into a boxer'. Several of his protégés fought matches of note as undercards and occasionally they were featured as the main event. One night Reilly was able to go to a match and went with several other members from the gym. Boxing would remain a banned sport in Illinois for several more years but that didn't keep these types of unsanctioned events from happening throughout the City. The ban was the result of rampant corruption in the sport in the late 1800s.

He was surprised when his grandfather asked if he could go along. Reilly and his grandfather had forged a wonderful relationship and were closer now than ever. Grandfather was spry for his age even though he or no one in the family knew what his true age was. Reilly tried to figure it out one time by asking his grandfather what his age might have been at the time of important historical events. The plan worked horribly as he either had no recollection of the event, or when he did, he had no idea of how old he had been at the time. All the family knew was that he was old; very old. Reilly was well into his high school years by this time, and the roles of the two had changed dramatically. As a child, his grandfather had been Reilly's protector, to the best of his ability, when out in the world. Now, as they were leaving for the boxing match, his father pulled Reilly to the side and asked him to watch out for his grandfather. They met three other boxers at the gym before they all made their way to the arena. The venue could hold hundreds of people, and there were plenty of seats still available for the earlier fights. Having gotten there early, they were able to secure seats close to the action. The second of the two undercard events was a tremendous match. It went the distance with each of the two lightweight boxers giving it their all. After the final bell, both men were called to the center of the ring. By this time, the place was packed well beyond capacity. Acrid blue-grey smoke hung like a heavy sheet over the ring. Reilly felt the thrill of expectation as he couldn't decide which of the men deserved the victory. The ref held each fighter's wrist. Finally, he raised one arm as a cheer went up from the crowd. Reilly's cheer was for both men. In a time honored tradition, the two men faced each other, touched gloves, and headed back to their corner to be either congratulated or consoled.

The anticipation in the arena grew as the main event drew closer. Vendors went through the crowd selling beer in bottles. They were doing a brisk trade, and Reilly was surprised when his grandfather produced a quarter and made his purchase. He smiled at Reilly and his friends, raising the bottle in a salute. His grandfather was having a grand time and had an animated reaction to every punch thrown. The men from the gym appreciated his enthusiasm and laughed as he shadow boxed from his seat. Now, an announcer entered the ring as the crowd hushed. As he introduced Uppercut and his fighter, the crowd turned their attention to the area where the fighters would make their entrance. They made their way up the aisle to a smattering of applause. The moment was magical for Reilly as a sense of pride swept over him at the sight of his trainer. He recognized the fighter from the gym, a heavy weight by the name of Angel Vasquez with huge shoulders and big hands. He looked resplendent in a deep blue robe. Emblazoned across the back of the robe were the words 'Al's Gym', the name of the gym where Reilly worked. A stool was produced, and the big man took a seat. Uppercut leaned over so he was face to face with his fighter, giving him directions as the second fighter entered the ring. Reilly, from his seat, could 'feel' the intensity of UC's final instructions. One of Uppercut's trainees from the gym, a welter-weight named Andre Montero, leaned over to Reilly and told him the favorite always entered the ring last.

"Do you think we have a chance?" asked Reilly.

"Angel's gonna have his hands full. If he's still around after the first two rounds, he might be able to pull it off," he replied, and went on to say that he was going to be just about impossible to knock out after the second round. "The other guy knows that, and he's going to give him everything he has in the early rounds. This should be one hell of a fight."

At the opening bell, the favorite came out of his corner like he was launched from a slingshot. He pummeled Angel with blow after blow with Uppercut screaming, "Cover, cover, cover," throughout the entire round.

Both fighters made their way to their corners after the first round. Reilly turned to Andre, saying, "Angel's getting killed out there. He barely threw a punch."

"Keep watching," was all Montero said.

The second round was a carbon copy of the first, which left Reilly wondering why he had ever allowed Uppercut to be his trainer. When Andre saw the bewildered look on Reilly's face, he asked him if he was starting to notice anything.

Reilly answered, "You mean besides Angel being beaten half to death?"

At the start of the third round, the favorite once again charged out of his corner and began raining blows down on Angel. Before the half-way point of the round, he was still punching but now with a lot less energy. Andre elbowed Reilly in the ribs, "Are you watching this?" he asked. Uppercut was up and screaming, "Step in! Step in!" and Angel did. Before the end of the round, Angel threw a series of well-placed, well-calculated punches. Each found their target with one rocking the favorite back on his heels. The fourth round found the favorite being danced backwards around the ring as Angel continued his surgical assault. At the two minute mark of the fifth round, the challenger had backed his opponent into a corner where he landed alternating blows to his head and mid-section. The favorite was having trouble keeping his hands up defensively when Angel wheeled back and let a ferocious blow fly. His target was the man's chin, and he landed a direct hit. He was ready to follow this with a second assault when he saw his opponents eyes roll back in his head. The man's arms dropped limply to his side. Angel stepped back, allowing room for gravity to finish its work. As the big man collapsed onto the mat, the entire ring shook.

# Chapter Five

The next day Reilly hurried to the gym and immediately sought out his trainer. "Uppercut, that was amazing last night," he complimented the old man.

"I saw you boys there," replied the trainer. "Did you get your road work in yesterday?"

The look on Reilly's face gave the old man his answer. Reilly started to explain that between school and working and the boxing match, he hadn't had time. Before he could finish, Uppercut turned and began walking away. The young trainee was flooded with a variety of emotions. He was angry at Uppercut as he had worked so hard and had faithfully done everything he had been asked. Mostly, he felt disappointment in himself for letting Uppercut down.

Uppercut turned and walked back to Reilly, "So what did you learn last night?" he asked his young protégé. Reilly thought for a moment and replied that you needed to be smart in the ring. Uppercut smiled at him and told him that maybe there was hope for him yet. As Uppercut walked away, he called back over his shoulder, "Four-miles today. That's two; two-mile runs with wind sprints in between." Reilly smiled at the man's back. He couldn't wait to get started.

One day, as Reilly was getting close to graduating high school, two events happened that would change his life. The year is 1923. Reilly walked into *Al's Gym* after school, and displayed on the wall near the locker room was a poster advertising something called the *Golden Gloves*. The first Golden Gloves tournament was held in the Chicago Stadium. A columnist and boxing fan by the name of Arch Ward came up with the idea, and his newspaper, the Chicago Tribune, sponsored the event. This amateur event tested the state's anti-boxing laws. It would take four more years for amateur boxing to become legal.

Reilly knew upon seeing the poster that he wanted to know more about the event. He was anxious to test himself outside of the relative safety of *Al's Gym*. His training had moved well past road work, sit-ups, pull-ups, and jumping rope. Now, as part of his normal workout, there was time spent pounding away on the heavy bag as well as the speed bag. His technique on the speed bag, which he loved, was among the best in the gym. Even though his routine included almost no weight training, Reilly had grown strong and muscular. Occasionally, he would spar with Andre Montero, the only other welterweight in the gym. Andre was older by several years and lighter by four pounds on most days. Their bouts were spirited and good natured as the older boy played the part of a mentor to the young boxer. On days that he was scheduled to spar, Reilly's grandfather would make the trip to the gym and stay in Reilly's corner, much to Uppercut's consternation. It was UC's style to bring both boxers together between rounds and give instructions. It was grandfather's style to contradict him. The two would often argue to the point that Andre and Reilly would need to separate the two men. On the day that his grandfather invited Uppercut into the ring to settle a dispute, Reilly pulled his grandfather to the side and threatened to ban him from the gym if he didn't behave himself. After much convincing and more threats, he persuaded his grandfather to shake hands with Uppercut and apologize. He wasn't happy about it, but Uppercut was very gracious. Following that, grandfather began showing up at the gym more often even at times when Reilly wasn't around. Reilly was happy when he realized the two men were becoming friends.

The second event that changed Reilly's life, much more profoundly than the Golden Gloves poster, happened one day as he and Andre were sparing. Lighter fighters tend to be quicker, and at 143 pounds, Andre's hands moved like lightning. It was difficult for Reilly to be too offensive in the ring as Montero could turn any assault from Reilly into an opportunity to land a punch. That being the case, it forced Reilly to be cautiously defensive during their bouts. Their fights were like chess matches. As was tradition, most training would be suspended during a match, and the fraternity of boxers from throughout the gym would gravitate to the ring to offer encouragement to the contenders. The fighters were barely conscious of their audience, but on this particular day between rounds, Reilly caught site of a girl standing at ringside. He had rarely seen a girl in the gym, and when he saw her, he could barely concentrate on anything except her. He thought she was beautiful.

"Reilly, are you paying attention! What's wrong with you today?" demanded Uppercut.

Almost as if shaken out of a trance, he looked at Uppercut as if he was surprised to see him. "Sorry, UC," he mumbled.

At the sound of the bell, both fighters met at center ring and touched gloves. That might have been construed as the closest Reilly came to throwing a punch. Andre stepped in cautiously, saw an opportunity, and landed a right followed by a series of three quick left jabs. None were knockout punches nor did Reilly make much of an effort to block them. Andre took a step backwards trying to understand this new ploy by the young fighter. To his amazement, Reilly was spending more time looking at the young girl at ringside than he was at him. To complete the bizarre picture, Reilly had what can only be described as the goofiest look in the world on his face. Reilly didn't notice that Andre had quit punching him. He didn't notice that the other fighters in the gym were having a good laugh at his expense. What did get his attention was seeing Uppercut standing next to the girl with his arms folded across his chest. He does not look happy. Uppercut whispers something to the girl, who then departs quickly. Reilly slowly comes out of his trance, but the goofy look is still plastered onto his face. One of the first things he notices is the sound of laughter and can't imagine what's so funny. He sees Andre looking at him, gloved hands on his knees, laughing harder than anyone. His grandfather is shaking his head with a bewildered look on his face. Even Uppercut looks less mad and more amazed by what has just happened. Reilly doesn't care because he knows something that none of the other's do. He has just seen the girl he is going to spend the rest of his life with.

"If you think I'm gonna let my granddaughter get mixed up with a fighter, you got rocks in your head, boy," Uppercut replied when Reilly sought him out at the end of his workout and boldly asked about the young lady he had seen at ringside.

"I'm not a fighter," answered Reilly. "I'm going to be a policeman."

"You're damn right you're not a fighter. You looked like a damn fool in the ring today. Everyone laughing and carrying on. You disrupted the whole place. I'm mad at Andre too for not knocking the hell out of you when you were standing there looking stupid."

They are all huddled together in a small equipment room at the back of the gym. Reilly's grandfather is at his shoulder. "Well, that's good that you feel that way because if she's your granddaughter, then she ain't near good enough for my grandson," he tells Uppercut.

Reilly groans.

Now the two men are nose to nose, animatedly explaining why each of their progenies is too good for the other.

The next day Reilly enters the gym, blessedly without his grandfather, and once again seeks out Uppercut. He asks again about his granddaughter and is encouraged that this time UC doesn't seem angry. "Sit down Reilly," he tells the boy. "Sissy is precious to me. She grew up without a daddy, and I've always been protective of her, probably too protective. Last night when I got home, I thought about the kind of boy I'd like to see her with, and I had to admit that boy would be a lot like you."

Reilly grins broadly.

"Now see, there you go again with that stupid look on your face," said the trainer. "I guess you made an impression on her as well because she asked me about you. Now don't let that go to your head. She wanted to know if there was something wrong in that melon of yours to stand there in the middle of a boxing ring letting the other guy hit you like that. I told her I knew your grandfather was crazy and that maybe it ran in the family."

With great trepidation, Reilly asks if it would be all right if he was to call on her; perhaps take her out for a walk along the lake. Uppercut's advice is to come by the house on Sunday afternoon after church. He cautions the lad with, "If you think I'm protective of her, wait until you meet her mama."

## Chapter Six

Reilly courted Sissy through the rest of high school. She didn't like the idea of him boxing but knew he didn't have long term plans of staying with the sport. She was in the audience the night he fought in the first Golden Gloves event ever held. This inaugural event was a six-night mini–Olympics where young people from one ethnic neighborhood could go toe to toe with young boxers from other areas of the city. The event, which started in Chicago in 1923, would eventually reach all corners of the globe.

Sissy was sandwiched in between grandfather and Andre Montero. Uppercut was in Reilly's corner to offer encouragement and help anyway he could. UC was not able to study or watch Reilly's opponent prior to the fight, which was frustrating.

"Reilly, I don't know anything about this kid except that he's a Dago from the south side. He's probably poor and hungry to make a name for himself. He wants to use you, Reilly. He wants to give you the beating of your life because you're standing in between him and what he wants. Don't look at me, Reilly, look at him. To him, you're just some nappy haired nigger that's trying to take what's his."

At this last comment, Reilly snapped his head towards Uppercut.

"Why are you looking at me, boy? I told you to look at him. You see that look on his face. That look means he don't respect you. He thinks you're a nothing from nowhere, and he's about to show the world that he's arrived." Uppercut continued, "You're strong, Reilly. You're strong and you're fast but more important than that; you're smart. He don't think niggers are smart, but you're smart as hell and about to show the world that Reilly Thorn is one strong, fast, smart nigger."

Sissy's heart sank as the bell heralded the start of the bout. She began a silent prayer as the two fighters approached one another. She didn't get too far into her petition as before the halfway mark of the first round, Reilly stood over the motionless form of his opponent. In his corner, Uppercut's assistant leaned over and whispered into his ear, "He does realize that you're the one who called him a nigger, right?" At that, both men laughed as Reilly's arm was raised into the air.

Also in the audience that night was Tommy McMahon, who waited for Reilly outside of the venue. Officer McMahon had kept in touch with Reilly off and on throughout the years. He would occasionally stop in at the gym and either watch Reilly train or to simply say hello. He took pride in Reilly's development over the years. Now, as Reilly was about to graduate from high school, he was still committed to becoming a police officer, and Tommy McMahon had committed to being his sponsor. Black officers were still a bit of an oddity in the department, but if a young man of color had a clean record, he might get on the force. Having a white officer pulling for him from the inside didn't hurt either.

As Reilly approached, McMahon noticed the pretty young girl walking with him and assumed this was Sissy. Reilly had mentioned her several times, and the big cop suspected his young protégé was in love. Of course, rounding out the threesome was the ancient form of the grandfather.

As introductions are made, McMahon smiles at Sissy and says, "Reilly said you were pretty but didn't do you justice." Both Reilly and Sissy blush at the comment.

"Did you see Reilly tonight, Officer?" asked grandfather, who always referred to the big man as 'officer'. "I've been helping with his training you know," grandfather continued as Reilly snuck a sly smile at the policeman.

"I could tell," said McMahon, "Reilly, did you have a past with that boy? I've never seen you look angry before, but you looked to have a personal vendetta against him." Reilly mumbled a 'no' as he thought back to Uppercut's words before the bout. He realized now that his trainer had pushed all the right buttons before the match. Thinking back to the young Italian fighter laying in a clump in the middle of the ring, he felt bad.

Following the event, Reilly's interest in boxing waned even though Uppercut told him in all seriousness that he had the potential to make a living in the sport. "I told you when I first met you that I would train you if you showed me heart, and you showed it to me in spades. You got more heart than any fighter I ever trained." When Reilly asked his ancient trainer, friend, and mentor if he was disappointed in him, he smiled at the boy and said, "The only way you'd disappoint me is if you'd ever disrespect my little Sissy, but I can't ever picture that happening. If you ever do, you and me will be climbing in that ring together. You hear me, boy?"

"UC, there's something I need to talk to you about," began Reilly tentatively, "I love Sissy more than anything in the world and want to spend the rest of my life with her as my wife." Reilly was barely past his eighteenth birthday when he said this. Sissy was just seventeen.

The smile on Uppercut's face told Reilly all he needed to know. UC did tell him that he wanted Sissy to finish high school, explaining that no one in the family had ever achieved this lofty educational milestone before. He had dreams of her going beyond just high school as she was a bright girl and a good student. Reilly said his plan included, first and foremost, getting through the police academy. With Tommy McMahon's help, he hoped to be accepted and would be starting as soon as a spot became available. "I want to be through my training and already working before we get married. If I'm going to have a wife, I want to be able to support her."

Uppercut approved of the plan but never got a chance to see any of that happen. One afternoon, shortly after their conversation as Reilly was sweeping up at the gym, there was a commotion near the ring. Reilly was one of several members who rushed to the back of the gym. There, lying motionless at the near corner of the ring, is Uppercut.

# Chapter Seven

Reilly began his police training shortly after the funeral. He was the only Negro in his class with all others being white. He sensed how little most of the other recruits wanted him there, but there was nothing alien about that sensation. He had never felt welcome in any white environment at any time in his young life. Maybe that wasn't fair as the gym had blacks, whites, and Latinos all training together. Of course, the other guys might be marginally tolerant of different races but were still trying to rearrange your face once you stepped into the ring.

In the academy classroom, Reilly was solid academically. Athletically, after years of training under Uppercut, no one came near to his ability. He was fast, and he was strong. His core was rock solid, so sit-ups, pull-ups, or climbing rope came easily to him. The same was true for distance running. Part of the training included putting on boxing gear and getting into the ring. Reilly's prowess was evident from the beginning as he was the only one in the class who had trained at any serious level. Word of his Golden Gloves experience began to circulate, and during the second session the instructor turned the reins of the class over to him. Reilly made a good impression on his classmates in large part due to his understated demeanor during the class. He was well spoken and patient as he went through the basics of throwing and defending a punch. His hands were a blur as he worked the speed bag, and there was little doubt that if he was to hit you, like he hit the heavy bag, it would leave a mark.

Their academy instructor was a real hard-ass, ex-military type by the name of Gregory Maloney, who was universally disliked by all the trainees. Even Reilly, who had a calm and easy-going manner, didn't particularly like him. Maloney was a monster. He was tall and big across the shoulders. He was a few years past his prime but still heavily muscled. He had no neck. During training, one of the recruits tried goading Maloney into getting into the ring with Reilly. Reilly had grown beyond his welterweight status, and now at close to 160lbs, he was at the top of a middle-weight classification. Maloney was a true heavyweight at well over 220lbs. Reilly paused to consider the Black credo, *'you got to go along to get along'*, and the inherent danger he found himself being thrust into. Two scenarios crossed his mind. He had little doubt that he could out maneuver and out spar the bigger man but worried that if he was to embarrass him it could have repercussions down the road. The second option was to let his guard down, but Maloney, at his size and weight, could do serious damage with even one punch. At first, he tried to beg off saying that there was too much difference in weight for it to be a fair fight. He knew he looked cowardly, but he could live with that. Maloney felt no such compunction as he was already getting into his gear and preparing to step into the ring.

There is no bell. There is no referee. The two men, more accurately one man and one boy, move cautiously out of their corners and approach one another. Maloney had his share of fights and knows no fear, but he still needs to respect Reilly's quickness. They circle each other waiting for their opportunity. Reilly looks like a boxer; Maloney like a wrecking ball. He charges and swings wildly. Reilly easily ducks the punch and realizes that years of training are hard to abandon as instinctually he releases a three punch combination. The left jab straightens the big man up. This is followed by a right to the gut, which doubles him up and sets Reilly up for the uppercut. The recruits cheer as Maloney staggers. Reilly hopes he'll drop to the canvas, but he maintains his balance, shakes his head, and comes at Reilly. Maloney is bleeding from either the nose or mouth. Reilly knows he won't be seeing out of his left eye too well over the next several days. Maloney changes tactics and tries to capture Reilly in a clinch, but he is perhaps the slowest opponent Reilly has ever faced. He quickly ducks the grasp, gets a lightning fast jab to the side of his head and moves to the far corner of the ring. Maloney looks confused as he has grasped nothing. He is surprised to find Reilly across the ring waiting for him. The scene is comical, and the plebes laugh. Reilly realizes this is bad business. Maloney is enraged and, like a bull, charges Reilly. There is no doubt in his mind that this has moved well beyond a sparring match as Maloney wears a mask of pure hatred. Reilly is confident that he can continue to avoid the big man and get punches in pretty much as he pleases, but he also knows that Maloney will never quit coming at him. Once again, Reilly sidesteps the move and dances away, this time without throwing a punch. He can see the big man is getting winded as a possible way out of this mess starts to form in his mind. Reilly adopts a boxing stance in the center of the ring as Maloney comes at him. Reilly goes into a cover as he allows Maloney to throw punches at will. Few of these punches land with much force as the big man's tank is nearing empty. Reilly offers him his chin. Maloney lands a punch squarely into Reilly's jaw, or at least that's the way he hopes it appears to those watching. Reilly sees the punch coming and turns his head with the incoming fist. This mitigates the force of the punch. As the punch 'lands', Reilly snaps his head back, giving the appearance that the blow has landed with extreme force. As Reilly spins, he drops to the canvas and doesn't move. He hopes the big man doesn't drop onto him and continue his assault. Instead, Maloney stands over his prone opponent breathing heavily and watching cautiously. The recruits look on in shocked silence.

"You and you," barks Maloney at two of the recruits, "Help Thorn up. Alright, any of you other dog-pukes want to go next?" The offer is met with silence as Reilly is helped to first his knees and then his feet.

As he is helped out of the ring, Maloney says, "Thorn, good job today. Go take a shower. You're done for the day. The rest of you pukes give me a mile and a half. That's six laps ladies and don't take all day with it either."

Still hurting from the loss of his trainer and mentor, Reilly suffered a second profound loss shortly before his academy graduation. His grandfather went to bed early one night and never woke up. That loving, gentle, and caring man had followed Uppercut into the eternal light. The losses, coming so close together, solidified the bond between Reilly and Sissy as they leaned heavily on one another for support as they grieved.

The loss marred the graduation ceremony as Reilly had always envisioned both Uppercut and his grandfather in the audience cheering louder than everyone. That is of course if they weren't arguing over one trivial matter or another. His bond with UC had grown strong over the years, and Sissy had captured his grandfather's heart. Sitting with his parents were Sissy and her mother along with Officer McMahon. He wore his dress uniform as did other officers who had sponsored one of the graduates. The program had been intense, and not everyone who had joined the academy had completed the training. Tommy McMahon was fiercely proud of Reilly. He sensed upon meeting him as a young boy that Reilly was a special kid, and now seeing him standing in formation in a police uniform; his feelings are validated. McMahon and Greg Maloney were cadets in the same academy class and had remained friends over the years. Tommy had kept tabs on Reilly's progress during his training. He had sought out the instructor two-days after his fight with Reilly and laughed as Maloney told the story.

"Honest to God, Tommy, the kid really bailed me out. I was getting my butt whipped when he takes a dive. He did a good job as him and me are the only ones that know the truth."

"What were you thinking stepping into the ring with that kid? Gregory, do you own a mirror? Look in it, you're a wee bit past your prime," laughed McMahon. "I've watched him fight. I'm glad he decided to become a cop but can't help but wonder how far he would have gone if he had stayed with boxing."

"Screw boxing," said Maloney, "If you think Chicago politics are crooked as hell, they still take a distant second to that cesspool they call boxing."

## Chapter Eight

Reilly found a position on the force. On most days, he walked a beat in a poor neighborhood near to his home. In the years since coming to Chicago, his parents had worked hard and saved well and were finally able to buy a small bungalow. Reilly helped as much as he could by contributing from his meager earnings from the gym. Prices in the 1920s were ridiculously low by future standards but so were wages. A loaf of bread was 10 cents; a quart of milk 14 cents. A pound of ground beef costs 15 cents. For larger purchases, a new Ford automobile would run about $550.00, a stove was $26.00, and a home, on average, $3,000.00. As wonderful as these prices sound, a good annual income for a man was $1,574.00 a year. Reilly's father worked six days a week, for no less than 10 hours a day at a wage of $4.00 a day. His wife made less than that.

Sissy went on to graduate high school and almost immediately began making plans to trade her cap and gown for a wedding gown. The two were married in a simple ceremony at their local Baptist church. Andre was his best man. Following that, there was a spirited reception at the church with family, neighbors, and friends. One of the two white faces in attendance at the church was Officer Tommy McMahon. The other was Dominic Augustino, a friend Reilly had made in the academy. McMahon stayed for the reception; Dominic left shortly after the church service. Several men brought instruments, which included everything from guitars to banjos to squeeze boxes and even a saw with a bow.

Sissy found a job working in a predominately black school. She was fortunate as not many white teachers wanted to work with Negros. They decided to move in with Reilly's parents for several reasons, including wanting to help with his parent's bills, while saving money for a home of their own.

Another reason for them to all live together was the growing list of ailments exhibited by Reilly's father. Workers at the time, be they black or white, were used by American manufacturers until they were used up. Day in and day out they toiled in harsh conditions. Poor ventilation and poor lighting, coupled with long work days and long work weeks, would eventually wear a man down. The senior Thorn hurt his back. His production slowed. Workman's Compensation laws were passed in Illinois in 1912. This was in large part due to the public outcry over the conditions described in Upton Sinclair's, "The Jungle". Thorn applied for compensation, but his claim was denied. It was not uncommon for worker's negligence to be identified as the cause of an accident. He was let go. Following that, he was relegated to day laborer jobs when he could find them. Suddenly, the Thorns had a lot less money coming in.

Aside from this, things were going well for the Thorns as Reilly settled in on the force. He made a few friends and discovered pretty quickly that there was a strong bond between policemen. Typically, there were two cops on a beat at any time. The officer Reilly was with was usually white. One day, in a tough Irish neighborhood on the near south side, Reilly and his partner stopped to question several boys. Evidently, the boys felt no strong compulsion to treat Reilly with respect. They asked his partner, an officer by the name of Donofrio, what he had done wrong to get stuck with a nigger. Donofrio unsheathed his nightstick and brought it down on the offending boy's head.

"You don't talk to no cops like that never," was his advice to the other boys. The irony, unknown to anyone except Donofrio, was that his dislike of Irish was second only to his dislike of blacks. At the end of a work day, not only cops but workers from all over the city found their way back to their own ethnic or racial ghetto. Donofrio, in particular, couldn't wait to get back to the Italian stronghold he made home and complain to anyone who cared to listen about how he had to work with a Negro. Of course he didn't put it in such delicate terms.

Reilly, who had not approved of Donofrio's method, bent to help the boy to his feet. In unison the boy's friends asked him to please leave him be, and they would tend to their friend. One of the boys, still very much aware of the nightstick, chose his words carefully. Reading the nametag, he very respectfully said, "Officer Thorn, if it is OK with you we will help our friend back home."

Reilly acquiesced and stepped away. He knew they didn't want a black person touching their friend. As they continued their rounds, Donofrio laughed and said, "I must be losing my touch. I was trying to crack his head open."

Reilly wisely remained silent.

# Chapter Nine

Carl Sandburg would describe Chicago in his poem '*Chicago*' as, '*hog butcher for the world*'. The 'Back of the Yards' neighborhood was where the butchering took place. The area would maintain a high level of activity even during the not too distant Depression as the old adage, '*people gotta eat*' was, and always will be, an absolute truth. The bouquet of swine and beef and lamb permeated huge areas on the near southwest side of the city. Mixed with the aroma is the sweat of fear as thousands of animals are led to their death daily. The men who work the chutes have long since quit noticing the smell of warm blood and pig shit. By rail and by truck, more livestock are delivered to their sacrificial fate day after day; week in and week out. Here, the business of killing has been honed to a fine art. At the end of their shifts, men pour out of the slaughterhouses. Many head back to their ghettos while some stop at a local gin mill for a cold beer and a smoke.

One of the popular watering holes is a place simply known as '*Augie's*'. Of course, there is no sign on the outside of the building as Prohibition is still the law of the land and many years away from ending. Patrons gain entry by finding their way to the end of an alley and then going through a nondescript doorway in what appears to be an abandoned building. August '*Augie*' Augustino, the uncle of Dominic, Reilly's friend from the academy, is the proprietor.

Augie had been a bar owner long before the days of Prohibition and had made a nice living at it. He was the quintessential bartender. He was affable. He could tell a joke, but more importantly he knew when to talk and when to listen. Good bartenders are good listeners. Short and plump, he would laugh and say that people liked to be around him because it made them feel better about themselves. It was a small shot and a beer joint but had a loyal customer base. At lunch, his wife put out a buffet which attracted a good number of stockyard and factory workers. It was long hours, but it's what put food on the table. Then the 18th Amendment passed and the manufacturing and sale of alcohol became illegal. Shortly before the law was to go into effect, Augustino was going over his books one day in the middle of the afternoon. This was typically a quiet time, and on this particular afternoon he had only one customer, nursing a beer, at the end of the bar. Augustino knew many of his customers but had no recollection of this lone patron.

"So, what happens to you with Prohibition?" asked the stranger.

His question in the quiet bar startled Augustino. "Oh, sorry, I was engrossed in this, do you need another beer?"

"I asked, what's going to happen to you now that Prohibition has passed?"

"Mister, I've been asking myself the same question for weeks. I'm embarrassed to say it's been so long since I did anything besides run a beer joint that I don't know how to do anything else."

The stranger smiled. It was a warm and friendly smile. He was handsome with what many would describe as chiseled good looks. Augie hadn't paid much attention to the man when he walked in but took a closer look now. He had noticed the jacket and tie when he entered but thought he might be a salesman out making calls. On closer inspection, he could see the shirt was smartly stitched. The jacket finely tailored. He wore a large ring. It looked expensive. The same could be said for his tie-pin and cuff links. Augustino's advice to anyone wearing high-end jewelry in this neighborhood would be, 'don't'. Better yet, leave it at home, but somehow he had the feeling this guy was not too concerned about it. He suspected that this guy might welcome someone trying to take these prizes.

"I have some business associates that could use a man with your unique talents," replied the stranger, "maybe we can help each other out." With that, he left the bar. Augie realized afterwards that he had never paid for his beer.

The results of this innocent conversation would change Augustino's life in a myriad of ways. Later that night, the stranger appeared at closing time with two of his business associates. He introduced himself with the lyrical name of Johnny Octaviano. The other two received no introductions, but Augustino deduced pretty quickly who the boss was. He said nothing directly to Augustino. Instead, he would whisper to Octaviano in Italian, and Octaviano would then translate for Augustino. Augie correctly deduced that these men were Sicilian. Augustino's family was from the mainland, and he spoke Italian fluently, but Italy has many local dialects, so even though he could hear the whisperings, he did not understand all of what was being said. What the three offered wasn't a business proposal per se as that would give the impression that Augie would have the option to think about what was being suggested and then make a decision.

Octaviano told Augie that they were simply business men. Now that Prohibition was here men would still want alcohol, and they could provide it. He explained that drinking should be a social activity. "People like to go out, have a few drinks, listen to music, and maybe dance a little. That's where you come in," explained Johnny.

Augie had never felt so uncomfortable in his life and asked if he could think about it. The third man in attendance rose, asking, "Anybody want a beer?" Without waiting for an answer, he took his jacket off. In a holster, pressed to his left side, was a revolver. He neatly folded his jacket over the back of the chair, made his way behind the bar, expertly drew a beer from the tap, took a sip, and then flung the glass at the mirror behind the bar. The boss never even flinched. A light in the stairwell came on, and Augie's wife called down asking if he was OK.

"I broke a glass. Go on to bed."

"Guido, why do you have to do things like that?" Johnny asked the hulking figure behind the bar. "We're having a business meeting here, and you go ahead and break the man's mirror." Turning to Augie, he said, "Of course you can think this over. We'll be leaving now, but I want you to go upstairs and discuss this with Rose. She needs to agree with your decision. That's what a happy marriage is all about. Your whole family should be comfortable with this, too. Your folks, they live in the little bungalow over on 38th near Halsted, right? You should talk to them, too."

34

Octaviano had never met Rose. There should be no reason for him to know her name. The same was true of his parents. These thoughts chilled the bartender.

Augie closed *'Augie's'* in accordance with the new laws. His new business partners found him a spot in a warehouse district near the stockyards. Much of his furniture, along with the bar itself and his entire inventory, was moved into the new location. On the first night in the new place, the bar was packed. Johnnie had 'asked' if the boss could use the bar to entertain his friends, and of course Augie had no choice but to agree. Manning the door was the mirror breaker, eyeing everyone through a special sliding window in the door before they were allowed entry. The men looked annoyed as they were finally granted access, but the women thought the peep-hole entry was somehow exciting. Trays of food were brought in from local eateries, and the booze ran freely. The women were young, stylish, and shapely. The men, many of them, were old and paunchy but with a look of affluence and power. Augie was pretty sure he recognized several patrons from the local paper. They might have been politicians, or they might have been gangsters, or as is true around the world, they might have been both.

The next morning Augie's cupboard was quite bare. The hard liquor was either drunk or appropriated as Augie had watched many leave with a full bottle. Besides a half barrel of beer there wasn't much left. Johnnie came in around noon, and Augie explained his dilemma.

Octaviano, who was so affable and friendly when compared to some of his associates, simply laughed and said, "Augie, last night was a very successful opening night. There were some real big shots here, and tell me you didn't notice some of those skirts. You are off to a really great start."

"But Johnnie," he complained, "all my drink is gone, and I have no money."

"Don't you worry about that," said Johnny with a smile. He finished his beer and departed leaving a fifty dollar bill behind on the bar.

Augie looked at the bill like he might have looked at a rodent that had made its way onto the bar. It was the biggest tip Augie had ever received, so why not just take it and slip it into his apron. Rose would be thrilled. He left the note where it was and busied himself with washing glasses and straightening up. When his tasks took him past the bill, he would give it as wide a berth as he could. He wouldn't look at the bill directly, choosing instead to glance at it sideways as he passed. He felt silly as he finally took a position directly in front of the fifty and simply stared at it. His arms were folded across his chest and over his rather generous paunch. He pretended to not know why he felt conflicted, but he knew exactly what the issue was. As a bartender, he had seen many men over the years who had taken the wrong path in life. They had either started drinking too much, or gambling, or stepping out on their wives. Augustino, who was not well educated and would never be considered scholarly, had read a poem in the Sunday paper several years before about some guy who's walking through the woods. The guy comes to a fork and needs to make a decision on which path to take. If someone had told Augie he was referring to *The Road Not Taken,* by Robert Frost, he would have said, "Yeah, that's the guy," and then he would make a point of remembering the name, but he would invariably forget. He liked the poem so much that he cut it out of the paper and would read it occasionally. The clipping went missing at some point along the way, but that was OK because he still knew the gist of it. He often thought of this poem when he would see men making bad choices in life. He was shaken out of his stupor when the mirror breaker came into the bar to man the front door. Without another thought, Augie's hand shot out and snatched the note off the bar and stuffed it into his pocket. As simply as that, Augie had chosen his path.

Later that same afternoon, several men appeared and began unloading assorted spirits. Being a warehouse there was a lot of unused square footage behind the bar area. A second, and then a third truck followed, and by the end of the day, a shortage of booze was no longer a problem. The problem was that each had handed Augie a piece of paper for him to sign before leaving. They were invoices. The sum of these invoices was more than Augie made in a year.

Johnnie appeared the next day and again told Augie there was nothing to worry about. Three additional trucks appeared that afternoon along with three additional invoices. Booze was like gold during the Prohibition, and, like gold, needed protection. There were never less than three men at the warehouse. They weren't always the same men, but they were all cut from the same cloth with dark hair and dark eyes and heavy beards. Many spoke only Sicilian. Some were large and imposing, others smaller and more furtive in their mannerisms. They all looked dangerous.

Booze came in and booze went out. Sometimes, small trucks would appear with license plates from New Jersey or Iowa or any one of a dozen other states. Several bakery trucks made frequent pickups. There was even a hearse that would appear periodically. The men loading the hearse would cross themselves often and looked relieved to see it pull away.

In the evening, *Augie's* did a brisk business. After three o'clock it was mostly blue collar types looking for a sip before heading home. Augie was typically behind the bar during that time and would charge for drinks. Later in the evening, there was a better class of clientele or at least they were better dressed. Johnnie had other men serving the booze for these patrons. Augie would watch and learned who they charged and who they did not.

Beside the stack of invoices for the booze that was being delivered, Augie receive a bill for the rent monthly along with utility bills. He approached Johnnie, who was now at the bar often, with his concern over the mounting bills all of which were in his name. Octaviano would laugh it off and tell Augie he worried too much. Augie's life settled into a pattern, which he was for the most part comfortable with. No one ever asked him for money for the booze deliveries or for anything else. He pocketed the money from the afternoon business, and Johnnie slipped him money often. Octaviano would pull out a fat wad of bills and start peeling off twenties, which he would stuff into Augie's breast pocket with a pat on the shoulder.

"You make sure you buy Rose something nice," he would tell Augustino with a smile.

Augie wasn't stupid. He knew who these men were and what they were. Somehow he was able to look past all that. He liked Johnnie, who always treated Augie like he was in charge of the bar even though both of them knew who was actually running things. He sensed correctly that Johnnie liked him as well. Octaviano was such a pleasant fellow, and Augie would find himself wondering why he had chosen the life he had. Most of the time, what they were doing all seemed so legitimate that Augie would allow himself to forget how illegal this whole business was. Johnnie had walled off a section of the warehouse and made a private office for the boss with a stylish conference room. There was a small bar at the end of the conference room, and occasionally Octaviano would tell Augie that the boss was having a meeting and that he should go home. It would be close to midnight when the meetings would start. Augie was glad not to know who was at these gatherings or what was discussed.

As the bar became more established, other services were made available. Johnnie took another section of the warehouse and created a small but well-appointed private casino. There was a poker table, which was rumored to host high stake games. It was a classy affair. Augustino watched as framing began for what would be a series of small rooms. His curiosity was sated as following the plastering, painting, and finish carpentry, he watched as a truck delivered a half dozen mattresses and frames.

One afternoon, a police officer walked into the bar. Augustino recognized the man as he would stop in occasionally, but he hadn't known until today that he was a cop. Augie was almost relieved that they had been discovered even if it meant being arrested. Instead, Octaviano met him at the door with a warm smile and a handshake. He led him to the bar where he personally poured the man a beer; something he only did for important customers. Augie watched as Johnnie slid an envelope across the bar top along with the beer. The two men talked like old friends. Johnnie signaled to one of the painted ladies as Augie thought of them. She sidled up next to the policeman and whispered something in his ear. Her hand rested on his inner thigh. The cop laughed as his beer was topped off, and the two disappeared into the back. She took his policeman's hat and placed it on her head, and they both laughed as the curtain swung closed. This scene would repeat itself weekly. It was always the same cop, a young guy who didn't look old enough to be involved in such deceits. The cop rarely wore a uniform, but the bar patrons knew who and what he was. The man sensed that Augustino was intimidated by him and liked to make the portly bartender sweat a little bit when he came in. The truth was Augie was terrified of this rogue cop. As the weeks went by, he became more arrogant and demanding. He wasn't a pleasant fellow, and several of the girls would disappear when he walked in. Augie wasn't sure what happened when they went in the back, but there was an incident after one session that resulted in one of the girls crying. The girl he mistreated was named Mary; Mary with the big tits as she was commonly known. The other girls went to console her, and Johnnie stepped in to try to placate matters. The two men had a rather animated conversation in a quiet corner of the bar. The cop left looking unconcerned about what had just happened. He glared at the whores as he left. Later that night, Mary appeared wearing heavy makeup in a failed attempt to cover up a black eye.

Augie, who would admit that he wasn't the brightest guy in the world, was beginning to see how the whole process was orchestrated. It made him wonder. Prohibition had its roots as a massive social experiment and, like many experiments of this nature throughout history, had the lofty goal of creating a more utopian world. Even Augustino could see how Prohibition missed the mark miserably. The bartender thought back to his pre-Prohibition days of running a small shot and a beer joint and compared that to what he now saw happening. Hard liquor became the drink of choice because it was more concentrated and therefore easier to bootleg and transport. People now drank at home in greater numbers than ever before, and when they did drink in public it tended to be in greater excess. Men and women, drinking together, often led to moral lapses in judgment. By definition, almost the entire country was now criminals as most people were still drinking in clear violation of the law. There were no regulations or control over how alcohol was being distilled. Over 10,000 people died during Prohibition from drinking alcohol distilled from wood. Wood alcohol had the potential to create permanent blindness or severe organ damage. Legislating morality typically does not work well. Prohibition clogged the courts and the penal system while promoting corruption within law enforcement agencies.

Perhaps Will Rodgers, the comic-philosopher of the day, summed it up best, "Prohibition is better than no alcohol at all."

There was a complexity to manufacturing and distributing alcohol for an entire nation which fueled the need for more organized crime syndicates. Augie was getting a firsthand look at this, and what he saw was big business in every sense of the word. Teams were dedicated to every part of the industry from shipping and receiving, manufacturing, distributing, security, and payroll. Accountants and book keepers were a common site in the back offices behind the bar. Month after month, year after year, the business flourished, and like clockwork, Augie would be delivered stacks of vouchers, statements, and invoices which he would dutifully sign. He quit caring or worrying about it as no one had ever asked him for a nickel in all the years since the relationship began. Johnnie would laugh and tell him, "See, didn't I tell you that there was nothing to worry about?" Financially, Augie was doing well. He didn't draw a pay check in the traditional sense, but Johnnie took good care of him. Every Friday there would be an envelope waiting for him at the beginning of his shift. Beyond that, Johnnie was quick to peel off a couple of twenties for Augie, always with the caveat, "Remember, you buy Rose something nice. You got a lovely wife there, and dames like pretty things." Rose liked cash and was thrilled with what she could buy with the extra money. Augie resolutely refused to let her anywhere near the bar. She wisely didn't know what went on there, nor did she want to know.

Augie spent most of his time in the tavern part of the building. If he wasn't there, he could usually be found checking stock in the back. There was a tremendous amount of inventory on hand at any one time. He was in the far recesses of the warehouse one afternoon looking for a store of good rum from Cuba. A pipeline between the US and Cuba, known as *Flota del Ron* or The Rum Fleet, had developed during this period. This was the good stuff and intentionally kept in the back as there was less of a chance of it walking off. It fetched a high dollar. This was close to some back rooms that Augie had never ventured into. He was surprised to hear a commotion coming from behind a closed door. Not stopping to think, he opened the door and there he saw four men, three of whom he recognized. The two large men were part of what he thought of as the security force for the warehouse. They each held the arm of a badly beaten man. Augie had little doubt that if they let go of the man he would collapse to the floor. The fourth man, the man orchestrating the beating, was Johnnie Octaviano. Johnnie turned quickly towards the opening door. He looked nothing like the handsome and easy-going man that Augie had come to like so much over the years. He looked unhinged. He was breathing heavily. His normally neatly combed hair hung in sweaty strands in his face. Blood was splattered on his crisply starched shirt.

"Get out," he hissed.

Later that afternoon, Augie stood behind the bar fearful of what Johnnie would do after the earlier incident. He felt sick to his stomach. He wanted to go home. And now, here came Johnnie as good looking and finely tailored as ever. He called over to the bouncer at the door with a laugh, "Hey Guido, you're not sleeping over there are you?" He patted another patron on the back as he made his way over to where Augie stood looking ashen and nervous.

"There's the best damn bartender in the world. How are you doing today, Augie?" With a wink and a conspiratorial smile he leaned across the bar and whispered, "See anything interesting today?" and with that, burst into a fit of laughter. He slid his hand across the bar and left a stack of bills in front of the bartender with the admonition, as always, "Remember, I think you should surprise Rose with something extra special today."

"One other thing," he said laughing, "next time, maybe you should knock first."

With that, he made his way around the bar stopping to chat with some of the customers. Augie was torn between being confused and relieved. In his hand were five crisp twenty dollar bills. Several days later, Augie saw an article in the paper describing a badly beaten corpse that was found in a dumpster in a neighborhood west of the stockyards. The police were looking for anyone that had information that might help identify the man or solve the case.

Augie knew nothing.

Life settled back in after the incident. There was never another word spoken concerning it, and it seemed to have little effect on the relationship between Octaviano and Augustino. Augie, who was unhappy with the path he was on, realized that there was no turning back. *Way*, as Frost had opined, *had led to way*. He didn't consider himself to be a gangster. He still thought of himself as a bartender, perhaps a bartender who had lost his way. On most days, it was easy to pretend that he was still the same old simple barkeep. On other days it was not quite so easy, like the day that Johnnie came in with a suit jacket for Augie. Trying to make light of the situation, he led the bartender into the back where, after fitting him with a holster and revolver, he slipped the jacket on.

"I don't want to carry a gun," complained Augie, "I wouldn't know how to use it."

"What are you talking about?" said Johnnie, "If something's breathing, and you don't want it to breathe no more, you take the gun, point it, and pull the trigger. Now what's hard about that? Just don't shoot any of my customers. Try not to shoot yourself either for that matter."

In addition to the sidearm, there were now two sawed-off shotguns behind the bar. Johnnie advised Augie that these required almost no aiming at all as long as the weapon was pointed in the right general direction. It was during this period that Augie began seeing more dangerous looking men around the bar. These men said little. Some patrolled the outside while others would station themselves around the bar at various places. They each had beer in front of them in an effort to make them look like customers. On strict orders from Johnnie, the beer went untouched. Mattresses were brought in and set up dormitory style in the back. Everyone seemed tense. Even Johnnie was not his usual relaxed self. Seeing one of the thugs sleeping at his post, Johnnie walked directly to him, took his revolver out and slammed the butt end of the gun into the side of the man's head.

"Pay attention! The next guy I see sleeping, I'm gonna use the business end of this thing. You got that? For Christ sakes he's bleeding all over the place. Take him in the back and get him cleaned up," he shouted.

The tension lasted several weeks putting a strain on everyone. Deliveries and pickups slowed down, and before a truck was let in, it was stopped at the end of the alley and inspected. A parade of men would come in to meet with Johnnie and be gone just that quickly. Other groups would filter in and out several times a day. One night a car stopped at the entrance to the alley, and a trench coated man stepped onto the running board and fired a tommy-gun down the alley. No one was hurt, and Augie hadn't even realized that what he was hearing was gunfire.

Augustino, who had done a good job of not sticking his nose in back room matters, became more and more concerned about Johnnie. The stress was starting to take its toll on the young man. He looked like he hadn't slept in days. Out of concern, he asked, "Johnnie, are you OK? I'm worried about you."

"Augie, you worry about everything. That's what I love about you," he said with a weak smile. "Just make sure the beer is cold and the customer's glasses are full." With that, he hustled off leaving a twenty behind on the bar.

The murder rate nationally during these years almost doubled. Violent crimes like battery and assault rose 13%. The federal inmate population increased a staggering 516%, from what it was before prohibition, which burdened all branches of government. New taxes were created to make up for the shortfall. On the other hand, bootleggers and other criminals were doing just fine. By 1930, the manufacturing and distribution of alcohol had become a finely honed business. During its peak it is generally believed that bootlegging was a four-billion dollar a year industry. Across the country it is estimated that there were now 10,000 speakeasies operating. In Chicago, there were hundreds of bars that simply stayed open during prohibition or, like *Augie's*, moved to a more clandestine location. *Augie's* became what was known as a 'blind-pig' tavern, which meant there were no markings on the outside of the building. There were hundreds of 'blind-pigs' in Chicago.

Bodies began popping up all over the city as the newspapers chronicled the daily death toll associated with what they labeled gang or turf wars. Most notably was the St. Valentine's Day Massacre where seven members of the Bugs Moran gang were gunned down in a north side garage by a rival gang who had dressed as police officers for the occasion. It was generally believed that Al 'Scarface' Capone was responsible for the murders, but he denied any part in the slayings. No one was ever charged with these murders. During the prohibition gang wars in Chicago, 215 gangsters were killed.

As tensions continued to run high in the bar, Augustino, like the rest of the city, monitored the progress of these gang wars and the rising death tolls. On a Monday, after a particularly bloody weekend, Johnnie came bouncing into the bar like his old self. It was early, and the place was empty so he grabbed a seat at the bar as Augie poured him a beer. When the bartender's sport jacket swung open, Johnnie saw the gun and laughed, saying, "Augie, are you still toting that pistol around with you? Maybe you were expecting trouble?"

When Augie wasn't sure how to respond, the gangster said with a smile, "You better give me that heater, Augie. I was afraid you were going to shoot yourself in the leg anyway."

# Chapter Ten

Even though life continued to be tough for the Thorns, none would describe it as a bad life. Their quarters were cramped as there were four of them sharing a relatively small home. Reilly and Sissy's plan to buy their own home was on hold indefinitely. They might have been able to manage the purchase, but there was no way his parents could afford to keep their house. Work was still sporadic for the senior Thorn due to his overall health. His parents, who had lived in grandfather's sharecropper one room shack, were used to close quarters and communal living. Similarly, Sissy was accustomed to small spaces as the home she grew up in with her mother and Uppercut was even smaller than the Thorn's home. There was little friction in the family and what little drama there was, was nothing compared to the love in the home. Sissy was treated like a daughter, and she developed a strong love for her in-laws. It was easy for Sissy to see where Reilly got his character from.

Sissy and her mother-in-law formed an especially strong bond. In the evening, they could be heard in the kitchen talking and laughing. They both loved to bake, and Sissy learned to make many wonderful dishes from her mother-in-law. One day, Sissy showed her a recipe for skillet cornbread that she had cut out of the paper. "Well, what do you think?" asked Sissy.

"Oh, you know me," her mother-in law replied while handing the recipe back, "I never used no recipe for nothing I cook." Saying this, she lowered her eyes and turned away.

Sissy was accustomed to many in her life butchering the English language as there were those who had not had the benefit of an education. "I'm sorry," she said, "it looked interesting."

"Well, you try it, honey, and I'll watch. How does that sound?"

"Wonderful," said Sissy with a smile, "You sit, and I'll get the skillet." Handing the recipe back to the senior Mrs. Thorn, she said, "Here, you read off the ingredients, and I'll get everything out that we need."

Reilly's mother stared at the news print. She said nothing. Looking at the paper, she saw one or two words that she recognized. A look of sadness stole over her face, marring her natural prettiness.

Sissy came to a slow realization. Her mother-in-law couldn't read and like many illiterate people had gone to extreme measures to keep it a secret. Sissy approached her and gently took the paper from her hand. "It's not important," she said, "your cornbread is probably a lot better than that stupid recipe."

Mrs. Thorn slowly raised her head and looked at her daughter-in-law. The love and compassion she saw in her face made her realize that Sissy would never judge a person on how well they read. "I just never learned," she stated simply, "there weren't no opportunity down south, leastwise not for me. At night, I watch when you pick up a book and get all cozy and read. You look so happy, so peaceful."

The next day, Sissy presented her mother-in-law with a first grade primer. She cleared a space on the back porch and sat with her in the evenings doing simple exercises. The porch was off-limits to the men in the house during these tutoring sessions. Sissy had confided to Reilly what was going on, and she assumed that her father-in-law knew what was happening as well. Reilly knew his mother couldn't read or write but didn't think about it much. He was surprised to find out that this bothered her as Reilly considered his mother to be very intelligent in spite of not having these basic skills. Because her mother-in-law was embarrassed by this shortcoming, there was an unspoken agreement on everyone's part to pretend they didn't know what was going on out on the back porch.

Reilly's mother was intelligent and learned quickly. The pairing of a talented teacher with a motivated student is a powerful combination. Sissy had her recognizing and reading quite a few words by the end of the first session. The more she learned; the more she wanted to learn. One day Sissy presented her mother-in-law with a first grade reader. Mrs. Thorn held the book and stared at the cover. This seemed to be beyond her comprehension and well beyond her ability. Sissy told her she was going to do fine and left her on the back porch. Sissy went to sit with the men in the parlor. A short time later, her mother-in-law came in cradling the book. She had the appearance of someone carrying a precious talisman. Without saying a word, she found her favorite chair, opened the book, and began to read silently. No one reacted, but if you were to look, you would see the two men were smiling broadly. A tear slowly slid down Sissy's face.

One night a short time later, Sissy asked for her mother-in-law's help in making a cake. They loved their time together in the kitchen. Sissy seemed nervous, which was unusual for the young girl. She fussed over the frosting and went to extra care trying to make it perfect. Her mother-in-law laughed, and said, "The way those two men eat, I doubt if they'll even notice the fuss you're making."

Sissy remained edgy during dinner. The two women shooed the men out of the kitchen as they cleared the table. Sissy put on a pot of coffee, and when everything was just right, she called the men in for dessert. Mrs. Thorn had guessed wrong as both men commented on how beautiful the cake looked.

While they were enjoying their cake, Sissy slipped her mother-in-law a piece of paper, "Mama, will you read this, please?"

Mrs. Thorn looked nervous as she took the paper. She had never read anything in front of anyone besides Sissy.

"It's OK, you'll do fine," encouraged Sissy.

Her mother-in-law cautiously unfolded the piece of paper. She looked at the short note and began to cry.

"What does it say?" both men asked with concern.

"It says," she announced, "I'm going to be a Grandmother."

# Chapter Eleven

"Because it ain't like that no more," said Andre as he and Reilly stood near the ring at the back of *Al's Gym*. Andre had slowly moved into the role of trainer following the passing of Uppercut. It was a good fit for him as he knew the clients and he knew the fight game. Andre had kept in great shape and still sparred with a lot of the young fighters that he trained. His pragmatic view was that it was the best way he knew of seeing what the fighter was doing right or wrong.

"That night we went to watch a fight with your grandfather was a whole different world," Andre said. "That was an ugly business at that time too but nowhere near as messed up as it is today."

Reilly simply stood there listening, mulling over what his friend had to say.

"Why do you want to do this anyway?" asked Andre even though he knew the answer. Montero knew the Thorns were hurting. His father rarely worked, and when he did, it broke Reilly's heart because he was expected to kill himself for very little money. His mother brought in next to nothing. Sissy made little in the school system. She was offered college classes to supplement her wages, and Reilly encouraged her to take advantage of the opportunity.

"Look Reilly, you're my friend, and I hope you'll listen to me. What you're talking about is *underground* boxing, and it's a dirty business. One of my guys tried it, and he still ain't right in the head. He took a shot in the temple from a guy who hid brass knuckles in his gloves. Some of these fights are bare-knuckled. There ain't no ref, not one that does anything anyway. When a guy goes down the fight ain't over. I heard about one fight where the guy was unconscious on the mat, and the other guy kept punching and kicking. The ref wanted no part of it and left the ring. The guy's corner tried to get their boy out, and the crowd held them back. They ended up taking a beating, too. Believe me, you don't want no part of that," said Andre, and finished with, "besides, you're a cop and that shit's illegal."

"I got my reasons," was all Reilly could think of to say.

"Yeah, let me guess, you need the money, right?" asked Andre. "I got a few bucks I can let you have if you promise to get this goofy idea out of your head."

Reilly was touched by the gesture as he was pretty sure Andre was in as bad of shape financially as the Thorns, probably worse.

"Reilly, you ain't fought or trained seriously in years. You still look to be in OK shape, but it don't look like you missed too many meals lately." With that said, Andre started jabbing at his young friend's modest gut. Reilly was fending off the well intentioned punches as best as he could but was having trouble as both men were laughing. "What makes you think you can even do this anymore?"

"Got to. Got me a baby coming."

"Go home and forget all this nonsense," was Andre's last bit of advice for Reilly before he left the gym.

A lot of what Andre said resonated with Reilly. The fact that underground boxing was illegal bothered him a great deal. Reilly saw a lot of illegal activity day in and day out. During the 1920's, Prohibition had made a lot of average people criminals.

During a normal shift it wasn't unusual for Reilly and his partner to encounter people who were either drunk or in possession of alcohol. Additionally, what Reilly saw from his vantage point were people with enough money to buy both alcohol and a car and then set out to enjoy both at the same time. Annual arrests for drunkenness in Chicago tripled between 1920 to 1925, from roughly 30,000 to 90,000. This was by no means indicative of everyone who could have or should have been arrested. The courts and jails were already bursting, so the prevailing thought amongst cops was to let minor infractions slide. Reilly understood the need to evaluate and respond appropriately when dealing with alcohol related incidents. If the guy or girl looked like they could make it home under their own power, he would let them go. On one memorable occasion, Reilly encountered a drunk on the street who was having some serious navigation issues. Reilly stopped, exited his vehicle with Dominic Augustino who was his partner that night, and approached the drunk. The man had no alcohol on him, and when the officers discovered he lived nearby, they opted to drive the man home. It was near the end of their shift, which was an additional motivation for just seeing the man home as compared to arresting him. Augustino gave the man strict orders to not get sick in the squad car, which Reilly found funny to say the least. When they pulled up in front of his home, the man sobered up enough to realize where he was and scrambled to get out of the car. The back doors were set up to only be opened from the outside, and when Reilly opened the door, the man fell out of the car. He got to his feet quicker than either policeman would have thought possible and began ambling away. When Augustino asked the man where he thought he was going, he replied, "To jail. I know my rights." Before the two officers were even at the top of the stairs, the front door flew open and a large woman, wearing a bathrobe with a head full of hair curlers, grabbed the drunk by his collar and yanked him into the house. Reilly and Dominic could still hear the screaming as they drove away.

"Justice comes in many flavors," said Augustino somewhat philosophically and both men laughed.

Reilly liked having Dominic as his partner as they tended to be on the same page when it came to being police officers and how they vetted out justice. On occasions when they did find a small amount of open liquor on a person, they would pour it down a sewer and toss the bottle. Not all cops Reilly worked with played that scenario the same way. Some would keep the alcohol for themselves. Others might shake the person down for a payoff. In addition, confronting and confounding police officers by the mid-twenties was proliferation of automobiles.

It could be said that the manufacturing of automobiles, and all the attendant businesses centered on the industry, is what put the roar in the Roaring Twenties. Cars, punningly, fueled the need for gas stations, which were being constructed everywhere. Motels, a word invented to describe a roadside motor-hotel, also sprang up across the nation along with drive-in diners. Roads needed to be built or upgraded. The 1920s started on an economic downturn with unemployment rates at 11%. Economic policies pushed by then Commerce Secretary and future President Herbert Hoover, convinced industry leaders to raise worker's wages and put more money in the hands of the working man. These policies coupled with unprecedented manufacturing growth, not only in the automobile industry but across the country, ushered in an era of wealth. This wealth, perhaps for the first time in civilized history, filtered down to the middle class. Mass production techniques, first used by Henry Ford in the manufacturing of the Model-T, found their way into a multitude of other industries. Mass production led to lowered manufacturing costs, which meant lower prices. The American public now had the assets to purchase items like cars, washing machines, refrigerators, radios, and numerous other mass produced items. Unemployment stayed below 5% during most of the decade. The American worker now had more free time and mobility than ever before. Labor movements from earlier decades had shortened the average work week for many, and labor saving appliances meant more time available for relaxation and recreation.

The country's financial elite prospered as never before as their factories couldn't keep up with demands. These were the one percent who invested in the stock market. The Dow Jones peaked at six times higher in 1929, than what it was in 1921. Statistical data is sketchy and unreliable during this period, but it is generally believed that there was a greater separation between the ultra-wealthy and the working class than ever before.

# Chapter Twelve

Life at home was good for the Thorns as they busied themselves for their first child. Reilly thought Sissy had never looked more beautiful. She had a glow about her, and Reilly couldn't understand the horror stories that he had heard about pregnant women. Sissy was a special person by nature; patient and easy going. Her pregnancy seemed to amplify these noble traits.

Reilly's mother was more excited than anyone and entertained the family with a seemingly endless number of ways of predicting whether Sissy was having a boy or a girl. If Sissy ate something sweet, it meant they were expecting a girl. If she craved something salty, it meant a boy was on the way. It seemed that no matter what Sissy did or said or felt or ate, the senior Mrs. Thorn saw it as a predictor. Everything was an indicator, from whether her feet were warm or cold, or how shiny her hair was on any given day. One day, she asked Sissy in all seriousness if her right breast was growing bigger than her left. The fact that the prediction changed from week to week, or even from day to day, did not seem to bother the soon-to-be Grandmother.

Everyone had their way of preparing for the baby's arrival. Mr. Thorn cleaned out a small room that could best be described as a fair-sized closet and began turning it into a nursery. It was good to see him engaged as more often than not he was unemployed. He scrubbed the room from top to bottom and then with Sissy's blessing, painted the walls a pale violet color. The trim work was painted a bright white. It looked beautiful. He rummaged a rocking chair, which he hand-sanded smooth and painted white with lilac accents. He envisioned Sissy needing a private place to nurse the baby and pictured them using this repurposed rocker. His wife sewed lovely lace curtains to cover the only window in the room.

Reilly, for his part, fawned over his wife constantly. On many days, he drove Sissy a little crazy, but she knew this was his way of contributing, so she quietly endured his doting ways. If she started to get out of a chair to get something to drink, he would jump up and offer to accommodate any need. If she insisted on getting up, he would offer her his arm and help her up. He would follow her to the kitchen and 'help' her get a glass of water. How could she get mad at her husband when he told her often how much he loved her and how beautiful she looked?

One day as she began to rise from a chair, there was Reilly practically pushing her back down. "Whatever you need, I'll get for you," he told his wife.

With a hint of exasperation, she told him she needed to use the bathroom.

At night, she loved him best of all as they would climb into their small bed. He would hold her and caress her swollen belly. She would lament the fact that she was getting fat, and he would truthfully tell her that he had never seen her look more beautiful. He would rest his head on her chest and talk to the baby. He would tell his soon to be born baby that he couldn't wait to meet her. He would promise to read to her and take her to the park and push her on the swings. He told her he would protect her and never let anything bad happen to her. When Sissy would laugh at him and tell him he was being silly, he would insist that the baby could hear and understand what he was saying. Whatever the reality was, Sissy was charmed by this and knew that Reilly was going to be a wonderful father.

One night, being in a playful mood as they lay in bed, Reilly said to his unborn baby, "This is Officer Reilly Thorn. Come in, Baby Thorn."

"We have a two-eleven in progress on 22nd and Ashland. Officer Daddy needs back-up."

He continued in this vein even pretending to answer comments from the baby that only he could hear.

He had Sissy laughing so hard that she had to get up to use the bathroom. When she climbed back in bed, she teasingly chastised him for making a pregnant woman laugh that hard. He looked contrite and apologized even though he was still smiling. She held and caressed him. They kissed, and then more passionately, they kissed again. No matter how hard they held each other they still weren't close enough. If they could, they would have merged into one single being. He told her once again how beautiful she was. Their caresses and gyrations grew steadily more ardent. Their breathing; heavy and husky, joined in syncopation, becoming more hurried and more urgent. Sharing a small home they fought the need to scream out in orgiastic joy. Now, gradually their breathing slowed. They lay together enjoying the simple pleasure of holding each other.

Reilly, propped himself on one elbow, looked seriously at Sissy, and said, "I don't think we should do things like that in front of the baby."

That resulted in more laughter and yet another unscheduled trip to the bathroom.

Sissy continued to work until late in her pregnancy against the objections of Reilly. She felt fine, and the family could use the money that she brought in. Her doctor was considered more progressive for that era as he felt women should function to their ability while pregnant. Seeing that Sissy looked and felt healthy and strong, he told her not to push it too hard but not to pamper herself either. One day, close to the end of her gestation period, she woke up feeling it would be best not to go to work. Reilly was already at work, and her mother-in-law had just left for her job at the hotel laundry. Reilly's father was in the kitchen cleaning up breakfast dishes. He looked up from his chores, prepared to offer his daughter-in-law some breakfast. Stopping in mid-sentence, he goes to Sissy and leads her to a chair.

Sissy offered him a weak smile in return and assured him she was fine. As she said this, a slight grimace crossed her face.

"Ok, let's go," was all the senior Thorn said. With that he grabbed the bag that had been packed and prepared several weeks prior and led Sissy out the door. In spite of everything, Sissy couldn't help but smile at the sight of the bag and the memory of Reilly packing and repacking it numerous times. Checking it and double checking it.

Until the middle of the twentieth century, blacks did not have a lot of choices when it came to hospital care. Many Chicago hospitals refused to treat black patients or hire black doctors and nurses. The choice to take Sissy to Provident Hospital on the near south-side was therefore an easy one. Provident was established in 1891 by Daniel Hale Williams, one of the country's first Negro surgeons, whose goal it was to create an environment welcoming to minority patients and professionals.

Upon arrival, her father-in-law stayed with Sissy while she was being admitted. He made sure she was in good hands and comfortable before heading off to find a telephone. Reilly's father was on strict orders to call the precinct and ask for the dispatcher if anything should happen. Reilly had stopped by the radio desk at the beginning of every shift for the past month to remind them to contact him immediately if they should receive word from anyone in his family. Reilly was so predictable that when he would duck his head in, the dispatcher's would preemptively cut him off with, "We know, we know...call you." It was good natured teasing even though Reilly drove them a little crazy with his constant fretting.

"This is Thorn, go ahead dispatch. Over," Reilly said into the radio. Radios became available in police cars in the late 1920s.

"Officer Thorn, we need you to respond to an emergency call at Provident Hospital. Over," came the long awaited call. When Dispatch didn't get a reply, they followed it with, "Thorn, did you copy that? Over."

"Sorry," said Reilly, "I dropped the radio." Of course, Reilly couldn't hear it, but the entire dispatch area laughed at the response. Reilly would be teased unmercifully when he returned to work with most comments having a common theme of cautioning Reilly to be careful to not drop the baby.

He was on patrol with Dominic Augustino when the call came in. Reilly insisted on driving to the hospital, but Augustino resolutely refused.

"Just sit back, relax, and enjoy the ride," advised Dominic as he engaged the siren and sped away. Officer Augustino may have posted a land-speed record time getting to the hospital, but Reilly still begged him to go faster. Dominic wanted to tell his partner to shut the hell up but took a more friendly approach and reminded him that getting them both killed wasn't going to do anyone any good.

As they pulled up to the hospital, Reilly was exiting the squad car before it even came to a full stop. He never heard when Augustino called after him, "Don't worry, I'll park the car."

If Reilly hadn't been wearing a police uniform, they might have called security and escorted him out of the hospital. Reilly Thorn, a man most would describe as rather passive and easy going, looked deranged as he went from white coat to white coat demanding to know where Sissy was. Augustino came up behind Reilly, took his arm, and led him down a corridor.

"Where are you taking me?" demanded Thorn.

"To find Sissy. You did want to find your wife, right?"

"But how...?"

"I stopped at the visitor's desk. They have all sorts of good information," said Augustino with a smile.

After what seemed like an eternity, Reilly found Sissy's room. She smiled as he entered. The sight of his father, standing next to the bed holding Sissy's hand, did much to calm the expectant father. Reilly leaned over and kissed his wife on the top of the head.

"It'll be any time now," said Sissy.

Dominic Augustino, who had followed Reilly into the room, approached the bed, "How you doing, Sissy?" he asked. After a very brief visit, he departed saying, "I need to get back on patrol. Reilly, I'll call the precinct and let them know you're out for the rest of the day."

Reilly never even heard or replied. It was Sissy who thanked Dominic for getting him there in one piece.

Shortly after Officer Augustino left, Sissy had a contraction. The senior Thorn grabbed his son before he went running out of the room to report this to anyone who would care to listen. Expectant fathers, especially first-time expectant fathers, during these years hadn't a clue as to the mechanisms of child birth. A second contraction followed a short time later, and that's when Reilly's father told his son to stay with Sissy, and he would inform the staff that it was time.

Now alone, Reilly squeezed his wife's hand and brushed hair back from her brow. He could feel perspiration on her forehead. She grimaced slightly as another milder contraction came and went. He knew he had done this to his precious Sissy and thought back to Uppercut when he had warned him, "If you ever do anything to hurt Sissy, you and me are going to climb into that ring."

"Sissy, I'm sorry," he said. Seeing his wife in pain was heart breaking.

Through a series of quick rapid breaths, she smiled and started to tell him not to worry when she was spasmed by the strongest contraction yet. Now, it was Reilly's turn to grimace as she squeezed his hand well beyond the point of pain.

At that moment, several orderlies and a nurse entered the small room. The nurse, a substantially overweight black woman, lit up the room with her smile.

"Alright everybody, what do you say we have us a baby today?" she asked as she made her way to Sissy's bedside. "Oh my, you're a pretty one," she said, "and such a handsome father. You two are going to have a beautiful baby."

Looking at Reilly, she said, "Papa, you need to follow Grandpa now. I showed him where to go to wait. Go on now, she's in good hands."

Reilly looked at Sissy. He told her that he loved her. He didn't want to leave.

"C'mon son," said the senior Thorn as he led him out of the room.

The waiting was torture. Reilly was like a caged animal as he paced the small waiting area. Back and forth. Back and forth. His father would ask him to please sit and try to relax. Visitors came and went. Dominic Augustino stopped by after his shift to see how things were progressing. He told Reilly that the whole precinct was anxiously waiting for news. When she got home after work, Mrs. Thorn had found the hastily written note from her husband on the kitchen counter, and she was now sitting vigil with her husband and son. Andre had received a call and appeared with several sandwiches. His call had come from Sissy's mother who was now also in attendance. Andre seemed to have a calming effect on Reilly and actually got him to sit down and have part of a sandwich. Officer Tommy McMahon also stopped by having heard the dispatch call earlier.

Reilly said little. He was trying to quiet the horrible voices in his head that were intent on convincing him that something terrible was happening right down the hall. Something he was powerless to help with. At one moment, he was convinced he was going to lose Sissy. The next moment, he was sure the baby would be lost. The darkest thought was that he would lose them both and take all his reasons for living with them.

Hours passed. His mother told him this was common especially with the first child. All in the room tried to adopt a brave face, but dark thoughts couldn't be kept entirely at bay as the hours crept by.

Finally, the heavyset nurse from earlier in the day appeared in the doorway. There was not a trace of her larger than life smile as she surveyed the room. Standing with her hands on her ample hips, she announced, "Now is this any way for a family to welcome a beautiful baby girl into the world?"

Reilly was so prepared for bad news it took a moment for the words to sink in. A baby girl?

When the nurse next announced that both mother and child were doing fine, it was too much for Reilly as he buried his face in his hands and wept. His mother went to him and held him as sobs of joy and relief wracked her son's body. She said nothing as tears streamed down her own face.

The tears quickly abated. Hugs and handshakes and congratulations followed.

Mrs. Thorn didn't understand why her husband and son laughed when she reminded them that she had been saying all along that Sissy was going to have a little girl.

Before leaving, the nurse told them that they would need to wait as Sissy was being moved back to her room.

After what seemed like a long time, she reappeared asking, "Daddy, would you like to meet your daughter?"

Reilly looked to his father for guidance, "Go ahead, son. Your wife and daughter are waiting. Don't worry, we'll get to meet her shortly."

Reilly opened the door slowly, tentatively. The room was dimly lit. There was Sissy, propped up in bed cradling a tiny package. Mother and father simply looked at one another. A smile slowly appeared on Sissy's face. The smile was weak and tired and beautiful.

"Hope has been waiting to meet you," she said.

He realized they had never completely decided on a name but thought 'Hope' could not be more perfect. He was across the room in two strides and kneeling at mother and daughter's bedside. Tears flowed freely down his face as he held Sissy and gazed at Hope for the first time.

## Chapter Thirteen

The two federal agents sat in their small office assessing their situation. Prohibition had been good to them; very good indeed. The mob had set up a huge organization to manufacture and distribute alcohol, and Agents Wojick and Wroblonski were part of that organization. They might be a small cog in that wheel, but that was ok. As a matter of fact, small but vital was the best way to live in that world. Being small made them difficult to notice; being vital had rewarded them handsomely.

Curiously, the agenda of this two-person meeting was remarkably similar to clandestine meetings being held all over the country. A meeting akin to this was already scheduled to happen in the small but well adorned conference room at *Augie's* in the next several weeks.

Prohibition was ending. There was little doubt of that.

"I worry about a lot of stuff. Prohibition ending ain't one of them," said Agent Stanley Wojick with more confidence than he felt.

"How you figure, Stan?" asked his partner and cohort.

Teddy Wroblonski and Stanley Wojick had come up through the ranks together. They realized early on in their relationship that they were of a similar mindset when it came to law enforcement. They were friends even though Wroblonski, like many others, didn't consider Wojick very bright.

"Look, the mob has other interests for after prohibition. Stuff they're doing already but maybe on a bigger scale. Like take gambling for instance. You don't think there's a lot more money in gambling than what they're making now?" Wojick paused to let that resonate with his partner before continuing. "And what about ...you know a bunch of other stuff, too."

Wroblonski had to smile. They had both discussed the gambling angle numerous times. They both felt there would be a place for them in that world. Wroblonski found it funny that his dimwitted partner couldn't see beyond that. On the other hand, Teddy Wroblonski knew organized crime didn't plan on stopping with gambling. There were labor unions, many in their infancy, which needed the guidance and protection of the mob. Of course, you could always depend on the tried and true old chestnuts. Prostitution has had its place in the world since the beginning of time. The same was true of loan sharking.

The mob had plenty of legitimate businesses as well. They were heavily invested in construction, trucking, garbage collection, and restaurants in addition to the garment business. These legitimate businesses were used to 'launder' money acquired through illegal enterprises. Money obtained from criminal activities needs to be 'cleaned'. Once the money is cleaned, banks and other financial institutions will accept the funds without suspicion. Laundering money is a complex process which typically involves 'placing', 'layering' and finally 'integrating' the money back into circulation.

Drugs were an option even though both Wojick and Wroblonski were not inclined to dabble in that world. Many crime families felt the same way. A big part of the Mafia's success and rise to power in the 1920s was in large part due to their ability to bribe corrupt public officials and law enforcement leaders. They may not enjoy that same protection when it came to drug trafficking even though there was millions to be made.

On the global scene, drugs were finding their place in the world. In Germany, during the Weimar Years, which began after the First World War and extended through much of the 1930s, drugs like cocaine, morphine, and opium were widely available in places like corruption ridden Berlin. Stateside, cocaine and marijuana were available in massive quantities from Mexican neighbors. Both drugs were misunderstood in the 1920s. Wroblonski knew it was hard to be inconspicuous when it came to peddling drugs. He credited a lot of his success and his survival to being discreet.

Small but vital.

Wroblonski and Wojick had recently been reassigned to the Chicago branch after spending the last several years stationed in Atlantic City. The east coast had been good to them, but the reassignment had come at a good time. Atlantic City, perhaps the most corrupt little city in America, had caught the attention of the law enforcement world. Corruption and attention are a bad combination. Attention is like rust on the shiny chrome bumper of corruption. People notice. Maybe you could get by unnoticed with a little bit of rust, but the problem with rust is that it spreads. Tomorrow and each subsequent day the patch gets a little bigger and a lot more noticeable. Wroblonski and Wojick had managed to leg it out of Atlantic City at about the same time federal agents were showing up in mass. Many of these fresh recruits didn't share Wroblonski and Wojick's laisse faire philosophy towards law enforcement.

Wrobolski was a pragmatist, and his pragmatic world view was that there was enough to go around for everyone. He had no conflict, no internal struggle, with being a cop on the take. There were no sleepless nights; no moral dilemmas. If nobody got greedy; nobody got hurt, was another of the simple homilies he lived his life by. There was more than enough to go around to keep everyone fat and happy. He remembered what Enoch 'Nucky' Johnson had told him once in Atlantic City, "Fighting only gets you fighting."

Small but vital.

When he and Wojick had appeared on the Chicago scene, they first busied themselves with quietly making connections with the bootleggers. Of course the mob knew they were in town long before local law enforcement became aware of their presence. Confidants from their east coast days had set them up with introductions with the Chicago mob. Wroblonski considered them to be like job applicants showing up with solid resumes, great on-the-job experience, and impeccable recommendations. They were a shoo-in to get hired on.

So, that's why the first thing Wroblonski and Wojick do when they get to town is to go and talk to the mob guys who they are supposed to be investigating. Wroblonski figures if people aren't willing to talk there might be misunderstandings. Misunderstandings are bad for everyone. Misunderstandings in his line of work can get people killed. One of the first people they met with was Johnnie Octaviano. That guy Octaviano seemed like he was going to be easy to deal with. One thing Wrobolski liked about dealing with the mob was they understood how to play the game.

They were on the same page.

They sang out of the same hymn book.

Wroblonski and Wojick were part of the cost of the mob doing business; just one more expenditure.

The first meeting with Johnnie Octaviano couldn't have gone better. They weren't surprised to find out Octaviano was already paying off some local cop. They assured him they'd take care of that. They told him that he could expect better protection from now on. The feds had access to information that could really benefit a guy like Octaviano. Octaviano was glad to have these guys on his payroll. In Chicago, like in Atlantic City, there was a new breed of federal agent showing up. These guys didn't seem to understand how the game was played. Octaviano and Wroblonski were both well aware of a recent name on the Chicago law enforcement scene. Some guy named Eliot Ness, who came across as being a real choir boy. Capone had tried to bribe the son of a bitch, and what does he do? He takes it to the press as a way to show the world that the Chicago mob is afraid of him. The stones on that guy. Wroblonski knew that guys like Ness usually didn't stay vertical for too long, and as evidence of this, there were already a number of unsuccessful assassination attempts on his life. In 1929, Ness studied the background of every Prohibition agent and, after weeding out all the corruption, was only able to come up with a team of nine men that he felt he could trust. These nine became known as the Untouchables.

Neither Wojick nor Wroblonski spent very much time at *Augie's*. It wasn't necessary. It wasn't smart. One afternoon, after they had established a good relationship with the mobster, Wojick asked Octaviano who the big boss was. The three were sitting in one of the back rooms behind the bar sipping some very smooth and no doubt very expensive, high end whiskey.

Wroblonski had specifically told Wojick *not* to ask that question. He knew what omerta was, and he knew these mob guys all lived by this code of silence. Wroblonski worried that one day Wojick was going to say something stupid enough to get them both in trouble …or worse.

"You don't have to answer that," Wroblonski told the mobster.

Johnnie, without hesitation, answered, "August Augustino."

They were surprised as this was the first time hearing the name. Wroblonski had done his homework before he got to town and prided himself in knowing all of the major players. He told Octaviano honestly that he had never heard the name before.

Now, it was Octaviano's turn to feign surprise. "That's odd," he told the two, "you've each met him several times." Octaviano rose and went to some file cabinets and grabbed several thick files. As Wroblonski and his partner thumbed through them, they saw numerous receipts for everything from rent to electric bills all displaying the name of August Augustino.

Suddenly, Wroblonski started to laugh.

"What's so funny?" asked Wojick. Stanley Wojick was used to not getting the joke as more often than he liked to admit he didn't know what people were laughing about.

"Oh, that's clever," Wroblonski told Octaviano.

"What?" asked Wojick.

Augie had served the two federal agents on several of their infrequent trips to the bar. They, like most people, liked Augie.

Agent Wroblonski indulgently explained to his partner, "You know Augie? The guy who tends bar? Well, we better start treating him with a little more respect. As it turns out, he's a Mafioso king-pin. He's, what the hell do you people call it? Oh yeah, he's the 'capo di tutti capa'."

Octaviano liked the title, *the boss of all bosses*, and was impressed that this Pollack knew any Italian at all. He laughed at the comment.

Agent Wojick, still not sure what all this meant, laughed along with the others. When he would ask Wroblonski for clarification later, his partner would patiently explain that the fat bartender wasn't really a crime boss. Finally, a look of understanding crossed Wojick's face. Later, he would claim to have understood what was going on from the very beginning. Several days after that, he would explain to Wroblonski how Augustino was just a patsy in the whole scheme. This didn't bother Wroblonski. As a matter of fact, he was glad as it meant his partner really did understand.

# Chapter Fourteen

Reilly, along with the rest of the family, sat in the small living room. Hope, sensing she had a captivated audience, crawled over to the coffee table. Her grandfather, who spent many of his days caring for the child, said, "Come on Sunshine, show everyone what you learned today." Reilly's father had given Hope the nickname 'Sunshine' pretty much on day one. The name fit the toddler well. As Reilly watched, he reflected on the passage of time. It didn't seem all that long ago that his own grandfather had taken on a similar role with him. Hope treated her audience to a big toothless grin as she rocked back and forth in her seated position. Her next move was to get on her haunches and then onto her knees. Using both her arms and legs, along with the support of the table, she manages to stand. Reilly and Sissy, along with the grandmother, applaud their appreciation. It's a short performance as the effort to stand on tiny, wobbly legs for any length of time proves to be too much. Without warning, she plops back down onto her butt. They can't help but to laugh at the confused look on her face. Hope, not truly understanding what's so funny, laughs along with them.

Reilly slides out of his chair and onto the floor. Hope recognizes this game. It's one of her favorites. She quickly crawls across the floor. She doesn't stop when she gets to her father. Instead, she continues to climb onto his chest. Now, both horizontal but face to face, Baby Hope touches her father's nose. Reilly tells her 'nose'. Next, she touches his mouth, and he tells her, 'mouth'. They go through the same ritual with ear and chin and cheek. Finally, she grabs a handful of her father's hair. Reilly responds by saying, "Ow, ow, ow," which Hope thinks is the funniest thing in the world.

Sissy, looking on and smiling, tells her daughter, "Hope, don't hurt Daddy." Hope, who has come to think of this as part of the game, laughs harder. Sissy never had a doubt that Reilly would be a wonderful father. Good to his promise from Sissy's pre-natal period, Reilly takes his precious daughter for walks every day that the weather permits. He can sit and interact with her for hours. Reilly loves to put his daughter on his lap and page through her modest collection of books.

No one reads to the baby more than her grandmother. She patiently points out the animals and spells each name for her granddaughter. "Cow, C-O-W, cow, and see there's a dog, D-O-G, dog." She relishes the role of teacher, understanding it was not that long ago she was the student. She brought Hope the first book she would ever read. It was the Elson-Gray basic reader published in 1930. It chronicled the adventures of *Dick and Jane*. Hope, in truth, didn't actually read the book. Grandmother read it to her so many times the baby had memorized it.

Reilly loves his daughter with an intensity he didn't know was possible. Their modest home had always had so much love. The addition of

Baby Hope has amplified that love a hundredfold. Her grandfather's nickname for her was perfect. Hope did cast Sunshine wherever she went.

## Chapter Fifteen

Donofrio was born angry. His mother had given him the hopeful name of Michael Angelo Donofrio, a name he always hated. Donofrio, like Reilly Thorn, was inspired by a police officer as a young man to become a police officer. As a boy, Donofrio wasn't sure how old he was on that fateful afternoon, he clearly remembered walking down the street with his father, a man he both feared and hated. It must have still been winter as he recalled wearing a warm coat and gloves. It was dark but not late, perhaps early January. The senior Donofrio, who could best be described as a real piece of work, pilfered a sad looking, late season apple off a meager fruit stand as the two walked. Unbeknownst to the pair, a police officer saw the infraction and maneuvered himself to be able to intercept the duo at the entrance to the next alley.

The cop stepped in front of the two and as cordially as possible, asked, "How are the both of you today?" He made a failed attempt at a smile as he said this.

Neither of the Donofrio's knew what to say, so they said nothing.

"That's a tasty looking apple you have there. May I ask where you purchased it?"

The senior Donofrio, a liar by nature, replied without hesitation, "It's from home, Officer."

Michael Angelo watched the scenario unfold with keen interest. His loathsome father was starting to look a little pale as the cop simply let the obvious lie hang in the air. The policeman said nothing. He just looked at his father. He never broke eye contact.

With a shaky voice, he said, "Well, have a nice day, Officer," and made a move to walk around the policeman.

"Don't move you fat fucking liar," the officer quietly demanded. He still had that crazed smile on his face. From across the street it probably did look like a smile, but up close it was all wrong. Somehow forced and predatory.

"Now look here, I don't approve of that kind of language around the boy," stammered Michael Angelo's father. The young Donofrio was stunned by his old man's response as he had heard every imaginable curse word from his father on a daily basis starting from when he was still in a crib.

The cop tilted his head towards the alley saying, "Get in there." When this request was not immediately obeyed, he placed his hand on the butt of his sidearm, and repeated, "I said, get in there." Without waiting, the cop began to walk down the alley.

The senior Donofrio thought about using this opportunity to simply run away but couldn't summon the courage for such a bold move. He was not by nature a courageous man. He slowly began to follow the cop into the alley, but before he did, he turned to his son and in a rare moment of gentleness, said, "Son, you can wait for me here."

Michael Angelo looked at his father and, mustering a compassion he did not feel, said, "No dad, I want to go with you." Evidently, he did look compassionate as he said this as his father looked like he wanted to cry. The truth was that young Donofrio wouldn't have missed this show for anything. In his eyes, the policeman was perhaps the greatest thing he had ever seen in his young life.

The cop stopped halfway down the alley and, without turning around, said, "I saw you steal that apple." When from behind him the denials started, the cop spun around quickly and grabbed the liar by his coat collar. He slammed him against the wall, and with his face inches away from the terrified man, hissed, "Did you steal my apple?"

"Yes, yes, I did," squealed Michael Angelo's father. "Please don't treat me like this in front of the boy," he pleaded.

The cop turned towards Michael Angelo, and seemingly seeing the boy for the first time, asked, "Are you learning a lesson, boy? It's important to learn life's lessons early."

Michael Angelo enthusiastically nodded his head up and down to affirm that he was learning the greatest lesson of his life.

"It was just an apple," mumbled the thief.

Now the cop, who had surrendered any semblance of sanity, turned his attention back to the frightened man. "Just an apple? Do you think I give a damn if you steal an apple or a car or rob a bank? I own this street and everything on it. Do you understand that?" Removing his night stick he placed it under the terrified man's chin.

"There's a price to pay," said the cop, "always a price to pay."

The senior Donofrio had never been treated like this in his life. As a matter of fact, he was the one who handed out the abuse on most days. Being employed as a low-level manager at a small manufacturing company gave him enough authority to hand out orders, justice, and punishments as he saw fit. There were few things he liked better than to torment workers who found themselves on hard times. If he heard there was health or financial problems in one of their households, he might call the worker into his small office for an impromptu evaluation. The evaluations were always bad and would include veiled threats about suspensions or even terminations. There were times, glorious memorable times, that he had reduced brawny plant workers to tears. Oh, how he could make them beg and plead for their jobs. The ultimate payoff was when he would hesitatingly agree to overlook the performance issue and allow them to keep their job. Then, they would thank him and pump his hand and vow to improve in any way he felt necessary. If he asked, and he was tempted to ask on several occasions, they would have taken a knee and kissed his ring. He didn't fully understand the reason nor did he complain about it or admit it to anyone, but he would find himself fully aroused during these sessions. He often fanaticized about what would happen if he had women reporting to him. These daydreams were lurid and delicious.

Work had its satisfactions but he knew all too well that he wasn't the absolute ruler in that environment. He thought he should be. His boss was an idiot, and the owners at the highest level of the company were morons.

Home was another matter.

There he could rule with an iron fist. His wife was a pathetic mouse-like creature who had cursed him with a weak and disappointing son. He was disgusted at the end of each day when he would walk in the door and see the look of sick fear on her face. Her inability to understand where his anger came from only made him angrier. Dinner was as bland as the woman herself; the house every bit as disheveled as she. The better days for both of them included little dialogue. He would eat and settle in with either the newspaper or the radio as she would busy herself with cleaning and ironing. The apartment was small, making it difficult to stay too far away from one another or to keep from intruding on each other's space. He was a volatile man ready to fly into a fury over the smallest infraction.

"Do you have to make that much noise washing dishes?" he might bellow from the next room.

One night while ironing, she dropped the sprinkler bottle, shattering it on the kitchen floor. This was enough to send him into a rage. In a flash, he was in the kitchen asking her rhetorically how he could have ever been tricked into marrying someone like her. She fought tears as she hurried to sop up the water and shards of glass. He would remind her of the women he had turned away and wondered what he could have possibly been thinking to have *'hitched his wagon to such a nag'*. On those nights, he would send the boy to his room. Following that, he would order his wife into their bedroom. She walked with the gait of someone being led to the gallows. Following closely behind, he espies the way her buttocks move under her house dress. Her waist is slender. He begrudgingly admits that she has a certain attractiveness to her. He has seen other men look at her as well. This either angers or excites him depending on his mood at that moment. Once the door was closed, he would explain that she had erred and that he would now have to teach her a lesson. Looking appropriately burdened by this responsibility he would order her to undress. He knows she is afraid. Her chest heaves with each breath, and as it does, her bosom strains against the thin material. "Slowly," he would caution her. As her dress slipped off, he would remind her of the paradise he provided to her and the boy and the little thanks he received for all his troubles. He orders her to approach. Her fear is palpable. He loves this moment and forces himself to proceed slowly. He says nothing as he knows his silence tortures her. As she stands waiting subserviently, he mentally thumbs through his Rolodex of depravity. The demands he makes are meant to humiliate and degrade her. He knows she is not comfortable doing these acts. He reminds her, *'If you were, it wouldn't serve as much of a punishment, would it'*? He calls her a whore. He tells her she's disgusting and stupid. On the nights she cries, which are often, he becomes both more enraged and more aroused.

The paradise described by the senior Donofrio is actually a cheap run-down apartment in an impoverished section of town. The walls are thin.

On the other side of one of these thin walls sits Michael Angelo listening with contempt and concern. Most, but not all, of the contempt is for his father. He sees the weakness in his mother and saves some of his disdain for her. The concern is genuine and all for her. Michael Angelo loves his mother deeply. On the nights his father turns his anger towards him; his mother will seek him out and hold him while he cries. She comes to his room once she is convinced her husband is asleep. She smothers his face against her bosom so as not to wake her abusive husband. Michael Angelo tells her he hates him. She tells him that his father is a good man and a good provider. They both know this is a lie. The boy suspects that his mother hates him as much or more than he does.

One night, after a particularly bad episode between his parents, Michael Angelo tells her, "I'm going to kill him. I swear to God, I'm going to kill him one day." He does not know what happened on the other side of the wall that night, but he knows he hurt her. Michael Angelo could hear the whimpering. He heard the hushed pleading of his mother to please be gentle. Her pleas went ignored as the boy placed his hands over his ears in an effort to block the sounds of her suffering.

Seeing the anger in the boy's face, she begs him to never say those words again. She makes the sign of the cross and looks to heaven.

"Always a price, always a price, always a price," the cop repeats.

"Anything," offers the senior Donofrio. "I'll give you anything," he says as he begins to cry.

The cop takes a step back and looks at the blabbering man. "You know I could run you in, right?" says the cop. "I could throw the book at you. It would be a mess. There would be bail and court costs. Maybe some jail time."

The senior Donofrio was tempted to remind the cop again that it was just an apple but wisely chose not to. Besides, the cop looked less crazy at the moment, and he didn't want to risk having him slip back into the insanity he just witnessed.

He cautiously asks, "Officer, is there some way I might be able to pay a fine now?"

The cop seems to study the question. He looks to the sky as perhaps the solution to this problem is to be found there. He rubs his chin. He turns his gaze back towards the thief. The senior Donofrio can still see the imbalance in those hard eyes. The look scares him.

"Please officer, I need to get the boy home. His mother is a worrier. You know how women are," he says.

If either man had bothered to look at the boy, they might not have understood the look on his face. Michael Angelo watches with rapt attention. He looks enthralled. He doesn't want this play to end. Earlier, when the cop withdrew his night stick, the boy had a vision of the policeman bringing the club down on his father's head. In his mind's eye, he heard the crack of the club against the skull. As the cop pulled the club back for a second blow, he could picture hair and blood plastered to the wood. The second blow would be followed by a third. By this time his father would be a sniveling mass lying on the ground. By the fourth blow, he would no longer react to the hits, but the cop would continue to rain abuse with even more gusto on the evil and vile form of his father. Splattering blood would cover the wall and the alley. Some of the spray would hit Michael Angelo, and he would rejoice in the carnage.

Sadly, regrettably, none of that happened.

Instead, the cop holsters the night stick and demands, "Give me your wallet."

The senior Donofrio looks sick as he hands over his billfold. He usually carries a lot of cash. It's not that the family is well off, but occasionally he has the opportunity to flash these bills. He likes those moments, and Michael Angelo had witnessed numerous times when his father would buy a few pieces of penny candy and then apologize to the store clerk that he didn't have anything smaller than a twenty. To validate the point, he would open his wallet and show the hapless clerk two or three large bills. There are other times when the senior Donofrio would fantasize about being held-up out on the street. In these vivid daydreams he would heroically pummel the mugger, or muggers as often the fantasy included being accosted by a whole gang of ne'er-do-wells. Today, there are four twenty dollar bills in his wallet. He says a silent prayer as he hands over the billfold. Those eighty dollars need to pay this month's rent and buy groceries and pay bills. It will be a tough month for the Donofrio's if the cop takes it all.

The cop looks at the cash and quietly whistles. "You shouldn't be carrying this much cash around with you," cautions the police officer. "There are a lot of dishonest people out on these streets. I'd hate to see anything bad happen to you."

The apple thief thanks him for his concern. He hurriedly tells the policeman that he was on the way to the doctor's office. The boy's been sick he explains despondently; the medicine expensive.

"Doctor?" asks the cop, "I thought you were hurrying home? Something about his mother being a worrier."

The senior Donofrio feels sick to his stomach as the cop turns his attention to the boy.

"Are you sick, boy?" asks the cop.

Michael Angelo realizes that for the first time in his life he has power over his father. He doesn't have the kind of power the cop has, but he's getting a small taste of what it would be like, and he's hooked. The boy has learned to think fast and calculate odds quickly to try to avoid beatings from his father. He uses those skills now as he considers the probabilities. He can tell the cop that he's in perfect health with the hope that the police officer will rain abuse on his father, but he knows there are too many variables outside of his control in that scenario. He'll fantasize about what that course of action would have been like later, but at this moment in time, his gut tells him to play this another way.

"I have been sick, Officer," says Michael Angelo. "It's been going on for a while and the doctors can't figure out what's wrong. I have seizures. They think there's something wrong with my brain."

Michael Angelo has inherited the 'liar gene' from his father. The words roll off his tongue easily. Now, the fabrication is out there hanging in the air and being assessed by the cop.

"I think I'm getting better. I really do," adds Michael Angelo with just a tinge of false hope in his voice. "It's been hard on the family, but they don't complain. They just want me to get better."

The cop opens the wallet and extracts a twenty. He hands the billfold back to the senior Donofrio. He cautions him to behave himself in the future. He tells Michael Angelo, "I had a friend years ago who had what you have. He's okay now," and with that, he turns and exits the alley.

Father and son walk home in silence. Much later that night, he hears his mother's hushed pleas through the thin walls. "Please not that. *Please*." This is a particularly bad session. He hears the whimpering. He hears primal grunting from his father. He's old enough now to suspect what the nature of this abuse might be. He is both sickened and excited about what might be happening in the adjacent room. The next morning Michael Angelo finds a five-dollar bill on his night stand. He turns the bill over in his hands and ponders the meaning. He understands that his father, for the moment and in his own way, appreciates what he did for him yesterday. He also knows that the appreciation will turn into resentment and the resentment into something very ugly. His mother found that out last night; his turn is coming.

## Chapter Sixteen

Cars, long, black, and somehow sinister looking, had been arriving one after the other for the past fifteen minutes with each off-loading adhering to a well-defined protocol. An oversized sedan pulls up and two men exit. One of the men is a soldier, not in any traditional military sense but still deserving of the title. These soldiers are 'made' men who have sworn allegiance to their family. Each made man has gone through a ritual where they have vowed to honor omerta; the Sicilian code of loyalty and silence. The second man exiting the vehicle is the consigliere whose role it was to act as an advisor to the head of the family. The consiglieri are second only to the underboss, which in turn, are second only to the head of the family. The underboss will not be in attendance this evening.

Now out of their vehicle, Capos or Captains frisk the two men for weapons. There are five Capos present this evening; one from each of the families that would be represented at the meeting. Capos could be trusted to perform this search, at least as much as you can trust anyone in this line of work. Only the driver and a lone figure, silhouetted in the back seat, remain in the car. The driver exits next and is frisked. Following that, he opens the back door for the head of the family who walks directly into *Augie's* with his consigliere following closely behind. It would be considered disrespectful to frisk the family's head. The driver and soldier reenter the vehicle and drive off, making way for the next family to arrive and the ritual to begin again.

Augie Augustino tried to look everywhere except the door as it was opened to let another mob boss in. Johnnie Octaviano was there to greet each duo. There was a reverence to each greeting as if a distinguished dignitary was being welcomed. Normally, Johnnie would be smiling and laughing while he performed this ritual, but tonight there was a solemnity which would make laughing and smiling seem inappropriate. All the families were coming out of a difficult time. Things were said, boundaries had been crossed; men, good and brave men, had been lost.

Adding to the other-worldliness feel to the evening was the fact that the bar was completely empty. Augustino was surprised when Johnnie had asked him to make himself available for this evening's summit. In the past, Johnnie would slip Augie a few bucks and tell him to go home early. On those evenings, one of Johnnie's soldiers would take over the bar. Typically, it was a slender and stooped shouldered man that Augie knew only as Sal. Sal said little as he would position himself behind the bar. The first thing Sal would do was to take off his suit jacket, revealing a shoulder holster and shiny revolver. This hardware came off next and would be stashed behind the bar. The donning of an apron did little to make Sal look like a bartender. A scar ran down the right side of his face from the ear to his jaw. The next thing Sal would busy himself with was to rearrange everything behind the bar, which annoyed Augustino to no end. Augie would never say anything to Sal about this as Sal looked both a little pazzo and a lot dangerous.

But Sal wasn't there tonight. Augustino was, even though he wished he was anyplace else.

Once Johnnie escorted the boss and his consigliere into the meeting, he would come back and ask Augustino to prepare their drink orders. There was no friendly chatter between the two men as the drinks were mixed. Johnnie would deliver the drinks and then go to the door awaiting the arrival of the next duo. Finally, all the principals have arrived and are now behind the closed door. Johnnie is with them. Augie wishes he wasn't as this left only him and Guido 'The Mirror Buster' Santori in the now empty bar.

On the first night Augustino met Johnnie and his associates; Guido had taken a beer stein and broken the mirror behind the bar. This was at Augie's 'legitimate' bar in the days shortly before Prohibition was enacted.

Augie didn't like Guido. Guido had spent most of life looking through a peep-hole at patrons wanting access to the bar. He thought this made him important even though Augie thought you could train a monkey to do his job. Bartending, on the other hand, was a time-honored art; a true skill. Any moron could do what Santori did. Augie wisely kept these opinions to himself. Another reason Augustino had for not liking him was the constant barrage of insults Santori would hurl at him. Guido would delight in belittling Augie in front of customers. When he let people into the bar, he would tell them they would need to talk to the fat-ass behind the bar to get a drink.

"His name is Doggie," he would tell them, and many of the customers, not knowing any better, would call him Doggie. When Augie corrected them, Guido would laugh hysterically.

'Fat-Ass' was Guido's favorite nickname for Augie but by no means the only one. At various times, he would address him as 'barrel-ass', 'dumb-ass', or 'The Amazing Rotundo'. Santori had a seemingly endless collection of derogatory nicknames for Augie Augustino. Augie knew he could afford to shed a few pounds but didn't like to have this pointed out on a daily basis. He was sensitive about his weight, and it would hurt when customers would laugh at these barbs. It was most hurtful when Johnnie laughed. Augustino would laugh along with them because that's what a good bartender did.

Augie remembered all too well the day he told Santori that he was the last guy in the world that should make fun of fat people. "Why don't you look in the mirror once in a while?" asked Augustino. Then for good measure, he adds, "Just make sure you find a really wide mirror." Augie remembers the day because he still gets a ringing in the left ear from the beer bottle Santori slammed into the side of his head. This all happened in the middle of the afternoon when the tavern was pretty much empty. It was fortunate that one of the prostitutes, a sweet girl named Mary who was friendly with Augie, was in the bar because it didn't look like the one-shot had appeased Guido's anger at the comment.

Mary, all five-foot-three of her, shoved Guido with all her might. "Why would you do that to Augie, you big ape?" screamed Mary.

Guido took one hesitant step towards her.

"Go ahead and see what Johnnie says."

This was enough to stop Guido. Guido couldn't understand why but everyone seemed to like Augustino. He saw the way Johnnie was with Augie, and if Santori was to be completely honest, he would admit to himself that he was jealous of their relationship. The same was true of the hookers the bar kept in their stable. They were always talking and laughing with Augustino. When the girls would teasingly invite Augie into the back, he would laugh and ask, "Where were you twenty-years ago when I could have really used you?"

Mary goes to Augie, who is still on the floor after the attack from Santori. She kneels next to him and cradles his head against her ample bosom. Mary's not the prettiest girl in the stable or the shapeliest, but her gigantic boobs keep the men coming back.

"How you doing, Augie?" she asks as she gently presses his head against her chest.

"I'm fine," he tells her but adds, "I wouldn't complain if you held me like this a while longer."

Mary laughs and helps him up. Augie is trying to shake the cobwebs.

Mary fixes Guido with a stare. "Tell him you're sorry," she demands.

"No."

"Tell him, or I'm gonna tell Johnnie."

"He said I was fat," complained Santori.

"You are fat; now tell him you're sorry."

It hurt to know Mary thought he was fat, and it scared him to think of what Johnnie would do if he found out. "I'm sorry, Augie," he said meekly.

The irony in all this was that Santori was so stupid he thought that he and Augie were friends. Augie thought he was an asshole. This was another opinion he kept to himself.

Now that the main bar is empty, Guido feels comfortable leaving his post. The Capos are still outside, so there's little to worry about.

"Hey, abbondanza, how about a shot?" he whispers to Augustino.

"Forget it, Johnnie wouldn't like that." Augie enjoys the fact that he could tell him no. That would teach him for calling him 'abundance'; yet another shot at Augie's weight.

"Good boy, I was just testing you. Congratulations, you passed, now give me a beer."

Augie gives him an exasperated look. Santori, to the best of his ability, smiles in return. A smile on Guido's face is the proverbial square peg in a round hole. It just doesn't fit.

Now, leaning over the bar, Santori asks, "So tell me Fat-Ass, do you know what this meeting is all about? I'd bet you'd like to know. Huh, I bet you're dying to know."

"It's none of my business," replies Augie. He knows he should let the conversation end right there but adds, "I wish Johnnie would have asked Sal to bartend tonight."

"Sal? Sal ain't never bartendin' no more. Unless maybe the Angels get thirsty for a drink."

Augie mulls the comment over but doesn't reply.

"Angels?" continues Santori and chuckles, "There's no fuckin' way that son of a bitch got through the Pearly Gates."

Again, Augie says nothing. He busies himself with cleaning an already clean glass.

"With all the shit that guy did, he's mixing drinks for Satan himself right now. God damn right he is."

Santori, getting frustrated over the silent treatment, asks, "What the hell's wrong with you tonight?"

"There's nothing wrong. I just don't think Johnnie wants us talking about this. Johnnie tells me what I need to know. Other than that, I mind my own business. That's all."

The truth was Augustino wasn't inclined to mind his own business. He knew more than a few details about all of his regular customers. People drink, drinkers talk ...sometimes too much. Augustino, like many bartenders, knew how to open the vaults to a drinker's heart and soul. Late at night, when most patrons have staggered off to bed, a drinker might tell Augustino things he would never tell his parish priest even under the anonymity of Confession. Stories of unfulfilled dreams or misdeeds. Regrets about not being a better father or husband or friend. Often this litany would be spoken with head down directly into a half empty beer stein; never making eye contact with Augustino. Sometimes the drinker would become agitated, angry at the injustices the world had hurled at him. Other times, the melancholia became too great and would reduce the penitent to tears. At those times, Augie would put a hand on the man's shoulder and assure him that everything would be okay even though he had spent enough time around drunks to know that this prediction was unlikely to come true.

"Shit Augie, you're the nosiest bastard I know," said Santori. "You're dying to know what's going on in there." Guido leans further over the bar and asks conspiratorially, "You want I should tell you?"

Augie had to admit that he was a nosy bastard just as Santori had said. There were many times over the years he wanted to ask Octaviano more about what was going on but knew he was better off not knowing. At those times, he would casually ask Johnnie if everything was OK. Johnnie would grace him with that million dollar smile and answer that things had never been better.

He thought back to the day Johnnie, in all seriousness, said, "Augie, I need you to know something. It's crucially important so pay attention."

"Anything Johnnie, you can tell me anything at all." Augustino was both excited and a little afraid to be taken into Johnnie's confidence like this.

Johnnie looked around the bar, making sure no one was in listening distance. "You're putting too much Vermouth in the martinis," he said, and then when the effort of looking so serious became too great, laughed uproariously. "Augie, I don't want you to worry about anything around here except being the best bartender in the world. People don't go to a bar for the booze; they go for the bartender."

Tonight, with *Il Uomo* in attendance, especially under these circumstances even Augie was bright enough to know something big was going on. Augustino knew 'The Man' by no other name, and *Il Uomo* had no idea what Augustino's name was. This was fine with Augie. He knew *Il Uomo* was Johnnie's boss, but beyond that, he knew little else. The times he was at the bar he did no socializing. He would walk straight through the tavern making no eye contact. He would end up in the small conference room with Johnnie. They were often joined by the bookkeepers. If the meeting went on long enough, lunch would be brought in. Johnnie would leave the small room long enough to get a bottle of wine and several glasses and then disappear back into the meeting. When the meeting was over, Johnnie would escort *Il Uomo* to the door where they would say their goodbyes. Johnnie, as a sign of deep respect, would bend and kiss the ring of *Il Uomo*. The Man would take Johnnie's lapel and pull the much taller man towards him. After giving him a kiss on each cheek, he would leave the bar.

Guido again repeated the offer, "So, you want I should tell you what's going on?"

"What happened to Sal?" he asked, not really sure he wanted to know the answer. Augustino could not remember when time had ever gone so slowly.

"Fuck Sal. Sal got stupid, and stupid can get you dead in this business," answered Santori with more than a little resentment. "Just remember this Bubble Ass; don't ever cross Johnnie."

"I like Johnnie. He's good to me," said Augie a bit defensively. "I'd never cross Johnnie."

"He ain't no choir boy is all I'm sayin'."

Augustino thought back to the afternoon he had walked in on Johnnie orchestrating a beating in one of the back rooms with two thugs he had seen around the bar. He thought about the article he had seen in the paper several days later about a badly beaten corpse found not far from the tavern. After an awkward moment of silence, Augie hesitantly asked what tonight's big meeting was all about.

"I thought you minded your own business," answered Santori. "You know what's been happening around here the past few months, right?"

"Yeah, sure I know. Well, I know Johnnie's been on edge, but all that seems better now," said Augie. As proof of better times, he added, "Johnnie took my heater away." Augie had been both relieved and sorry to have lost his gun. It made him feel like a tough guy, probably for the first time in his life.

Santori laughed when he heard the word heater. "You mean that pea-shooter Johnnie gave you?"

"The newspaper called it 'turf wars'," said Augie, to show he knew what was going on. From Augustino's point of view it looked like everybody was making money, so he couldn't understand why the families were fighting.

"Hey there Big Butt, maybe you're not so stupid after all."

"Again with the fat jokes. You should be nicer. Then maybe people would like you more," said Augie.

This comment hurt Santori more than Augustino would have guessed. "People like me," he said defensively. "Mary likes me."

"That doesn't count. You have to pay Mary."

Santori said nothing. He was in his forties and had never married. He daydreamed often about a different life from the one he had chosen. A life that included a wife and kids. Sometimes when he lay with Mary, he would fanaticize that they were married. No one would suspect it but Guido was a gentle and caring lover. He only slept with Mary and prided himself on being faithful to her. One day, after making love to Mary, he told her that they should run off together. "We could build a new life someplace where no one knows us or knows our past," he told her. "Maybe we could go to Michigan. I got a cousin out there who owns a flooring place. I could maybe get a job there. If you were with me, I could be happy selling linoleum."

'Johns' fell in love with hookers all the time, and Mary recognized this for what it was. There was no other life for her; probably not for Guido either. On the day Guido 'proposed', she stood on the bed so they could be eye to eye; such was the difference in their heights. Putting her arms around the hulking figure, she gave him a big hug and told him he was sweet. "Guido, I hope you do find that girl someday and get out of this crazy racket. You and me both know I'm not that girl." She kissed him and ruffled his hair, saying, "If you don't find her, you come see me next week. Okay?"

Time crawled.

"Prohibition's ending," announced Santori.

"Hey, that's great news," said Augie a little too loudly.

"Shhhh," admonished Santori. "Great news? What the hell's wrong with you? How could you possibly think that's good news?"

Augie had dreamt of the day Prohibition would be over. He pictured himself with a little shot and a beer joint like in the days before the Volstead Act had become law. Augustino couldn't understand why it wouldn't be good news for everyone. He shared these thoughts with Santori.

"Augie, just when I think that maybe you ain't the dumbest guy in the world, you say something stupid."

When Augie looked confused, Santori continued, "Do you know how much money these guys make off of illegal booze?" he jerked a thumb at the closed meeting room door in case Augustino was too stupid to figure out who he was talking about. "So let me ask you this. When this shit's legal again, who makes the money?"

CHRIS DRNASO

Augie nodded slowly. He had never thought of those circumstances when Prohibition finally ended. He wondered what Johnnie would do. "So when does this happen?" asked Augie.

"That's just it, nobody knows. That's why the families are meeting. They want to put the fighting behind them and figure out how they're going...."

Guido didn't get a chance to finish his thought as the door to the meeting room opened. Johnnie alone came into the room, "Guido, cars," was all he said before going back into the conference room.

Guido went to the door to tell the capos to start bringing the cars around. Augie tried to look busy behind the bar even though he had cleaned every glass twice and wiped down the entire bar two or three times.

The principals began exiting the conference room. It was a solemn procession, which given the fact that these men typically looked solemn, meant nothing. Two by two, the men left the building until it was just Johnnie and *Il Uomo* at the door. Johnnie helped him into his overcoat. If any words were exchanged between the two men, it was done so quietly that Augustino couldn't hear. There was the emblematic ritual of kissing the ring and the kissing of each cheek before Johnnie walked him out and saw him safely into his waiting car.

Guido looked at Johnnie as he came back into the tavern and was relieved to see the worry lines melting from his face. "How about a beer?" Augustino offered.

"Sure, a beer will probably wash down that double-whiskey you're going to pour me very nicely," said Octaviano.

"Guido, there's some sandwiches and a beautiful tray of cannoli in the conference room. Why don't you grab them?" asked Johnnie and added, "Nobody even touched the cannoli."

"I'm on it boss," he replied, and headed into the conference room.

"Did you kids play together nicely tonight?" Johnnie asked Augustino. Johnnie knew that Santori liked to tease his bartender. He also knew that it bothered Augie more than Guido realized.

"Oh sure, Johnnie. There was no problem."

Just as Guido was coming back into the room with a tray of sandwiches in one hand and the pastries in the other, there was a pounding at the door.

77

"I'll get it," Octaviano said, "you got your hands full."

"That's my job boss," answered Guido as he slid the trays onto the nearest table. "It's probably some rummy looking for booze or pussy."

Now at the door, Guido looks back at Augustino and Octaviano, saying he'll send whoever it is packing. As he slides the peephole open, he turns to see who's keeping him from tucking into the sandwiches and desserts.

The explosion of the double barrel shot gun sounds like thunder against the late night quiet of the bar. Johnnie is off his bar stool in a flash and pulling his revolver from its holster. Before he is halfway to the door, the sound of a powerful engine and squealing tires fills the night.

# Chapter Seventeen

It felt good. It was comfortable, like slipping on a well-worn and favored pair of shoes. He'd been away a long time and didn't realize how much he missed the sights, and even the smells, of his old gym. Most, but not all, of the faces were new, and it was like old home week when he ran into someone he knew from his boxing days. Invariably, they would spend a few minutes reminiscing about the good old days. The conversation often turned to memories of Uppercut as stories, both funny and poignant, were shared. Many of the old crowd asked what he was doing there, and Reilly simply passed it off as a guy getting older and trying to get in better shape. It was a good cover story that both young and old could relate to. Reilly wasn't in anywhere near the same shape as he was during his boxing days, but he was still in good shape. Part of this was because he had kept up with his roadwork since stepping away from the gym. He had always liked to exercise and especially enjoyed running. He worked a revolving shift and, like many who had constantly changing schedules, found it affected his sleep. Running, especially during the first few days of a shift change, helped mitigate the effects.

At first, Andre had resolutely refused to have anything to do with his training. He knew Reilly was looking to help the family by entering the world of illicit boxing. Andre wanted nothing to do with that world. He had begged his old friend to walk away. He threatened to ban him from the gym; a gesture he knew was meaningless as there were other gyms available to

Reilly. In his heart, Andre knew the best chance Reilly had of not being killed in the ring was to be his trainer.

Andre, who had cut his teeth in the boxing world with Uppercut, told all new members at the gym the same thing Uppercut had told him years ago. *'If you're willing to work hard and have heart, I'll train you. If not, I won't waste my time'*.

Andre said these words to Reilly now. Memories of his beloved manager Uppercut rushed back at Reilly. He knew Andre was serious when he asked, "Do you have heart, Reilly?"

Their training started the next day. It was a different chapter in their lives. They had been friends for years. They had trained together as young men and, being in the same weight class, had sparred together often. There were still a few long time members at the gym who remembered the spirited sparring matches the two would put on. In those days, they were both lightning fast and smart, which usually makes for an entertaining combination. When Reilly and Andre sparred, everyone in the gym would be at ringside knowing they were in for a treat.

Reilly knew he was a long ways from sparring with anyone. Andre was rebuilding his friend from the ground up and treated him like he would any raw recruit. Andre knew this wasn't fair but hoped it would frustrate Reilly into walking away from this whole plan. Reilly was in for many miles of roadwork, hours of jumping rope, building his core with thousands of sit ups, and exhausting work with the medicine ball. There would be little work with the weights, just like when he trained with Uppercut.

One day, several weeks into their training, Andre spied his trainee looking at the speed bag.

"Forget it," he told Reilly, "you're a ways away from working the bag."

Reilly, who up to this point had obediently followed all of Andre's instructions, walked to the bag and began working it. Slowly at first, he just used his right hand before he switched to his left. Several in the gym, realizing there is something going on between the two friends, turn to watch. Reilly began some simple combinations; right-right-left, followed by left-left-right. Andre, arms crossed, stood to the side watching the show; his expression unreadable. Reilly, now at one with the bag, has picked up his speed as his combinations get steadily more complex. The bag is a blur. His audience is mesmerized, but Reilly has more to show them as he folds elaborate footwork into the demonstration. Several applaud as calls of encouragement come from the appreciative audience. As quickly as the show started, it stopped. Reilly grabs the bag to steady it. He is sweating and breathing heavily. It's eerily quiet in the gym. It's never quiet in the gym. Andre has a reputation as a no nonsense trainer and is the first to tell new trainees, *It's my way or no way*. Those assembled are anxious to see how this scenario will play out.

Reilly realizes he was wrong. What he did was disrespectful, and all he can think to do next is to say, "Sorry Boss. That was just something I had to get out of my system." The comment goes a long way towards defusing the situation as many, including Andre, laugh.

Andre, addressing the assemblage, warns, "Reilly's my best friend and might be able to get away with this ...once. I don't recommend anyone else try it. OK, is this a gym or a sewing circle? Let's get back to work."

Now, showered and ready to leave for the day, Reilly appears in the doorway of the small office at the back of the gym that was once occupied by Uppercut. He taps lightly to get Andre's attention. "Could we talk?" asks Reilly.

The room is small, tiny really, but Andre has managed to maneuver another chair into the space for visitors. He grabs a stack of freshly laundered towels from the chair and sets them to the side before offering his friend a seat.

Once seated, Reilly begins, "I know you're intentionally slowing down my training. You're trying to discourage me, and I know why you're doing it."

Andre breaks the eye contact first, perhaps looking a little guilty.

"If it's all the same to you, I'd rather not help my friend get himself killed," the trainer replied in all seriousness. "Wouldn't a cop say that would make me an accessory to murder?"

Reilly would have laughed if his friend didn't look so affected. He knew he was putting him in a tough spot. "I'm getting into the ring, Andre. That's a fact. If you train me to the best of your ability, I'll be fine. All this roadwork and other stuff you got me doing will help, but we both know I need to be training in the ring. I need to be going toe-to-toe with your best guy."

The age difference between the two men had been very apparent when they first met. Reilly was just a kid at the time. This age difference disappeared as Reilly got older, and the two men became friends. Now Andre felt like the older brother or perhaps a young uncle.

"I'm about 170 pounds. I'd be a light heavyweight by my way of thinking. So, who's your best guy in that class?" asked Reilly.

"By your way of thinking? That's the problem Reilly, you're not thinking. Weight class? If you think this is like real boxing, you need to get that idea out of your head right now. They might throw you into a ring with a guy who weighs in at 220. I'm not talking about some slug. I'm talking about a monster of a guy who knows how to take a punch and throw a punch. You want to spar? How about if I throw you into the ring with Angel?"

Reilly remembered Angel from the 'old-days' and was surprised to see he was still at the gym after all these years. Angel could box. There was no question about that. Being honest with himself, he had to admit he'd want nothing to do with fighting a guy like Angel Vasquez.

Andre was glad to see his words were having an effect on his young friend.

"I'll tell you what. I'll put you in the ring with a guy your weight, but he's going to be wearing these." Andre slid the top drawer of his desk open and pulled out a set of brass knuckles. He dropped them onto the desktop with a clang. "I took these beauties off one of the guys in the gym. He was training for the kind of boxing you're looking to do. He took most of the padding out of his gloves. I could tell by the sound his hits made on the heavy bag that something wasn't kosher. That and the fact that nobody wanted to spar with the guy."

Reilly stared at the knuckles sitting on the desk. He had always loved boxing. He and Andre had both learned to respect boxing from Uppercut, a man who loved the sport more than anyone. The sight of these things made him sick.

"Are you free Saturday night?" asked Andre.

Both men said little as they walked away from the warehouse turned boxing ring. It was going on eleven o'clock, and the streets were crowded with others who had attended the night's matches. Pent up excitement, along with a lot of testosterone, had spilled out of the arena and onto the street. Alcohol, which was still illegal, had flowed freely during the entire night as beer vendors roamed the aisles. They had done a brisk business. Now, out on the streets, shoving and shouting matches were everywhere. Several fights had broken out. The cop in Reilly compelled him to step in between two of these street fighters, but Andre pulled him back with a shake of the head.

"That ain't none of our business," he said as he led his friend away from the fracas.

As they put more distance between themselves and the venue, the streets became less and less crowded until it was just the two men walking side by side. It was a silent march. Both men were still processing the events of the evening. The location itself could best be described as industrial. A makeshift ring had been constructed in the center of a large open warehouse area. Four barnyard lights, suspended from the dark ceiling, illuminated the ring. There were multiple rows of chairs encircling the ring. VIPs and high rollers would have a seat. Many others would stand. Some had climbed onto catwalks and crossbeams to watch the event. Against the back walls were cages where bets could be placed. The bookies, like the beer vendors, appeared to be doing a good business.

There had been three fights on the card. The first match, a spirited affair between two like sized and evenly matched fighters, ended abruptly late in the fourth round.

Andre whispered to his friend, "Can you guess what the over-under was for this fight and where most of the action was?"

The idea had crossed Reilly's mind as he saw one of the fighters drop his shoulder and offer his chin to the other. This would have been a 'red-flag' to an experienced fighter but most in the crowd would have never suspected that the fix had been in on the first bout. It stirred a memory of his academy days when he had stepped into the ring with his instructor.

The second bout looked legitimate to both Reilly and Andre. Both men were about evenly sized but not evenly skilled. The better boxer might have finished the fight earlier but it ended up going a full 10-rounds and ending with a decision. Most of the action had been for a win by knockout. The crowd, either anxious for blood or the next fight, screamed their disapproval. One discontented fan threw his beer bottle at the ring. Within seconds, two burly bouncers pounced on the man, pummeling him with night sticks. This helped to satisfy the crowd's blood lust as they turned their attention to the action in the audience. Reilly was close to where this all took place and got a good look at the unconscious man as they dragged him from the arena. His entire face was a mask of blood. He wasn't sure if the man was still breathing or even alive. He suspected that there might be a second beating in the man's future once they got him outside.

Reilly and Andre continued their silent march. With each step that took Reilly further away from the warehouse, the better he felt. He didn't feel good but at least better. He would never feel good about what he had seen this evening. He thought about Uppercut and what he would have said about tonight's proceedings. He knew that Uppercut would be ashamed to know Reilly planned on stepping through those ropes.

If the night had ended after the first two bouts, Reilly could have shrugged off what he saw with little afterthought. Sports, all sports, had the potential to be fixed. Reilly would never forget the Black Sox scandal of 1919. He liked baseball as a kid and considered players on that team to be his heroes. He was crushed to discover they had tainted a game he loved.

The third bout was what would haunt Reilly's dreams for a long time.

There was an extended break after the second fight. There would be plenty of action on this fight, and the promoters wanted to make sure there was enough time for everyone to place bets. Beer and food vendors hustled through the crowd knowing this was their best last chance to make some money on this night. Finally, the lights over the ring flashed on and off several times, signaling the main event was about to begin. The first fighter to enter the ring could best be described as big and shapeless. Reilly didn't judge. He had played enough sports to know that surprisingly good athletes could come in some pretty bad packaging.

Leaning into Andre, he says, "That guy looks like Leo."

"Oh Christ, it is Leo! What the hell is he doing here?" asked Andre

Leo Frankowicz had trained at the gym for years. Leo was a very good boxer. Leo was fat. Leo was very fat. It would make Uppercut crazy when Leo would walk into the gym prior to his workout chowing down on one treat or another. Leo would describe it as a light snack. Uppercut would shake his head and claim Leo could feed half the gym with his light snack. Many opponents would make the mistake of judging Leo on appearance, but those who had stood toe to toe with him knew that he was surprisingly quick in the ring. Reilly marveled at anyone who could eat like that before one of Uppercut's training sessions without throwing up.

The ring announcer now heralds the arrival of the favorite into the arena. The crowd erupts as the fighter makes his way to the ring. The guy's a monster. A chant of *Bruiser, Bruiser, Bruiser,* starts in the back of the venue and spreads quickly throughout the arena. Shedding the robe, Bruiser poses for the crowd. Every part of the fighter is heavily muscled. He's massive across the back and shoulders.

Like with the first fighter, Reilly reserves judgment as he's also seen some pure physical specimens, like the Bruiser, who weren't particularly good boxers.

Bruiser points at Leo's rolls of fat and laughs. He grabs his own washboard mid-section and pantomimes a man jiggling his belly. There is little to jiggle on Bruiser's stomach.

Leo responds by shaking a fist at his opponent. He grabs his ample midsection with a gloved hand and starts to shake his blubber. When the crowd laughs, Leo throws his hands in the air. The mass cheers.

Bruiser has the look of a man who doesn't appreciate the antics of the fat man.

Before the bout starts, both men are called to the center of the ring. The underdog extends his hands to Bruiser for the ceremonial touching of the gloves....

Reilly and Andre are now at the point on their walk home where they split up and go separate ways. These best friends, usually so comfortable with each other, have said little to one another. Andre fights the temptation to ask his old friend if he has seen enough this evening to convince him to give up this crazy idea. Reilly and Andre both respect boxing. They love the sport. Uppercut had instilled in both men the idea that boxing was a time-honored and somehow noble sport. There was nothing noble in what the two friends had witnessed tonight. Reilly watches as Andre walked away. Walking alone and feeling very alone, Reilly turns his collar up against the cool night air and heads for the sanctuary of his humble home.

# Chapter Eighteen

Donofrio, never one prone to good moods, is feeling particularly ornery as of late. It seemed like the whole goddamned universe was conspiring against him. It was one thing after another. He was still pissed at that sonofabitch Octaviano for making a big deal out of him slapping some whore around. That's what guys did with broads. Maybe you wouldn't do it with your wife all the time, but who gave a damn about what you did with a prostitute. Besides, he didn't have a wife, so he had to go to hookers for a little fun. Now, when he made his weekly stop at *Augie's*, the broads were icing him out. That bitch Mary with the big tits was the worst. She was like the union-steward or something. Who the fuck died and made her boss? She was going to get hers, too. Donofrio had given a lot of thought to what he'd like to do with that little whore if he ever got her behind closed doors. That particular fantasy never failed to bring a smile to his face. He thought him and Johnnie were friends. They had a nice relationship; mutual respect. He couldn't believe it when Octaviano stood up for the whores over him. They're whores for god's sake. Octaviano said they were like private contractors who just leased space in the back. He had no control over who they bedded and who they didn't. What a crock of bullshit that was. Octaviano owned that pussy; pure and simple.

He used to like making his collections there. Well, he liked Augie anyway. Who wouldn't like that big, dumb sonofabitch? He heard what happened to Guido, and he was glad to hear that guy got his. He'd like to shake the hand of the man that was on the business end of the shotgun that night. Guido Santori, who did that guy think he was? He had the balls to tell him to stay away from Mary. He had told Donofrio if he ever touched Mary he'd kill him. Donofrio had assured him he wanted nothing to do with that slut. They both knew it was a lie. He thought about running the sonofabitch in for threatening a police officer. What kind of world was this where guys had so little respect for a cop?

He had no choice. Weekly collections still needed to be made, and he was expected to make them. So every week Donofrio would go to *Augie's*, like he was some flunky errand boy or something. Oh, Johnnie was still there to greet him and still acting as friendly as ever. Slapping him on the back and offering him a beer. Donofrio knew it was all a big act. The phony sonofabitch.

As if he didn't have enough on his plate, now he has to deal with his old man. Donofrio had witnessed up close and personal the abuse his father had heaped upon his mother. He had moved out as soon as he had the money to get away. He still remembered the look of fear and hopelessness on his mother's face on the day he told his parents he had found his own place. Even though he was now physically removed from the home, he knew the abuse hadn't stopped or even slowed down. The opposite was probably true. There was a time when he felt sorry for his mother. It was harder and harder for him to muster sympathy for her. She needed to take some accountability for what was happening. It used to be when Donofrio saw a bruise on her; he'd ask what his father had done. Lately, he would ask his mother what she had done to deserve it. It was always the same answer. "I didn't do anything, Michael Angelo," she would claim.

She still called him Michael Angelo even though she knew how much he hated that name. He had to fight the urge to give her the back of his hand at those moments. Donofrio never hit his mother. He remembered all too clearly those horrifying nights as a child when his father would beat him for a real or imagined infraction. He remembered his mother comforting him in the darkness of his small room. He remembered her smell and the softness of her breasts as she would try to muffle his sobs. She continued to do this even after the night his father had burst into the room and dragged her out. Michael Angelo had buried his head in his pillow that night, but it was not enough to drown out the anguish coming from the next room.

Michael Angelo loved his mother. She was so warm and loving when it was just the two of them. He had wonderful after school memories. Times when he would help her bake or she would help him with his homework. The mood in the house would grow progressively darker as the time for his father's return approached. It broke his heart, even as a young boy, to see the emotional and physical change that his mother went through as the hour of his arrival grew nearer. She would beg Michael Angelo to *please* not do anything to anger his father when he got home. She knew it was an unfair thing to ask as there was no control over the man's moods or his temper. His mother would race around the house trying to make sure everything was perfect. She would straighten things that needed no straightening; fluff couch pillows that needed no fluffing. Dinner would be checked and double checked as the expectation was that it be served hot and fresh as soon as her tyrannical husband walked in the door. She would send Michael Angelo to his room to do homework, and then she would stand and wait for the key to turn in the lock. She had become so in tune with his habits that she could almost sense his mood just by the sound the tumblers made as he turned the deadbolt.

Michael Angelo had seen this scenario play out the same way day after day throughout his entire childhood. His father was almost always gruff, even if not always abusive, when he walked in at the end of the day. On rare occasions he was in a good mood. He remembered one day when his father had brought his wife roses. She wept as she hugged him. That night Michael Angelo had listened through the thin walls. He heard cooing and passionate whisperings coming from the next room. For some enigmatic reason, these sounds infuriated the boy even more than the agonized sounds he normally heard.

His mother, like so many abused spouses, remembered their courtship days when he would tell her she was the prettiest girl in the world. It had been a long time since her husband had told her that. She held fast to the hope that they would one day rekindle their lost passions; rediscover their earlier love.

Donofrio knew this was going to be a bad one. It had to be for his mother to call the station house. When Donofrio finished his shift, there was the simple message waiting for him; *Call your mother. IMPORTANT*. He checked the time and figured his father was probably still at work. That was good. He wanted to be there when he got home. This would give him a chance to get his mother's side of the story, not that her story ever changed much. '*I didn't do anything. I swear; I did nothing*'. He was tired of both of their bullshit. He was going to tell her that when he got there. At least that was his plan until he opened the door to the small apartment.

There was his mother sitting on the sofa, her left hand shielding his view of her face.

"C'mon mom, let's see what the bastard did this time," Donofrio said as he gently took her hand. As soon as he saw her face, he felt the fury rise in him. Jesus, she was a mess. The entire side of her face was purple. Her left eye was almost entirely swollen shut. The little he could see was pooled with blood. There was a trickle of dry blood in her ear. Angry bruises showed on her arm. This was the worst by far that Donofrio had ever witnessed. He had been a cop long enough to see plenty of carnage out on the street. He was unaffected by most of what he saw on the job, but the sight of this sickened him. His mother sat staring straight ahead. She said nothing. She didn't seem all that aware that her son was in the room. He took her chin and, as gently as he could, tilted her face towards his.

A look of surprise crossed her features. "Michael Angelo, when did you get here?" she said, just as sweetly as you please. "How was school today?" she asked.

The question chilled him. His rage for the moment was replaced with concern. This was his mother. What did that sonofabitch do to his mother?

He went to the kitchen and prepared an icepack. "This is going to be cold, mom," he said as he gently held the pack to her damaged face. She grimaced in pain, either from the cold or from the pressure against her bruises. Probably a little of both thought her worried son. He asked her some simple questions and was relieved to see that she was starting to get her wits about her. He helped her to her feet. "Mom, I want you to go lay down in the bed," he instructed. She limped badly, and Donofrio noticed for the first time the swelling and discoloration of her right ankle. *'Christ, what the hell happened here?'* he wondered.

Donofrio understood that every once in a while you needed to straighten out the old lady. That was, by his upside-down way of thinking, all part of married life. Wifey gets a little cocky or mouths off at the wrong time and a husband had the right, no, the obligation, to nip that shit in the bud. Whatever had happened here went way beyond acceptable limits.

With difficulty he helped get his mother into bed. She asked to use the bathroom. He flushes the toilet for her and sees there is blood in the urine. There seemed to be little of the woman that wasn't bruised, so it was almost impossible to handle her gently enough to not cause her pain. He managed to get three aspirin down her throat. He sat on the edge of the bed and held her hand.

She told him she loved him. "You're a good boy," she whispered.

"Ma, I need you to sleep now," he said. He was angry and embarrassed to feel tears welling in his eyes. He continued to sit with her as she slowly drifted off to sleep. He could still see the torment in her face and wondered if there was something stronger in the house besides aspirin. He wished there was something he could give her to make her forget what had happened here, not just last night but over the years. Donofrio allowed himself to wonder, not for the first time, what it would have been like to have had a better home life. He wondered what it would be like to live without the fear and dread both he and his mother had to endure every day of their lives at the hands of his father. The compassion for his mother slowly ebbed, replaced by a white hot hatred for the man who had done this.

Donofrio was outside the building smoking a cigarette as his father came around the corner. When he saw his son waiting, he felt fresh anger at his wife. Why'd she drag the kid into this?

"What are you doing here?" he asked his son as he approached.

"I'm here because you beat the hell out of mom last night."

"That's none of your concern. That's between me and your mother."

The words angered him, but the younger Donofrio said nothing as he took a long pull off his cigarette. The time for words had passed. He knew his father had no respect for him nor did he have any respect for the uniform. He took no pride in his son being a police officer. None of that mattered any more as Officer Michael Angelo Donofrio saw the future come into focus with pristine clarity.

When the boy said nothing, he went to shoulder his way past his son. "Get out of my way," he gruffly said.

"I'll make sure you see it coming, pops," his son said quietly. "That's a promise."

This seemed to get his father's attention. "See what coming?" he asked.

"The bullet," was all the younger Donofrio said as he dropped his cigarette, toed it out, and turned towards home.

As he walked away, he could hear his father's protestations. "You can't talk to me like that. You're a cop for god's sake. You think that uniform makes you a big man? You're a punk."

His final comment to his son was one they both knew wasn't true, "Even you ain't crazy enough to do that."

# Chapter Nineteen

Officer Dominic Augustino looked at the two federal agents questioningly as he stood quietly in front of the small desk. The man behind the desk continued to read from several papers he was holding. He held one finger in the air as a signal for Augustino to wait until he finished reading. If Augustino would have seen these two men out on the street, he might not have immediately pegged either as cops. Today in this room, there was no doubt they were in law enforcement. This mystery did not require great detective skills to unravel as there, on the desk in plain sight, was a gold badge inscribed with the words, *Federal Agent*. Augustino had not been offered a chair when he entered even though there were empty chairs available. One man, the reader, was seated at the desk. The other man, a hulking figure with broad shoulders, stood at the only window in the room. He seemed captivated by the street scene one-story below. Dominic took in his surroundings at a glance. One desk, several chairs, a lamp, and one small file cabinet made up the furniture. The half-glass door to the room was one of four in the second floor corridor. The others had the names of businesses stenciled on them. The door Augustino entered only displayed the number '3'.

Officer Augustino had found a note in his locker telling him to make himself available for this meeting. The note went on to caution him to tell no one of the invitation. He was not to wear his uniform. As he stood in the small office waiting for the seated man to finish reading, he ran the events of the past several weeks over in his mind trying to isolate any incident that might have landed him here. He had stood in front of the small desk long enough to where it was getting awkward.

Agent Wroblonski placed the papers face down on the desk and, at last, looked at the nervous young policeman. He studied Augustino for a moment. His expression, hard to read.

"Do you know Officer Michael Donofrio?" asked Wroblonski.

"Yes sir, I do," replied Augustino, and after a slight hesitation, he added, "He's a fine officer."

The man behind the desk paused a second. He appeared to be assessing both the response and Augustino. "I suspect we both know that's not true, but we'll get to that in a moment."

The big man at the window, who up to this point hadn't even acknowledged that Augustino was in the room, suddenly wheeled on the cop, pointed a beefy finger, and said, "You're in big trouble, boy! Don't try playing dumb with us, that's our job."

The peculiar comment hung in the air.

"Christ, Wojick, do you ever stop and think before you talk?" He next looked directly at the surprised cop and, by way of introduction, said, "I'm Special Agent Wroblonski, and you just heard from my partner, Agent Wojick. Look Officer, I'm not your captain, so I'm not sure how much trouble you are or aren't in. I don't really care too much about that right now. This meeting is simply a way for us to get to know one another."

Augustino remained quiet. He would speak when he knew more. For the moment, he said nothing. Wroblonski respected that. More often than not someone in Augustino's position would start running off at the mouth and, before you knew it, would say a lot more than they should. He had interrogated enough suspects to know that the really smart ones said little; the stupid ones, as one might expect, said stupid things. The ones who thought they were smart were the ones whose mouth really got them into trouble.

"So, let me tell you what we know so far. Donofrio is a dirty cop. He's on the take with bootleggers operating here in Chicago. He's small time, but the agency we work for doesn't tolerate any indiscretions on the part of any officer sworn to uphold the law."

Wojick interrupted, "Pay attention, boy."

Neither man responded. Wroblonski knew his partner was trying to intimidate the young cop. Stanley Wojick was a long way from being the brightest guy in law enforcement, but his brutishness got people's attention. Wroblonski had a different approach. This dichotomy was one reason they made a good team.

"Officer Augustino is with us so far, Stanley. He's hanging on every word. Isn't that true, Dominic?"

"Where were we?" asked Wroblonski. "Oh right, we were discussing Donofrio. As I was starting to say, Donofrio has been putting the pinch on one of the local mob families. He takes a payoff in exchange for information or in some cases protection. We've already met with Officer Donofrio and have convinced him of the error of his ways. We've turned him back to the good side of things."

Part of this was true. Agents Wroblonski and Wojick had met with Donofrio. Their agenda wasn't to put him back on the path to salvation. The truth was crooked cops like Donofrio made their job a lot easier. Donofrio would take the risks. If things went bad, Donofrio would take the fall.

"Donofrio still has the same relationship with this crime family. The difference now is he's bringing information back that we can use in fighting crime."

Again, there was some partial truth to this. Donofrio was still visiting the *Augie's* once a week. He wasn't bringing back information. He was bringing back a fatter envelope. The envelope now contained additional funds to pay for the services of Wroblonski and Wojick as well.

"Officer Donofrio told us something of interest concerning you, Dominic."

That statement captured Augustino's full attention.

Wroblonski continued, "Are you related to a gentleman by the name of August Augustino, known in most circles as Augie Augustino?"

The meeting adjourned ten-minutes later. It was a life altering ten minutes for the young police officer.

"We need to let you go as we have a meeting set up with," and here Wroblonski paused to reference some papers on his desk, "Captain Benjamin Rush. I assume you do know Captain Rush?"

Ben Rush was the captain in Dominic's precinct. "Yes sir, I know Captain Rush," he replied.

"Rush is just one of Chicago's finest that we'll be meeting with. This is standard operating procedure to let local law enforcement know we'll be working in the area. We'll say nothing to Rush about our little talk, the same way you'll say nothing about this meeting. Is that understood?" asked Wroblonski.

"Understood," said Augustino.

"Just one more thing before you're dismissed. We want you to say nothing to Officer Donofrio about today's conversation. I don't know if you two are friends but friends talk, right? The same rules apply with your Uncle Augie. That might be tougher because he's family, but we are ordering you to say nothing. Is that understood?"

Another half-truth told by Wroblonski had to do with the meeting with Ben Rush, Augustino's station captain. The reality was that meeting had already taken place.

Augustino's commanding officer seemed like a good man, but most of the men in the precinct didn't really know him. Occasionally, he attended meetings that were held at shift changes. Most of the time he looked distracted at these briefings and was the first person out of the room when the meeting ended. He surprised Reilly one morning when he addressed him by name. Reilly shared this story with his friend Dominic Augustino, who laughed and said, "Reilly, you're the only Negro in the precinct. Everyone knows your name."

Rush did know Reilly's name. What would have surprised all the patrolmen under his command was, that he not only knew their names, he also knew a great deal about them. He could have told them where they lived, if they were married, how many kids they had and, in many cases, the age and names of their children. Ben Rush very quietly kept his finger on the pulse of everything that happened in the precinct. What Rush had discovered over his years in law enforcement is that, far and away, most cops are honest ...as long as you looked the other way on what he considered minor indiscretions. Ben Rush did look the other way on cops that fixed an occasional traffic violation or took advantage of a 'Blue-Uniform' special at a store or restaurant. He understood what a difficult and dangerous job this was and believed if a cop was to get a free meal, or a good deal on a nice suit, it was deserved. In Rush's view, it was all about setting limits. He had seen cops that had fallen in love with what some called, 'The Big Store'. This, Ben Rush could not or would not tolerate. Rush cared about his men, which was the main reason he took the time to learn so much about them. There was a second, darker reason. It allowed him to keep his antenna up for 'Red Flags'. If one of his men recently bought an expensive car or moved into a bigger house in a nicer neighborhood, Rush knew about it. He had the resources available to do some clandestine investigating into a patrolman's finances.

Rush had been in a command position for most of the nineteen-twenties, and what he saw happening in his beloved Chicago troubled him.

Prior to World War One, the city made meaningful strides in the war against vice. Sadly, whatever ground gained during this period was soon lost with the election of Mayor William 'Big Bill' Hale Thompson. Thompson was mayor from 1915 until the early 1930s, with the exception of a few years in the middle of the 1920s. Thompson was a cowboy; a cowboy in the literal sense of the word as he had worked at that trade in New Mexico. Bill was not only big but bigger than life. One day, he entered the halls of the city council on horseback. And he was a big man, standing at over six-foot and weighing in at 300lbs. He was an outstanding athlete. He was closely aligned with organized crime in general and Al Capone in particular. When Big Bill sought to regain the mayoral seat in 1927, Capone contributed $100,000.00 for his reelection. In 1993, a panel of historians named Thompson the most corrupt politician in Chicago's history. Of course Ben Rush didn't know that the future held this dubious honor in store for Thompson. He only knew that Chicago had become a safe harbor for some seriously bad individuals. Rush had seen good cops stymied by inefficiencies in a corrupt system even when trying to make arrests in gangland murder cases. Big Bill Thompson was ousted as mayor from the years 1923 to 1927, in favor of a new administration who tried to suppress bootlegging. The murder rate actually rose during these years. Big Bill, with the aforementioned help of Capone, regained control of the city in 1927.

Rush himself had given a lot of thought to his meeting with the two federal agents. More national law enforcement agencies had begun to surface around the country. Chicago, being a hot bed of organized crime, corruption, and bootlegging, attracted the attention of these relatively new agencies. For the most part, Rush didn't like it. Men would show up and try to take over. They were arrogant and tended to treat the embedded police force condescendingly. Rank is everything in a police department just as it is in a military setting. With these federal agents you didn't know where they sat in the hierarchy of rank, and this bothered Rush. It made Rush sick to see the way Chicago police brass, all the way up to the commissioner, kowtowed to these G-Men. Ben Rush also knew that corruption, like a cancer, didn't discriminate on who or what it poisoned. He had seen it infect everyone from high ranking elected officials to petty autocrats who had found themselves with some minimal amount of authority.

Rush, on occasion, still thought about a man named Gierke who worked in the city's building department. Gierke had a tiny office in the basement of City Hall. It had been used for janitorial supplies prior to Gierke convincing his boss to let him reinvent the space as an office. The job was purely a patronage position. His wife, a cousin of a city councilman, had managed his campaign, and he thanked her by getting Gierke his job. The city was booming, and the building office was busy. The way it worked was that no one could get their permit until Gierke gave his stamp of approval. He wasn't an inspector or an engineer. The truth is he could barely decipher a simple set of blueprints. None of that mattered because Gierke was bright enough to figure out that he could either approve a project or delay it. Delays would cost the builder money for every day they waited for their approved permit. The smart play was for the developer to visit Gierke in his little rat hole of an office with a small gift of appreciation for the fine work Gierke was doing. If they left with their permit, well that was all part of the price of doing business in Chicago.

Ben Rush would have never even been aware of Gierke's existence except that he had made friends with a developer who had complained of the delays he had to endure at the hands of this petty tyrant. When the builder described the blatant shakedowns, Rush was moved to pay Gierke a visit. He wore his uniform. Gierke was unimpressed as he described to Rush how the process to obtain a permit was complex and could be painfully slow. Gierke next went to a stack of folders, which sat on the corner of his tiny desk. The third or fourth folder from the top was his friend's application. Gierke opened the folder and stared intently at the content. His brow was furrowed. After a moment, he closed the folder.

"This application will need a lot of additional review before it can be approved," expressed Gierke with a contrived sense of concern. Having said this, he slid the folder back into the stack. When he was done, it now rested at the bottom of the pile.

Rush's first impulse was to reach for the man's collar, pull him forward while sending a punch into his smug little face. Instead, he thanked him for his time and left. Rush wasn't a fool, and he knew what and who he was dealing with that morning before he ever walked into the building department. He understood how the city worked and knew full-well that this little worm of a clerk was connected. Rush was not without his own resources. Before leaving City Hall, he visited one of his own connections; a city official who owed Rush a favor or two. The next day Rush's friend received a call letting him know his application had been approved. When Gierke left work that day, he laughed as he found a parking ticket on his windshield. Rush knew it was a meaningless message to send as Gierke would have the ticket 'fixed' before the ink on the citation was even dry.

Rush saw more and more instances of how this was the way things got done in Chicago. Everyone knew someone; everyone was connected. As is often the case, Gierke squeezed too hard or squeezed the wrong people, and he ended up losing his cushy patronage job in the building department. This wasn't a problem because in a growing city like Chicago, his city councilman benefactor simply moved him to another department.

Rush ran this over in his mind as he thought about these G-Men. He had seen too much to simply take these men at their word. What bothered him was that he didn't have the same resources available to him to validate these men. Rush liked to be well informed before venturing into any situation. He lived by and survived with the credo, *'Do your homework'*, but in this case, his homework was sketchy and incomplete.

Rush wasn't sure what to make of Wojick and Wroblonski. Wojick, who didn't seem particularly bright, said little. Wroblonski, who spoke a great deal, said even less.

After the meeting, Augustino found himself out on the street wondering what had just happened. The more the G-man spoke, the more confused he became about what his role might be in all this. He was warned repeatedly to say nothing. He was told they would be in touch. On that ambiguous note the meeting ended and, just that quickly, he was shown the door. He was relieved to be out of the meeting. The air felt good. The meeting had ended abruptly, almost as if they were suddenly in a hurry to get rid of him. He began to amble away. He hadn't gotten too far when the question of why they rushed him out suddenly seemed important. The story of Captain Rush being scheduled to come in following his interview didn't ring true with Augustino. He had been a cop long enough by this time to trust his instincts, and here his inner voice told him to hang around for a bit. There was a small diner across the street from the meeting location.

Augustino went in and found a seat at the counter where he had a good view of the building's entrance.  The pie and coffee were so good that he almost missed him. The fact that he wore a fedora and had his collar turned up made it difficult to pick him out. The only way Augustino was sure was that, before walking into the building, he stopped and looked up and down the street. His survey included looking directly at the diner. Even though Dominic was seated far enough back from the window, he still took pause as Officer Donofrio appeared to look directly at him. Donofrio slid in through the doorway and was gone. Augustino finished his coffee and quickly exited the café, digesting both his pie and what he had just witnessed.

## Chapter Twenty

Dominic Augustino loved his Uncle Augie. For as long as Dominic could remember, Augle was the focal point of family get-togethers. He had a seemingly endless number of jokes and stories that he shared with the men, women, and children of the family. The women and children might get the edited, censored rendition of the story while Augie saved the bawdier version for the men. Dominic could picture Augie, off in a corner of the room, telling a joke in whispered tones to the men in the family. He kept a vigilante eye out for his wife, Dominic's Aunt Rose. If Rose should espy him, she would chastise him with admonitions like, "Augie! You better not be telling any of those dirty jokes over there." The reprimands from his wife did little to discourage Augie. Many of Augie's funniest stories were about life with Rose. People, including Rose would laugh as she, like just about everyone else, had a fondness for the lovable Augie. Uncle Augie was the proverbial life of the party.

There was speculation about just what Augie did for his livelihood. It was no secret that he owned a modestly successful bar prior to Prohibition. This was in the Back of the Yards neighborhood where  Augie would occasionally host a family party at his tavern on Sunday afternoons. It was a nice bar and might be described as nothing fancy; words that one might use to also describe Augie. Barkeep was a good fit for Augie as he had no other skills to speak of. He had a wrench behind the bar that he used to tap kegs with. It was the only tool Augie owned. The only tool he felt he needed in his life and in his profession. He wasn't good at getting up early and didn't mind staying up late. Following the enactment of the Volstead Act, there was some conjecture about how he supported his family. Some of the rumors were uncomfortable to think about as they cast Augie in an unfavorable light. One truth that was hard to ignore was that whatever Augie was doing, he was doing pretty well at it. In 1926, Chrysler introduced its Imperial model and Augie showed up at a family function driving one. Two years later, he sold the barely used luxury car and bought the even more costly Imperial Phaeton. Augie was never going to be accused of being a slave to fashion. Clothes, even nice or expensive clothes, just don't do much for certain people. Augie qualified as one of those folks. Rose would tease him with, "Augie, you are the only man I know that can put on a brand new tuxedo and ten-minutes later look like an unmade bed." And this was true, his shirts refused to stay tucked; his ties hung askew no matter how much Rose straightened them. Rose, on the other hand, had an eye towards the finer things in life. As Augie pulled up in a new car, Rose might step out of the car with an expensive fur or a lavish new piece of jewelry. Rose, like others, didn't ask what her husband was doing, and Augie didn't tell. Whatever Augie was involved in, he seemed to be doing just fine for himself.

There was one thing that those closest to Augie couldn't deny. With each passing year he looked more worried; more haggard.

Dominic, following his meeting with the two federal agents, had no doubt about his uncle's doings. He could understand now why his carefree uncle was looking a bit stressed of late. Wojick and Wroblonski had shown the young police officer folders full of receipts all bearing the name of August Augustino. Dominic's lovable uncle had gotten mixed up with some bad guys. The two federal agents had painted a picture of his uncle as a mafia kingpin. The idea, in Dominic's mind, was laughable. Wojick and Wroblonski had told Officer Augustino to say nothing about what they had found out about his uncle. Dominic tried to explain that his uncle just wasn't bright enough to orchestrate any large scale underworld operation. It hurt Dominic to describe his uncle in these terms, but it was the truth. The two agents listened politely and then dismissed the young police officer. Before they let him go, they reemphasized, "Say nothing. We will contact you. This may happen tomorrow or next week or perhaps never. Be prepared to aide national law enforcement efforts and tell no one of this meeting."

Dominic struggled through a myriad of emotions before reaching out to his uncle. The Augustino's were not Sicilian but, like nationalities and families around the world, had their own version of *omerta*. There was truth in the old adage about blood being thicker than water. Dominic couldn't help his uncle until he understood exactly what was happening in his uncle's world.

Augie squinted as he left the warmth of the sunny day and entered the coffee shop. It took him a moment for his eyes to adjust before he saw his nephew signaling to him from a booth near the back. Augie smiled broadly as he made his way to the table. Dominic assessed what he saw. A heavy set, doughy man somewhere on the wrong side of being middle aged. His pants were baggy. There was a shine to them at the knees. His shirt was untucked on the right side. It occurred to Dominic that Augie's shirt was always untucked on the right side. His hair seemed to defy the gel his uncle used as cowlicks stuck out in several random directions. He carried his fedora in his hand. Dominic rose as his uncle neared the table. He looked as his uncle's face. It was a good face. It was the kind of face that one intuitively knew would help a friend or family member or even a complete stranger. It was a face that was creased with years of laugh lines. Dominic loved that face and loved it more than ever as his uncle treated him to a broad smile. Augie took his nephew by the shoulders and planted a kiss on the young man's cheek. Dominic completed the ritual by kissing his uncle's cheek.

Dominic gestured that his uncle should take a seat.

"What, you're not working today?" asked Augie, making note of the fact his nephew was not in uniform. "Is everything OK on the job? You doing OK?"

"No problems, Uncle Augie. The job's great," replied Dominic.

"You need money? It's good you come to your Uncle Augie. How much you need?"

Dominic had to laugh as he told his uncle he didn't invite him to lunch to ask for a loan. The offer didn't surprise Dominic as Augie was quick to offer loans. The loans always came with zero interest and no expectations on when the money might be paid back. No matter how many times Augie might get stiffed on a loan, he never hesitated to offer to help the next person. This was true even when the next person was someone who had reneged on an earlier advance.

"We need to talk, Uncle Augie," Dominic said.

Augie laughed, "You young people always look so serious. Besides, no one should talk on an empty stomach." With that said, Augie reached for the menu that was held against the wall by a collection of condiments and a napkin holder. "So, what's good here?" he asked.

"Not the coffee," answered his nephew as he took another cautious sip.

Augie quickly perused the menu, which offered a modest collection of soups and sandwiches. "You think they'd have one pasta dish on this menu? What, they don't have a pot to cook a little linguini in?"

The lunch conversation was light. Augie mentioned several times how nice it was for Dominic to invite him out. After the table was cleared and Augie was finished lamenting that they had no cannoli, the two settled in to why they were here.

Dominic started simply, "Uncle Augie, you're in trouble."

Augie was not a bright man but knew there would come a day that his affairs would become public. There were times he could convince himself that there was nothing wrong with what he was doing. Augie knew he was involved with bad men but didn't consider himself an outlaw. He was a bartender, that's all, a simple bartender. How much trouble could a guy get in by serving beer and telling a few jokes to his patrons? He was fortunate that on most days he could block out what he saw going on around him. He convinced himself that Johnnie Octaviano was just a businessman and that the dangerous looking men he saw around the bar were simply business associates. He could block out a lot. Mary was just a girl trying to make a living. He liked Mary and chose not to think of what went on in the back room as she giggled enticingly while escorting a 'date' out of the bar and into her erotic realm. Augie was good at convincing himself that there was nothing wrong with what went on in his life. After all, he was just a simple barkeep. But sometimes at night, when Augie crawled into bed, the reality of it all came crashing in. He closed his eyes and would see the flash of the shotgun. He would hear again, for the thousandth time, the deafening blast. He would remember the way Guido Santori slammed against the wall as the acrid smell of gunpowder and the lingering, bluish smoke drifted through the bar. He saw with accursed vividness the way the big man slid down the wall and the almost comical way he came to rest on the floor. Augie saw the disgusting trail of blood and brains left on the wall by Santori. The residue created a surreal road map showing the route Santori traversed as he slowly made his way from this world into the next. Yes, Augie was usually, but not always, quite good at convincing himself that he was just a bartender; a simple bartender.

Dominic had let his words hang in the air. He could see the internal struggle his uncle was going through and knew he had to let the man process the simple declaration. Augie started to speak, stopped, started again and then sat silently looking at the scuffed and coffee stained table top in the hope that a clue on how to proceed was to be found there.

As the silence grew longer, Dominic asked, "Tell me how all this happened."

"It was that goddam Prohibition," answered Augie.

Dominic refused to think of his uncle as a perp or criminal, but the cop in Dominic recognized this as the moment when the person being questioned opened up. Smart cops knew this was the time to say nothing. After a short pause his uncle continued.

"Everything was fine. I had a small bar, and me and your Aunt Rose we did OK. We weren't rich or nothing, but we did alright for ourselves. I was lucky. I liked what I did for a living. There's a saying that if you like what you do, you'll never work a day in your life. Well, that was me. I was good at it, too. Then that goddamn Prohibition hit. Those goddamn do-gooders got to stick their nose in my business. What's wrong if a guy wants to stop and have a beer on his way home? It don't hurt nobody. It's not like booze ever killed nobody, no-how, no-way."

Dominic had seen the damage alcohol did to people's lives every day while out on his beat. Everything from car crashes to spousal abuse to infidelity to disorderly conduct often could be traced to the bottle. He was pretty sure his uncle had seen as much or even more. Dominic wasn't here to debate that with his uncle.

"So, then I gotta figure out what I'm gonna do. The only thing I know how to do is run a bar, and the government is telling me I can't do that no more."

For the first time since he started talking, Augie raised his head and looked at his nephew. He saw the look of concern on the young man's face, and he loved his nephew for it. Dominic knew his uncle was coming into a part of the story that was more difficult to tell. He again was patient as he waited for his uncle to work up the resolve to continue.

"So one day this guy walks into the bar ...hey, that sounds like I'm telling you one of my bar jokes, huh?" Augie said as he smiled at his nephew. It was good to see the lovable man smile. It was short lived as he now continued. "His name was Johnnie, Johnnie Octaviano, and it was like he was sent from heaven to help me. Johnnie's class, Dominic, pure class. He's really handsome. The broads love this guy. He got money and dresses real nice."

Dominic didn't want to write down the name in front of his uncle but made a mental note to find out more about this Mr. Octaviano.

"He asks me what am I gonna do when Prohibition starts? When I told him I didn't know, he said he could help. He asks me how I would like to go on running a bar. He respected what I do Dominic. He told me that they could use a guy with my skills. Everybody thinks there's nothing to running a tavern, but you gotta be on the ball. You got to order the booze and take inventory. It's long hours and then you gotta deal with all sorts of people. Sometimes those drunks can get pretty nasty. They can be *aggressivo*, you know, not very nice. I got robbed one night. Oh yeah, this guy comes in at closing time and sticks a gun in my gut. Scared the hell out of me. When I told Johnnie that story, he laughed and told me that I would never have to worry about getting robbed again. Johnnie's got a great laugh, Dominic. I think you'd really like him."

"Maybe I could meet him someday," Dominic replies. He sips his water waiting for his uncle to continue.

"I told him sure, sure I'd like to keep running a bar, but how's that gonna happen? Later that night, Johnnie comes in at closing time with this older guy and this other guy. The other guy's a big guy. His name was Guido Santori. I didn't know what the old guy's name was. He didn't say much. I found out later that he was Johnnie's boss."

Augie's talking faster now. His thoughts seem scattered, and he's rambling, but Dominic is just letting him run with it. He'll try to sort some of this out later.

"They called the old guy *Il Uomo,* you know, 'The Man', because he is the main guy I guess. Johnnie always treats him with respect. Johnnie would kiss his ring. I seen him do it a few times. Now that's respect. The other guy, the big guy, Guido, he was an asshole, Dominic. He broke my mirror that first night. He threw a beer mug at it. Johnnie got mad at him for doing it, too. He told him he shouldn't have oughta done that. Guido was always givin' me a hard time. He was a bully. I kind of feel bad about thinking he was an asshole because of what happened and all."

"What happened?"

"Oh that, he got his brains blown out one night in the bar," said Augie. "Damn, I could really go for a nice cannoli right now."

"Wait a minute. Someone was shot and killed in the bar? And you witnessed this."

"Yeah, there was some big meeting. It was a big deal. All these important guys met in the back room. Even Johnnie was nervous about it, and Johnnie's always very cool. Johnnie asked me to bartend for the meeting. I was honored because it was a big deal and all. Usually, he would have asked this guy Sal to do it, but Guido told me Sal had gotten himself killed somehow. Guido told me that before they blew his brains out. Christ, what am I sayin' here, of course it was before he got his brains blown out."

"When did that happen?"

"It was the same night as this big meeting. Everyone had finally left, and it was just me, Johnnie, and Guido alone in the bar. I could see Johnnie was starting to relax. I poured him a drink, and Guido went to get us some leftover sandwiches from the meeting room. There was a knock on the door, and Johnnie got up to see who it was. Guido told him he'd get it because that was his job and all. Guido thought he was a big shot because he knew how to answer a door. Christ, a three year-old knows how to answer a door. So Guido slides the little peephole open, and there's this loud explosion, and well, that was how Guido got his brains blown out."

Dominic looked at his uncle. He wanted to ask a hundred questions but couldn't formulate even one.

"I felt bad about that for a long time," continued Augie, "I had bad dreams and couldn't sleep. I felt bad too about thinking Guido was an asshole and all. You know, the funny thing is that I kind of miss him. I know Mary misses him."

"Was Mary his wife?"

"I think Guido would have liked that, but no, she wasn't his wife. She's one of the prostitutes that work at the bar," replied Augie matter-of-factly. "She's a friend of mine. Mary's really nice. All the guys like Mary. She has huge boobs."

Dominic wasn't sure what to expect when he approached his uncle, but this was a lot more than he bargained for. Booze, the mob, gangland slayings, and prostitution. Part of Dominic wanted to know more while the other part was hoping his uncle was done talking.

"Uncle Augie, you're in a lot of trouble," Dominic repeated.

"What trouble? I didn't do nothin', and besides, Johnnie will take care of it. You don't understand, Dominic, these guys got connections all over the city. They're 'Big-Time' connected."

Dominic felt badly for his uncle. Here's this sweet, funny, and unbelievably naïve man sitting across from him and he has no idea of what's really going on.

"May I ask you a question?" asked the young police officer. When Augie nodded his approval, Dominic asked, "Did you ever sign your name to anything at the bar?"

"Oh sure, I sign for just about everything," Augie replied.

"I met with two federal agents who have been assigned to investigate crime and corruption in Chicago," said Dominic. "At the meeting they showed me folders full of receipts all signed by you, Uncle Augie. They think you're running the whole operation. I don't know what will happen next, but when they come, they'll be coming after you."

Augie smiled at his nephew, "I told you not to worry. Johnnie will take care of this."

"Uncle Augie, I think you're the fall-guy in all this, and it might be Johnnie who's been setting you up."

Suddenly, Augie becomes agitated, "That's ridiculous. Johnnie's my friend. He'd never do that. You should have seen how mad he got at that asshole Santori when he broke my mirror."

Dominic could sense that he was losing his uncle. "I'm sorry. I didn't mean to say anything bad about your friend. I have to ask you to do something, OK? I don't want you to say anything about this conversation to anyone. That means Johnnie Octaviano or Aunt Rose or anyone else. Will you give me your word?"

After Augie gave his word, Dominic navigated the conversation into calmer waters. They made small talk until Augie announced he had to get going. The two men rose and embraced. They exchanged kisses on each other's cheeks. Augie took his nephew by the shoulders and, looking him directly in the eye, said, "You're a good boy, Dominic. I know you love your old uncle, but I'm telling you, you got nothing to worry about."

On that note, the two men parted.

# Chapter Twenty-One

The two federal agents and Donofrio had formed an unholy trinity in the short time since they first met. Wroblonski knew they were playing a dangerous game; a game that had the potential to not end well. Wroblonski, who was far and away the brightest of the three, had of late spent a lot of time thinking of all the possible eventualities. There was a new breed of honest cop emerging. Guys like Eliot Ness who couldn't be bought. Guys like that didn't care if they were busting crooks or crooked cops. Wroblonski did not want to end his career as a disgraced cop. His mother was proud of him and bragged about him to family, friends, and strangers. It would kill her if he was to get busted. She'd never live down the shame of it. On the other side of things was the mob. Any relationship with these violent men could go sour quickly and without warning. Wroblonski had run afoul of one of the smaller operators in Atlantic City and suffered through some harrowing moments in the weeks before making the move to Chicago. While assigned to New Jersey, there was several times where a cop just disappeared. One day they were there, and the next they were gone without even a body left behind for a proper burial. The neighboring ocean did not give up its secrets or its dead. He knew that end would kill his mother as well.

Neither an end at the hands of the saints or the sinners had much appeal to Theodore Wroblonski. He questioned whether it was some special sixth sense warning him to give up this game, or perhaps he was simply losing his nerve. Regardless of what the real reasons were for his trepidation; he knew it was time to move on.

The other two members of this bizarre threesome did not suffer from the same concerns as Wroblonski. In truth, it looked like Agent Wojick and Officer Donofrio were having the time of their life. They had become friends, and this worried Wroblonski. The combination of Wojick not being the sharpest tool in the shed and Donofrio seeming not quite right in the head should have troubled him. Wojick had always been the perfect complement to Wroblonski. He was happy to play second fiddle. He did what Wroblonski asked without question. He understood the importance of keeping a low profile. He was ...controllable. With the addition of Donofrio into the mix, their core relationship seemed to be changing. Oftentimes in the evening, Wroblonski and Wojick would have gone out for dinner. After that, they might have caught a vaudeville act. Following the release of "Don Juan" in 1926, they also had the option of going to a movie house in the evening to watch a 'talkie'. Even though this 1926 Warner Brother's release was the first talking motion picture, it was Al Jolson's "The Jazz Singer" the following year that convinced movie makers that talking pictures were what the world wanted. Wojick would now beg-off from spending the evenings with his longtime partner in favor of hitting the town with the young policeman. Wroblonski wasn't sure what these two were up to, but he didn't trust his partner to be smart, and he sure didn't trust Donofrio to be sane. There were more than a few mornings when Wojick staggered into the office still wearing the same clothes from the day before. His eyes, looking like roadmaps, told the story of the drinking that must have gone on throughout the night. On the morning Wojick came in with a gash under his left eye, Wroblonski tried talking to his partner.

"Rough night last night?" he asked the hungover man.

"Great night. You got no idea."

"You think maybe you should give this a rest. I mean with you and Donofrio and all?"

"Donofrio's a good kid. We're having us a high time out there. Teddy, you worry too goddamn much. What's wrong with a couple of guys being out on the town?"

"The difference is we're cops. We're cops that might have good reasons to keep a low profile," answered Wroblonski. He fought to keep the agitation out of his voice.

"Fuck that, we can get away with this shit because we are cops. You ever think of that?" asked Wojick. "You should hang out with us some night instead of going home to your knitting. You don't know what the hell you're missing."

"I'm telling you to give this a rest. I don't want you hanging out with that Donofrio. We can't risk that. We got too much to lose. Besides, he ain't right in the head."

"Yeah, you got that last part right. You got no idea how right you are on that last thing you said about him not being right in the head," rambled the big man.

Wroblonski didn't like the way this conversation was going. He especially didn't like the last comment his partner had made because he realized his partner was right. He really didn't know just how crazy Donofrio was. Crazy could get a guy killed out there. He was about to get a taste of just how *pazzo* Donofrio was.

"We need to talk," was the first thing Octaviano said when Wroblonski answered the phone. They made arrangements to meet at *Augie's* tavern even though Wroblonski avoided being seen there too often.

The bar was mostly empty when he entered. He espied Johnnie behind the bar and nodded towards the door leading into the back offices.

Now, situated in the small conference room, Octaviano pours them both a drink. "We got a problem," he told the federal agent.

Two nights prior, Agent Wojick and Officer Donofrio are drinking. Wojick is very drunk. He believes that his new best friend is just as inebriated, but he is wrong. Donofrio has given the impression that he has matched the agent beer for beer and shot for shot, but he has carefully controlled the amount of booze he has consumed. They are sitting in one of the hundred 'blind-pigs' that still operate in the city. They are not known to be cops in this establishment. Wroblonski has convinced his partner to stay away from places like *Augie's* or any other place they were offering protection.

"She had no right to talk to you like that," said Wojick in response to the story Donofrio told about the incident between him and Mary.

"I'm the only guy in the world that can't get laid in a whorehouse," said Donofrio laughing. The two men click glasses as a toast to the unfairness of it all. Wojick alone drains his glass. "That's no bullshit. Not only that, she's got all the other hookers icing me out, too. I walk in there and they all scatter. And what was the big deal? So what, so things got a little," here he hesitated looking for the right word and finished with, "physical."

"That ain't right," agreed the agent.

"And I'll tell you something else. She loved it. I was giving her the ride of her life, and she loved every minute of it."

The truth was Donofrio, not for the first time, was having some performance issues. The more he worked at it, the more hopeless it seemed. Mary, like all hookers, had seen this scenario repeat itself with clients. Alcohol dulls the libido. The spirit is willing, but the flesh is weak. A lot of 'johns' will simply fall asleep; others, embarrassed and humiliated, will mumble an apology and leave. Then there's the breed who feel the fault belongs to the hooker. They offer instructions and criticisms. When that fails, it oftentimes will lead to something darker. The night Donofrio took Mary into the back rooms at *Augie's*, things started well. They laughed and kissed. He, like most of the men who visited Mary, rejoiced in her oversized breasts. At first, he was fully aroused but began to lose the sensation. By the time they were both naked, it was evident that the spirit had left him entirely. Hookers have a veritable arsenal of tricks and techniques they employ in these situations. Often, but not always, they are successful. Mary was striking out, and Donofrio, in no uncertain terms, let her know the fault lay with her. He lied, saying that this had never happened to him before. Now, the pattern was coming full circle. As he hurled insults at her, calling her fat and stupid, he began feeling an awakening in his loins. There was a time when this was enough to motivate him to bring the coupling to fruition. Lately, he seemed to need more. That night with Mary he knew he was moving into a strange new realm. He squeezed her hard and pinched her in sensitive places. When she complained and reacted, he ignored her and inflicted more cruelty. Her pain was his pleasure. Donofrio wrapped his hands around her throat as he neared the completion of this violent session. Mary, fearing suffocation, struggled to free herself. Donofrio, now existing completely outside of himself, punches Mary in the face. She falls back on the bed as Donofrio grunts several times and collapses on top of her. He is sweating and breathing heavily. Mary is crying softly. Donofrio feels sick, and he knows why. He sees all too clearly his father in himself. The man he always hated. The man he swore he'd never become.

"I heard you gave her a shiner," said Wojick.

"No, I didn't give her a black eye. I mean, 'yes', she ended up with a black eye, but that was an accident. You know things were getting really heated up. I got to tell you; she's wild. Well, she moved one way and I moved the other, and BAM, we ended up butting our heads together. We were laughing about it when it happened. Anyway, I felt terrible about it because I know it must have hurt. The next thing I know, she tells everybody I punched her, and that's how she got the black eye. All of a sudden everyone's pissed at me."

"I knew there must be more to the story," slurred the big agent, "You're a good kid. I knew you wouldn't do that."

Donofrio hangs his head. When he looks up at his drinking partner, he says with unquestionable sincerity, "All I wanted to do was apologize. That fucking Octaviano wouldn't even let me do that. I just wish I could see her again for a few minutes to tell her again how sorry I am." Donofrio had not only inherited the 'liar-gene' from his father, he had inherited an enhanced strain of the gene. Again, Donofrio hangs his head.

Wojick reaches out and pats the young man on the shoulder. "Yeah, that ain't fair. You're just trying to square the books with this broad. You're trying to do the right thing."

Donofrio senses this is the right moment, and asks hopefully, "Are you saying what I think you're saying?"

Wojick, who isn't particularly bright when he's sober, is even more muddled in his thinking when in this condition. Seeing the hope in the young cop's face and not wanting to disappoint him, he says, "Damn right that's what I'm saying," and clicks his stein against Donofrio's glass. He feels good about himself when he sees Donofrio smile for the first time since telling the story.

"If I could just get a few minutes of her time, you know, to explain and apologize."

"She's a hooker. You pay her; she makes time," said the agent.

Donofrio proceeds cautiously. He knows Wojick isn't bright, but he also knows he's a cop, and even dense cops can recognize bullshit when they smell it. "I see what you're saying. So what's your plan?"

The question surprised Wojick as he didn't have a plan. Donofrio, unlike his longtime partner, always treated Stan Wojick like he was smart, so he didn't want to appear stupid now. "You know where I'm going with this, right?" he answered ambiguously.

"I do," answered Donofrio, looking both grateful and excited.

"What's the problem?" asked Wroblonski. Even before Octaviano answered, he knows it had to do with Wojick and Donofrio doing something stupid. He wondered just how stupid.

A short time later, Donofrio and Wojick are sitting in an idling car a short distance from *Augie's*. He has convinced the federal agent that it was his plan that had brought them here. Donofrio fears Wojick may be too drunk or too stupid to pull it off, but if he does, it will reap a reward that the young cop has fantasized about for a long time.

Wojick enters the bar. It's getting late, and it's a work night so the place is pretty empty. He sees Augustino at the bar. He grabs a stool and orders a beer. Looking around he's glad there's no sign of Octaviano. He's not too drunk to know that the greasy wop might say something to Wroblonski. His partner's orders were crystal clear, '*Stay out of bars we're putting the pinch on*'. As he surveys the room, he sees Mary at one of the round tables with two of the other hookers. He makes eye contract and smiles. Wojick has a nice smile. It softens the lines in his face, giving him a boyish look. Mary likes his smile.

"You know we're not supposed to do this," she says as he holds the car door open for her.

"You probably do a lot of stuff your mother told you that you shouldn't ought not to do," replies Wojick, making Mary laugh. Mary knows he's drunk but hopes he's not too drunk to perform. All women, even whores, have a certain type they are attracted to. This man, who introduced himself as 'Stan', fits the bill for Mary. He's kind of cute in a Neanderthal kind of way; brutish with big shoulders and a thick neck. More importantly, he made her laugh several times at the bar. Mary likes to laugh and tends to trust men who are funny.

According to the plan, as Wojick was seducing Mary at Augustino's, Donofrio was hustling to a small hotel several blocks away. He was now waiting in the shadows as the door swings open. Wojick opened the door and gallantly bowed, saying, "After you my dear."

As Mary walks in laughing, Wojick says, "You're going to thank me for this tomorrow," and closes the door. Wojick turns and descends the steps feeling good about himself. He's done a good deed by helping to patch things up between these two.

She turns to the closed door, saying, "Stan? What are you doing, Stan?"

From behind her she hears, "Stan's not coming back."

Fear paralyzes her as she recognizes the voice.

"I've missed you, Mary."

Both men had settled into an uneasy silence. The small second floor office seemed a lot smaller this day. Wojick sits with his arms folded across his chest. Wroblonski recognizes the posture from his years of interrogation. His partner has shut down. He's quit talking. What had started as a discussion had quickly degenerated into shouting match. He knew his partner was hungover, and the yelling must have been killing his headache, but Wroblonski was glad of it. He knew Wojick was as stubborn as he was stupid. He also knew at some level Wojick knew he had really screwed up and was still processing the events.

Wroblonski hadn't actually seen Mary but Octaviano had, and what he described sickened the federal agent. He always suspected Donofrio wasn't playing with a full deck, but what the mobster told him about what went on behind those closed doors was sick; it was perverse. He knew Wojick might not be bright, but his partner had never seemed intentionally cruel. Wojick had often used his size and his physical presence to full advantage during interrogations. A sick look of fear would appear on a difficult suspect's face, just by Wojick taking off his sport jacket and rolling up his sleeves. He knew the effect the sight of his barrel chest and those beefy hands and massive forearms had on a person. Wroblonski understood his partner was putting on a show. Wojick would crack his knuckles and then make his neck crack. He would study his big ring. First, taking it off and then, giving it a second thought, he would slip the ring back onto his finger. Wojick would say little during this performance. Oftentimes, that's all it took to get the canary to sing. Wojick took pride in his ability to intimidate a suspect into talking. He told Wroblonski once that it was no fun slapping around a suspect to make him talk. "It's like a game," he explained, "I win the game by making someone talk without laying a finger on them." Wroblonski had his own role to play and complimented the show by advising the suspect that he could avoid a lot of heartache, and healing time, by telling what he knew. Wroblonski understood that his partner hoped that this intimidation was enough to make the perp squeal as he took little pleasure in roughing up a suspect. Wroblonski liked that about his partner. He realized his partner was blessed with a special gift that few others possessed.

Knowing this about his partner is what concerned him when he told him about Mary.

The Stan Wojick he had known for years would have been deeply affected by what had happened. Now, after spending the past several months with Donofrio, Wojick showed little emotion or feelings as he listened to the details. The answers he gave, the rationales he proffered, sounded like they were coming directly from Donofrio instead of Wojick. Donofrio had awoken something in his partner; something dark and angry, perhaps something violent. Wroblonski knew he was losing control of his partner to the entity the young policeman had unleashed.

Wroblonski wasn't quite ready to let this pass. He retreated to a more gentle approach. "Stan, you know we have got to be careful, right?" When Wojick said nothing in response, he continued, "Things are changing, and some of these changes really got me worried. I'll tell you the truth Stan, I think it's time for us to get out of this racket all together. There are too many factors that are out of our control."

Wojick looked at his partner like he was seeing him for the first time. Finally, he said, "You know Teddy, I think you're right. You do need to go find something else to do. You held us back for too long. I got a new partner now who ain't afraid of his own shadow. We got plans Teddy, plans that guys like you would never have the balls to pull off. The days of me being happy with a few table scraps are over." On that note the big man rose. Still being hungover from the night before it took him a moment to steady himself.

"Stan, I think you're making a mistake."

Before reaching the door, he paused without turning. "I'm fixing mistakes," is all he said before setting his fedora on his head and exiting the room.

## Chapter Twenty-Two

Donofrio walked into *Augie's* like nothing had happened. As he approached the bar, he could see the look of sick fear mar Augie's typically friendly features. He liked the reaction. People should fear hlm when he walked into a room. Fear and respect him. He suspected everyone in the bar knew about what had happened between him and Mary. He was glad they knew. He hoped there was a lesson learned for these rubes in all this. He was a cop, and the last time he checked, a cop could do pretty much whatever he wanted to.

"Tell Octaviano I want to talk to him," he ordered the nervous barkeep.

"He's in the back, but he's with someone." Augustino wanted to berate the arrogant cop for what he had done to his friend Mary, but he was afraid to say anything. He thought about the wrench he kept behind the bar. It was the only tool Augie had ever owned or knew how to use. An image flashed of him grabbing the wrench and bringing it down full force onto the smug cop's head. Instead, he said, "I'll let him know you're here."

Octaviano eyed the crooked cop. He, like Augie and others in the bar, would have enjoyed bringing a wrench down on the arrogant young man's head. Donofrio may be corrupt and unlikable but he was still a cop, and cops had a brotherhood second only to that of a Sicilian crime family. If this had just been a case of one of his girls getting slapped around a little bit, he would have let it pass. The girls all knew that was a risk that went along with the job. Some of the johns who tried it got more than they bargained for.

These broads were tough and more than willing to stand up for themselves. If the john decided he didn't want to pay or tried to get the girl to perform acts that crossed the line of decency, they might feel the sting of a weighted handbag to the back of the head. Octaviano remembered the night Big Sally dragged a john through the bar by the heels. He struggled to get free and pull his pants up at the same time. Guido had opened the door as she approached. She never hesitated as she proceeded to pull him straight out the door and into the alley. When Sally walked back into the bar the patrons greeted her with cheers and whistles. She took a deep bow to even greater applause. The incident in the end turned out to be a great marketing ploy for Sally. As word spread of the indignity she had heaped on her client, other men, in need of disciplining, came looking for Big Sally.

Sally didn't seem to even like men. There were whisperings and innuendo about the petite woman she shared an apartment with over a bakery several blocks away. If a man came to Sally looking to be punished or humiliated, he came to the right place as she was more than happy to oblige. Octaviano knew that a good whore house stocked their shelves with a variety of diverse choices. The men who visited the women at *Augie's* tavern all seemed to want something different. Johnnie made sure on a Saturday night he had a selection of younger, older, but not too old, tall, short, thin, and heavyset women available to satisfy as many demands as possible. On occasion, he brought in an Asian woman, and even though blacks were not welcome at *Augie's,* a Negress was kept out of sight in the back for those who wished to sample a bit of forbidden fruit. She did a great business. The girls who did the best were the ones who either filled a certain niche or satisfied a certain craving.

While Big Sally doled out punishment, many other women in the house seemed to be punishing themselves, perhaps out of guilt over the life they had chosen.

Mary wasn't Big Sally or really like any of the other girls. Mary was different. Mary seemed at peace with her career path. Mary was sweet and affectionate. She was warm and loving and funny. She was a mother-figure to the other girls, and Johnnie always thought these maternal qualities were what attracted many of her clients to her. She wasn't the prettiest girl in the stable but did a brisker business than some of the nicer looking girls. The crime boss knew a lot of women gravitated to this trade because they were insecure about their looks or had an abusive childhood at the hands of an overly affectionate uncle. Some found their way to the tiny back rooms at *Augie's* because they had no other marketable skills.

Octaviano never knew, and he never asked, why Mary had chosen this path.

Mary grew up in south Philly. She was raised in a big and loving Christian family. Her father had insisted on a Catholic education for Mary and her siblings. She did well in school. She was popular and was at the center of a group of close friends. She had developed early and sported sizable breasts by the seventh grade. While her girlfriends teased her good naturedly, the boys started noticing Mary for the first time. Some of the boys, who in the past had rarely said hello to Mary, now sought her company. Mary, not yet a teenager, loved the attention. She didn't mind that they had trouble maintaining eye contact. So what if their eyes would gravitate to her chest, stealing glances at every opportunity. It just felt good, especially when one young man in particular found his way to her. One afternoon after school, Mary sat alone in the library. Her concentration was broken as she heard the chair next to her being pulled away from the table.

As Robbie Tuccio sat down, he asked, "Hi Mary, do you mind if I sit here?"

Robbie, the cutest boy in the class, not only knew her name but wanted to sit next to her. That was just the first of so many magical moments that afternoon. The late afternoon sunlight performed a prismatic ballet on the chipped, gold-leafed lettering of the well-worn, leather-bound books as it filtered through the drafty and dirty window panes. Dust, spotlighted by the refracted light and hearing the invisible music, joined the dance. While this silent waltz went on around them, they laughed and talked as quietly as they could as they were in a library, albeit a nearly empty library. Like other boys, Robbie's eyes would drift often to her shirt front. Mary found this flattering and actually rearranged herself in an effort to display her assets in the best possible light for her young suitor. As he looked, she would puff her chest out causing her breasts to strain against the thin white material. Mary knew this was wrong but guiltily admitted to herself that she found this game stimulating. Mary, for the first time while not in the privacy of her small bedroom, felt familiar urges washing over her. She felt flushed and hoped her face and neck did not appear as red as they felt to her. Her nipples were so hard they hurt, and she knew what seemed like an urge to urinate was something completely different. Robbie for his part seemed so cool and collected. He smiled warmly as she struggled to keep up her end of the conversation. Her concentration was weak; her thoughts muddled. Robbie had slid nearer, and now his chair was touching Mary's. He boldly put his arm on the back of her seat and then on her shoulder. Mary was torn between wanting this to stop or wanting it to go on forever. My God he was good looking, with thick, blue-black hair and deep set eyes. Mary envied him for his long eyelashes. Robbie leans in and, without ever breaking eye contact, kisses her quickly on the lips. He pulls away and waits for her reaction. When she makes no objection, he leans in again. This time the kiss is longer and more passionate. She knows on one level that they are just kids, but at the same time, she feels very real and very adult stirrings course through her young body. She is helpless to keep a soft moan from escaping as Robbie kisses her again and again. She is embarrassed at the moistness she feels between her legs. She presses her thighs tightly together in an effort to quench the growing heat but it creates the opposite reaction. She buries her face in his neck, and as she snuggles, she feels his hands gently caress her breasts. She is affronted or at least she tells herself she should be. She's young and confused. He's being so gentle, and even though she does not want to admit this to herself, it feels good. She knows this is all wrong. She knows the names given to girls that let boys do this. She should slap his face and berate him and let him know that she is not that kind of girl. Instead, Robbie kneads her breasts more ardently. Mary fights the stirrings within her, but it is a fight she is losing. From the front desk, Sister Mary Xavier makes the announcement that the library is closing. Robbie and Mary disentangle themselves from one another. They both have a disheveled look and pause to straighten out their hair and clothes before leaving. Robbie brushes a strand of hair back from her forehead. It's a nice gesture. Mary stands and wonders why Robbie remains seated. When he does rise, Mary can see the bulge pressing against the thin fabric of his gabardine trousers. She has an incomplete understanding of what she's looking at, but Mary does know that she has aroused her classmate. This thought is both frightening and exciting at the same time. A perverse sense of pride comes from knowing that she had produced this reaction. Mary hopes she didn't look too guilty as she passed the front desk and said good night to Sister Xavier. The nun asked where they had been hiding as she wasn't sure anyone was still there besides her.

Now, outside the building, Robbie asked if Mary would like to walk to the park with him. There is a desperation to the way he asks. She considers the invitation. Mary is flattered but tells him no as her mother would be getting worried if she got home too late. Besides, she had stayed late at school to finish her homework, and now, she still had to get that completed. Robbie sheepishly apologized for interrupting her. They both laughed at the comment. Mary can hardly feel her feet touch the ground as she makes her way home. She giggles as she rehearses the name *Mrs.* Mary Tuccio. She knows she's being silly.

That night in bed, Mary replays every moment from that afternoon over again in her head. She luxuriates over the thoughts of Robbie touching her and her reactions to those touches. She knows it's wrong, but she allows her hands to move across her body. In her mind, they are Robbie's hands. This afternoon, he stopped at just touching her breasts, but he is being ever so much bolder in the darkness of this small, dark room. Mary encourages the boy to explore, and he does so with great enthusiasm. Sated, Mary falls into a deep and dreamless sleep as her phantom lover fades into the blackness.

Mary couldn't get out of the house fast enough the following morning. On her way to school, she indulged herself with a fantasy about seeing Robbie in the distance. He is standing with a group of boys from class. When he spied Mary, he would leave his circle of friends and run to her. He would take her books and unashamedly kiss her on the cheek. Together, they would walk into the building hand in hand. The images were rich and vivid and wonderful.

As Mary continues her walk still lost in her make-believe world, she sees Violet Bognano walking towards her. Violet is, on most days, her best friend. Other days, they don't get along very well. Violet is walking with purposeful strides towards her friend. Mary can't wait to tell her the exciting news. Violet, like just about every other girl in class, had a crush on Robbie Tuccio.

Still several houses away, Violet demands, "What did you do?"

Mary is confused by the question. "What?" she asks.

Violet clarifies the situation for her. "What did you and Robbie do yesterday in the *library*? Everyone's talking about it."

Mary, suddenly defensive and a little afraid, replies weakly, "We didn't do anything."

Last night had been beautiful and special and magical. Now, the crisp morning sun is casting a much different light on the previous afternoon's events.

And just that quickly, Mary went from being the funny and quirky and popular girl in school, to being the class slut. As happens often with the telling and retelling of a story, the line between truth and fiction gets more and more blurred as one embellishment begets another. By the end of the week, the somewhat innocent petting of two young people became something much darker. While Robbie relished these enhancements, Mary denied them and tried valiantly to defend her honor. It was futile. It was like scrubbing sap or glue or pine tar off her hands and finding out that the more she scoured, the bigger the mess she made.

She was tough and tried hard to hide how much it hurt to hear the whisperings and the snickers as she walked the halls. Girls in her class avoided her. Violet, sweet Violet, stayed true to her friend, but she was an exception. Boys would seek Mary out whenever she was alone. The bold ones might show up at her door in the evening with their heads filled with unrealistic expectations. Meeker boys might wait for her on her route home and hesitantly ask if they might carry her books and escort her the remainder of the way. Mary knew what they wanted as bold and meek alike could barely contain their anticipations. Mary hated their motivations but admitted to herself that she wanted their affections. She played a coquettish game with her young suitors. She teased them enough to keep them interested, but they received very little in return.

Mary felt empowered. She liked the feeling.

The stigma of that afternoon in the library stayed with Mary throughout high school. As she grew older, she became less of a novelty as more girls let more boys do more with each passing year. Mary's line of admirers grew less over time. She realized how much she missed the attention and was loathe to lose the affections of these suitors. Her solution was to let boys take more liberties with her. Her pragmatic view: if people think I'm a tramp, and I seem powerless to change my reputation; why fight it. It was liberating for her. She had devotees who took her to dinner and brought her flowers. She craved the attention. If they expected something in return, and they usually did, so be it. She knew she wasn't beautiful in any classical sense of the word, but there was a certain prettiness about her, especially when she smiled. She had always had a fetching smile.

There was something else that Mary was not comfortable dwelling on; she liked it. She liked the feel of a man's hands on her. Some boys were tentative and gentle. Others were coarser and bolder. She wondered if other girls reacted to touches or caresses or kisses the same way she did. It didn't seem to take much to get Mary's motor running. Mary knew that girls weren't supposed to enjoy these activities. The nuns, along with the church, made that abundantly clear. The act of coupling was reserved for married couples and strictly for the purpose of procreation. Mary often thought that it were these stringent taboos that made the act so stimulating. She had urges from the time she was very young. She didn't fully understand what was happening, and she suspected it was a sin, but that didn't stop her from letting her hands explore her tender young flesh.

One night, Mary climbed into bed knowing she was unprepared for the next day's classwork. She became anxious. The anxiety manifested itself in a bizarre and wonderful way. It was her first orgasm, and even with all the guilt that went along with it, she loved it. The guilt explained the Decade of the Rosary she said before going to sleep but did little to explain her climbing into bed the next night intentionally unprepared for a test scheduled for the following day. She hoped to capture the same magic from the previous night, but that didn't happen. Another mystery.

Mary would have never put it in these terms but she looked at her situation idiomatically: if girls who liked sex were whores, and she liked sex, then she was a whore. If, A=B, and B=C, then A=C. She didn't consider the flowers or candy or dinners as payment for the favors she granted to her young suitors, but there was a day that she knew she had crossed that line. There was a pair of shoes on display in the window of the neighborhood department store. They were beautiful. They went for the staggering price of twelve-dollars. Mary loved them. She wanted them and told herself she'd do anything for them. Three doors down from Mary's home lived Mr. Phillips. Mary had known him all her life but never knew his first name. Mr. Philips was not married, but there were times a taxi would stop in front of his home and a woman would exit the car. It was never the same woman, but it was always a woman of a certain type. He took great pride in his yard and would often take the time to show Mary different plants and what would bloom next. He was nice to the kids in the neighborhood and would sometimes offer Mary a piece of hard candy as they would tour his yard. As Mary started to develop, Mr. Phillips, like so many of the boys and men that Mary encountered, took a keen interest in her budding womanhood. One afternoon, as Mary passed his yard, they struck-up a conversation. Mr. Phillips was boldly focused on her chest. Most boys would sneak glances, but that was not the case with her neighbor. He made a point of commenting on how she certainly wasn't a little girl anymore.

"Mary, you have really developed into a beautiful young woman," he told her appreciatively while his eyes drank in every part of her.

Mary blushed and thanked him. It felt wonderful to be described as beautiful. She knew full well what was going on and what her neighbor wanted. When Mr. Phillips asked where she was headed she laughed and embarrassingly told him that she was on her way to the department store to see if the shoes were still on display. "I don't know why I'd care. They cost a fortune."

"Hmmm," was Phillips only comment.

Later that afternoon, Mary sat in her room and slowly un-wrapped the shoe-box shaped package. They were beautiful. When she slipped them on and sashayed across the room, they made her feel beautiful. She expected to feel guilty, but she did not. What she had done with her neighbor that afternoon was unquestionably wrong, but somehow the shoes made up for all of that. Up to this point, she had restricted her dalliances to boys, but Mr. Phillips was not a boy. He was a grown man. Mary took pride in the fact that a grown man found her attractive.

Several days later, Mary once again saw Mr. Phillips in his yard. He waved and gave her a friendly hello. Mary thought it might be awkward, but he acted very naturally as if nothing had happened between the two of them. He casually mentioned that a good friend would be visiting and asked

Mary to stop by if she happened to be free. He told Mary his friend would very much like to meet her.

"Oh, why would anyone want to meet me?" she asked. Mary fully understood 'why' and told herself that she would make a point of *not* stopping by.

The following week, Phillips was once again tending his garden, and as he had said, there was another man with him. Mr. Phillips introduced him as Tom, just Tom. Tom, like her neighbor, seemed enchanted by Mary.

"Phillips here told me you were beautiful, but you are really stunning," he said sincerely.

Later that night, Mary made her way to Tom's small apartment. When she left, she had enough for a new dress to go along with her new shoes.

She never would, but if years later she had told these circumstances to Augie, he might have mentioned a poem he had once read. It was a poem about a guy walking in the woods and then coming to a place where he had to make a decision on which of two paths to choose. Augie liked this poem. He had kept a copy, but it had gone missing at some point. He could never remember the name, but if someone had said he was thinking of *The Road Not Taken* by Robert Frost, he would have said, not for the first time, 'Yeah, that's the guy,' and then promise himself that he would remember. He would again, not for the first time, invariably forget. That was OK. He knew the gist of what the poem was trying to say.

Octaviano liked Mary but had never bedded her. He knew how the late Guido Santori felt about her and thought he would violate a trust by sleeping with her. Omerta, which could extend beyond this world and into the next, was one reason. Another darker reason was that Johnnie would always remember how close he had come to answering Augie's door the night death had come a knocking. The night Santori was gunned down. Johnnie had dodged a bullet that night, literally and figuratively. He owed Santori for his sacrifice.

The other issue was, now that he had gotten to know Mary so well over the years, he looked at her like she was more of a sister. They were friends. Feeling as he did about Mary, and having to sit here with the vile creature that had violated her so badly, was almost more than Octaviano could stomach.

"She's in pretty bad shape."

"Who?" replied the cop. He actually had the balls to chuckle slightly as he said this.

Octaviano fought the primal instincts stirring within him. He was an enigma. He made his living in a violent business but was not, by nature, a violent man. He only resorted to muscle as a last option. It took incredible discipline to keep from pummeling the smirking face that sat across from him. He knew he had a fierce side. He wasn't proud of it. He took more pride in being a good negotiator. He sometimes thought back to the day he had beaten a man to death with his bare hands. Looking back on it, he wished he hadn't. He couldn't change the past. More disturbing than the act itself was the memory of how wonderful it felt to unleash that brutality. He couldn't deny the euphoria he felt as his henchmen dragged the lifeless body away.

Donofrio was good at justifications. In his mind's eye, he was already seeing the events of that night with the whore in a much gentler light. The memories were less violent. It was just a couple of people who got a little wild in their lovemaking. He'd be damned if he was going to take a lot of grief for a little harmless lovemaking. Who did this greasy wop think he was? He was a fucking gangster, and now he thinks he can sit in judgment of a police officer.

"What do you want me to say?" asked Donofrio, "She's a whore, so I treated her like a whore. I don't want to hear nothing no more about that, you understand?"

Octaviano didn't say anything. He knew Donofrio was touched in the head, and Johnnie had plenty of experience dealing with men and women who weren't right upstairs. Instead he said, "Okay, if you don't want to talk about it, then we don't talk about it."

Donofrio slowly digested this response. He eyed the gangster with a combination of surprise and suspicion. Octaviano simply looked back. His expression, like that of a savvy poker player, was unreadable. The problem with all these people is that they don't know who they're dealing with, but they were going to find out. His old man, this grease-ball, his mother, Wroblonski, and even that shine cop were all going to find out first hand who and what they were dealing with. There was a lesson all these people needed to learn and Donofrio was the right guy to teach them. He'd love to take that black bastard Thorn down a peg or two. He saw the way the guys in the precinct went out of their way to be friendly to him. They were nicer to him than they were to a *white* cop, and that was just wrong. And why, just because he was some kind of freak novelty at the station house? He hated Reilly and plenty of those other nigger lovers for treating him like he was special. Yeah, there were lessons to be taught and he was going to teach them all. Thorn could wait. Even this greasy wop could wait. He'd get to them in due time. There was a much older score he needed to settle. He had a lifetime of unfinished business to take care of, and the day of reckoning was approaching.

Johnnie Octaviano was not a man who feared much, but looking at Donofrio, he saw something frightening in the man's expression.

# Brother can you spare a dime? 1929

Circumstances beyond their control, in the form of the Great Depression, derailed the Thorn family's financial progress by the end of the decade. The year is 1929, and Chicago, because of its dependence on manufacturing, is one of the hardest hit areas of the country. As manufacturing faltered, men powered down their lathes and presses and poured out onto the streets to search for non-existent jobs. Reilly's mother, who worked in the laundry of a quality downtown hotel, had her hours reduced. She would have been out of work completely if her supervisor wasn't fond of her.

Sissy kept her job in the schools but wasn't always paid. Educators often received reduced wages or no pay, in part because the city's tax base was so dramatically reduced. She was so committed to the welfare and education of her students that she asked Reilly if she could continue to teach under these circumstances. Reilly supported her for a variety of reasons, not the least of which was that he loved her dearly. He knew how much she loved the children and how important her work was to her. The practical reason for her to stay in the school system was that there were no other jobs for her to seek out. Her reduced wages were still better than no wages.

Reilly on the other hand, had no work slowdown. The streets became progressively more dangerous as desperate times created a measure of desperation, and good, God-fearing men to turned to crime to put food on the table. Transients from around the country hitch-hiked rides into Chicago on railroads in the hopes of finding work. Shanty towns sprang up throughout the city.

The family met one evening around the small kitchen table to discuss finances over coffee and an apple pie that Sissy and her mother-in-law had baked that day. The pie was wonderful. The outlook was not.

All this happened with all the subtlety of someone dropping an anvil on their foot. The nation's economy simply fell apart. Over the next three years, industrial production in the US dropped by 46% while unemployment rose a staggering 607%.

Reilly was frustrated as he was living with the results of the Great Depression, but he didn't understand the causes. He would ask Sissy to explain it to him. She claimed that no one really knew what went wrong and, she was right as decades later the debate would continue amongst economists as to what happened and why. The interrelated complexity of many factors makes it difficult to isolate a single cause as, like dominoes, one factor affected another, perhaps several others. Even the weather played a part in the downward spiral as the drought in the Mississippi Valley, popularized in the Steinbeck classic, "The Grapes of Wrath", was the catalyst that caused thousands to abandon their family homesteads and set out on a brutal and unforgiving road.

After the night they went to the makeshift boxing arena, Reilly had told Andre that he had given up any thought of underground boxing. On the day he said it, he believed it. What he saw that night sickened him, which made the decision to abandon the plan an easy one.

Since that night the landscape had changed but his resolve hadn't. It would be tough but the Thorns would get by, and Reilly would figure out a way to help the family without having to climb through the ropes.

# Thorn
# Part II

# Chapter Twenty-Three, 1930

Prohibition, along with the Great Depression, was now into a new decade. The frustration of being broke and sober tore at the fabric of American life. In news that shocked the country, the infant son of famous aviator Charles Lindberg is kidnapped. The nation mourns as several months later the lifeless corpse of his infant son is discovered. Three thousand unemployed auto workers march in Dearborn, Michigan. Police open fire and four are killed. The 'Bonus Army', 15,000 World War I veterans, descends on Washington DC, demanding their military bonus. Herbert Hoover orders Douglas McArthur to forcibly disperse the protestors. Unemployment is still widespread as 14,000,000 remain out of work. Jobless rates, which were at 3.2% in 1929, are now estimated at over 24%.

Franklin Roosevelt unveiled the New Deal with the popular slogan, *'The only thing we have to fear is fear itself'*. Most Americans would have added hunger and homelessness to the list of what was to be feared.

The United States does not have the market cornered on suffering and unrest. In Germany, the Nazi party is now in control. Famine devastates the USSR. Japanese troops occupy Manchuria. Four-thousand protesting farmers are killed by the army in El Salvador. Popular fiction chronicles the hard life and political change a half-a-world away in China in the Pulitzer Prize winning *The Good Earth* by Pearl Buck.

America needed heroes and found them in the most unlikely places. Organized crime provided a cast of characters that filled this need for modern day Robin Hoods. Characters that would ride in, like the heroes on their favorite radio serials, and save the day. Newspapers embellished the mystique of these often ruthless killers by painting them in a much different light. The names given to these mobsters made them somehow more enchanting. Nicknames like 'Baby-Face' Nelson, Al 'Scarface' Capone, George 'Machine Gun' Kelly, 'Lucky' Luciano, 'Ma' Barker, and Vincent 'Mad-Dog' Col captured the nation's imagination.

The depiction of Bonnie and Clyde in the press was at considerable odds to the reality of their atrocities while on the lam. Several iconic photos of the couple were found in an abandoned hideout. These photos, often showing the couple in playful moods, were embraced by the press and distributed in newspapers across the country. This type of exposure only added to their romanticized public persona. Bonnie, like many crime figures from the era, was considered quite fashionable as she posed wearing the latest styles. The reality was that Bonnie and Clyde led a band of thieving murderers. The death of nine police officers and several civilians were attributed to their gang.

Perhaps the most telling example of this phenomenon was Charles Arthur 'Pretty Boy' Floyd. Floyd, who arguably had the most interesting of gangland nicknames, was considered a criminal spawned by the depression. Stories abounded of Floyd handing out money to bystanders as he executed his crimes. 'Pretty Boy' Floyd was gunned down by law enforcement at an Ohio farm. Thousands of people showed up at his funeral. A mourner claimed, according to the urban myth, that Floyd was so popular that he could have been elected governor of Oklahoma, and added, "He probably would have made a good one."

The world was in a topsy-turvy state of imbalance. The crooks glorified; the cops vilified. Even the solar system offered what appeared to be dramatic commentaries with a full solar eclipse as well as a shower of meteorites that crashed into the United States.

Reilly Thorn sat on the rickety back steps of his small home. He gave nary a thought to what was happening in the big bad world. Being with his precious Hope, watching her tottering around the yard, could make him forget about all the insanity in the world. Hope as always had Mrs. Fish with her. It was her favorite doll. Hope had named it when she had barely learned to talk. It sounded like she said her name was 'Mrs. Fish' and, regardless of what Hope was actually trying to say, the name Mrs. Fish stuck.

"Flowers, daddy?" she asked as she pointed to a small patch of dandelions sprouting from the sparse lawn. "Pretty flowers, daddy?"

"Yes Hope, they're beautiful flowers," he answered.

"Papa doesn't like these flowers, daddy," claims Hope with an air of assuredness. Papa was Hope's name for her grandfather. "Daddy, are you watching Hope?" she asked, making Reilly realize that he was studying his daughter intently.

"Yes, sweetie, daddy's watching you play," but as he said it, he knew it was more than that.

At that moment, the back door opened and Sissy called to her daughter, "Come in, Hope. Papa has an apple all cut up for you." This was a favorite treat between the family's patriarch and the little girl.

Hope beams at her mother, asking, "Cin'm sugar?" as she heads for the stairs. "S'cuse me, daddy," she says, navigating her way past Reilly on the narrow stairs. "Cin'm sugar apple," she explains to her father.

Sissy corrects her, "Hope, the word is '*cinnamon*,'" and then repeats the word a second time, "cinnamon."

Hope agrees wholeheartedly. "Cin'm," she says adding, "and sugar," to make sure there is no misunderstanding. Reilly demands a kiss from his daughter before letting her pass him on the stairs. Hope kisses him quickly, but it is a barely there kiss as she is now solely focused on her 'cin'm, sugar apple'. As she works her way past, Reilly tells the toddler that he loves her. He says this quietly and looks away as he says it. Reilly assumes she did not hear. Hope surprises him as she turns at the top step and says, "I love you, too, daddy," and then, "I gotta go," disappearing into the house.

After the conversation from the previous night, he says nothing to Sissy. Sissy knows last night was difficult for Reilly. She knows to give him his space this morning. He needs to process. Sissy waited as long as she dared before going to her husband with her concerns about Hope. Simply stated, physically she was not where a child her age should be. She was small. At her physicals she was consistently at the low end of the growth chart. The doctor had many opportunities to examine Hope as the little girl was at the clinic often. At first, the doctor dismissed it as allowing each child to grow at their own rate. On their last visit, the doctor once again reassured Sissy that Hope was fine even though Sissy felt he might be shielding his concerns. Sissy said little about this to Reilly. She loved her husband and didn't want to concern him unnecessarily. After all, Hope was a bright, curious, and happy child. If it was just a matter of Hope being small, it would be much easier to overlook or rationalize. She would either catch up to other kids or she might remain on the petite side the rest of her life. Sissy began to notice more than just her diminutive size. Hope seemed to tire easily. She was a 'good-sleeper' from the time she was born. She went to bed early and slept well into the morning. In the afternoon, she would take a minimum of one nap, often two. Sissy came to know many young mothers in the neighborhood and, as young parents are inclined to do, would compare notes. She was proud that Hope could cognitively hold her own with any of the other children. Hope was very communicative and would often voice complex thoughts in well-articulated sentences. When Sissy asked other mothers about nap time, she often heard nightmare stories about what they went through. Other children, now in their terrible twos or traumatic threes, vigorously fought naptime. Sissy was told how lucky she was when she mentioned that Hope never fought naps.

Sissy didn't feel lucky; she felt concern.

Last night Sissy had asked Reilly to take a walk after Hope had been put to bed. Her in-laws were more than happy to watch over their little grandbaby. It felt good to walk through the quiet neighborhood. They said little as they strolled. They held hands. They did not have a destination in mind but ended up at a small toddler's park where they often brought Hope. Given the lateness of the hour, the park was empty. Reilly joked that they better not tell Hope they had gone to the park without her or she'd be mad. Sissy was usually quick to laugh at Reilly's comments, but tonight she did not react to the quip. She led him to a bench, and they both sat.

"Sissy, I don't need to be a cop to see you have something on your mind," said Reilly.

His lovely wife said nothing. She stared straight ahead, and when Reilly turned towards his wife, he saw a tear form and slowly roll down her cheek.

"Sissy, talk to me, please. You're making me nervous." The truth was she was scaring him. Still, she said nothing. The cop in Reilly knew she would talk in her own time. She wasn't there yet, but she would get there. He took his wife's hand. It was cold even though the evening was mild. He caressed her hand lovingly until it started to warm.

Finally, after what seemed to be a long time, Sissy simply stated, "I'm worried about Hope," and this being said, the tears flowed freely. Reilly put his arm around her. She was shaking to the point of trembling.

"She'll grow. You'll see. We talked about this before. I don't really want to talk about it again. She's fine," he told Sissy. They had talked about Hope's slow growth rate in the past. Reilly wasn't concerned about it. Hope was perfect in every way. The most perfect little girl the good Lord had ever created. Reilly, who loved Sissy with his entire being, didn't appreciate this conversation. When she tried to express concerns about Hope in the past, Reilly was quick to change the subject. He did not tolerate hearing his baby was less than perfect from anyone, even Sissy. Reilly was never curt or dismissive with his wife except when she spoke of concerns about Hope. At those times, he would end the discussion with extreme prejudice.

When Sissy replied that it was more than just her size, Reilly rose from the bench and stepped away. Sissy tried to take his sleeve, but he abruptly jerked it away.

"Reilly stop, please don't shut me out like this." Sissy had rehearsed what she was going to say and, more importantly, how she would say it. That script was now out the window. "Reilly, do you remember the day you brought her to the park, and Hope took a hard fall off the slide?"

He hadn't turned around, but he hadn't kept walking either. He looked past the quiet swings to the empty slide. He remembered the day. Hope had bruised her knee. Kids fell down and hurt themselves all the time, so what was the big deal. She had cried. He gave her ice cream and everything was fine. Why would Sissy bring this non-event up now?

Sissy proceeded cautiously, "It took a long time for that bruise to heel. Do you remember that?"

Reilly did remember. *'Hope got a boo-boo at the park on the slide with daddy',* Hope would tell everyone who cared to listen. Of course Reilly remembered because weeks later she still asked her father to kiss her boo-boo.

"All those earaches Reilly, the doctor said it was her lymph nodes. Reilly, her lymph nodes are swollen, and it makes her ears hurt." Before she could continue, Reilly began to walk away. She knew her husband well enough to know this conversation was over. She was almost relieved that for the moment anyway it was over. She knew what needed to be said next. They were words that would break her heart to speak aloud. Sissy, because of her more flexible schedule, was the one who typically took Hope to the doctor. It was Sissy who initially made the diagnosis. She sensed, as only a mother can know, that something wasn't right. She visited the local branch of the library but not finding the detail of information that she was looking for, made the trip downtown to the main library. When she brought in Hope for the ear issues and the doctor attributed the pain to swollen lymph nodes, she checked off an item on the mental list that she kept to herself. The bruise that wouldn't heal checked another box. Hope tiring so easily and the nose bleed that wouldn't stop checked off two more boxes. If it had only been one symptom or perhaps two, it would have been easy to dismiss her findings. Mothers, especially first time mothers, tend to stress a lot over little things, proverbially making mountains out of molehills. But it wasn't one or two things.

Hope exhibited, to varying degrees, every symptom related to childhood leukemia.

When she mentioned her suspicions to Hope's doctor, he was quick to dismiss her fears as unfounded. Sissy was not to be put off. She had read that early diagnosis might be crucial. She demanded that the doctor order a blood and bone marrow test. The doctor, if for no other reason than to get rid of a paranoid mother, ordered the test. Sissy had the paperwork in her purse. When she looked at the order or even thought about it, she felt sick to her stomach. She knew she couldn't go through this on her own. She wasn't strong enough by herself. Reilly was the strongest, most stoic man she could imagine, and even he wasn't durable enough to absorb this kind of blow. She needed him. She needed his strength because she knew that if she had to endure this on her own, it would kill her. She felt that even thinking about little Hope being seriously ill was a betrayal to her daughter. She must be a terrible mother to have even thought this. The doctor told her she was being silly. Perhaps he was right. She prayed with all her faith he was right.

They walked back home in an uncomfortable silence.

Sissy was crying softly. Reilly wasn't proud of himself but resolutely refused to comfort her. She knew how he felt and was not surprised that he had reacted this way. He loved Hope with his heart and soul. His intense love for his daughter made Sissy love him even more. She fell into step next to him as they approached the house. She wove her arm through his. She felt how rigid he was. Reilly was powerfully built, and she needed to draw from that physical strength now.

At the bottom step she held him back. "I'm sorry."

"It's late Sissy, and it's been a long day," was all he said as he started up the steps.

Sissy watched Reilly disappear into the house. She wasn't ready to follow just yet. Instead, she sat on the second step and let the night envelope her. The darkness felt comforting and somehow secure. There was warmth and safety in the darkness. The gloom lent anonymity to the familiar houses and landmarks up and down their street. That obscurity helped to dull the pain and fear and worry she felt. She would have opted to live in this darkness, but at some point the dawn would arrive, and upon that arrival, would illuminate the shadowed recesses in her mind where the darkest of her thoughts had taken root, like the dandelions in the yard that Hope was so taken with. She held onto the image of Hope examining the dandelions, and saying, *'pretty flowers.'* Sissy finally made her way into the house and climbed into her sleepless bed.

## Chapter Twenty-Four

"You're a putz, Leo."

Leonard 'Leo' Frankowicz sat across from Andre in the small office at the rear of the gym. In the background, the sound of leather on leather, along with the whirling of jump ropes, could be heard. It had been a while since Leo had made an appearance at *Al's Gym*. In fact, Leo hadn't been at the gym since the night Andre and Reilly had found him being used as a punching bag in a smoke-filled, dimly lit warehouse on the near southwest side of the city. When Andre hadn't seen him, he thought Leo was either hurt or, knowing that his trainer was upset to find one of his fighters mixed up in illegal boxing, had decided to make himself scarce until things had a chance to cool off. It also crossed his mind that Leo might have joined a different gym. In truth, this last thought bothered him, and he hoped it didn't turn out to be the case. Every gym needs a 'Leo'; the guy who everyone knows and everyone likes. That was Leo. He was an institution at *Al's Gym* and had been around for as long as anyone could remember. Andre took in the sight before him. Leo had come in to apologize to his long time trainer. Most guys under these circumstances wouldn't have stopped to pick up a sausage and pepper sandwich on the way to mend fences, but there sat Leo, talking with his mouth full between bites of the oversized, sloppy sandwich. Grease and red-sauce coated his chin and hands. At one point, he offered Andre a bite. Andre told him he was disgusting and should learn how to use a napkin. Leo laughed at the barb. Leo rarely showed up at the gym without a satchel of food; a large satchel. Even though the bag typically contained enough to feed a family of four for several days, Leo was not one inclined to share. The fact that he offered Andre a bite of his sandwich told the trainer that Leo was truly repentant and wanted to make amends.

"Money," was the one word answer Leo gave when Andre asked why he did it.

Andre really had no need to ask the question. There were very few people or families, that he was aware of, that were living comfortably. Many were barely surviving. When Leo disappeared from the gym, Andre, knowing where he lived, altered his own route home one evening in order to walk past his house. Several newspapers littered the front porch, and the windows had no dressings on them. The home looked sad and unloved as empty homes often do. A flower pot, sprouting nothing but the vestiges of some long abandoned bloom, sat near the front door. Andre, calling to a neighbor two houses down asked if he had seen Leo. The man, looking fearful and suspicious, disappeared quickly into a home that was every bit as forlorn as Leo's.

When Andre didn't respond to his short answer, Leo chuckled and said, "I've been flying my 'Hoover-Flags' for a long time now, Andre."

Hoover-Flags, a running gag at the time, were really a harsh editorial about the country's feelings towards the way Herbert Hoover, the nation's thirty-first president, was handling issues related to hunger, unemployment, and homelessness. A man would turn his pants pockets inside-out and ask, "How do you like my Hoover-Flags?" Families would at times be forced, after losing their home, to move to an open area and build a shelter out of discarded cardboard, wood, or metal sheeting. These cobbled together collections of shanties were unaffectionately known as 'Hoovervilles'. In yet one other indictment against Hoover, men sleeping in the open would cover themselves in newspapers which they dubbed 'Hoover-Blankets'. Few Presidents have received greater accolades or harsher criticisms than Herbert Hoover.

"I'd like to come back to the gym," he told Andre. He lowered his eyes as he said this, and the trainer could guess what was coming next. "But I got no money."

Andre was used to this as there were many currently at the gym that were in arrears on their dues. The owner, Al, collected what he could, whenever he could, from whoever might have a few bucks to their names. Most months it barely was enough to keep the doors open.

"Did you talk to Al?"

"Yeah, you know me and Al go way back, and he said it was OK, but I had to square it wit' you because you might be mad at me and might not want to train me no more."

"What did you do with the money from fighting?" Andre asked. "If you want to go out there and get kicked around for money, then you should have enough to pay Al."

"Yeah, about that, they don't pay me much for fighting. As a matter of fact, that night when you and Reilly came, remember that night, well they never paid me for that night. They said they couldn't pay me because I didn't finish the fight. I wanted to ask them, how'm I going to finish the fight when I'm knocked out like that?"

Andre was incredulous.

"Those guys were pissed-off because I was supposed to make it past the second round. I guess that's where the line was for the fight. That big dumb Slovak bastard, he don't understand English so good. That's that guy Bruiser. You remember him, right? All of a sudden, he clocks me in the side of the head. He was not supposed to do that. So they tell me they can't pay me. Ain't that some crazy shit? I bet they paid that big dumb Pollack. I bet he got his money."

Andre said a silent prayer thanking God that Reilly seemed to have come to his senses. The thought of his best friend messed up in all this was enough to make him sick. Looking at Leo, he understood and sympathized with his predicament. Leo, like many others had, might have made worse choices when it came to providing for himself or his family. Crime rates were on the rise as good men, driven by despair and desperation, stepped over the line between right and wrong. Even though divorce rates fell during the Depression, there were many husbands and fathers who opted for a 'poor-man's' divorce by simply leaving their family and just disappearing into the landscape. Even more tragic were the many who sought the ultimate solace and release through suicide. Music has always supplied a soundtrack to any era's social and political climate and the early 1930s were no exception. The best, and arguably most iconic, example was the release of E.Y. Harberg's 1931 classic, "Brother Can You Spare a Dime?"

Leo continued, "The last time I was there I seen that...,"

Andre cut him off abruptly, "What do you mean, *'the last time you were there'*? Do you mean to tell me you went back there? Leo, are you nuts? You almost got killed that night."

Realizing that his trainer was unhappy with his last comment, Leo tried to soften his approach, "Well, yeah, I had to go by there to see about getting my money. It worked out good, too. One guy there, his name is Johnnie, he gave me twenty-dollars and told me I done all right. He wants me to fight as soon as I feel better and…"

Again, Andre interrupted him, "Fight again? Leo, you can't possibly be thinking about fighting again."

"Ahhhhh…"

"Stop right there Leo. I don't want to hear what you have to say next. You've said plenty already. Look Leo, I can't tell you what to do, but please promise me you'll stay away from there."

"Oh sure, sure, you don't have to worry about that. You think I'd go back there? No, I'm done with that."

The look on Andre's face told Leo that he didn't believe a word of it.

Leo, looking like he might know a way to smooth things over with Andre, says, "I want you to know that I didn't say nothin' about the nigger, I mean Reilly, when they asked me." Looking pleased with himself, and a little anxious to move on, Leo begins to rise from his chair.

"That's good Leo. Wait. What? Who asked?"

"Those guys that set all that stuff up. You know the promoters."

"They asked about Reilly. What did they want to know?"

"Who he was, they wanted to know who he was."

"OK, now think Leo, why did they want to know?"

"Oh, they want him to fight."

Andre thinks back to the events from that night. Leo and Bruiser make their way to the center of the ring to touch gloves before the start of the bout. Bruiser responds by slamming a left hook into the side of Leo's head. As the underdog drops to one knee, the referee begins to step in between the two men. Bruiser effortlessly sweeps him to the side. The crowd cheers. Bruiser moves towards the stunned boxer. Reilly looks around and is sickened to see the crowd's reaction as they scream their approval.

Leo still has enough of his senses about him to cover up as Bruiser rains blows on the still kneeling man. The defense doesn't last long as Bruiser, frustrated at the insolence of the man for trying to shield himself, delivers a kick into the man's side. This sends the already prone fighter sprawling onto all fours.

Reilly is out of his seat and headed for the ring. All he can think is that Leo is in serious trouble, and he needs to get him out of there. Andre is on his heels. He's not sure what Reilly's plan is, but he's not letting him go this alone.

Getting closer, he sees that Bruiser has straddled the man's back and pretends he's riding a hobby horse. This brings peals of laughter from the crowd. Leo struggles desperately to free himself, which only makes the entire scene even more absurd. Above the noise, Reilly hears the ringside bell signaling the end of the first round. Bruiser sends a devastating blow into the back of the Leo's head before climbing off his opponent. He heads back to his corner playing to the crowd the entire time. He flexes his massive biceps. He ripples his washboard abs. He raises both arms in victory. The chant of *'Bruiser'* begins again.

The blow to the back of the head has knocked the overweight fighter senseless. Meanwhile, in the opposite corner of the ring, Leo's entourage for the night are trying to revive their fighter at least enough to get him out of the ring. Bruiser, now aware of what's going on, rushes to their corner. He's having too much fun to end the carnage this soon.

Such is the timing that Reilly has arrived in the ring to step in between Bruiser and Leo. Reilly, remembering the stories of brass knuckles and buckshot being sewn into gloves, is hyper aware of where the big man's hands are. As he inhales deeply, a calmness descends over Reilly. Events begin to move in slow motion. Bruiser swings wildly at the interloper. Reilly easily ducks the punch and sends a bare knuckle blow into Bruiser's midsection. He feels the air escape from the man. The punch hurt both men, but Reilly doesn't stop to take inventory as he sends another fist into the side of Bruiser's head. In his altered state Reilly has time to think, *'that one was for you, Leo'*.

Meanwhile behind Reilly, Andre is helping to get Leo out of the ring. Montero keeps a wary eye on the big man's corner, prepared to jump in if they should try to help their fighter. So far they seem content to stay out of it. Andre doesn't blame them as on the heels of the blow to Bruiser's temple, Reilly joins both hands together and brings them down on the back of Bruiser's head. Andre, seeing this thinks that Reilly didn't learn that move at *Al's Gym*.

The entire ring shakes as the big man falls forward. He's not unconscious, but Reilly has beaten the last of the fight out of him. The crowd is beside themselves. Cheers erupt from every corner of the warehouse. Stamping feet lend to the deafening noise.

Bruiser's corner men cautiously come through the ropes. They hold their hands in the air in a sign of surrender. Reilly, still with his fists at the ready, give the men a slight nod. Bruiser is now making his way onto all fours.

Andre grabs Reilly by the shoulder to tell him it's time to go. Reilly, believing there is a new attacker to contend with, spins ready to launch another fist. Andre, also with his hands-up, screams over the din of the crowd, "LET'S GO!"

The small group makes their way to an exit. The noise has barely diminished as they approach an exit. Leo's trainer and corner man peel off towards whatever has been cobbled together as a locker room.

As Andre and Reilly leave the venue, Bruiser is now back on his feet but just barely. He staggers around the ring bellowing. The crowd laughs as the punch-drunk fighter looks around the ring for his opponent; any opponent. He's not sure at the moment of exactly what happened, but he is keenly aware that these peasants should fear and worship him. Instead, all he hears is laughter. He may not remember much from this night, but he will remember the crowd laughing at him. He will also acutely remember the black man who spoiled this special night for him. He will remember that bastard. He will find him, and he will punish him.

Learning from Leo the date and time for the next bout that Bruiser is scheduled to fight, Andre alone makes his way to the venue. No one laughs this night as Bruiser beats an inferior fighter. He is once again a crowd favorite. The beating he took that night at the hands of Reilly has done little to diminish his arrogance as once again he struts and poses for the audience. Before leaving the ring he faces each side of the squared circle and demands,

"I want the nigger! Find me that goddamn coward!" The crowd, many of whom may have been there the night Reilly climbed into the ring to help a friend, know exactly what Bruiser wants. The crowd wants the same thing, and the blood lust lathers them into a frenzy. Andre has seen enough and exits the gym thinking, "You may want him, but you ain't gonna get him." The thought comforts him as he walks away from the 'arena' for what he mistakenly believes is the last time.

From another corner of the arena, an impeccably dressed and handsome young man watches the crowd. He has made a good living giving people what they want; booze, broads, protection. It didn't much matter what people wanted. The important thing; the profitable thing, was to be able to provide it. He hadn't been there the night some black guy climbed into the ring and gave Bruiser a beating. That took balls. Johnnie had been told about the incident afterwards but truthfully, he didn't give it a lot of thought. Most people would have forgotten about it as well if Bruiser hadn't been offering the same challenge at the end of each fight, *'find me that black bastard'*. Sometimes, the process of supply and demand works in reverse. Bruiser was creating a demand; Octaviano's function was to supply what was wanted. Johnnie Octaviano had slipped Leo twenty-bucks and asked him who the Africano was. Leo claimed he didn't know. Johnnie knew that wasn't true; he just didn't want to say. Johnnie respected that; it was Leo's own code of omerta. He'd approach Leo again. He'd offer him another twenty-dollar bill, who knows, maybe fifty the next time. Johnnie prided himself in taking a non-violent approach to problem solving. He liked Leo. Leo reminded him in a lot of ways of Augie Augustino. Leo would tell him where he could find the *Africano*. Why wouldn't he? This was a wonderful business opportunity for everyone, so why wouldn't Leo tell him? Johnnie didn't care if everyone made a few bucks off this fight as long as the family made the lion's share of the profit. Johnnie, like Andre, would visit Leo's house. He would look through the same filthy window and into the vacant living room. Octaviano, unlike Andre, would not take note of the withering flower pot. The site of the abandoned house encourages Octaviano. He knows Leo is destitute. He also knows that desperate men will do just about anything to make a few bucks in these impoverished times. He doesn't see any reason to coerce the information out of Leo. Leo will see the wisdom of telling Johnnie what he wants to know. He hoped that was the case anyway because he liked Leo. And, after all, Johnnie is a man not prone to violence.

# Chapter Twenty-Five

The office was small and more than a bit forlorn, but that was okay. Ben Rush might describe himself the same way; small and forlorn. He felt particularly blue today, as tired of a blue as the worn wool uniforms his men wore. Sometimes he wondered if he wouldn't be better off turning a blind eye towards some of what went on in his precinct. He thought, not for the first time, of one of the few heroes on his side of the law, Eliot Ness and his trouble finding honest agents. After weeding out all the corrupt candidates, Ness was able to assemble a team of nine.

Christ that was pathetic.

He needed to push these thoughts out of his head this morning. There was a homicide during the night. That in itself was not news, not in this day and age. It seemed like Benjamin Rush came into a homicide every morning.

This one was different.

A squawk box sprang to life on his desk. "He's here, Captain," came the succinct message. Rush was glad no one was there to see him jump when the box spoke. He was getting edgy in his old age. Old age, my God I'm only fifty he thought and with that thought wondered how many more years he could endure in this job.

Two light raps on the door before it opened slowly, tentatively. "You wanted to see me, Captain?" said Officer Donofrio as he slid into the small space.

"Please come in. Have a seat," he said as he gestured towards one of the two stiff-backed wooden chairs opposite his own well-worn leather chair. "I have some news to share with you," said the seasoned officer.

Hesitantly, Rush went around the desk. He parked his backside on the only small section of the desktop that was not covered with stacks of paper. Once there, he regretted moving closer as he was now nearer to Donofrio than he wanted to be. "I'm sorry to say it's bad news."

The captain began, "Last night two officers were dispatched to investigate a disturbing the peace call. The disturbance was coming from an alley behind a closed florist shop near 29$^{th}$ and Emerald Ave." Rush looked at the notes in front of him before continuing. His hand trembled slightly. He had briefed his patrolman numerous times on crimes that happened both in and outside of his precinct. This was different. He continued, "At approximately 2:37am, Officers Franklin and Jacobi entered the aforementioned alley."

What was he doing? Had he really become so detached from the human condition that the best he could do was to deliver a clinical account of these gruesome details? "A short way into the alleyway the two officers came upon a homicide victim. The victim had been shot several times," said Rush. What the captain didn't say was that the victim had been shot numerous times in the face. "The only proof of identity was a wallet found near the victim. Whatever money that might have been in the wallet was gone. We are considering this as a robbery that went wrong."

Officer Donofrio said nothing. Rush wasn't sure he wanted him to respond or if he was grateful for the silence.

"Officer Donofrio," and then, feeling this needed to be more personal, "Michael Angelo, it pains me to the core to deliver this news, but ...the victim was your father, Joseph Donofrio."

Donofrio simply looked at his commanding officer. His expression was unreadable.

Donofrio shook his head. He actually smiled slightly as he replied, "Captain, you must be mistaken. I'm sure my father is at home. At home with my mother," looking at the clock on the wall he noted the time and continued, "he's probably getting ready for work right now. I could call over there, Captain. I'm not sure how my father's wallet ended up in that alley or who the victim is, but I know it's not my father. He's at home. He's getting ready for work."

When Rush made no reply, Donofrio trailed off. He hung his head. Rush watched as his shoulders began to shake. Rush took a handkerchief from his pocket and handed it to the young man. There was one more bit of nasty business to take care of before Rush could end this interview. He asked if there was a family member that could identify the victim. No, it was a small family. Donofrio was an only child. The officer said he would go to the morgue and make the identification. There was no way he would ask his mother to perform this gruesome task.

Benjamin Rush thanked him. He shook his hand. He told his charge to take the remainder of the day off. Donofrio was anxious to get to the city morgue and clear this whole thing up. He held fast to the belief that this was a case of mistaken identity, and he'd be glad to get the whole sordid mess straightened out. He asked Rush to say nothing for the moment to his mother.

Rush watched Donofrio leave. There were things about Officer Donofrio, almost from the beginning, that bothered the captain. Rush, in his inconspicuous and clandestine ways, kept tabs on his troops. Beyond making sure they were true to the uniform, he wanted to understand what motivated each of his men to be a police officer. Being a cop was a tough job. It was oftentimes dangerous, tedious, depressing, or frustrating. It was at all times stressful. Even men who joined the force for all the right reasons would all too often find themselves being lured in the wrong direction. Alcoholism rates among police officers, by some accounts, are higher, perhaps much higher, than in the general population. A divorce rate that hovers above the national average may be related to the frequency of spousal abuse in law enforcement households. Suicide rates among these professionals, while not as high as some studies claim, are in fact higher than the norm. When the black guy Thorn had joined the force, Rush had a candid conversation with his mentor Tommy McMahon. Tommy shared the events that led to Thorn becoming a police officer. It was a good story; a noble calling, and everything Rush had seen over the years confirmed what McMahon had said. Rush's life would be simpler if more officers were as principled as Thorn.

Donofrio was a different story. He had a hard edge to him. There were stories of 'concerning behavior' right from the beginning that made their way back to Rush. The captain received feedback early on that some of the more senior officers were not keen on being assigned to patrol with Donofrio. Rush paired rookies with seasoned officers as a training tool. Most rookies were grateful for this mentoring. Donofrio didn't seem to be. Rush tried to instill an image of community service in his department. He wanted the neighborhood to see his patrolmen as allies; men who could be trusted to act on their behalf. Many of the business owners would reciprocate by offering patrolmen a piece of fruit or a slice of pie. It was a comfortable give-and-take relationship. Rush's attitude was as long as these handouts didn't become excessive, he was okay with it. He would never tolerate an exchange of money or expensive goods. Donofrio, on one of his first afternoons near the end of his shift, and the patrolman he was assigned to work with for the day, entered one of the many small grocery stores on their beat. The owner knew the senior officer. They addressed each other by their first names and shook hands. They made small talk. Donofrio was introduced. He was cool towards the shop owner, but that didn't keep the proprietor from offering the men either a candy bar or an apple. The older officer declined, saying he would be sitting down for dinner soon. He just wanted to stop in and introduce the new man. Donofrio, on the other hand, stepped behind the counter and took a brown paper bag. Saying nothing, he went up and down the aisles placing fruit and several other small items in the bag. He called the owner over to the modest meat counter where a good-sized Porterhouse steak was on display. "Gimme that," he said. Neither the owner nor the mentor quite knew how to react. The senior officer was thinking perhaps Donofrio had decided to get some shopping done. That seemed peculiar as now he would need to carry his groceries around for the remainder of the shift. The grocer as instructed, took the Porterhouse and, after placing a piece of butcher's paper on the scale, proceeded to weigh the costly piece of meat. Following that, he wrapped the steak and, removing his wax pencil from a pocket on his white apron, wrote the price on the paper. Donofrio added the package to his bag and headed to the front counter where he selected several candy bars to his parcel, and without comment, he proceeded to the door and exited the building.

When his partner overtook him on the street, Donofrio laughed and said, "Well, I guess I don't have to worry about dinner tonight."

Word of this indiscretion quickly circulated around the station house, so it was no surprise several days later, at the daily briefings before each shift, the sergeant made inappropriate behavior an agenda item. There was no doubt as to whom this message was directed at. Perhaps most concerning about the Donofrio story was the degree of arrogance he displayed during his brazen act. This coupled with the fact that he was so new to the job. There were other officers in the briefing who were guilty of much worse behavior, but these other officers had waded slowly into the waters of corruption. Donofrio had jumped into the deep end of that pool.

This act, so early in the career of a new recruit, caught Rush's attention in a big way. It didn't take long for the dossier on Donofrio to grow. Stories of how he strong-armed shop owners and, in some cases, threatened and intimidated members of the community abounded. One woman, who knew an officer in the same precinct, showed him three tickets Donofrio had written her for traffic violations. He had not actually propositioned the woman, but there was little doubt of what she would need to do in order to make the tickets go away. Her policeman friend brought the tickets and the story back to Captain Rush. Rush took the tickets telling the officer to apologize for Donofrio's behavior. Another page in the growing file he kept on the rogue cop.

# Chapter Twenty-Six

Sissy, with little Hope in tow, had made the long journey to the clinic. Now, two buses and one train later, she sat patiently in a crowded waiting room. The room smelled of strong antiseptic. It wasn't a bad smell. Perhaps more of a clean smell; astringently clean and certainly unique to the environment. There was a long counter in front of her where several women, all in white, worked at either typing or organizing tall stacks of paper. The women behind the counter resolutely did not look at the people in the waiting room, lest they give them false hope of being seen by a doctor anytime soon. The amount of activity behind the counter was in direct contrast to the amount of inactivity in the waiting room. Occasionally, a nurse would enter the area from one of the long corridors that branched away from the seating area. She would call out a number. Each time a number was announced, Sissy would look at the small tattered card in her hand wishing for the number to change. Mother and daughter had been there over an hour and very few numbers had been called.

Sissy as she waited kept vigil on a small patch of sunlight that made its way slowly across the floor as time dragged on.

Hope, looking exhausted, was able to lay her head on her mother's lap and stretch out enough to nap. This was one occasion where Sissy was happy that her daughter could sleep anytime and anywhere. She looked angelic. Anyone looking at that beautiful little face, so at peace as she rested, would never suspect the dark fears that had brought them here today. Sissy prayed as she looked at her daughter. She brushed hair back from her face. She straightened her skirt. It was Hope's favorite. A frilly pink skirt normally saved for special occasions. When Hope heard that they were going on the train, she had put the skirt on explaining to her mother that a train ride should certainly qualify as a special occasion. Sissy agreed and told her daughter that she looked beautiful. Mrs. Fish, as always, made the trip with them.

"Is daddy going on the train, too?" asked Hope.

Sissy replied that it was just the girls going out for the day because daddy had to work, and this was in essence true. A greater truth was that Sissy had debated telling Reilly about her trip to the clinic. After the walk to the park that night and her failed attempts to broach the subject, she decided against saying anything to her husband. Sissy, a woman of deep faith, prayed that she was wrong about everything. She tried to convince herself that the doctors would find some simple explanation for the symptoms Hope was experiencing. They would give her some pills and send her home, shaking their heads at another paranoid mother who had wasted everyone's time. Sissy, with every fiber of her mind and body, wanted this to be the outcome. She pictured Reilly holding her and telling her how silly she had been this whole time. Years from now, when Hope was through school and happily married, all this would just be a deeply faded memory. My God, she needed this to be true.

The patch of sunlight continued its journey across the well-worn linoleum, taking on a more trapezoidal shape as the afternoon wore on.

Sissy hoped the test wouldn't hurt. Hope was such a delicate child. She complained often of being sore or achy, and the family had learned to handle her gently for fear of leaving a bruise. Hope woke at one point. Sissy had brought a cut-up apple with plenty of 'cin'm' sugar. She offered Hope a piece now. Hope ate it half-heartedly. There was a water cooler in the waiting room, and Sissy brought her daughter a cool drink. It was warm in the crowded room, and Hope's hair was plastered to her head. Sissy ran a brush through her daughter's hair as Hope finished her drink.

"More, sweetie?"

"No, thank you, Mama," Hope replied politely as she handed her mother the paper cup.

145

They sat. They waited. Hope leaned against her mother and looked off into the middle distance in front of her.

"Seventy-one, number seventy-one," came the long awaited announcement.

It took a second for Sissy to process the information before excitedly realizing that she was number seventy-one. She had been so focused on her little patch of sunlight as her celestial time-tracker had run out of floor and was now starting to ascend the wall.

"Here we are," Sissy replied anxiously as she scrambled to gather up her purse along with Hope, fearing that if she dawdled she would be relegated to the end of the line. "Come on, Hope. It's our turn."

Hope wasn't sure what that meant exactly but showed enthusiasm about doing anything besides sitting on the uncomfortable chair.

The nurse took a second to bend and say hello to Hope. "My name's Anne," said the nurse. "My, my, don't you look pretty today?" she asked the toddler.

They laughed when Hope replied seriously, "Yes, I do."

The three entered a small examining room. The smell of antiseptic was particularly strong in this confined space.

"Do you like my dress?" Hope asked the nurse.

"I think that might be the most beautiful dress I've ever seen."

Hope beamed at the compliment. "Hope, did you know I have a little girl who is right about the same age as you?"

"Is she here? Can I play with her? Does she have a doll? This is Mrs. Fish," said Hope as she showed the nurse her favorite doll.

Hope didn't understand that this woman's white little girl would never be allowed to play with a little black girl.

The nurse surprised Sissy when she replied, "I'm sorry, honey. She's at home right now. If I knew you were going to be here today, I would have brought her. I know she would have liked to play with you, too."

Sissy was relieved to find the nurse being so nice. She smiled at her, and the nurse smiled back. It was a warm and tender smile.

Hope was not inclined to take off her pink dress and put on the small white gown until the nurse told her that the dress might get dirty if she kept it on.

"You wouldn't want to get the prettiest dress in the world dirty, would you?"

The doctor arrived, looked at the chart, and said little as he examined Hope. He looked in her throat and felt the lymph nodes on her neck. He looked at the order and asked the nurse if she had secured the blood sample. She had. Hope had cried as the needle penetrated her arm. The doctor proceeded to gather the bone marrow for testing. He told Sissy that the results would be ready in six to ten days. Sissy wanted him to tell her not to worry. She wanted to hear the words that everything was fine. She needed reassurance. He offered no comforting words of optimism before mumbling a goodbye and exiting the room.

Now, it was just the three of them again. The nurse told Sissy that he was a very good doctor. "They have so many patients to see in a day that they can't dally or people would be waiting even longer," she explained.

Before they left, the nurse gave Hope a hug, which she liked and a piece of hard-candy, which she loved. She took Sissy's hand in hers and held her gaze for a moment. "I'll keep Hope and you in my prayers," she said. Sissy thanked her and on that note began the long journey back home.

## Chapter Twenty-Seven

Johnnie Octaviano visited Bruiser after his next fight. They found the boxer and his trainer in a small area at the back of the warehouse turned arena. Bruiser, whose real name was Vladimir Petrova, was the son of Russian immigrants. The man was a monster with a thick neck, broad shoulders, and a narrow waist. His gloves had already been removed. His trainer was in the process of cutting away the tape on his hands. The brass knuckles could be seen. The trainer stopped his work and threw a towel over the incriminating knuckles. Octaviano didn't approve but said nothing.

"Get the fuck out," said the fighter in a thick accent. It sounded like he said, 'Ged da faag aught'.

His trainer, another Russian by the name of Pietir, had been around the fight game for a long time. He recognized Octaviano and knew the man had connections. He said something to his fighter in what Johnnie assumed was Russian. The fighter replied angrily in the same language. The only word from the exchange that Johnnie recognized was 'nyet, which the fighter said several times.

He finally turned to Octaviano and asked, "What do you want? I ain't got time for this bullshit."

Johnnie understood that Petrova was one seriously deranged individual, but that was ok. That might actually pay a dividend for what Octaviano had in mind. Octaviano took the precaution of bringing along two of the biggest henchmen he had on his payroll. When they entered, Johnnie found the fighter sitting on a table and took up a position in front of the man. Each of his associates flanked the fighter; one on his left and the other to his right.

Johnnie treated the hulk to an engaging smile and replied simply, "We want to talk to you. That's all. We just want a few minutes of your time."

Bruiser made a move towards Johnnie but hadn't gotten far before feeling the cold steel of a gun barrel against his temple. The gangster to his right had his gun trained on the manager, who again said something to the fighter in Russian.

The gunman told the trainer that this was America, and he should speak American. "If you say one more word that ain't American, you ain't gonna say nothin' no more."

"You ready to talk now?" asked Johnnie calmly.

When the fighter made no reply, Johnnie said, "Good," and continued. "You're a joke Petrova. You fight punching bags with no talent and even then you wear the knuckles. You're pathetic," said Johnnie in a calm and conversational tone. "What about this?" asked Octaviano as he picked up one of his boxing gloves and let it fall on the table. It sounded like a weight being dropped. "What's that? A little buckshot sewn into your glove." Picking up the glove again he slipped it onto his hand and, with just the hint of a smile on his face, approached the fighter. "You make me sick," he said. Without warning, Johnnie reeled back and slammed the weighted glove into the side of Bruiser's face. The hard blow would have knocked most men unconscious, but Petrova had the wherewithal to make a move towards Octaviano. He was rewarded with the butt of a gun crashing into the back of his head. He fell from the table onto one knee.

"Ah, ah, ah," said the gangster with the gun as he once again pressed the barrel against the prone fighter's head.

Octaviano continued, "We got off to a bad start here, but that's ok. Maybe we understand each other a little better now that we've had our little talk. Maybe we can help each other out." Saying this, Octaviano helped Bruiser to his feet and back onto the table. He was glad to see the two blows they had delivered had gotten the Russian's attention. Like a wild stallion, Petrova had been broken. He was safe to ride now.

Vladimir Petrova was not a man to scare easily, but these men had made that happen. Now back on to the table, he cradled his head. His hand came away bloody. Octaviano saw towels folded on a chair, took one and handed it to the trainer. He told the man to clean his fighter up. "It looks like he doesn't have too much fight left in him tonight," Octaviano told the trainer. "That's good."

Petrova eyed the gangster fearfully. His vision was hazy. Octaviano kept blurring between one person and then two people standing in front of him.

"We're here to talk to you about your fight against Leo Frankowicz."

Hearing the name got the Russian's attention. Octaviano could see the hatred roiling in the boxer's eyes.

"Good, I can see you still remember that night?"

Johnnie had taken his top coat off when they entered and placed it over the back of a chair. He went to it now and was shrugging his way into it. As he did so, he looked at Petrova and casually mentioned, "We found your nigger."

The big man's questions went unanswered as the three men prepared to leave. "Vladimir, get a good night's sleep, and we'll talk soon," said Johnnie as they took their leave.

Johnnie had found Reilly Thorn. He had dispatched several of his men and assigned them to watch *Al's Gym*. He told them, "If you see a fat guy walking in, it's probably Leo," and sure enough they witnessed an overweight guy making his way down the street while eating a sandwich. This might have challenged most people, but Leo had become very adept at eating while doing just about anything. His wife took exception on the night she and Leo were about to be intimate. Leo came into the room with a plate of cheese and crackers. He told her it would enhance the experience, at which point she told him he had two choices. He could make love to her or the Gorgonzola. It took him a bit too long to decide as he looked longingly from his wife to the cheese. His wife made the choice for him, and Leo slept on the drafty back porch that night.

Ninety-minutes later as he ambled away from the gym, Leo was approached by two men. A car, with its back door open, idled at the curb. "Are you Leo Frankowicz?"

He was; he was then told that someone wanted to talk to him and to get in the car. Most people would have resisted or asked a few questions, but Leo simply climbed into the back seat. One of the men joined him in the back while the other joined the driver in the front seat. Before they pulled away, Leo asked, "Could you guys make a right at the next corner? I want to stop at the Jew's deli."

The three men in the car said nothing until they pulled up to a nondescript door in a deeply shadowed alleyway. "Get out," was their simple instruction.

Leo, once inside, was surprised to find himself in a very nice bar.

"Leo! Welcome," said the well-dressed man behind the bar, "let me get you a beer."

Leo made his way to the bar, while Johnnie expertly poured a beer. There was a second man behind the bar.

Johnnie, as he handed over the beer, introduced the two saying, "Leo Frankowicz, I'd like you to meet Augie Augustino." As they looked at each other, they collectively had the same thought, *'that guy could stand to lose some weight'*.

Johnnie took Leo, with beer in hand, into the back where he had a plate of fruits, cheeses, and small sandwiches sitting on a tray. Next to the tray was a small plate of powdered cannoli and biscotti arranged attractively on paper doilies.

Before Johnnie could even broach the subject, Leo started talking, "You know that was very nice of you to give me that money when that prick Russian stiffed me after our fight."

Johnnie correctly assumed that Petrova had nothing to do with whether or not Leo had gotten paid that night but said nothing.

"I'm not afraid of that guy. He's not a good boxer. That's why he cheats. Everyone knows he weights his gloves. The night he hit me it felt like I was being hit with a hammer. Next time, I'm not going to be so stupid. I was stupid last time. You can't take your eye off that guy for a second. The cheating bastard. Plus, I'm going to get my money up front next time. You think you could help me get another fight with that guy?"

Johnnie told him that might be a very real possibility, but that was not why he had invited Leo to this meeting. As Leo methodically worked his way through the tray of food, Johnnie said, "Leo, the last time we spoke, I asked you who it was that climbed into the ring and saved your ass that night. You remember that right?" Leo nodded, and Octaviano continued, "You told me you didn't know who it was."

"Oh sure, I remember that."

"I think maybe you didn't tell me the truth that night. Is that right, Leo?"

Blushing at having been caught lying to someone who had been nice to him embarrassed Leo.

"Leo, I respect that you didn't say anything, but you could really help me out by telling me what you know about this mystery man."

Leo's only reaction was to eat more slowly.

"Leo, I'm a businessman, and what I have for your friend is a business proposition. This could work out where everyone wins. Hell Leo, there might even be a few bucks in this for you," and saying this, Johnnie reached into his billfold and slid a fifty dollar bill across the desk.

It was the most money Leo had seen in one place in a long time. If Augie had joined them at that moment, he might have told Leo about Frost's 'The Road Not Taken' and how it related to the crisp bill in front of him. He would have soon discovered that Leo was not nearly bright enough to grasp the moral implications between the poem and the money. In truth, Leo completely misunderstood why Octaviano had offered the money. He picked up the bill, slipped it into his shirt pocket, and said, "Thanks Mr. Octaviano. This squares me for what that Pollack bastard cheated me out of."

Johnnie, incredulous, managed to muster the patience to ask again, "Leo, who was the Negro that climbed into the ring with you that night?"

"You mean the cop?" asked Leo in return.

"No, not the cop. The fighter, the black fighter."

"Yeah that's right. He's a cop."

Johnnie took a second to absorb this latest bit of information.

When Johnnie didn't respond, Leo felt the need to explain in more detail, "The black guy, the one who got in the ring that night, he's a boxer *and* a cop. He works out at *Al's*. He's a good fighter. He used to be there all the time, and then he wasn't there for a long time and now he is again." Leo had told himself to not tell them who the Negro boxer was. Every few moments since arriving at the bar, Leo would remind himself of that commitment. But at the end of the day, Leo was Leo, and just that unintentionally the information simply slipped out.

"His name is Reilly Thorn."

# Chapter Twenty-Eight

Donofrio wasn't accustomed to having his fellow officers engage him in conversation. Following the death of his father, his brotherhood of navy-blue, woolen-uniformed coworkers pulled together to show their sympathy. Most of these men, in truth, didn't care for Donofrio, but when someone suffers that kind of devastating loss, the right thing to do is to put aside petty squabbles and do what you can to help ease the pain of grief. Donofrio, in his own way, was touched by this show of support. The men had all signed a beautiful sympathy card and took up a collection for his recently widowed mother. Both he and his mother were touched that so many from the precinct attended the service. Each man made a point of expressing their sympathy to his mother. Many others told Mrs. Donofrio that it was a privilege and honor to serve with her son. When they saw the effects the words had on the grieving widow, they embellished their endorsements by telling her how well liked her son was and how he was an inspiration to the rest of the men. It was fortunate that the precinct made this show of support as there were very few others in attendance. The Donofrio's had little family and fewer friends. Several neighbors appeared at the wake. Most of those attendees had heard the symphony of abuse coming from the Donofrio's small apartment. Many had encountered the departed man's wife the day after one of these events when the abused women would purposefully turn her face in a vain effort to hide a black eye or bruised cheek. But tonight was not the night to dwell on those memories. Tonight was a time for neighbors to assure Mrs. Donofrio that her husband was a saint who would be missed by all. The widow knew there was little truth in what they said, but she understood and appreciated their willingness to say these things. She would warmly hold their hands and meet their gaze and agree, saying, "Yes, he was a wonderful man and a good provider."

Michael Angelo, overhearing many of these conversations, was sickened to witness his mother extolling the virtues of such a vile and abusive husband. The senior Donofrio's boss approached him to express his sympathy and assure the young man that his father would leave a huge void down at the plant. It was all Michael Angelo could do to keep from grabbing the man and pummeling him. Instead he asked, "So, can I expect to see many of my father's coworkers here tonight?" The truth the boss knew, and Donofrio suspected, was that his father was universally disliked in the workplace. Even the manager didn't want to be here but felt obligated upon finding out that no one else had any interest in making an appearance.

There were others in attendance that neither Donofrio nor his mother recognized. Because of the horrific nature of the death, the newspapers picked up the story and ran an article. Some, attracted by the violence of the death, appeared out of some morbid sense of curiosity.

Benjamin Rush arrived at the chapel towards the tail end of the visitation. When he arrived, there were only a handful of people remaining and many of those were saying their goodbyes. Several were at the closed casket, offering a final prayer. Rush found Donofrio talking with a familiar face, Stanley Wojick. He dutifully expressed his condolences to Officer Donofrio. He then shook Wojick's hand, asking, "If memory serves, you are Special Agent Wojick. Is that correct?" Rush could sense a tension between the two men. Following an awkward pause, Rush took a seat next to the widow.

When Rush moved off, Wojick asked quietly, "Who's that guy?" What he really wanted to know was how he knew his name.

"We'll talk later. For now you'd better go."

Benjamin Rush spoke quietly to Mrs. Donofrio, telling her all the things she needed to hear. Her son was a fine officer; her husband a good man. Rush, who liked to know what was going on with his officers, knew about the domestic abuse happening at the Donofrio home. The captain was in the habit of going over the previous day's activity reports. His secretary would have the reports neatly stacked on his desk and waiting for him each morning. Several times, he had come across the name Donofrio as his men had been dispatched to the address for a domestic disturbance reported by a neighbor. The wife, Donofrio's mother, had never pressed charges even though there would be comments in the reports detailing serious abuse.

Ben Rush had visited Mrs. Donofrio after one of these incidences. He was unprepared for her natural prettiness. She was going on fifty but had a lovely complexion and, even though she had been crying, Rush could see the doe-like softness in her eyes. He asked if he could come in, and she told him no. He could see an ugly purple bruise on the side of her face. He tried not to look at it but couldn't help himself. The sight of the bruise angered him. He told her the law would protect her if she should elect to press charges. She insisted that everything was fine and that things had just gotten a little out of hand the night before. He apologized for barging in on her morning. He gave her a card and told her, "Call me if you ever need anything."

As he turned to leave, she stopped him, "Thank you, Captain. Your kindness means a great deal to me."

"Please, call me Ben." Rush was glad to linger in the doorway, even for a few more seconds.

Helen Donofrio treated him to a hint of a smile before he left. It was a nice smile.

The morning following the wake, Rush told himself it was just the circumstances. He was simply trying to be nice to someone who had suffered a painful loss. He tried to convince himself of these things but thought of her often throughout the morning. He glanced at the clock and correctly assumed that she would be getting ready for the funeral. He thought about attending the service. He told himself that the department should be represented at the burial, and as no one else would be there, he should take on the responsibility. These were all the right reasons for being there, but they weren't the real reasons. He felt embarrassed over his feelings towards a woman who had so recently lost her husband. He found himself getting angry at the thought of anyone being unkind to her. He felt guilty over his feelings about her son. At one point, he chastised himself for not giving more thought to Agent Wojick being at the wake. Now, he leaned back in his chair and wondered at the events that might have brought these two together. By the end of the week, after having reviewed the coroner's report, Rush would give more thought to what had brought one of his officers together with a federal agent. Rush would also give more thought to the widow Donofrio as, no matter how much he tried to block her out of his thoughts, she continued to cross his mind.

# Chapter Twenty-Nine

A home phone was very much still considered a luxury in the 1930s, but the Thorns felt it was important as Reilly might get offered some extra shifts at work simply because the precinct was able to reach him. The same was true for Sissy and her teaching career, which as the Depression wore on, was still on-again, off-again. Occasionally, it would be for Grandfather Thorn concerning a day-laborer job. Now, Sissy looked at the phone as a harbinger of bad times yet to be heralded. Black and silent and somehow sinister, its idleness mocked her; it tormented her.

The seven days following the visit to the clinic might have been the longest week of Sissy's life. She slept horribly and ate poorly. She looked at the world through a haze. She said little. Reilly's parents tried to reach out to her. They tried to understand why their normally cheerful daughter-in-law was so down. Even more concerning was the fact that their son did not seem particularly worried about his wife. Reilly had always loved Sissy, worshipped was closer to the truth, but now he seemed content to let her wallow in her misery. Hope for her part was still the focal point of the family. Even though she seemed lethargic of late, she was still their little ray of 'Sunshine'.

Eight days after her visit to the clinic, Sissy walked into their modest home and said nothing as she gathered up Hope and disappeared into her bedroom. They both fell asleep almost immediately. A short time later, there was a quiet tapping at the door. Sissy awoke slowly, thinking of the Edgar Allan Poe poem, *The Raven*.

*'While I nodded nearly napping, suddenly there came a tapping'*

Again, she heard the gentle knocking at the door. This time she heard Grandfather whisper, *"Sissy?"*

Leaving Morpheus to weave dreams for Hope, Sissy slowly sits on the edge of the bed. She felt more like she had passed out instead of napped and, given her bad sleep over the past week, this may have been close to the truth. Again, came the slight rapping at her chamber door.

"I'm coming," she said quietly and made her way to the door. She loved the senior Thorn deeply. Her heart broke a bit when she opened the door a crack and saw the look of concern on his face.

"I'm sorry to disturb you. I didn't even know you had come home. I thought this was important enough to wake you up. A woman called for you. Her name was Anne, Anne Reston. She said it was important and that you should call her when you got home." Her father-in-law hesitated briefly before continuing, "Sissy honey, she said she was from some kind of clinic." He saw her shoulders slump as she took the note.

She said nothing. Instead, she turned to look at Hope sleeping peacefully on the bed. With her back turned to the family's patriarch, her shoulders began to tremble. He could hear the soft sobs that Sissy so desperately tried to stifle. He tentatively, gently, put his hand on her back. Sissy, who told herself that she was strong enough to fight this battle alone, knew now that she was not. Suddenly, she felt small and weak and scared. Feeling the loving hand on her back was the permission she needed to share the pain and fear that had tormented her. Turning, she allowed her father-in-law to envelope her in his aged but still powerful arms. He tenderly cradled her head against his chest and let Sissy weep. Great shuddering sobs shook her entire frame. As Hope was sleeping, he steered his daughter-in-law out of the room and into the hallway. He closed the door so as to not disturb his granddaughter. Sissy's mother-in-law had returned from work and looked at her husband questioningly as he continued to hold his daughter-in-law. Her husband indicated with his eyes that he wasn't sure exactly what was happening but the 'why' of it did not concern his wife. All she knew was that Sissy, a girl who was in every sense of the word her daughter, was suffering. She went to the pair.

"Sissy, Sissy, Sissy," she repeated, and took her precious daughter-in-law into her own arms. Feeling the embrace of her mother-in-law, Sissy began to cry even harder. Her mother-in-law joined in her tears. Two women weeping; one cried for Hope, the other for Sissy. Two, seeking a strength that one alone could not find.

Later, Reilly came in to discover the three of them seated at the small kitchen table with Hope. The late afternoon sunlight that filtered in through the window over the sink did little to warm or cheer the room.

Hope, with Mrs. Fish sitting on her lap, was busy eating a 'cin'm' apple with sugar. "Look what Papa gave me," she said, barely looking at her father.

Reilly planted a kiss on the top of his daughter's head.

Normally, this scene of familial bliss would have gladdened Reilly, but today there seemed to be an almost palpable tension pulsating beneath a thin veneer of civility. Neither his father or mother nor Sissy looked at Reilly. Collectively, they said nothing to the police officer.

"So, did I miss something here?" asked Reilly, addressing the elephant in the room.

Between chews, Hope answered honestly and innocently as only a child can, "I think they're mad at you, Daddy."

Abruptly, Sissy slid her chair back and hurriedly left the room.

"Wait!" demanded Reilly and made a move to follow her.

His father stood, effectively blocking his son. "Son, why don't you give Sissy a little space right now?"

Reilly's mother, muttering a comment about 'men', followed Sissy, leaving the two men, father and son, in the kitchen with Hope.

"We need to talk, boy," said his father, and suddenly, Reilly was no longer an adult. His father's tone had transported him back to when he was just a kid and in trouble for one infraction or another.

156

"Hope, how about if you finish your apple outside with daddy and me?" Her grandfather had built a child-sized picnic table for Hope that she would beg to eat her meals or snacks at. "You can sit at your picnic table," he added.

The two men settled on the back steps. Neither knew exactly what to say, so they opted to say nothing. It was more comfortable, safer, to simply watch Hope eat her cin'm apple with sugar.

Before Reilly arrived home that afternoon, Sissy had regained enough composure to speak guardedly to her in-laws. She told them about how her fears had started innocently enough and how easy it was at that time to convince herself that Hope was fine. So what if she slept more than other children. So what if she tired easily or needed to visit the doctor so frequently. That was in the beginning, but all of these things taken collectively had begun to concern Sissy more and more. She told them how she went to the library to try to understand what might be happening to her little Hope. She told them how she had gone to see Hope's doctor one more time to demand that he order certain tests for her daughter.

"He did order the tests, and I did take Hope to the clinic," she told her in-laws. "That was who called today, Papa. That woman Anne, she was the nurse at the clinic."

They listened as Sissy talked about her daughter. Hope's grandparents were an ingrained part of her life. This was especially true of her grandfather. They had seen much of what Sissy described and also had worries about their precious Hope. Like their son, they found it more comfortable to ignore what they saw. About the time Sissy had completed telling of her concerns, the bedroom door opened and little sleepy-eyed Hope emerged holding her doll. She went to her grandmother, hugging her leg and resting against her skirt.

"Hi Grandma," she said, "I took a nap with mommy."

The timing of Hope's arrival could not have been any more perfect as they were at the point in the conversation where they would next ask a question that neither wanted answered, 'What did Sissy believe the problem was?'

"She needs you, son. They both do."
Reilly said nothing.

For the moment, he was content to watch Hope at her undersized picnic table enjoying her snack. Hope would take a slice of apple and encourage Mrs. Fish to take a bite. "That's a good girl," she would say, "apples are good for you." She mimicked what her grandfather would say, "An apple a day keeps the doctor away."

What had always seemed like such a cute ritual between his daughter and her doll now seemed like a cruel joke meant to hurt and anger him. Reilly began to stand.

"Son?"

"I have to go, dad. I'm going to the gym." All Reilly wanted to do at that moment was to go one-on-one with the heavy-bag until his arms ached and legs gave out; until the sweat pooled at his feet; until he forgot why he was there. He wanted to punish that bag. He wanted to be somewhere where he only had to think about punching and then punching some more.

# Chapter Thirty

People noticed Johnnie Octaviano. He was handsome, in an almost boyish athletic way. He dressed well and carried himself with a certain bearing. So primped and groomed that he might almost be mistaken for a dandy in the vernacular of the day. That thought was vanquished quickly once one noticed the set of his square jaw and the steely depth of his gaze. *Al's Gym* was typically a noisy place but dropped by several decibel levels when Johnnie walked through the door. One trainee stopped jumping rope; another let the speed bag pendulum to a stop. He made his way slowly past several men working out. He took in their faces as he took inventory of the well-worn equipment. Sweaty, brooding faces, carrying the scars of battles from both in and out of the ring, stole glances at Octaviano. He didn't appear in a hurry. He exuded an aura of someone who had every right to be there. Finally, he was approached, and was asked.

"Can I help you?"

Octaviano treated the inquirer to an engaging smile, "My guess is you might be Andre. Is that correct?" As he said this, he removed his fine felt fedora and extended his hand, offering a handshake to the smaller man.

Andre looked at the hand suspiciously before tentatively extending his own hand. Upon shaking hands, Octaviano held the trainer's hand firmly as he leaned in and whispered conspiratorially, "Is there a place we might have a private word?"

Andre, who always had a sense of importance because of having an office to call his own, felt a bit of embarrassment as he and Octaviano entered the small space. Sliding behind the cluttered desk, he gestured towards the only other chair in the office. It would have been difficult to add even one more chair to the tiny area. Johnnie took it all in as he looked around. His features remained expressionless; his demeanor, non-judgmental. On the wall was a picture of Johnny Coulon, *'The Cherry Picker from Logan's Square'*.

Looking at the faded picture and smiling slightly, Octaviano, with a bit of awe in his voice, said, "I saw Coulon fight. Five-foot and 110 pounds. I was just a kid at the time, but I'll never forget him. He was amazing."

The photograph actually belonged to Uppercut, but Andre kept the picture of the diminutive fighter in his office as an example for all boxers that there was a place for everyone in the ring. Andre felt a pang of jealousy upon hearing that this man had seen one of his idols fight.

"A lot of people know that he was a great fighter but don't realize what a great trainer he became after his boxing career was over," said Andre. The Chicago boxing world could be a small place, and Andre had the pleasure of meeting his idol Coulon several times. Coulon opened a boxing gym on the south side of Chicago following his career. Many of the greatest boxers in the world had spent time at Johnny Coulon's over a fifty year time span.

Now, with the reminiscing about Coulon at an end, Octaviano turned his attention to Andre, smiled, and said, "I'm sure you're wondering why I'm here."

Shortly after Octaviano left the gym, Reilly arrived. In all the years that Reilly worked out at *Al's Gym*, he would make it a point to seek out his old friend and sparring partner to say hello and talk for a few minutes before starting his workout. Today, Reilly walked in acknowledging no one. Several fighters said hello to Reilly as he walked by, expecting a hello in return. They were disappointed as Reilly kept his head down and said nothing. Making his way to the locker room, he again said nothing to the other fighters who were either changing or getting ready to shower. Their greetings were met with silence as well. Slamming his locker door shut, he walked purposefully towards the heavy bag. Fighters, prudently, warmed up and stretched before starting their workout. It was something before today that Reilly did religiously. Today, Reilly walked to the heavy bag like he was approaching someone who had done him a grievous wrong and, without ritual or preamble, slammed a resounding right roundhouse into the inanimate leather. He hit the bag so hard that several in the gym turned to see what the commotion was. Reilly knew immediately that the solutions to his pain and misery were not to be found in abusing the lifeless bag, but it felt good regardless. It felt so good that he followed up his punishing right with a second blow, and then a third, and then a fourth. There was none of the fancy footwork that many in the gym had come to expect from Reilly. It was just a man senselessly, mercilessly pounding a heavy bag. Like moths to a flame, several from the gym gravitated towards the spectacle. Several others stopped their own workout and simply watched in stunned silence. A puddle of sweat began to form at the pugilist's feet. Reilly was oblivious to both the gathering crowd and the eerie silence surrounding him. Trancelike, he sent one punch after another after another into the bag. The carnage continued and by all rights, given the ferocity of the attack, should have begun to ebb in intensity. The opposite was true. Each punch seemed to escalate in both power and passion. Some in the gathering congregation, all seasoned fighters, actually cringed a bit when a particularly viscous blow found its mark.

Andre appeared and shouldered his way through the ring of fighters. It took him a second to take in the scene before quickly realizing something was wrong. One glimpse at Reilly's face told him that. His normally friendly features were contorted into a grizzly mask of hatred. Behind the look of anger was something else. What Andre saw behind that mask scared him even more.

"Reilly," he said. When he received no reply, he repeated his friend's name and, again receiving no reply, shouted, "REILLY!"

Reilly, like a man slowly coming out of a trance, turned to see Andre looking at him. As he slowly continued to gather his wits, he saw the rest of the assemblage staring at him. He didn't fully understand why he was the center of attention. He also couldn't quite fathom the look of concern on the faces of these men, many of whom he had known since he was little more than a boy. Saying nothing, Reilly sluggishly made his way to Andre.

"C'mon," was all Andre said as he put his hand on his friend's shoulder and led him towards the security of the minuscule office at the rear of the gym.

If either man had looked back, they would have seen a trickle of sand cascading down the heavy leather bag and mixing with the pool of sweat on the floor. Trainees from around the gym looked at this in amazement.

Reilly Thorn had punched a hole in the bag.

Octaviano had left *Al's Gym* having not heard what he wanted to hear. He wasn't used to that. He felt a certain frustration when people could not see a good business opportunity when it was presented to them. Octaviano was convinced that there was money, very likely a lot of money, to be made by getting that Africano into the ring.

Andre had been polite and professional. He told the gangster that Reilly had thought about boxing to help with the family's bills but had gone cold on the idea. Andre told Octaviano about the night they had gone to see Leo fight and how Reilly had intervened to help a friend. These were all things Johnnie already knew and, quite honestly, didn't care about. Andre told the well-dressed visitor that what he and Reilly had seen that night had sickened both of them. Channeling the memory of Uppercut, he went on to describe boxing as a time-honored and noble sport.

"Mr. Octaviano, what you do to boxing makes me sick."

Johnnie simply nodded. "I don't blame you for feeling that way. There is little nobility in the sport today," he agreed.

When Andre said nothing, Johnnie continued, "The thing is Andre, people want to see your boy Reilly step through the ropes and answer Bruiser's challenge. It took some effort to track you down. I was fortunate to find you. Thorn didn't leave a calling card the night he ambushed Bruiser."

Realizing the 'ambush' comment was meant to bait him, Andre let it slide, instead asking, "And how much did you pay Leo for what you wanted to know?"

"Leo may be a better business man than you think. He's bright enough to know a good deal when he sees one."

"Leo doesn't see much beyond the giant sandwich he's usually devouring. Congratulations, you managed to weasel some information out of a slow-witted, punch-drunk boxer. Look, let's get this straight, Reilly is not 'my boy'. I'm not his manager. I'm his friend and training partner. You're talking to the wrong guy, but I'll save you the trouble of talking to Reilly. He ain't interested."

Rising, Octaviano said, "I'm in the business of getting people what they want. There is too much interest in making this fight happen to simply walk away. Please tell Reilly that I'll be in touch, won't you."

On that note, Johnnie extended his hand. When Andre didn't reciprocate, he turned towards the door.

"You know he's a cop, right?" asked Andre.

Stopping and half turning, it appeared the gangster wanted to say something. Whatever it was, it went unspoken as he exited the small office and then the gym.

Now out on the street, Octaviano waved the waiting car away. "You two go back to the bar. I'll walk," he told the two men he had brought along with him. This didn't surprise the henchmen, nor did they question it as this was not the first time their boss had opted to walk. They understood that he had things on his mind that he needed to mull over. The two had a vague idea of what this visit to the gym was about, but they knew not to ask

Octaviano questions. He told them what they needed to know. As the car pulled away, Johnnie turned and began walking away unhurriedly. He gave little thought to the people he passed on the street, including the angry looking black man, carrying a gym bag that strode by.

Andre's small office was getting a lot of use this day as he and Reilly were now both seated on opposite sides of the desk. Sweat continued to pour out of the black fighter following his attack on the heavy bag. Grabbing a freshly laundered towel from a stack, he handed it to Reilly. Still breathing heavily, Reilly began to towel off. Andre said nothing as Reilly ran the towel across his toned chest and arms. He mopped his face and head. He did not look at Andre. The several moments of silence that elapsed seemed like a very long time. Reilly finally raised his head and, seeing the unmistakable look of concern on his friend's face, buried his face in his towel and wept.

# Chapter Thirty-One

"He was a prick."

"He was your father."

Donofrio had never seen Stan Wojick this angry. It was intimidating. The special agent appeared to grow in mass in proportion to his aggravation. His already huge chest and beefy arms seemingly inflated before the small cop's eyes. Donofrio had done a good job of manipulating the special agent up to this point but now realized that there was inherent danger in dealing with a physical force like Wojick. Like the guy who thinks he has total command over his vicious dog but starts to feel differently on the day the dog lowers his gaze, raises his hackles, growls gutturally, and begins walking menacingly towards his master. At that moment, the dog's owner knew his next actions were disproportionately important to how the scenario would ultimately play out.

Calculate your odds, thought Donofrio. The percentages spun in the cop's head like a roulette wheel. Donofrio, in his mind's eye, saw the wheel spin and could hear the ball tumbling as it looked for a resting place. Donofrio debated on whether to play black or red.

In what he could only describe as divine inspiration, he looked at Wojick and said, "My mother. He was going to kill my mother. She begged me to do this."

Donofrio barely got the explanation out before Wojick responded, "Bullshit! You are so full of shit. Like that bullshit with the hooker. I told you how pissed off Wroblonski got. And that was over a hooker. Who even gives a shit about a hooker?"

"I don't blame you. You're right. I knew this was wrong, and I knew it was wrong to drag you into this," Donofrio said regretfully. "We were friends, Stan. You may have been the only friend I ever had in my life." The last comment genuinely had an effect on the Chicago cop as he recognized both the truth and the sadness of what was just admitted.

Wojick mulled over the comments. The truth was he did consider the much smaller man his friend. They had some great times together. He liked Donofrio.

Donofrio made a move to rise out of the small booth where they had stopped for lunch. "I'll go now, Stan. Don't worry; you're clean in this whole thing." Stopping himself, he turned back towards the special agent. "It's not bullshit. You got no idea of what that man did to my mother. He was a prick, a mean, heartless bastard. She should have left him years ago, but he would have killed her if she tried. I love my mother, Stan," and here his voice broke a bit before finishing, "I'll go now."

Stan Wojick was trying to grasp, process and react to everything Donofrio had just bombarded him with. Because analytics would never be his strong suit, it didn't take long. He quickly decided on a plan of action. Before Donofrio could exit the booth, the big federal agent stopped him. "Sit down," he said quietly.

A look of relief spread across Donofrio's face.

"You stay. I'm leaving," said Wojick. Before he exited, he fixed the smaller man with an intense stare. "I'm done with you, you sick bastard. You used me for the last time. You don't come around me no more. Do you understand what I'm saying?" Because they were in a restaurant, Wojick keep his voice lowered, but there was no mistaking the passion and finality of what he had to say. "You come around me again and I'll snap your neck. I'll snap your neck like a goddamned chicken bone."

Donofrio watched the big man as he made his leave. He felt a void; an emptiness. He reflected on the events that had led to this.

They were drunk. They often were. If Stan Wojick had kept a diary, something he was not likely to do, many of the entries over the past months would have started with, '*Went out with Donofrio last night. Got drunk*'.

The little cop loved to drink, and remarkably, he seemed to be able to out drink the much larger man, night-in and night-out. After a few drinks anything might happen. Often they would gamble. Sometimes they would end up in a brothel. Those nights tended to end badly, with girls crying and warnings being issued to the two to leave and not come back.

One night, after several drinks, Donofrio announced, "It's time to take a little law and order back to the streets." Laughing, Donofrio slid off the barstool and made his way to the door.

Wojick, who had no idea what this meant, asked, "What the hell are you talking about?" Receiving no reply, he dutifully followed his friend out the door.

It was more than curiosity that led him out into the night. Donofrio had a way of making life interesting for the federal agent. Even on nights when they didn't do anything noteworthy, there was an element of excitement and anticipation with the two just being together and hanging out. Some nights, the two might simply have a few drinks and do nothing more interesting than go out for dinner. Stan liked those quieter evenings. Unlike Wroblonski, Donofrio would really listen to what Wojick had to say. The smaller cop might ask Wojick for advice, almost putting the agent into the role of big brother. It was a role Wojick liked.

Now, out on the street, Wojick hurries to catch up, "Where we headed, Doni?" Wojick had taken to calling the cop 'Doni', something Donofrio would not have tolerated from anyone else. He was OK with the nickname but only when it came from Stan.

"Not sure but I'll know it when I get there."

A short time later, on a deserted street, a lone man came towards them. Alternately, the street lamps would illuminate him and then hide him. With each passing through the light, the man gained definition. He was of average size, making him somewhat larger than Donofrio but much smaller than Wojick. He wore the clothes of a manual laborer. There was a slight weave to his walk as perhaps he too had imbibed this evening. The cop and the agent waited in the shadows.

"Good evening, sir," said Donofrio as the man approached. The man gave a start, believing he was alone on the street.

The first thing the man noticed was the badge in Donofrio's hand.

"What can I do for you, Officer?" The man said, slurring his words slightly.

"We don't want to alarm you, but there's been a murder, and we're looking for witnesses. Have you seen anything suspicious?"

"A murder? No, no sir, I ain't seen nothin'."

Donofrio went on to describe the murder suspect they were looking for. It was a perfect description of the man they had stopped. Donofrio went on to describe the man in front of him to a tee. When he was done with the description, he bid the man good-night, advising him to be careful as there was a murderer on the loose.

164

The man was barely out of their shadow when Wojick slammed the man against a wall and placed a gun to the side of his head.

Excitedly, he looked at Donofrio, "This is him! This is the guy. Don't you see? It's the murderer!"

"Oh my God. I think you're right. Sir, we are going to need to see some identification."

"Back pocket. It's in my back pocket, but I didn't kill nobody. I swear to God I didn't kill nobody."

Advising his partner to keep the gun trained on the man, Donofrio worked the wallet out of his pocket. "How do I know this is you? Maybe you stole this wallet. What's your name?"

"Gerrard, Gerrard Pickens," Gerrard went on to give his address and his marital status, his kid's names and their ages. He even threw in where he worked and his boss's name.

While he did this, Donofrio helped himself to the few dollars the man kept in his wallet. Out of sight of the 'murder suspect', he showed the money to Wojick and smiled. The big federal agent just shook his head in return. You never knew what you might end up doing when you went out with Donofrio for the night.

"Officer Smith, I believe we have the wrong man," Donofrio said as he handed the wallet back to the grateful man. The man thanked them both profusely, promising them he would report any suspicious behavior immediately. Now free, he ran down the street and disappeared around a corner.

Once out of sight, the two cops laughed and celebrated the ruse they had just performed.

"So, what's he going to say when he finds his cash is gone?" Wojick asked.

Mulling the question over for a moment, Donofrio replied, "What do we care? We didn't heist his dough, Officer Smith did," which got them both laughing even harder.

Wojick was pretty sure there wasn't actually a murderer on the loose but was embarrassed to ask the question.

Donofrio, still sitting in the small coffee shop, thought about the first night that he and Wojick had played that particular game. Wojick loved it from the beginning. They never used their real names. Taking on false identities allowed the two to be whoever they wanted to be. Sometimes they were good cops on a noble mission; on other nights they might be more threatening and more dangerous. In the beginning, Donofrio did all the talking. In time, Wojick would ask to take over. He was surprisingly creative and a lot more intimidating than the much smaller Donofrio. It was a special bonding time for the two friends. Donofrio had begun to tire of the game. It was work for starters. They had started to call it 'trolling' based on the fishing practice, and like fishing, they were not always successful. Stanley liked it so much that Donofrio continued to troll with his friend even though his interest was waning.

Occasionally, Donofrio would visit his parents. Visit his mother would be more accurate. There was always some telltale sign of continued abuse. There might be an ugly bruise that hadn't quite healed yet or maybe a busted lampshade. His mother would say little about these things, especially since her husband had told her that her precious son had threatened to kill him.

Donofrio played down the threat he had made against his father as something stupid said in the heat of the moment. The reality was that Donofrio had meant it when he said it and knew a day of reckoning would come to the man. Sometimes, he would daydream about what that moment would feel like. He had often thought about killing someone. It was unfulfilling if the fantasy involved killing a stranger. The biggest rush came when he thought about making good on his threat to the old man.

He wasn't sure where the inspiration came from, but that was OK. If Wojick liked the trolling game, Donofrio would give him one final game he would never forget.

On the fateful night, Donofrio got Wojick drunker than usual while drinking almost nothing himself. He had gotten good at pretending to drink when out with the agent. Donofrio had studied his father's movements and was in position to intercept him on his way home along a quiet stretch of his route. Joseph Donofrio worked late into the evening one day a month for inventory. Michael Angelo and his mother looked forward to this monthly occurrence. Tonight was that night. The small cop was almost beside himself with anticipation. It took some doing to get Wojick into position as he was 'sloppy-drunk' by the time they hit the streets. He told Donofrio that he didn't feel well and wanted to go home.

"You're OK, big guy, just hang in there for a few more minutes. I got the feeling this is going to be a great night."

Wojick liked the sound of that. If he was even a little more sober, he might have picked up on the fact that this was not how they normally operated during the trolling game. Normally, they just walked around and hoped to find somebody on an isolated street. Tonight, they were camped out in one spot. Again, if Wojick was sober, it might have felt like a stake-out.

It was.

"Ok, Ok, here comes someone," Donofrio said excitedly as his father came into view. "Listen Stan, here's the plan for tonight. When he gets closer, show him your badge, and then lead him into the alley for questioning. I'll wait down the street and, don't worry, when I get into the alley, BAM! I'll have a big surprise for you."

Wojick smiled stupidly.

As the senior Donofrio approached, Wojick stepped out of the shadows, "Where you think you're going?" Wojick slurred the words so badly that the senior Donofrio was forced to ask him to repeat himself.

Swaying noticeably, he slurred out, "I'm a cop," and realizing he hadn't shown his badge, began the challenging process of shuffling through one pocket after another. Now, with badge in hand, he ordered the man into the alley.

"You're drunk. I'm not going into that alley." This was unusually brave talk coming from the senior Donofrio.

Wojick, like most cops whether drunk or sober, do not like to have their authority questioned. "I said, get in that alley," and shoved the suddenly terrified man into the dark entrance. He shoved him a second time and then again until they were in the deep recesses of the alleyway.

Wojick and Donofrio had performed this ballet more than a few times, but being this drunk, the standard script escaped the swaying federal agent. "You're a murderer," claimed Wojick.

"Look, I don't know what you're talking about. Do you want money? I can give you money."

"No, that part comes later," said Wojick, starting to chuckle. "How'd you know about that part anyway?"

"I don't understand."

"There's a murderer and he looks just like you. What kind of coat is that?"

"It's a wool overcoat," answered the senior Donofrio.

"Yeah, that's right. The murderer guy was wearing that coat."

"What murderer? Who got murdered?"

Stan, again with difficulty, was able to extract his weapon.

"You don't need that. Please put that away," begged the senior Donofrio.

Wojick came to the slow realization that the younger Donofrio had now joined him.

"Doni, I caught the murderer. This guy's a murderer," and again started to laugh.

"You did good, Stan," he replied. He had no trepidation about using real names as his father was never going to leave this alley. At least not vertically.

"Michael Angelo? Is that you? Oh, thank God. Please tell this man I'm not a murderer."

"Quiet," his son demanded. "What you done was a lot worse than murder."

Having said that, a lifetime of memories came flooding back to the young police officer. Memories of a scared boy waiting in his room, praying his father wouldn't barge in with belt in hand or fists clenched. Never knowing when this tyrant would fly into a rage over some real or imagined violation of his harsh rules. The physical bruises and emotional scars that would never heal. The nights he would hear his mother whimpering in the next room. Dear God, what was going on in that next room? He didn't want to know, yet wanted to know every sick detail. His mother, a woman he adored, being violated at the hands of this monster.

Wojick stood quietly trying to understand the unexpected twist the game had taken this evening. Did this guy call him Michael Angelo? He knew that was Donofrio's name, but he also knew he hated that name. Who was this guy?

Without warning, Donofrio had Wojick's 58 caliper Police Positive Special Revolver with a four-inch barrel in his hand. His father still had his face to the wall when his son slammed into his back. The terrified man could feel the gun barrel pressing into the small of his skull.

"You don't have to do this," the sobs were now coming uncontrollably. "Think of your mother. She'll be all alone."

'Mother?' thought Wojick. He wished he wasn't this drunk. If he was sober, maybe this would make more sense.

"My mother!" screamed Donofrio, and with that, he spun his father around. The look of terror on the bloated man's face was pure ecstasy to the young cop. Making good on his promise to 'see it coming', he pressed the gun barrel between his eyes and, without warning or overture, pulled the trigger.

"Oh my God!" cried Wojick. "What did you do?"

Donofrio didn't resist when the federal agent wrested the gun from his hand. Holstering the weapon, Wojick turned. He only went several feet before dropping to his knees. He vomited violently.

Donofrio held his father against the wall. Blood ran down the man's face and over the forearm that had him pinned to the wall. He studied his victim closely. He watched as the last bit of life exited his body. Even in death, he hated this face.

Wojick, moaning in the background, shakily made his way to his feet. "We got to go. We got to go, now!" and with that, he made his way out of the alley.

Donofrio slowly came out of his own daze. My God he felt good. He felt free. With pure euphoria, he reached for his service revolver. Putting the gun to the dead man's face, he pulled the trigger, and then he pulled it again and again until every shell had been spent. Even then, he continued to pull the trigger.

He looked around. Stan was gone. Suddenly, that seemed like a good idea. He let the lifeless body tumble to the pavement. Calculate the odds, he told himself. He turned his father onto his back and quickly found the wallet. Opening the billfold, he found a fist full of twenties. Good old dad, he thought. "This dough isn't going to impress anyone where you're going," and with that, he pocketed the wad of cash and let the wallet drop. Hearing the unmistakable sound of a siren blaring in the distance, he took a quick look around. He hoped it would look like a robbery gone bad. With that thought he turned and disappeared into the night.

# Chapter Thirty-Two

Sissy once again sits in the small waiting room at the clinic. She was both panicky and frightened when she returned Anne Reston's phone call and was told it would be best if she made another trip to the medical center. Hope was spending the day with her grandfather, something they would both delight in. Sitting on Sissy's right is her mother-in-law. Sissy told her she would be OK to make the trip alone, but her mother-in-law insisted on accompanying her. Sissy was grateful to have her with her now. Even though they had an appointment, Sissy was given a card with a number on it and told the doctor would see her shortly. Today's number was thirteen. Sissy wasn't prone to superstitions but Reilly's mother was. She crossed herself and looked to the heavens when Sissy showed her the ominous number.

On this day there was no patch of sunlight, like during her last visit, to help mark time as they sat. The day was grey and threatened rain, another harbinger of bad things to come according to her mother-in-law. She loved this woman dearly but didn't need her backwoods mumbo-jumbo today. She was nervous enough without these thoughts fueling her angst.

Finally, a familiar face appeared. Anne Reston took the empty seat next to Sissy. She extended her hand, and when Sissy accepted it, Anne held on. She apologized for the wait saying the doctor would see her shortly.

"How's our little Hope doing?" she asked.

"Well, I guess we're going to find that out shortly," replied Sissy. She was fighting to hold back tears. She chastised herself for breaking the promise she had made to herself to be strong. She hoped the nurse would tell her everything would be fine. She didn't. She gave her hand a tender squeeze and told her the doctor should be available soon. The look on her face spoke volumes of what was to come.

They sat.

They waited.

They prayed.

Nurse Reston appeared for a second time. She didn't announce the number. Instead, she went to Sissy, and bending close to her ear, whispered, "The doctor will see you now."

The walk to the examination room seemed long, but it was not nearly long enough.

Mother and grandmother entered the small room with Anne Reston. The doctor stood on the opposite side of a small adjustable table. He was studying a folder.

Reston closed the door quietly.

"Nurse, you don't need to be here for this," said the doctor.

"I'd like to stay if it's alright. Mrs. Thorn is a friend of mine."

This comment surprised everyone in the room. The doctor nodded his approval. Sissy snuck a glance towards Anne, who smiled slightly in return.

Sissy sat in stunned silence staring through the dirty glass window of the bus as the street scene outside blurred past. How could all these people go about their business as if this was just one more day? Two men were laughing outside a small grocery store while the store owner swept the sidewalk in front of his shop. How did they not know that something horrible had happened? A group of three boys, one with a baseball bat slung across his shoulder, looked to be on an important mission. Could they not see the suffering and pain all around them? A pretty young girl waiting at a bus stop, oblivious to the admiring looks from the handsome young man standing only several feet away. Somehow, they did not feel the tear in the fabric of the universe.

"Lawdy, Lawdy, Lawdy," said her mother-in-law as the sky finally delivered the rain it had promised since early in the day. "I knew this rain was a comin'. I felt the Lawd was trying to tell me something, and 'Oh Lawd', you sure did."

Please thought Sissy, not now. On the street, a bicyclist kept pace with the slow moving bus. The rider unaware of the burden carried by one of the bus's passengers.

When Sissy didn't react to the statement, her mother-in-law continued, "The Lawd is about to test us, Sissy. He surely is."

They passed a police officer casually walking his beat. Touching the brim of his cap, he bids an elderly woman a good-day.

Sissy thinks of Reilly. All her husband knows at this time is that Sissy has taken Hope to a clinic for testing. He knows the family is not happy with him. One of the few things Reilly has said to Sissy in the last week is that she has betrayed both him and their daughter. The words hurt. They are unfair. Letting the accusation stand, she said nothing.

Their relationship, which had always been so special, is now strained. What will happen next? Yes, the Lord is testing all of them.

Sissy sits on the front porch waiting for Reilly to return from work. She holds in her hand the envelope emblazoned with the name of the clinic in the upper corner. The envelope contains God's test. She tries to calm herself. She steadies her breathing and runs the words over in her head. She espies Reilly making his way down the street. She loves him but fears this encounter. Reilly she thinks, please stand by me. I need you. Hope needs you. Reilly is now at the base of the steps. Sissy tentatively looks at his face, his eyes. Reilly reaches for her hands. He pulls her towards him. She stands. She is on the first step while he remains still standing on the sidewalk. He folds his muscular arms around her. She draws from his strength. She can feel him crying. He has always been so strong, not only physically but emotionally. It scares her.

"Sissy," he whispers in her ear. "Please tell me everything is going to be okay."

All Sissy can do is hold him closer as she too begins to cry.

Hope is sleeping. She had asked to go to bed immediately following dinner saying she was tired. Reilly asked if she would like to take a quick trip to the park before turning in.

"Thanks daddy, but I'm *sooooo* sleepy," she said theatrically.

The simple statement, which made them laugh in spite of circumstances, said so much.

"C'mon," her grandmother said, "I'll read you a story. How does that sound?"

A short way into the story, Grandmother realized the child was asleep. Quietly closing the door, she goes to join the family. There are now four sitting around the small kitchen table.

Reilly, looking at the paperwork given to Sissy at the clinic, asks, "What does this mean?" pointing to a line reading, 'Bone Marrow Test Results' with the ancillary comment, 'extraordinarily high white blood cell count'.

"That was one of the tests they did on Hope. It was called a bone marrow test," she answered.

"But what does it mean? Is having a high white blood cell count good or bad?"

"Bad, that's why Hope is so achy all the time. Her bones hurt."

The family digested this bit of information while Reilly continued to pour over the paperwork.

"What about, 'Blood Count shows low hemoglobin and a low platelet count'. Is that good or bad?"

"Bad."

Reilly struggled with the pronunciation of the next category. "Petechiae? What is that?"

"Those are red or purple spots on the body," replied Sissy.

When Reilly replied that this didn't sound good, Sissy simply nodded.

"Lymphadenopathy?" asked Reilly, phonetically sounding out the long word to the best of his ability.

"The doctor felt her neck and under her arms, and it was swollen. Anne Reston told me he was feeling the lymph nodes."

"Bad?" asked Reilly.

"Yes, bad," Sissy agreed sadly.

Grandfather, saying nothing, stoically took it all in. Grandmother would occasionally throw in, 'Lawd have mercy,' or some other petition to the Good Lord.

Finally, Reilly made his way to the end of the report. "DIAGNOSIS: Acute Lymphocytic Leukemia", he read the line aloud, and then placed the papers on the table in front of him.

There was no need to ask the dreaded question. One look at Sissy told him everything he needed to know.

It was bad, real bad.

Overwhelmed and feeling helpless, the family prepared for bed. Sissy went to lie with Reilly. She held him. She let him cry. Finally, his breathing settled into a steady rhythm as a restless sleep fell over him. She was grateful as he had to work the next morning. Sissy lay in bed with no expectation of sleep. Surrendering any hope of sleep, she decided to get up. The house was deathly quiet, so she was surprised when she found Grandfather still sitting at the kitchen table. She took a seat across from him. Initially, they said nothing, but in time, the patriarch spoke of the sorrow he felt. His shoulders slumped as he spoke of the heaviness in his heart. Sissy could see the pain in his face and in his posture and in his soul.

The family had to endure so much this evening, but Sissy carried an additional burden that she hadn't had the strength or the will to bring up earlier.

"Papa, may I show you something?" she asked.

In seconds, she was back at the table. When she was sure they wouldn't be interrupted, she slid a single piece of paper across the table.

It was a bill. The name of the clinic was displayed across the top. At the bottom were the words, 'Amount Due' with a large number written next to it. The large amount was concerning. The old man studied the paper. Sliding it back across the table, he said, "I wouldn't worry about that. Reilly has insurance." He tried unsuccessfully to look hopeful as he said this.

In 1798, Congress established the U.S. Marine Hospital services for seaman. This was the earliest coverage for health services in the United States. The population of the United States in 1940 was 132 million with less than 10% (approximately 12 million) covered in some part by health insurance. The needle hadn't moved a great deal over a 142 year time span. Even those fortunate enough to have coverage often found the insurance lacking in time of need.

"That's what I told them at the clinic. I told them Reilly had insurance through work," said Sissy, "They said that would help, but it wouldn't be enough. They said we got to be prepared for more bills. Bigger bills than just what they gave me today. There's going to be bills for medicine too and treatments that wouldn't be covered all the way. Papa, they said this was going to cost the family money, a lot of money."

"And you haven't told Reilly this?"

"No," and with that said, Sissy took the paper and spirited it back to where she had hidden it.

# Chapter Thirty-Three

"Dominic, what are you doing here?" asked Augie as his nephew approached the bar. "It's good you come to see your uncle once in a while."

Dominic Augustino took a seat at the nearly empty bar. He refused the beer his uncle offered.

His nephew looked troubled.

"What's the matter? A young guy like you shouldn't have a care in the world."

"We need to talk, Uncle Augie."

At that moment, Mary approached, "Who's your friend, Augie?"

Augie, following the introductions, informed Mary, "Dominic's a cop."

With the memories of Donofrio still fresh in her mind, Mary told the police officer it was nice meeting him and then disappeared.

"I got a visit from your friend Johnnie Octaviano," said Dominic.

"That's great," Augie said enthusiastically, "I always wanted you two to meet."

"Uncle Augie, your friend's putting the squeeze on me. The story's complicated, but he's trying to arrange a boxing match. One of the boxers is a friend of mine, but he doesn't want to fight. He wants my help in convincing this friend to agree to the fight."

"The guy doesn't want to fight, then the guy doesn't want to fight," said Augie pragmatically.

"If I can't convince him to fight, he could make things bad for you."

"That's crazy talk," Augie laughed.

"It's not crazy. Your name is all over this place. When the heat comes down, you're the one who's going to burn."

"Johnnie would never let anything like that happen."

"Uncle Augie, I could care less about this fight, but I do care about you. That's why I'm here."

"It ain't such a good idea for a cop to be in a place like this," said Augie. "You should go now," and having said that, he ambled down to the far end of the bar and began slicing lemons.

# Chapter Thirty-Four

Michael Angelo Donofrio survived, in large part, because he understood how to calculate the odds. He thought out the consequences of his actions. It came naturally. He completely missed the 'big picture' of what the universe would be like without his father in it. He didn't grasp the interdependency between his mother and father. It was not a harmonious yin and yang they shared, but their bond, which pushed and then pulled, was still codependent. No matter how screwed up their relationship was, they preoccupied each other. They fulfilled one another. The result was that they didn't often bother their son. It was only after his father was out of the picture that he fully understood the roles of these two dysfunctional people in his world.

His father's passing had left a void in his mother's life.

She looked to her son to fill that void.

He didn't want the job.

Oftentimes at the end of his shift, there would now be a note at the dispatch desk, *'Donofrio...call your mother'*. At first, his fellow officers were sympathetic to both mother and son because of their loss. After a while, her neediness began to wear on them as well. Donofrio was both embarrassed and angry on the day the anonymous note read, *'Michael Angelo, your mommy wants you'*.

He would call, feeling marginally responsible for what had happened, but he couldn't give her what she wanted.

"Please come for dinner," she would beg. "Bring some of your friends from the station." As everyone had been so nice at the funeral and had said such wonderful things about her son, she was under the mistaken impression that her son had many friends at work. It appeared that he was in reality very popular amongst his fellow policemen.

Donofrio was lonely. He didn't realize how much his time spent with Stanley Wojick meant to him. He had gone through life without having a friend, so he had never come to appreciate the value of friendship. Now he was once again alone. He told himself that he didn't care but knew it wasn't true. He tried to convince himself that he didn't need anyone but knew that was also a lie. He hated himself for this need. Like his mother, Donofrio had suffered a loss that left a void in his life. His mother looked to her son to fill the emptiness. Donofrio filled the emptiness with anger or, at other times, self-pity. He filled it with hatred and with alcohol.

He still went out at night. He might gamble or visit a 'blind-pig', but by himself, the experience was greatly diminished. One night he tried the 'trolling' game, stopping an elderly man on a deserted street. He asked the man a few questions and, after handing him his identification, advised the man to be careful and go straight home. Without Wojick as part of the ruse it just wasn't the same.

On another night, loneliness and alcohol drove Donofrio to call his former friend.

"Stan, it's me, Doni," He started tentatively.

The agent's response was quick, "Are you out of your mind? Don't ever fucking call me again. I don't know you, you got that?"

The rebuff had hurt more than he would have ever thought.

It was close to midnight when Donofrio found a prostitute walking the streets. He showed her his badge. She was new to the trade, and the thought of being arrested and going to jail terrified the girl. Her fear excited the cop. He made a deal with her; come to my apartment and we drop the charges. She agreed. Behind closed doors the predictable failings began once again, and again predictably, he blamed the girl. He didn't understand why but knew it was the pain inflicted and the abuse delivered that excited him. Pushing the naked girl down on the bed, Donofrio wraps his hands around her throat. She gags. Her eyes bulge. In the dim room, Donofrio catches a glimpse of himself in the bureau mirror. In the reflection he sees his father. The maniacal look on the face in the glass scares him. If he is his father, then who is this creature he is choking the life out of? He doesn't want to look at the girl lest she wear the face of his mother. He turns his gaze slowly back towards the whore. He prays he does not see his mother looking back at him. It is the hooker. She is close to passing out, perhaps close to death. He jerks his hands away and scrambles from her. Rolling off the top of her, he crumples onto the floor. He hears her take in a long, life-giving breath. Half-standing on unsteady legs, he lurches towards the bathroom. The prostitute jumps at the sound of the slammed door. She can hear the retching sounds of the cop vomiting violently. Fearing what might come next, she grabs her clothes and handbag and, not stopping to dress, flees naked into the night.

Having no friends or interests, Donofrio found himself with a lot of time on his hands. Alcohol and time to think can be a bad combination. How did this happen? How did he fall so far, so fast? One night, being in a reflective mood, he thought long and deep over the death of his father. He analyzed the events that had led to that one defining moment in a dark and filthy alley. A pivotal, life changing, moment. He had not only lost his father that night; he had lost his best friend.

Why? He asked the empty efficiency apartment.

The answer came to him in a moment of clarity.

# Chapter Thirty-Five

Some knew Hope as Reilly would bring her in to work if he needed to go to the station on a day off. Typically, this was on a pay-day when he was not scheduled to work. Hope was always a big hit. She was never shy amongst the officers. She would walk around and talk to the men. Some of the cops kept hard candy at their desk and would offer her a piece. No matter what type of candy Hope received, she would emphatically assure the giver that it was her favorite candy in the whole world. On one visit, an officer gave her a butterscotch, and Hope thanked him and told him how butterscotch was her very favorite. Hearing this, the cop at the next desk offered her a peppermint.

"Peppermints are my very favorite candy ever," she assured the policeman.

When he teased her, asking how butterscotch and peppermint could both be her favorite, Hope without skipping a beat, replied, "It's candy! They're all my favorites."

Many of the men and women at the station knew Hope and were glad to see her. Her occasional visits made for a welcome interlude.

Reilly felt their genuine disappointment on the day he stopped in for his pay without Hope.

When Reilly explained that his little companion wasn't feeling well that day and had opted to stay home, they offered their well-wishes. No one thought much about it as little kids were always coming down with something. If they would have thought to look, they might have noticed the pained look on Reilly's face.

As the saying goes, word gets around, and this was true at the police station. At first, it was whisperings and innuendos. *'I heard Reilly's daughter is sick'*, was the gist of what they knew as the rumor spread through the station house. Even though they knew none of the details they were concerned. Word spread from cop to cop, department to department. They gave Reilly his space. They didn't need to be cops or a detective to figure out Reilly was not his usual self. Reilly, the coworker who was always quick with a smile and warm greeting, now seemed withdrawn and sullen.

Word that Reilly was going through a bad patch had reached the desk of Ben Rush. He knew nothing more than his men but, at the same time, had more resources at his disposal to find out precisely what was happening. Several well-placed phone calls later, he had a good idea of what Thorn's issues were.

Rush too had met Hope on one of her visits. She had walked into the captain's office and asked, "Hi, I'm Hope. Do you know my daddy? His name's Reilly Thorn." Without asking, Hope climbed into a chair across the desk from Rush. She looked so tiny in the oversized chair. She had trouble seeing Ben over the stacks of reports on his desk, prompting her to comment, "Wow, What is all this stuff? You sure do have a lot of paper."

"I sure do," Rush agreed.

"I can help you throw it out," Hope offered.

Rush was enchanted by the precocious little girl.

A short time later, Reilly found her and whisked her out of his commander's office, apologizing profusely for the interruption. Ben Rush assured him that it had been a pleasure. Hope surprised him by giving him a hug before leaving with her father.

Now, the thought that this sweet child had leukemia weighed heavily on Rush's heart. Rush liked Thorn and thought of him as a valued member of his team. He remembered being keenly aware of Reilly's color when he first arrived. He wasn't sure when it happened, but at some point, he quit thinking of Reilly as his 'black' officer. Thorn was defined by many characteristics, but his color was no longer one of those traits. He sensed that many others, but not all, never all, in the department felt the same way. In the beginning, there was grumbling from many of the officers if they were assigned to work with *'the black guy'*. Over time, that reaction had all but disappeared. Most of the men, like Ben Rush, had stopped paying all that much attention to the color of Reilly's skin. Of course, this was not true of all the officers as there were still those whose bias and bigotry was so deeply seeded, they would never be able to see Reilly as anything but a Negro. As Reilly had achieved a high degree of acceptance amongst many of his coworkers, those who felt differently prudently kept their prejudice to themselves.

Rush thought of some of the men he had seen promoted during the time Reilly Thorn had reported to him. Chicago, in the early 1930s, had more African-American police officers on duty than other big cities. Promoting these officers was another matter. It would be 1940 before a black Chicago police officer would reach the rank of Captain. Prior to that, black officers who made the rank of Sergeant would never be assigned to supervise white officers. In Rush's opinion, if Reilly had been white, he would be an easy consideration for promotion. Rush, open-minded and somewhat liberal considering the time-period, gave little thought to the inequality of this situation.

It was just the way of the world.

Word of Thorn's little girl concerned Rush as a person, but there was something else that reached his desk that disturbed him as a commander. Reilly was letting this affect his work. He faithfully showed up for his shift, but even though he was there, he was not completely there. A police officer out on the streets needs to be one-hundred percent engaged and aware at all times. Anything less could get you or your partner killed.

"What's this for?" asked Donofrio suspiciously.

"It's for Thorn's little girl. She's sick," Dominic Augustino explained. The fraternity of police officers had decided to 'pass the hat' and take up a collection for Hope.

Donofrio's first inclination was to tell this prick to go pound salt but realized pretty quickly that this response would make him even less popular with his coworkers. "So, what's the going rate?" he asked.

"Most of the guys are ponying up five-bucks. Rush threw in twenty. We don't turn down any donation."

Donofrio surprised Augustino by taking a ten out of his wallet and handing it over, with the comment, "Here you go. Reilly's a good guy."

The truth was he hated Thorn. He pretty much hated all his coworkers, but this was especially true of Thorn. Thorn had friends at the precinct, a hell of a lot more friends than he did. The thought of this black bastard being more popular than a white officer gnawed at Donofrio.

Donofrio figured ten-bucks entitled him to a little more information. "So, Reilly's really hurting for cash, huh?"

"Not sure exactly how bad it is, but you know what a cop takes home. There ain't much left over at the end of the week, especially for doctors and medicine."

The thought of Reilly having financial troubles gladdened Donofrio. Perversely, he saw it as a sign that there might actually be some modicum of justice in this unfair universe.

# Chapter Thirty-Six

Hope was born too soon. In the early years of the 1930s, leukemia was prevalent enough to be readily recognizable by the medical community. The doctors knew what Hope's condition was. Curing it was a whole different conversation. These were the years before chemotherapy; radiation treatment was in its infancy. The prognosis for anyone suffering from Acute Lymphocytic Leukemia was not encouraging during this period of medical history. In Switzerland, at this same time in a clinic in Zurich, a Doctor by the name of Gloor was presented with a leukemia patient. He was an American businessman by the name of Eugene Metzger. The combination of his blood counts, his anemia, and his fever were all typical of Acute Lymphocytic Leukemia. Gloor treated Metzger with a combination of radiation, arsenic, and thorium-X. (RAT). Following the treatments, Metzger went into remission. He returned to New York and continued to operate his successful lace business. The following year Metzger returned to Switzerland, still in remission. Dr. Gloor was so encouraged by the results that he published his findings. Instead of acclaim, Gloor was met with ridicule. He lost his job at the Zurich clinic and spent the rest of his life toiling in medical obscurity. Acute Lymphocytic Leukemia was fatal one-hundred percent of the time. Everyone knew that. If Gloor thought he had found a cure, he was a fool. Eugene Metzger might have argued that last point, and as it turned out, he would have plenty of time to formulate the argument. He lived to the age of 102, or about fifty-years after being treated by Gloor. He was a philanthropist, and he was wealthy. Mount Sinai Medical School has an administration building named after Metzger and his wife Rose. There is a possibility that Eugene Metzger was not cured but was actually in a state of prolonged remission. He might not have cared what the reality was. Arsenic, at various times over the decades, has either been embraced or discredited as a treatment option for leukemia. Many years later, it was found to be an effective treatment for promyelocytic leukemia.

None of this impacted Hope as the treatment option was unknown and unavailable. She had been born too soon.

# Chapter Thirty-Seven

Augie was good at reading people. That might have been true of bartenders in general, but it did not need to be true of necessity when Augustino saw Donofrio walk into the bar. He approached the bar without his normal swagger. His eyes were downcast.

"Is Johnnie around?" he asked.

"Sorry, he ain't been in yet." As usual, several of the girls working the club that afternoon disappeared into the backrooms when they saw Donofrio enter.

"Did he leave anything for me?" he asked, referring to the envelope that Donofrio was in the habit of picking up once a week.

Augustino, who knew that there would be no more envelopes waiting for Officer Donofrio, made a show of looking behind the bar for something he knew damn well wasn't there.

"Sorry, I don't see it."

Donofrio left saying he'd try back later.

The envelope in question had been picked up the day before by two men. One of the men sat at the bar and had a beer while the other went into the office with Octaviano.

The big man at the bar asked if Mary was available.

She was.

"Please tell her I'd like to talk to her," he asked, sounding apologetic in the way he asked.

Mary, peeking through the curtain at Stan Wojick, told Augie to deliver the message that she wanted nothing to do with him. Augie, given the size of the man, was hesitant to deliver that message. When he did approach Wojick, the big agent asked Augustino if he would tell Mary that he was sorry for what he did and the pain he had caused her.

"Tell her I don't blame her for being mad at me. What I did was bad, real bad," he told Augie.

Augie dutifully delivered the message, and Mary, being the soft-hearted creature that she was, found herself seated at a table in the far corner of the room with the hulking figure. Augie kept an eye on the two, his trusty wrench at the ready. He wouldn't need it as Mary, who started out looking angry, began smiling at one point and even laughed at some of what was being said. Later that evening, the big man returned to the bar with a box of candy under one arm and a bouquet of flowers in the other. The two disappeared through the curtain and were seen no more that night.

When Wojick and Wroblonski left the bar that afternoon, Johnnie delivered a clear message to Augie and others working the bar. Donofrio was 'out'. The two agents would make sure that this same communication was delivered loud and clear to the rogue cop.

Donofrio found his way to the small office occupied by Wojick and Wroblonski. He had the look of a schoolboy who had been sent to the principal's office as he meekly knocked and then entered the small space. Like during his first visit, Wroblonski sat behind the desk absorbed in the file he was reading. Wojick stood at the window. He gave no acknowledgement that anyone had entered the room. Donofrio, who hadn't been offered a seat, remained standing. Finally, Wroblonski shuffled the pages into a neat stack and placed them in a manila folder on his desk.

There were no pleasantries exchanged between the three as the time for that had passed.

A half hour later, Donofrio left the office a much changed man. It was no longer a three-person team. He had been cut from the squad, benched, put on waivers. He was the odd-man out; persona non grata.

Wroblonski was crystal clear in his instructions. Donofrio was not to offer any special services to any establishment where the federal agents were offering protection. No more kickbacks would be coming Donofrio's way. Those days were over. At various times during the meeting, Wroblonski took on the guise of a clean-cop chastising a crooked cop. At other times, he sounded like he might actually be a mob boss taking one of his henchmen to task for indiscretions. At those times, there were less than veiled innuendos about what might be in store for Donofrio if he was to step outside the lines. Finally, he spoke to Donofrio as a benevolent uncle might speak to a wayward nephew. He encouraged him to change his ways, to think before acting.

Wroblonski ended the session with, "You have to be smart if you want to walk on both sides of the street and not get busted or worst. You put us in a bad way with some of our clients. You don't want to ever be in a bad way with these guys. They know it ain't good business to 'off' a badge, but believe me, you fuck with these guys and you're going to end up wearing concrete boots at the bottom of Lake Michigan. Cop or no cop."

Wroblonski assumed that this was the end of his relationship with Donofrio.

Wojick had gone through the meeting without saying a word to his former friend. Wroblonski knew some of the mayhem these two had gotten into during their time together, but he never knew why Wojick had severed the relationship. One day, Stan made his way back to his longtime partner. He apologized, saying that he was done with the cop and realized he was putting everyone in jeopardy by his actions. Wroblonski figured that something big must have happened between the two for Wojick to terminate their partnership with such finality. Whatever happened had a profound effect on his partner as Wojick had been a real choirboy since coming back into the fold. Wojick never told his partner about the 'trolling' game, which had led to a dark alley behind a closed florist's shop. He never spoke of the sound of gunshots shattering the silence of a quiet night. He fiercely guarded the most disturbing secret; the man lying in an expanding pool of blood that night was in fact Donofrio's father.

# Chapter Thirty-Eight

Two men knew of a way to help Reilly pay his growing medical bills. Dominic Augustino pictured Reilly climbing through the ropes as a way to help his Uncle Augie. The second man's motivations were also altruistic.

Andre Montero, had never been so conflicted in his life. Reilly Thorn, his best friend for so many years, had serious problems. Andre, like others, knew of a possible solution to those problems. The solution, Reilly climbing into the ring, was one that Montero hated to the very center of his still powerful core. Andre thought long and hard about alternatives. He came up empty. He knew the precinct had taken up a collection as did the fellow fighters at the gym. People's willingness to help was admirable. Their ability to help was limited as the depression lingered on well into the nineteen-thirties. Most folks were hurting, and those who weren't, didn't have the resources to help all of those who were. The Thorn's predicament, when boiled down to the basest common elements, wasn't much different from thousands of others who were in as bad a shape as Reilly and his family.

Andre, with the hopes of finding something noble at the makeshift boxing arena, attended another match. Like at other times, he stood in the back of the arena and watched. He saw the mismatches in the ring. Men, with little to no boxing skills, had agreed to fight out of pure desperation. Often homeless or with a family to feed, they knew of no other way to provide for their loved ones. These men were either crazy or courageous to enter the squared circle. They knew they would take a beating. They knew they didn't have a chance against bigger and sometimes better trained boxers. If there was any honor in this viper pit, it was to be found in these hopeless men. Men who had made a decision to sacrifice themselves to keep a roof over their family's head or to put food in the bellies of their hungry children. There were times when they gave more than expected. There were times when they sacrificed everything as they were dragged out of the arena. The night, which started with them fighting, ended with them fighting for their lives.

What Andre found even more despicable than what he saw in the ring, was what he saw in the faces of the men who had made their way to the venue that night. Men who had barely scraped together the few coins necessary to attend. Men seeking a surrogate outlet for the pain and frustration in their own lives. The bloodlust painted on their faces told Andre what they expected in return for the price of their admission. These men were not there to watch a boxing match. They were there for blood. They would scream their fury if they received any less than complete and utter carnage. If a boxer hit the canvas, the expectation was for the prone fighter to be set upon and beaten senseless. They rarely left disappointed.

There was one new twist this evening. Whenever a match ended, the ring announcer would step to the center of the canvas. The crowd would quiet in anticipation of something important that was about to happen.

Pausing for dramatic effect, he would suddenly broadcast at full volume, "Who do you want?"

"BRUISER!" would come the response from the multitude.

"What does Bruiser want?" came the follow-up question.

"The Shine!" the crowd would roar.

"Who do you want?" the MC repeated.

"BRUISER!"

"What does Bruiser want?"

"The Shine!"

This chant repeated itself several times. It reminded Andre of tent revivals he would attend as a child. He remembered all too clearly the way a traveling evangelist could whip his congregation into a frenzy. If the men and women at those events had been filled with the spirit of the Lord, what vile entity occupied the hearts and minds of the men in the arena on this night?

The final bout on this night once again featured Bruiser. He was the star of the show. He pandered to the crowd. Strutting and flexing. Andre had to admit that he was an impressive physical specimen. Bruiser would stop his theatrics long enough to point a gloved hand at the crowd and scream, "Bring me the nigger!" The pack, who was already chanting 'Bruiser-Bruiser-Bruiser', responded with even greater passion.

Montero left before the last fight started. Bruiser's opponent that night didn't look to be much of an adversary. He was outweighed by no less than forty pounds. He had the physique of a manual laborer; perhaps a longshoreman who found his way to the venue on this night in the hopes of making a few bucks. Maybe a guy who handled himself pretty well in bar fights down at the docks. Some guy with a little bit of brawn and even fewer brains. Andre had a pretty good idea of how the night was going to end for this overmatched challenger and, knowing that, had no appetite to watch the final bout.

Andre hadn't gotten far when from behind he heard his name being called. Turning, he sees Johnnie Octaviano.

"Shouldn't you be in there watching the main event?" Andre asked. There was no mistaking the disdain in the tone of the question.

"Bruiser will do just fine without me," answered the gangster. "You want to know something, Montero? What Bruiser does makes me sick, too." Before Andre could reply, Octaviano continued. "I don't care if you believe me. I'd like nothing more than to get a quality fighter in the ring with that wretched excuse for a human being. Someone who could teach him about both boxing and humility."

When Andre said nothing, Octaviano finished with, "A guy like Thorn."

"I figured it wouldn't take you too long to bring this around to what you really want."

"It's not just what I want. You heard the crowd. They want the same thing."

"They want blood, pure and simple, and they don't much care if it's pouring out of a white guy or a black guy as long as it's red and there's plenty of it."

"This fight's going to happen. Don't you see? It has to. It's fated."

"What the hell are you talking about? Fated? We control our own destiny, and believe me, Thorn's destiny doesn't include climbing into that ring." The whole time this conversation was going on, all Andre could focus on was what the Thorns were going through.

The look on Octaviano's face was not easily read as he said to Andre, "Stop and think about this for a minute, Andre. The crowd in there thinks they love Bruiser, but they don't. They have placed the big Russian on a flimsy pedestal. Don't you see? That pack wants to see that arrogant bastard beaten. Right now, they don't know how much they hate Bruiser, but I see it. I see it every time Bruiser fights. Even tonight, there is a hope that somehow this new challenger will find a way to humble him. Don't you understand? Bruiser's opponent tonight is just like them. Just some guy who's trying to rise above all the pain and misery in his life. Like them, the odds are stacked against this guy. The difference is he's been given a chance. It's not much of a chance, but dammit, it's still a chance."

"Do you know who Bruiser's opponent is tonight?" When Octaviano didn't receive an answer, he continued. "His name is Mickey Coyle. He works in the yards and has gotten strong handling slabs of beef. Trust me, nobody fucks with Mickey Coyle on his home turf, but here tonight, he just a nothing from nowhere. Mickey has a job, at least part of the time, which makes him one of the lucky ones, but he likes to gamble, which makes him one of the stupid ones. He's not a good gambler. He likes the long shots and things just haven't worked out for him. He owes some bad people a fair amount of money. So he comes to me. He's a guy with a problem, and I'm the guy who might be able to help. I need guys who are willing to go toe-to-toe with Petrova, so I tell Mickey if he's willing to fight, I might be able to help him out. He likes the idea, and do you know why? He's a long shot, and Mickey likes the long shot. Mickey had every intention of beating Bruiser tonight. He fantasized about hearing the final bell with him being the one who's still standing. All he can picture is having his arm raised in victory at the end of the bout. I did that, Andre. I gave him that hope. I took a guy in trouble and I gave him a chance. That's not easy to do in this day and age. What he does with this gift, this opportunity that I gave to him, is up to him."

"Do you think Mickey Coyle has a chance tonight?" Octaviano asked. When Andre shook his head no, Octaviano said he agreed. "But you know what? I got no control over that. All I can do is give a guy a chance. The rest is up to him."

"Trust me Andre, the night Thorn climbs into the ring the crowd will hate him. They will want to see him smashed. They will chant Bruiser's name and scream and beg for him to destroy this black interloper. Do you know why? Because they think they love Bruiser. They are convinced that Bruiser is their champion, their hero. They'll get their first inkling that ain't the case when Thorn delivers his first combination. Oh, they'll still cheer for the Russian but maybe not all of them or maybe not as loud. Some will start to believe that Reilly has a chance the first time he delivers a solid punch. Some will 'ooh and aah' when Reilly uses that fancy footwork of his to keep the Russian out of striking range. When Reilly lands that punch that staggers Petrova, they will not only believe but they'll start to understand just how much they hate that Russian bastard. They'll be on their feet. Every punch that finds its mark will be a strike against the abuse and grief they get handed every day."

Montero didn't understand why he just didn't walk away, but he didn't.

"The chant will start again," continued Octaviano, "but the difference is they'll be screaming Reilly's name. They have no allegiance to Petrova. They never did. They'll be convinced that they not only hate Bruiser now but have always hated him. They have prayed for this day of deliverance and it is now upon them. Their tormentor, the cause of so much that is wrong in their lives, is being beaten. That feeling will cleanse them. It will liberate them."

For the second time this night, Andre thought back to the revival tents of his childhood.

"Reilly, by my way of thinking, was a hero the night he climbed into the ring to help Leo. Now, he has a chance to be a hero again."

The two men stood in a silence that did not last long.

"Hero?" asked Montero incredulously. "What in God's name is heroic about what you just described? What you created is the opposite of all that is good and noble about my sport. I've dedicated my life to the science of boxing. You think those animals are demanding the 'nigger' because they're hoping to see a spirited boxing match. They're disappointed to see anything less than death, and they look to you to be the merchant of death. You told me once that your job is to get people what they want, and you don't give a damn what it is. If they want booze or broads, you're their guy. If they want blood and horror and death, you're still their guy. You know what your problem is, Octaviano? Your problem is that you don't live in the real world. You don't understand that most people aren't like the animals that you surround yourself with. You're not making a hero when Reilly climbs into the ring." Andre can feel the passion building in him. "You're making a buck! At the end of the day isn't that all that you really give a damn about? You think you're some kind of humanitarian for giving Mickey Coyle his big chance tonight. The truth is if Coyle's lying dead at the end of the night it wouldn't mean a thing to you. And why should it. You said he owed you a gambling debt. If he pays the debt with his life, so be it as long as the books are squared in the end."

Octaviano wasn't used to people talking to him like this. It troubled him to see the truth in what Montero accused him of. He asked quietly, "I know why that crowd is in there tonight. I understand what they want. What do you want, Montero?"

When Andre didn't reply, Octaviano continued, "You're right about a lot of what you said. I do know what people want, and I've made a good living for myself by getting it for them. The trouble is, I'm looking at you and trying to understand what you want, and I'm coming up empty. You tell me what you don't want. You tell me what you don't like. None of that helps me understand what you do want." Looking intently at Andre, almost like he was inspecting a strange new animal that had just been discovered, he repeated the simple question, "What do you want, Montero?"

Octaviano continued to study this odd creature in front of him; this new species that had suddenly become very quiet. Montero turned and began walking away. Johnnie watched as his figure disappeared around the next corner. The gangster lived by some very simple truths and one of them was that everybody wants something. He had never met an exception to the rule. Everyone had a need, and Octaviano was the guy who supplied whatever was demanded. *"What do you want, Montero?"* he mused as he too turned and walked back towards the makeshift arena. *"You came here looking for something. Why are you here?"*

# Chapter Thirty-Nine

Michael Angelo Donofrio did not realize how close he was drifting to the edge of sanity. He was angry. He knew that, but he was used to that sensation as all of his life he had been one pissed-off guy. This was different. If he would have stopped and taken inventory of the events of his life over the last year, he might have gained some insight into his mental condition. He knew something was different. He knew his world was changing and that some of those changes were very concerning. He couldn't get the image of his father out of his head. It started the night he was with the hooker when he saw his father staring back at him from the mirror. That was the last night he had been with a woman, but it wasn't the last night his father had appeared to him. There was a second visitation and then a third. After that, the sightings had become more frequent.

Behind Donofrio's anger and hostility, there lived a scared little boy. He was, under the harsh veneer, still a frightened child who would lie in darkness and shake and pray that his father would not turn his abusive attention towards him. Some nights the need to urinate overwhelmed him, but fear kept him a prisoner in his tiny room as he listened to his father rampage through the house. His mother hid the pee-stained mattress from her husband, and without comment, she gave her son a jelly jar. He loved her for these kindnesses.

As an adult, Donofrio had finally freed himself from his tyrannical old man or at least he thought he had. After the first sighting, he did well at convincing himself that it was just a combination of alcohol and dim lighting that had conspired to play a trick on him. The second event happened while out shopping. Stopping to look at the goods in a store window, he noticed in the reflection the image of a man standing very close to him. The man was peering over his right shoulder. Donofrio didn't like people invading his space. Turning, before he could say anything, the person was gone. He hadn't clearly seen the man's face but that wasn't necessary to know it was his father. Mirrors became Donofrio's enemy as his father was partial to looking back at him as he shaved or washed. Sometimes his face became that of his fathers. At other times, he would see his father standing behind him. He believed, or needed to believe, that these apparitions would simply stop at some point. He couldn't understand why they had started to begin with.

On the day his father stepped out of the mirror and into the real world, Donofrio started to realize that he might be slipping. It was a pleasant afternoon. He and a fellow officer, his partner for the day, were walking their beat. Many of the officers still liked being assigned to walking duty. Donofrio wasn't one of them. He didn't care for being out amongst the citizenry, preferring the insulation of a patrol car. Today however, it was such a lovely day that even Donofrio admitted to himself that this wasn't a bad way to while-away his shift. And then, for no apparent reason and without warning, there was his father.

Donofrio froze, prompting his partner to ask what was wrong. The intruder, some thirty-feet away, simply stood there. He maintained eye contact the entire time with his son.

"Donofrio, what are you looking at?" asked his partner.

That seemed to shake Donofrio out of his stupor. Turning his attention to his partner, he says, "I see him there. He thinks he's going to get to me but he ain't. I got rid of him once. I can get rid of him again."

"Get rid of who?"

Donofrio stopped himself before saying it was his father that he would get rid of for a second time. Christ he had to be careful. His old man had almost tricked him.

He continued to be visited by the image of his deceased father. The appearances were random and unpredictable. He might see his father several times on one day and then not for the next week. At night in the dark, these visits had the most profound effect. One night he watched his father walk past his bedroom door. He simply walked past, never even stopping to glance into the bedroom as he went past the door. On another night as he lay in bed dozing, he heard a commotion in the kitchen. At first, it sounded like some somnambulist might be making a late night snack. He lay in the dark listening to indistinct whisperings. He heard drawers open and then close. The next morning Donofrio looked for signs that his father had been there but nothing was out of place.

He told himself repeatedly that this was all in his head, and he did believe that to be true. He got into the habit of repeating a less than comforting mantra. *"You are not real, you are not real, you are not real,"* he would close his eyes and say either to himself or out loud depending on where he was at the moment. Sometimes that would work as upon opening his eyes the apparition was gone. Donofrio wasn't sure how he kept from screaming on the night he closed his eyes and repeated his mantra only to feel rancid breath being exhaled into his face. He cried as he tried to convince himself that this phantom was not real. At last, the fetid breathing stopped. In an act that took all his nerve, he finally opened his eyes to find an empty room.

Though not a religious man, he tried to find peace in the sanctuary of a local church. He wasn't sleeping except for a few hours a night. He looked haggard. He felt worse. Crawling into a back pew, he had barely closed his eyes when he heard someone arranging themselves in a seat several rows in front of him. Cautiously peeking, he could see the unmistakable form of his father kneeling in prayer. There was something safer about this visit. Perhaps because they were in a sacred place or maybe it was because his father had his back to him and was paying no attention to his exhausted son.

Donofrio, worn out and at his wit's end, began to cry softly. How did this happen? Why was it happening, he asked himself?

When no answers were proffered to his silent questions, he looked through bloodshot and teary eyes at his father, and asked, "What do you want?"

She was surprised to see him at the door.

"Michael Angelo, why didn't you tell me you were coming?" asked his mother. Seeing the look on his face, she asked, "What's wrong? Are you OK?" She wanted to say more, to ask more as she had never seen her son look worse. He was unshaven; his hair unkempt. She smelled the husky unpleasant odor of a man who had not recently bathed. The collar of his shirt was filthy. Her worry over all of these concerns vanished when she looked at her son's eyes. Mothers have the intrinsic ability to overlook or rationalize shortcomings and failures in their children. This is integral to the role, happening at a genomic level. Symbiotic bonds are forged; bonds so strong that a mother could no sooner abhor her own self. Helen Donofrio knew from an early age that her son was different, but she never dwelt on what was wrong with her son, choosing instead to focus on what was right with the boy. The most important characteristic of her son was that he loved his mama. That one quality negated every other worry she ever had about her son. He loved his mother, and that was all that mattered.

But now looking into her son's eyes, she can no longer afford the luxury of denial. He has the look of a haunted man. She doesn't understand, nor would she believe, how astute this observation is.

"Michael Angelo, come in, sit down. What's wrong? Tell me," she asks in a voice bordering on begging.

Her son does not move. Standing in the doorway, he stares at his mother.

"Please come in," she asks hesitantly even though the idea of being with him behind closed doors scares her. She has never feared her son until today.

Donofrio steps, perhaps more accurately shuffles, into the room. Without turning, never taking his eyes off the woman who spawned him, he swings the door shut behind him. It closes hard, startling his mother. She jumps at the sound.

Donofrio looks at his mother like he is seeing her for the first time. He has gained clarity. He knows now why things haven't gone well for him. His father explained it to him, and now, for the first time in his life, he understands. He feels foolish for not having figured it out for himself. The answer, so simple, was there all along.

Without warning, he backhands his mother. She thought she had suffered the last of her black eyes, but she is wrong. She staggers backwards dropping to one knee. When she looks at her son, she gasps. Looking back at her is the face of her departed husband. The image clears, and she is once again looking at the twisted and deranged face of her son.

"Please," she begs, "please don't. Michael Angelo, please stop."

"Shut up!" he screams at her. He stoops and lifts her off the floor. He holds her up by the collar of her dress. His face is barely inches away from her face. His breath is horrible. She desperately tries to look away. Those eyes, those eyes are too difficult to look at, too dangerous. Half pulling and half dragging her across the living room, he flings her onto the sofa. She lands hard, awkwardly.

"Please don't," she begs again.

This creature, once her loving son, looks at the heap on the couch. There is no indication that he recognizes her.

Fear keeps her from saying anything. She doesn't move, adopting a posture common to abused women as a passive defense mechanism. She doesn't look at him for fear that he will hit her again. She is careful not to move lest some minor movement on her part should further enrage her tormentor. Her heart is breaking. This is her son, her son who had always loved her so much.

Helen sneaks glances at her son but only when she was convinced it was safe to do so. Donofrio begins to pace. She senses the struggle within her only child. He appears to be speaking, but he utters no words. He speaks at last, but he is not addressing her.

"Everything was fine," he said, in what could be described as a sane and convincing way. "It was fine," he says again, but again, he is not speaking directly to her. He repeats the word *fine* several times. Each time he says the word, he gives it a slightly different inflection. He was speaking to an empty room, but his mother has the sense that the room was not unoccupied in her son's world.

She can feel that he is beginning to get agitated. His pace quickens.

Looking at an empty corner of the room, Michael Angelo offers an answer to a question that only he can hear, "I know. I know all that. I said, I know. Then what the hell do you want me to say?" he mumbles to his unseen inquisitor. He walks around the room. He continues his soliloquy, "I was doing good, real good. I had friends. I had a lot of friends. And the broads, Christ, there were a lot of broads." He smiles at whatever images he is recalling.

Turning abruptly to another empty space within the small room, he shouts, "Shut up! I'm a cop for God's sake. It should have never gotten this fucked up but it did."

His mother wants to go to him, to hold him like she held him as a small child and tell him everything will be OK. He needs help, and she feels the pain and frustration of not knowing how to help. Against her better judgment, she says in a voice barely above a whisper, "Let me help you. Michael Angelo, please, let your mama help you."

"It was you," he says softly, "It was always you. I couldn't see that. I don't know how I could have had that so balled up."

She has barely moved from the position she was first in when he threw her onto the settee. Terror grips her as her son approaches. She is half sitting, half lying as her son takes a dominant position over her. "Sit up straight," he says as he takes her shoulders and helps her into a sitting position. "There, is that better?" he asks.

She should feel better, but she does not. There is something even more frightening in this new persona from her son. Looking down at her, he says, "I'm still mad at you about Stan. Stan was my friend, ma. He was my best friend."

She doesn't know who Stan is, and she is afraid to ask. She has a vague recollection of meeting a 'Stan' at her husband's wake, but it is a memory too distant to trust.

"But you had to fuck that up for me the way you fucked up all the other stuff," he says. "I didn't want to do it. Oh no, I would have never done it if you hadn't asked me. You were always selfish like that, ma. You always thought about you. It was you, you, you all the time."

She was afraid he would become agitated again, but he did not.

"You had to have it that way, didn't you? Was he really that bad, ma? Was he? I didn't have to do it. I could have said 'no'. What the hell, nobody had a goddamn gun to my head." He actually laughed at that last comment. It was a strange laugh. It was the laugh of the only person in the room to get the joke. "You don't think that's funny?" he asked. "I should have told you 'no', but you kept pushing me. You knew right from the start that one person couldn't do it. So who else was I going to get to help me? You knew goddamn well that I'd ask Stan. Who else can you ask to help with something like this? Stan was a good friend so right away he says, 'Sure, Doni,' that's what he called me, 'Doni'. He's the only guy that called me that, but it was OK because we were pals. That's what friends do for one another, ma. They help each other out. So I ask Stan, and he says, 'Sure, Doni, I'll help you. Whatever you need', he tells me."

"Stan asks me if I'm sure I want to do this, and I tell him I'm *not* sure, but I tell him that's what my ma wants. He tells me that I'm a good son. He was always saying stuff like that to me."

Donofrio turns and looks at his mother. Her eye is starting to discolor where he slapped her. "Geez ma, it looks like the old man smacked you around pretty good. I keep telling you to keep your yap shut. I don't even want to know what you did this time to piss him off."

Her son seems to struggle with something that doesn't make sense. He lets the thought and the curious statement be as he continues.

"Stan and me, we got to think about this because it is a big deal. We never done nothing like this before, so we have to start, you know, planning. All along I'm telling Stan that I don't think it's such a good idea, but the deeper we get into this the more Stan seems to like the idea. He tells me, '*Leopold and Loeb couldn't pull it off, but we can*'."

His mother understands the reference. Leopold and Loeb were two college students who thought they could commit the perfect crime. They were supposedly geniuses. They kidnapped a 14 year old kid. The duo then murdered the little boy. They didn't even know him. They just wanted to see if they could get away with it. The murder had happened in Chicago. Their perverse mission failed, and the two were apprehended.

Her son pauses. Even though she fears where this story is headed, she is comforted by the fact that her son has calmed in the last few moments.

Without warning, he looks again to an empty part of the room, and says, "I'm getting to it."

"Sorry ma, where were we? Oh yeah, the next thing I know, Stan and me are waiting on a dark street. I can't believe this is really happening. I tell Stan let's just go home and forget the whole thing, but he won't hear of it. So we wait and then, just like we planned, here comes pop."

His mother lets out a quiet cry, "No, please stop, please don't say anything else."

But he doesn't stop. He continues talking even though he is once again addressing spirits in the room that only he can see. "We walk into the alley. Nothing seems real. It's more like a goddamn dream. I beg Stan to stop, to just call the whole thing off. We can just walk away I tell him. But he won't listen. He puts dad up against the wall. He puts the barrel of the gun between his eyes, and just like that it's over."

His mother is sobbing as she quietly repeats 'no' over and over again.

"I feel sick. I'm shouting at Stan, 'What did you do?' I drop to my knees, and I can't help it, but I start throwing up. Stan looks at me and says, 'What's wrong Doni? This is what your mother wanted. You're a good son, Doni. You're a good boy."

"No," his mother moans, "no."

Michael Angelo sits quietly as his mother weeps. He has finished talking. Now that his story has been told, he seems at peace. Several long minutes pass. Michael Angelo Donofrio rises, says nothing, and without so much as a backwards glance walks out of the small apartment.

Helen Donofrio tries desperately to process what she has just been told. She is afraid; afraid to be in this room for fear the spirits her son spoke to might be present still. Does she believe her son? Yes. She questions some of the details, but she believes the crux of the story. She will try to sleep but will toss and turn throughout the night. In the morning, over a much needed and blessed cup of coffee, she will come to a decision on what to do. Making her way to the phone, she dials a number she is well acquainted with. "May I speak to Captain Benjamin Rush, please?"

# Chapter Forty

Universal Consciousness, postulated in ancient Greek philosophy, was first hypothesized in early Buddhist schools of thought. Although not quite legions, there were many who had an interest in seeing Reilly climb into the ring. Motivations ranged from the egocentric to the altruistic. Johnnie Octaviano saw the money to be made in promoting the fight, but that wasn't the only reason he wanted to see the event take place. Dominic Augustino hoped to leverage Reilly's participation into a way to get his Uncle Augie out of trouble. Even Andre Montero, the man most against having any part of this world, had motives beyond helping his longtime friend get out from under his mounting medical bills. Simple minded Bruiser was, predictably, spurred by a simple need. Beyond these few, there were the thousands whose thirst for blood required no other incentives.

"How bad is it?" asked Andre.

The two friends sat in a small café following a workout. Andre knew it was hard for Reilly to talk about the things happening in his life. Montero normally understood and accepted these boundaries, but today he couldn't help but ask as Reilly, who was like a brother to him, was so obviously hurting.

Reilly chose not to respond to the question, opting instead to stare into the inky blackness of his coffee cup. He stirred and stirred the mixture, seemingly mesmerized by the swirling liquid.

It had not been one of their better training sessions. Most concerning was the lack of focus and concentration that his partner displayed. The two were still evenly matched fighters but hadn't sparred today. Montero knew if they had, he would have easily bested his friend. Andre invited Reilly out for a bite to eat with the intention of getting a better understanding of the Thorn's predicament. He knew not to ask about Hope as Reilly would simply answer that his daughter was doing fine when anyone asked. Montero suspected that was not the case but would never press his friend on that subject.

Andre elected to qualify his question. "When I asked how bad it was, I wasn't asking about the coffee."

Reilly said nothing, so he tried a different tack, "Listen pal, I told you I'd treat, so you better start eating that damn sandwich."

Reilly looked up and managed a weak smile at the comment, "It's not good, and I ain't talking about the sandwich."

Montero made no reply.

"I'm not sure what's going to happen. The money's pouring out a lot faster than it's coming in. The cops at the precinct helped; so did the guys at the gym, but that money has come and gone." Reilly hesitated before saying, "You know the church has been dropping off groceries." Reilly hung his head like a man who had just confessed to a terrible crime. "Groceries, what kind of man can't even put food on his family's table?"

Andre felt the emotions coursing through his friend; a myriad of pain and anger and frustration all competing within this good and decent man.

Montero was loath to speak what was on his mind. He knew what he was about to suggest would shock Reilly. After weighing and measuring all possible options, Montero's sole consolation was that at least Reilly had an option. He thought back to his last conversation with Johnnie Octaviano outside the makeshift arena. It was the night the meat-packer Mickey Coyle stepped into the ring with Bruiser. He couldn't remember the exact words Octaviano had used, but he remembered the gist of it. He took a guy with no options and offered him a chance. Montero realized he didn't know how the fight between Coyle and Petrova ended up. The results of this kind of boxing didn't show up in the next day's sports page. He believed he was better off not knowing. Andre, who found any comparison to Johnnie Octaviano distasteful, felt like Octaviano as he took a deep breath and said to his friend, "Reilly, I know of a way to help."

And with that simple declaration, the die was cast.

Once again Dominic Augustino finds himself walking down a dank alley on his way to a nondescript door. There is a curious little eye-level cutout with a sliding panel. The peephole opens and he is allowed entry. The memory of his lunch with his Uncle Augie rushes at him. The lunch when his uncle told him of how one night the tap on the door was answered with the blast of a double-barreled shotgun. Feeling a shudder course through him, he makes his way to the bar. He greets his uncle. Augie is thrilled to see his favorite nephew. The tension from their last meeting was quickly forgotten. That's the beauty of Augie Augustino. Dominic declines the proffered beer while the two make small talk. Dominic hates being in this place. It's illegal; it shouldn't even exist, and he's a cop. Dominic is not making a social call. Like Judas Iscariot, he has information to share. Fate has made him the messenger. The message he has is for Johnnie Octaviano only.

The meeting is short. Dominic tells Octaviano about the Thorns troubles, but before doing so, he asks for assurance from the mobster to protect his uncle. Dominic Augustino has done what he had come here to do.

His involvement in this mess is over. He makes a point of telling Octaviano this. It's up to Johnnie to convince Reilly to fight.

Octaviano sits alone in his small but well-appointed office and mulls over this enticing bit of news. He closes his eyes and visualizes the big night. He knows he's getting ahead of himself as there is much to do between now and then. He can see past all of that because the single most important piece of the puzzle is now in place. He leans back in his finely-stitched leather chair and allows himself the indulgence of a small smile.

# Chapter Forty-One

"You should rest now," said Reilly as he tucked little Hope into bed.

"OK, but will you read me a story?" she asked with a sheepish smile. "I promise I'll stay awake."

Reilly smiled in return. No matter who put Hope to bed, she would ask for a story. When she asked her father, he would tease her and say 'no', citing the fact that she always fell asleep before the story's end. This mock dialog would go back and forth with Hope pleading and vowing to stay awake. Reilly would tell her 'no', there would be no story tonight. As part of the ritual, Reilly would eventually yield and agree. Hope would be delighted. He would further tease his daughter, warning her she would be in BIG trouble if she fell asleep. Reilly would demand a hug and a kiss before beginning. Of course, within minutes Hope would be sound asleep. It was a silly game that neither ever tired of.

There was a time, not so long ago, when Hope's insistence and Reilly's protests would become so animated that Sissy would appear in the doorway. She would remind them that this was bed time and that Reilly might want to pretend he was the adult in this situation. Reilly would look appropriately chastised and Hope would laugh. "We were just playing, mama." Sissy, in truth, thought this custom between the two was adorable.

Hope loved stories about knights and princesses and heroes on white steeds who would save the damsel while capturing each other's hearts in the bargain. If a dragon should appear, Reilly invented a friendly beast that would help to rescue the fair maiden. Once rescued, the dragon would be committed for life to the protection of the princess. Villains had no place in these stories. If one showed up, Reilly knew to dispatch him peacefully and to show him the errors of his way, converting him to a life of goodness.

Once asleep, Reilly would remain seated on the undersized chair, next to the little bed, in the tiny room, where he would simply watch his dear little girl sleep. He would wonder at the dreams she might be having. Perhaps the dreams were extensions of the story she just heard. Reilly believed this was true, and thus believing, he made sure to keep his stories virtuous, lest something wicked should creep into Hope's dream world.

On this night, he stayed longer than usual. The small room offered him sanctuary; an asylum from the reality that lurked just outside the thin door. Eventually, Sissy joined him. She said nothing. She stood behind her husband, both watching their daughter sleep. She looked so peaceful. Sissy placed her hand on Reilly's shoulder. He gathered strength from this simple touch. He placed his hand over hers and gave a gentle squeeze. The two exchange no words. Silently, Reilly rises. He drops to one knee, giving Hope a gentle kiss on the forehead. Now standing, he turns towards Sissy as she folds her arms around her husband. They take each other's hands and exit the room, softly closing the door behind them.

Grandma and Papa are at an age that on many nights they are in bed even earlier than Hope. This being one of those nights, Sissy and Reilly are the only two awake. They make their way to the kitchen. Sissy offers to make Reilly coffee but he declines. She pours them each a glass of juice. Reilly doesn't recognize the brand and asks about it. It was part of the groceries a church member dropped off. The juice, which Reilly initiatively thought was good, suddenly tastes bitter. He slides the glass towards the center of the table.

There is a growing stack of bills on the counter, and Reilly goes to retrieve them. Once again sitting across from Sissy, he begins to shuffle the papers. He makes no effort to add them up. He pages through each one reviewing the total. Some are old enough to have second and, in one case, a third notice attached to the original bill.

"I've been trying to ignore those things," Sissy says, in a weak attempt at levity.

"I fetched them for a reason," says Reilly. After a pause, he continues, "I might know of a way out from under all this."

He lets the statement hang in the air.

Sissy comments, "If it involves robbing a bank, they would probably frown on that down at the precinct."

"You know how I've been working out with Andre. Well, I've been training hard, and I'm ready to get back in ring." Reilly chooses his words carefully. Sissy grew up around the fight game and, with Uppercut for a grandfather, knew more about boxing than most. "There are fight clubs out there, and you can actually make a few bucks by fighting."

"Fight clubs?" she asks suspiciously. "So, we're not talking about sanctioned boxing, are we?"

Professional boxing, like just about everything else, was affected by the Great Depression. Purses were small, which prompted many to not fight.

In 1930, no one even held the heavyweight title. Following that, six-fighters would lay claim to the title over the next seven years. Many fans and fighters either boycotted pro boxing or simply ignored it. Later in the decade, boxing would win back many fans in large part because of the rivalry between Joe Lewis and Max Schmeling. Their bouts would become the stuff of legend.

"Well no, not sanctioned in the traditional sense, but a guy could do pretty well fighting in the clubs. I'd be a nobody in the professional ranks, and a nobody gets very few fights and makes even less money. A guy can make some real money in the clubs, especially if he wins, and I can win Sissy. I can fight. I've gone to these bouts, and these guys aren't boxers. They haven't had the training like I've had. Andre's been getting me ready for this."

"The Andre I know cut his teeth with Uppercut. This doesn't sound like something Andre would encourage anyone to do."

"He wouldn't. You're absolutely right. Normally, he wouldn't, but he knows we're in a bad way. That's the only reason I'd even consider something like this."

"And where exactly do these fights take place?" she asked with even more suspicion.

"Back of the Yards," he answers casually, "There's a warehouse district where they put this whole arena together."

"You're talking about underground boxing."

Reilly's hesitation tells her what she wants to know.

"Reilly, you can't possibly be serious. That's not boxing." Sissy thought back to her childhood, to the night that Uppercut tried to help the family out of a jam. It was shortly after her father left them and times got real hard for her mother. Uppercut, like Reilly, could fight. He made his way to one of these makeshift arenas and barely made it out of there alive. He was beaten so badly they thought he might not pull through. "Absolutely not! You can't do this. Reilly, I know you want to help, but we'll figure out a solution that doesn't include you being beaten half to death. The Lord will provide, Reilly. I believe this with all my heart."

"Maybe this is the Lord's way of providing. Maybe the Lord made me strong and fast because he knew I would need those skills now. Maybe if I don't do this, I'll be turning my back on God's gift. You need to think about that, Sissy!"

She did stop and think about what Reilly had just said. She didn't believe it was true, but she needed this pause before continuing. "Reilly, if I thought that you fighting would cure Hope, I'd beg you to do it. I'd beg you to climb into that ring and fight with everything you got. I'd be right next to you, and I would fight and claw and kick and bite if I thought it would fix Hope."

Sissy harbored thoughts so dark that she dared to never speak of them. She believed that if she kept these thoughts locked away and did not utter them; they would not come to pass. They were thoughts of despair and hopelessness. They were thoughts of surrender.

A fat tear rolled down her cheek as she voiced her ultimate fear aloud for the first time.

"Reilly, they can't cure Hope."

# Chapter Forty-Two

Ben Rush tried to keep his pulse in check as he climbed the stairs to the Donofrio's modest domicile. The note he received said little. He had thought about the Widow Donofrio often since the funeral. He didn't fully understand his attraction. Part of it was that she was vulnerable. She had suffered a tragic loss, and his heart did go out to her. There were several times when he had the phone in hand but had lost his nerve before dialing. What could he say when she answered that wouldn't sound foolish? He fought to keep her out of his thoughts, but in quiet moments, he would remember the softness of her eyes and the sheen of her olive complexion. There were other times he thought of her slender waist and full hips. If he was in high school, he would recognize these feelings as having a crush. Now, as a man on the wrong side of middle age, he wasn't sure what to call it.

"Cream or sugar?" Helen Donofrio asked as she poured Ben's coffee. The two sat at a small kitchen table. It was a pleasant room at this time of the day with sufficient sunshine streaming in from the single window.

"Black is fine," he answered as he took in the rest of the small apartment; an apartment not a great deal different from thousands of others just like it all over Chicago. Rush wasn't sure what he was hoping to find as he looked over the kitchen and living room. Perhaps it was the cop in him coming out; a cop looking for lingering evidence of the abuse that took place within these walls. That persona was never too far off. Any signs of the cruelty handed out by a brutal husband should be well-faded as it had been a while since the funeral. That wasn't the case. He discretely studied the bruise on the side of the widow's face. She had done the best she could to cover it with makeup. That wasn't done by her husband. He would have seen it at the wake. Rush assumed that the bruise was why she had summoned him here today. He tried to keep patient. The widow would explain the circumstances in her own time, and the captain would listen politely. Following that, he would find the bastard that did this and punish him. Any cop who had been around as long as Ben Rush was no stranger to spousal abuse. He never understood the exact dynamic, but cops were often guilty of this mistreatment. Rush had never married. He came to regret this over the past few years as he would often romanticize about a wife to share his upcoming retirement with. He told himself that he just hadn't met the right girl but knew this wasn't true. He just hadn't looked very hard. Earlier in his career, friends and family would go out of their way to act as matchmakers. In time, mostly because of the Ben's lack of enthusiasm, these would-be cupids lost interest as well. His career had taken precedence over family life. He had married the uniform.

Helen sat across from him. She stared into her coffee. Sunlight caused an aura to appear around her. She looked lovely. Without making eye-contact, she asked if he would like more coffee.

"Oh, what was I thinking? I have cookies that I was going to put out," she said as she started to rise.

Rush reach out and took her hand. He surprised himself with the boldness of this move. "Please Helen, sit," he said gently, "I'm fine."

She cautiously raised her head and briefly made eye contact. He had kind eyes; tired but kind. She too had thought about the captain since meeting him at her husband's service. At the visitation, he had been so very nice. He took the time to sit and speak with her. The words he chose were more than the typical platitudes that she had received from so many others in attendance. He seemed sincere. He carried himself as a man who had also lost something.

Apropos of nothing, she thought he was handsome. She didn't dwell on that as she could not imagine what a good-looking and successful man like Benjamin Rush would ever see in Helen Donofrio. Helen had spent the last twenty-five years being told that she was worthless. She was constantly reminded that she was ugly and stupid and insignificant. Over the years, she had accepted her uselessness as reality. She had been lucky, in truth blessed, to find any man that was willing to take her in and feed her and put a roof over her head. She came to believe that the abuse she suffered was a small price to pay in exchange for these blessings. Believing all these things, she pushed any thoughts about Ben Rush to the far recesses of her mind.

"Helen, would you like to talk?"

"I really don't know where to start," she answered timidly.

Rush, in what was a daring move for someone like the captain, lifted her chin. Helen still kept her eyes downcast. Gently, ever so gently, he caressed the damaged side of her face, asking, "Would you tell me how this happened?"

Old habits die hard as she replied defensively, "I didn't do anything. I swear to God I didn't do anything."

"I know you didn't, Helen. I'm just trying to understand what happened here." Later generations would come to study, diagnose, and analyze the psychology of abuse. These studies would identify patterns of behavior typical for both the punisher and the victim. Ben Rush, like most in the nineteen-thirties, had a shallow depth of understanding in matters related to dysfunctions within a family setting. He was in over his head. His patience and thoughtfulness made up for much of his ignorance. He let the moment marinate before asking again, "Helen, what happened here?"

"It was my husband."

Ben was unprepared for this reply. He knew it couldn't be true. He decided to be honest by asking her to be truthful to him.

"It was him," she began, "but it wasn't him."

Rush let the curious comment stand. He felt she was close to opening up, and he wanted to give her a clear path to say what she needed to say. Helen raised her head and took a long look at Ben. He knew that she was sizing him up. Could he be trusted? Would he be the source of even more pain in her already painful life? Rush knew he was being tested. He knew he had passed the test when Helen once again dropped her eyes and began to speak.

"It hasn't been an easy life for me," she began. She took Ben back to the beginning, to the time she first met her husband. "Those had been good times. We were young and in love, but it didn't take long before things began to change. The changes happened so slowly it was easy at first to convince myself everything was fine. In the beginning, it might just be a harsh comment. I would let these comments roll off. I was trying to be a good wife. If my husband was angry, I would have to try harder. That's what a wife should do; try to make her husband happy. In time, it became more than just the harsh comments. He would scream at me, sometimes over the smallest thing. Several times, a policeman appeared at the door in response to a neighbor's complaint. He would be happy to be told that there was no problem and then be on his way. These same neighbors would give me the most piteous looks when I saw them out on the street. I felt like a bad wife; a wife that didn't know how to make her husband happy. Still, they were just words, and I knew that if I was to try harder, things would get better. The early years hadn't been all bad. Sometimes, following one of his outbursts, he would appear with flowers or surprise me with dinner at a nice restaurant."

Rush listened as she mustered the strength to continue. He couldn't imagine what this delicate creature could have done to deserve such treatment.

"In the beginning, he never hit me," claimed Helen. "I told myself that if he ever hit me I would leave him. But, like the yelling, the ...the other stuff started slowly. At first, I convinced myself that the occasional painful pinch or rough grab wasn't enough to make a big deal out of."

For the first time since beginning, she raised her head enough to look at Ben Rush. "I really did try to be a good wife. I really did."

"I got pregnant. I was foolish enough to hope that this would change things between us. He pretty much ignored me during my pregnancy with the exception of some hurtful comments. He would point out how fat I was becoming and warn me that I had better lose this weight after the baby was born. But he didn't say, 'the baby'. Instead, he would look at my swollen belly and ask when *that thing* was finally going to show up."

"I didn't care. I was going to have a baby and suddenly my life had meaning. I was going to have a baby that I could hold and hug and love."

"Michael Angelo was born, and he was so beautiful. I know every mother feels that way, but I knew he was a special gift from God. A gift just for me and that was pretty much how it was. My husband took no pleasure in the birth of his son. When the baby would cry, he would order me to, *'shut that thing up'*. He would get angry when I would tell him that babies cry."

Helen struggled with what she had to say next. She had never told anyone of the nature of some of the punishments her perverse husband had subjected her to. She thought back to the nights he would prod her down the hallway towards their small bedroom. She shuddered at the memories of standing there cold and naked as he would study her; his vile mind mulling over what to do with her as he hurled insults at her. She remembered all too clearly his demands. Demands that came with veiled threats about what might happen to 'her precious baby' if she wasn't cooperative. She would do anything he asked if it meant he would not hurt her child. The memories of what he demanded flooded back at her now. The worst was the touch of his hands as he roughly threw her onto the bed. She tasted bile rise in her throat at these thoughts. She felt filthy afterwards. No amount of scrubbing cleansed her.

In the end, Helen could not bring herself to speak any of this out loud. Instead she said, "If possible, he became even less tolerant of both me and Michael Angelo. So you might be wondering why we didn't just pack our bags and leave. Oh, I thought about it plenty of times, but I didn't have the courage. I was afraid of my husband, but I was more afraid of trying to make it in the world without him. He sheltered us. He fed us."

Rush could see she was dealing with some particularly painful memories. He didn't know what she was recalling, and in truth, he didn't want to know. All he wanted was to go to her, to hold her and whisper that things were going to be better now. He almost convinced himself that this was true, but then he looked at the angry bruise on the side of her face. That was not the handiwork of her now deceased husband.

The widow went on describing life with her brutal husband as their only son went from baby to toddler to tot to teen. They lived cautiously, lest they wake the beast within the husband and father they shared this hovel with. She did whatever was necessary to protect the boy even though there were times when her sacrifice was not enough, and the boy would feel his father's ire. In moments, figuratively and literally dark, mother and son took strength from one another.

Rush believed Helen had finished talk of her husband. Her calmness at the retelling of these abuses had a chilling effect on the police captain. He expected her to cry as he felt tears well in his own eyes several times as she spoke. She didn't cry and, as near as Rush could tell, hadn't even come close to tears. Instead, she delivered this litany in a disassociated and monotone voice. After a moment of silence, Ben Rush reached across the table and took her hand. "Helen, I'm so sorry."

The statement sounded lame to his own ears, but she responded by giving his hand a gentle squeeze. "I should be apologizing to you, captain. I had no right to burden you like that. I can't imagine what a fool you believe me to be." For the second time that afternoon, Helen studied the captain's face. She liked what she saw there. The kindness she saw in that face upon first meeting him hadn't been an illusion.

"You are a nice man, Benjamin Rush."

They let several seconds pass, content to just look into each other's eyes. Rush knew from the beginning that there was something special about this woman. If he was forced to put into words what that was, he doubted if he would be able to. He didn't care. He suspected correctly that Helen did not want his sympathy. That wasn't why she had bared her soul as she had. Rush also believed, again correctly, that she had never told anyone the things she had told him this afternoon. Part of him felt honored, special, that the widow had trusted him enough to confide in him. Rush was a good cop. His intuitiveness told him that even though Helen had said plenty, there was more that she needed to say. He didn't have to wait long for her to continue.

"Ben, I know who killed my husband."

# Chapter Forty-Three

They debated on where to meet. Reilly, because he was a cop, refused to go to a tavern, and Andre, because he hated this whole nasty business, didn't want Octaviano in the gym. They opted to meet at the boxing venue.

This was the first meeting between Reilly and Octaviano.

Reilly was prepared to dislike Octaviano.

That did not turn out to be the case.

Johnnie, upon shaking his hand, held both his hand and his gaze. "Reilly," he began softly, "I know why you're here and what your little girl is going through. My heart goes out to you."

Reilly mumbled a thank you.

"I keep you and your family and little Hope in my prayers every day."

Reilly looked surprised, either because this man knew Hope's name or because an outlaw would mention prayer.

"Come on," said Octaviano, "I'll show you around." There wasn't a great deal to see. In the back was a makeshift locker room. The showers were little more than garden hoses cobbled together. There was a sheet surrounding the makeshift plumbing. In the floor was an open drain. "Here's where the fighters wait before their matches." It was a small room with a six-foot table as well as a smaller table. On the smaller table there was tape, gauze, and a pair of scissors. There was one metal locker and a mirror. Johnnie explained there were several rooms like this. He only showed them the one, and they rightly assumed they were all the same. The tour eventually took them ringside. Even though the windows were painted over, they still managed to allow in some hazy natural light. Beyond that, there were a couple of security lights that stayed on all the time. The dim lighting and eerie silence gave the ring a decidedly sinister feel.

Reilly climbed into the ring. He walked around. He tested the rigidity of the ropes. He bounced gently up and down to get a feel for the give in the canvas.

As Reilly looked over the surroundings, Octaviano looked over him. Petrova easily had thirty plus pounds on him, which had the gangster wondering if the cop would be able to hold his own against the bigger man. He knew Reilly had training that the Russian lacked but would that be enough?

Andre, who had been silent, now pointed out, "Reilly hasn't agreed to anything yet, so let's not get ahead of ourselves here." Andre had rehearsed Reilly for this moment before arriving. He told his friend, "This guy wants you in that ring real bad. We need to make sure it's on our terms."

Octaviano countered this maneuver with, "Reilly, no one's going to force you into that ring. We both know this is a dirty business. If you want to walk away, I'll understand completely." Octaviano knew he was rolling the dice with this last statement. He had done his homework and knew the Thorn's financial situation. Reilly did not appear to have a lot of options.

There was a good chance the Thorns could lose their home. Many did in the nineteen-thirties.

Reilly deviated from the pre-arranged script as he stated, "I need the money. If this can help my family out from under our bills, I'll do it."

Andre jumped in with, "We're not agreeing to anything. We need to settle on more than just the money."

"Reilly, you need to understand something right from the start. You're not here because you can fight. I believe you might be a good fighter. Who knows, maybe you can beat the Russian but understand this; I don't care much one way or the other. My job is to give people what they want, and what they want is to see you climb into the ring. This is a blood sport; pure and simple."

Reilly made no reply, so Octaviano continued.

"Fate and circumstance have conspired to bring you here. You and Andre show up one night for what? To see a fight or maybe out of curiosity. The next thing you know you're not just watching the story unfold; you're part of the story. The moment you stepped through the ropes to help a friend, the world took notice of Reilly Thorn. You gave the world a little taste, and the world wants more. You can thank the Russian for that. He's done more to create the demand for this fight to happen than I ever could. Everybody's got a reason for you to either climb into the ring or to walk away as fast as you can. I believe I know why you're here, but you may not know all the reasons I want to see this fight happen. I'll make money off this fight whether you win or lose, but it's not just about the money. My reasons, beyond the dough, are my own. Know this Reilly, I want you to fight."

"So, what do we do now?" Reilly asked as he and Andre left the arena.

"Train. Train hard and train smart," came the simple reply.

They had a month to get ready. Andre tried to negotiate for no less than six weeks. Octaviano didn't want to even sign off on the month delay. The gangster feared the multitude might lose interest in the fight if they had to wait for that length of time.

"You're the promoter. You can use the time to generate even more interest," countered Andre.

Octaviano laughed at the comment, telling the trainer that he might have missed his calling in life.

In truth, Andre had negotiated a very good deal for his friend.

There came a moment when everything that needed to be discussed had been discussed. It was a defining moment when Reilly, and Reilly alone, needed to make a commitment. If Augie Augustino had been there he might have handed the fighter a worn and wrinkled bit of newsprint. If Reilly was to unfold the tattered paper, he would have seen the heading, *"The Road Not Taken"* by Robert Frost. Reilly, like Augie, knew the verse. It was one of his favorites as well. Reilly didn't consciously think of the poem as he agreed to the fight, but he was fully aware that on this day, he, *'the one traveler'*, had chosen a path. Any doubt about the finality of this decision was erased when Octaviano counted out three hundred dollars and handed it to the black man.

"Reilly, Andre strong-armed me into giving you a cut of the gate. The three-hundred is an advance on your take. Andre took good care of you. I'm glad he's not representing all of these fighters. I'd go broke."

He also handed the trainer a hundred, saying that was to make sure Reilly was in top form the night of the fight.

Andre, beyond the money, brought up the subject of cheating. "I know the Russian weights his gloves. I know he uses the knuckles," referring to the brass knuckles that were not uncommon in underground fighting.

Octaviano agreed that he too wanted a fair fight. He committed to checking Petrova's gloves prior to the fight. As Montero and Thorn walked away, they all too clearly remembered Octaviano's last comments: *"You both need to understand something. The Russian's a cheater. I can check his gloves, but he's going to do anything he can to tip the scales in his favor. Be especially careful before and after the bell. Petrova knows fighters drop their gloves at the sound of the bell. He's used that before. He'd bring a gun into the ring if he thought he could get away with it."*

Andre asked the gangster about a tune-up fight prior to the big bout, saying, "It's been a long time since Reilly fought publically." The truth was that, except for his limited Golden Gloves experience, he had never fought in front of a crowd this size. Andre, remembering the throngs of people and the noise in the arena, feared that when the time came Reilly might be overcome by the moment.

Octaviano was disinclined to agree, and he had several motives for not wanting to see that happen. The reason he shared with Montero and Thorn was that there was no way he would have time to set up this bout prior to the Petrova fight. His true reasons, which he kept to himself, were a bit different. If he gave Reilly a taste of this, he might decide he didn't want anything to do with this business and simply return the earnest money and walk. Another reason being, what if Reilly just wasn't a very good fighter. Johnnie reminded himself that he had never actually seen Thorn fight. If he lost a preliminary match, it would squash the interest in the big fight. The outcome of an earlier fight would also affect the betting line. Fight fans considered Petrova unbeatable. They would line up to bet and bet big on the Russian. The majority of the crowd would be white, and the majority of them hated blacks. Their prejudice would serve as an additional motivation to back Petrova. The odds at fight time would be heavily in the Russian's favor. Octaviano had a month to promote this fight, but he didn't plan on promoting this as a boxing match. He would promote it as a public execution.

# Chapter Forty-Four

Benjamin Rush had arrived at the station in between shifts and retrieved the evidence envelope himself. He wanted to keep this investigation as secret as he could for as long as possible. He inventoried the items on his desk. He began by reading a transcript of the events from that evening. It didn't offer much. It started with a call in the middle of the night from a citizen who would not give their name. They reported that what sounded like gunshots could be heard coming from the alley. There were some comments about what the responding officers had discovered upon their arrival. Several neighbors had wandered into the alley when the police arrived. Their names were listed along with contact information. They heard the gunshots but had seen nothing. If the person who had called in the report was there, they hadn't identified themselves. There was one comment that caught the captain's attention. One of the *ear*-witnesses claimed that he heard a single shot and then nothing. A moment later, he heard a series of shots. 'Attempted Robbery' appeared on the report as an empty wallet had been found near the victim. Rush had harbored doubts from the very beginning about the robbery angle. If the victim had simply been shot once, perhaps twice, it would not have seemed suspicious to the seasoned officer. The victim, Donofrio's father, had been slaughtered. The coroner had dug seven bullets, from two different guns, out of the corpse.

Next, Rush turns his attention to the seven bullets on his desk. They help to validate the scant testimony from the night of the shooting. There was one shot followed by a series of shots. The captain picks up the odd-bullet off of the table. It is a fifty-eight caliber. The others are 38 calibers.

Bullets from a crime scene have limited value unless you have a suspected weapon in hand. Bullets leave clues that can be found in tiny markings. These are labeled as class and individual characteristics. Small imperfections inside the barrel of a gun will leave a unique pattern of markings on the bullet. If you were to examine two bullets fired from the same gun, they would show identical individual characteristics. Special microscopes, invented by Phillip Gravelle in the mid-1920s, allowed side by side comparisons of two bullets at the same time.

Rush, sitting at his desk, had two crucial pieces of information. He had the bullets from the crime scene. He also had a very good idea of who the shooter or shooters were that night.

Ben Rush thought back to what Helen Donofrio had told him. According to what her son had said, Special Agent Stanley Wojick was the murderer. The widow confirmed that her son was present in the alley on the night of the crime. She explained that her son had tried to stop the agent. There was much to question about the events of that evening. How exactly did these three men find themselves in this dark alley? Rush had thrown robbery out of the equation even before speaking to the widow. Rush wondered at the rage it would take for one man to take a gun and pump bullet after bullet in another man's face. He shuddered when he thought that this happened between father and son. Helen Donofrio had shared what life was like for her and her son. Living in constant fear, a small boy is forced to watch the mother he loves being tortured at the hands of a brutal and violent husband. Cops look for motives. Rush had found one.

This might be considered by some as a crime of passion, but it did not exactly meet the criteria. Crimes of passion, by definition happen without aforethought. Things get out of hand; tempers flare out of control. A normally sane person has a moment of insanity. A killing, when successfully argued in a court of law as a crime of passion, might be reduced to a charge of manslaughter. There was no doubt in Rush's mind that there was careful planning and pre-meditation that led to the death of the senior Donofrio.

Agent Wojick hadn't planned this execution; Donofrio had.

# Chapter Forty-Five

"Hue dun guud," said Petrova, in his heavily accented English, "Dees ez guud. Real guud." The huge boxer smiled as he said this. Octaviano realized he had never seen the Russian smile before. It wasn't a good look for the man.

"I told you I could make this happen. You have to have patience, and you have to believe," replied Johnnie. Octaviano went over the details including the date and time of the fight.

"Vladimir, we are going to do everything we can to promote this fight between now and then. I'm having posters made up. We're putting them in every blind pig in the city; in every gym. This is going to be big Bruiser. The biggest fight of your life," said Johnnie excitedly. He could see his enthusiasm was starting to excite the Russian. "You deserve this Bruiser after the way that cowardly black bastard attacked you that night. Then he ran away. It makes me sick to think of what he did. Now you have the chance to settle the score."

Petrova nodded slowly, no doubt remembering the events of that night.

Octaviano let his words sink in before continuing. "The nigger's scared. He agreed to fight only if I could guarantee him a fair fight."

"I always fight fair!" the Russian said indignantly. Petrova might have pressed the issue but Johnnie, like the last visit, had taken the precaution of bringing two of his biggest henchmen along for insurance. Petrova remembered all too vividly the feel of the revolver crashing into the back of his skull.

"We both know that's bullshit," replied Johnnie, "I guaranteed the shine that there would be no weights in the gloves. No knuckles. Do you agree to that?"

Petrova quickly agreed. Everyone in the room shared the unspoken understanding that the Russian wasn't only a cheat, he was also a liar.

"He's scared?" asked the fighter, looking for confirmation from what he was told earlier.

"Terrified, the only reason he's doing this is because he needs the money. He probably drank up all his money or gambled it all away. You know how these shines are. They can't hold on to money."

"Ya, well he's going to get a lot more than money that night. I'm going to beat that bastard to death. You make sure his widow gets his share, huh?" said Petrova laughing. His laugh was even more unnatural than his earlier smile.

All but one in the room laughed along with the boxer. Octaviano chanced a glance at the Russian's trainer. He wasn't getting the joke, and he didn't seem to share his fighter's confidence. Pietir the trainer knew boxing, and he knew fighters. He had seen the black man charge into the ring that night. That man did not have the appearance of someone who scared easily. The trainer thought back to how easily the intruder had adopted a boxer's stance. His hands were fast; his punches punishing. That man was a trained fighter. Everything had happened quickly that night. Pietir only had seconds to observe Thorn, but those few moments had taught him plenty about what kind of skills the black man had. Petrova had been quick to reinvent the events of that evening. The Russian, in hindsight, saw himself as a victim that had been cowardly attacked. Pietir knew Petrova's ego would never allow him to see the events any differently. The trainer also knew that Petrova might be a fighter, but he was never going to be a boxer. His feet were slow; his technique flawed. The big Russian had survived by being big and strong with an iron jaw. Cheating, coupled with being matched with inferior opponents, had also helped him succeed. Pietir had tried to work with his fighter to improve his skills, but the big Russian did not take instruction easily. Again, it was his ego. The fighter resented being told what to do even from his trainer. Pietir didn't trust the gangster. He knew he was lying but wasn't entirely sure why he was portraying the black fighter in such a bad light. There was a game afoot here, and Pietir committed to finding out more about this supposedly scared and broke opponent.

## Chapter Forty-Six

The gym looked, perhaps more accurately felt, somehow different today. Physically, it was pretty much the same as it had been years ago. As he made his way to the locker room, the memory of walking in here for the first time came rushing back at Reilly. He remembered how afraid he had been. He smiled at the confidence it must have taken to walk in and ask for a job.

"Job?" asked Al, the proprietor, "Doing what?"

Reilly had rehearsed what he was going to say. He could sweep up and clean in exchange for the chance to work out at the gym. He had planned on keeping his answers brief but started rambling. He told Al all about his grandfather, his school, how he had met Officer McMahon, and how he wanted to be a police officer one day.

"All right, all right," said Al finally, "I hope you can sweep as well as you talk."

These walls and what was contained within, had been so integral to his life. Of course, he didn't know any of that when he walked in to this dirty and dingy gym for the first time. He didn't know he would be privileged to train with a mentor like Uppercut. He didn't know he would meet Andre Montero, a man who would become a lifelong and trusted friend. And he certainly never suspected that this little hole-in-the-wall would introduce him to his precious Sissy, the greatest treasure he could ever imagine. Reilly knew none of this was in store for him on that first morning. Reilly had chosen a road and, as Frost had postulated, *'way leads on to way'*. He had learned so much more than boxing here. He had grown into a man.

His reverie was cut short when Montero burst into the locker room. "Let's go, Thorn! You ain't just some middle aged cop trying to stay in shape no more. We got us a fight to win."

Reilly was surprised when the two left the locker room and headed for Montero's small office. Telling Reilly to take a seat, Andre produced a chart. The first line item started with the day's date. Next to it were several bullet-points. The first bullet-point read, *'Orientation'*.

"Where'd you learn a big word like that?" asked Reilly.

Andre ignored the comment, "We have a month to get you ready. Listen to me, Reilly. If you stepped into that ring today, you'd lose. We have one-month to improve your chances. That means every day we have to work to change those odds. Are you ready for this?"

Reilly nodded his agreement.

"Good, I put this itinerary together, yeah, I know *'itinerary'* is a big word, too. You got anything to say about that? No? Good."

Following that, the two men went over the plan day-by-day, item by item. Andre told his friend that he needed his buy-in and his commitment. "Reilly, you know yourself better than anybody. You need to tell me what you like and what you don't. I'm OK with making adjustments. I'm not OK with having no game-plan at all."

Reilly was impressed with the obvious amount of thought and effort Andre had put into this. With the exception of a few minor edits, Reilly thought the plan looked solid. Beyond the workouts and the sparring sessions, there were also daily dietary requirements. Andre wanted Reilly to put on ten-pounds over the next four weeks. Reilly stated that it would be difficult to work out at this level and gain weight at the same time.

"You're right," agreed the trainer, "but I'll take what I can get, even if that means you stay the same weight. The important thing is to not lose any pounds.'

The men talked about the danger of overtraining. That would be a delicate balancing act especially during the final week before the fight. The last two days were penciled in with very light workouts.

The two friends trained together for the remainder of the afternoon, focusing primarily on footwork.

"Tomorrow's your first sparing session. Be ready."

"You best be ready," replied Reilly as he playfully started throwing jabs at his friend's midsection.

"Yeah, we'll see about that."

And on that cryptic note, day one of training was in the books.

The next day Reilly hurried to the gym following his shift. He was anxious to get his workout in and get home. One concern, that went unspoken the previous day while going over the training schedule, was the time all this would require. Reilly understood that every moment spent at the gym was one less minute he would have with his family; one less minute with Hope. Hope was struggling. The disease was zapping the little strength she had. The treatments, blood transfusions, and limited radiation seemed to have little benefit. The family did what they could to make the little girl comfortable. Sissy rarely left her side.

Reilly tried to vanquish these thoughts as he walked into the gym. He was scheduled to spar today and knew he had to be sharp. Andre may be a few years older and a hair slower than he was, but he was still a formidable opponent. Reilly changed.

Montero approached him as he stretched prior to warming up. "Looking good, Reilly. I want you to stretch for a few more minutes. Three minutes of jumping rope following that. Then we'll get you taped up. OK?"

Reilly nodded, and Andre went on with his instructions, telling him he wanted him on the speed bag for one-minute before the sparring session.

As Andre walked away, Reilly asked him if he was ready.

"Ready for what?"

"Sparring," Reilly explained.

"You're not sparring with me." Montero thrust his chin towards the ring.

The huge man paused his shadow boxing with one of the turnbuckles long enough to smile and wave at Thorn. Even though muffled through the mouth piece, Reilly could still make out Angel Vasquez' comment, "Whenever you're ready, Peaches."

Angel, a true heavyweight, was well past his prime but still a big and powerful man. Reilly often thought back to the night he had gone to a match with Andre and his grandfather to watch Angel box. Angel had won that night against a favored fighter. In part, this was because Angel was a good fighter and also in part because he had Uppercut in his corner.

Andre herded both men into the middle of the ring for instructions.

"Angel knows what's going on, and he wants to help any way he can," he began. "It won't be long before everyone in the gym knows about the fight, too."

Reilly looked at the much bigger man as Andre continued. He realized if anything, Angel might actually be a bit smaller than the Russian. The thought alarmed him as Angel was plenty big. He had watched the heavyweight train for many years. He knew the big man was more than just size and strength. Angel could box.

"Reilly, are you paying attention?" asked Montero.

"Ready here, boss."

"Angel, anything?"

"Reilly, I know why you're doing this, and like Andre said, I want to help. We've been friends for years, but just so you know, when the bell rings, I'm gonna try to take your head off. Be sharp, I don't want to hurt you. One more thing, you're not fighting Angel Vasquez this afternoon. You're fighting the Russian. Don't forget that."

The warning being issued by someone that big got Reilly's full attention. Several last minute instructions and Andre sent both men to their corners to await the bell. Reilly realized that the gym had become eerily quiet. Everyone was at ring side. Most had an incredulous look on their face.

One longtime member, a friend to both Reilly and Angel, hollered to Andre, "Why are these two sparring? Reilly's gonna get killed."

Montero ignored the comment.

Andre would stay in the ring and act as referee. He signaled the timekeeper, and the match was underway. Reilly had seen Angel fight often. Unlike a lot of big men, Vasquez didn't bull rush out of his corner at the sound of the bell.

That was until today.

The bell hadn't stopped reverberating before Vasquez was across the ring, trapping Reilly in his corner. Reilly's greatest assets in the ring were his reach and his footwork. Within the first five-seconds, Angel had neutralized both. Reilly's only option now was to cover and look for an opportunity to escape the corner before Andre had the chance to inflict too much damage. Reilly leaned his weight into the bigger man, but it was like pushing against a wall. The only good news in all this was Angel was too close to unleash full-force punches. Instead, he pummeled Reilly pretty much at will with a series of jabs. That much weight leaning into him was more exhausting than Reilly would have imagined. Reilly thought Andre might step in and separate the two men. He did not.

With only seconds left in the round, Reilly managed to extricate himself. He succeeded in throwing a few weak punches at Angel as the bell rang. Andre, at the sound of the bell, jumped in between the two fighters. Reilly turned to head for his corner when he felt Angel spin him around while sending a punishing right into his midsection.

The members watching from ringside in one-voice shouted their disapproval. They had never seen anyone in the gym take a cheaper shot than that. Andre would never allow that. As they looked at Montero awaiting his reaction, they were disappointed as Andre just stood there with his arms folded across his chest.

Reilly stood with his hands on his knees, trying to recapture his breath. Christ that hurt. Angel approached again. Reilly knew he needed to defend himself but was having trouble straightening up. Instead of attacking, Angel went to Reilly and placed his hand on his back. "I'm sorry," he said. "I tried to warn you before we started that you were fighting the Russian today."

Jeers and taunts rained down on Angel Vasquez before Andre was able to restore order.

"Everybody listen up. I asked Angel to throw that late punch. You all know Angel. He would never do something like that on his own. I would never ask him to do it without a good reason."

The assemblage heard the words, but they did little to explain what they had just seen.

A late arriving member shed some light on what had just happened as he shouldered his way to ringside. In his hand is a placard. He hands it through the ropes to Montero, asking, "Would you mind explaining this? A kid was tacking it to the bulletin board as I was walking in."

Montero read the message. Besides the date and place was the announcement:

## DON'T MISS THE FIGHT OF THE DECADE

## VLADIMIR 'THE BRUISER' PETROVA
## Vs.
## REILLY THORN

The sucker punch to Reilly's stomach ended the sparring for the day. Now, once again in the small office, the two old friends sat.

"Sorry Reilly, but you need to understand that there ain't going to be a lot of rules the night you fight Petrova. The only difference today is that Angel threw one punch and stopped. If Petrova sees you doubled over, he's going to keep on coming. Be warned. That's not the only surprise I have in store for you."

# Chapter Forty-Seven

Ben Rush no longer visited the widow on the pretext of furthering his investigation. As he was at heart a shy man, he hadn't yet declared his feelings for her. On his second visit, the two sat and talked about everything except the case. Ben had called and asked if he could stop by for a few minutes. He left the small apartment several hours later. Helen's bruise, presumably delivered by her son's hand, was almost completely faded. Helen had never explained the bruise, and he hadn't pressed. It was comfortable for both of them to pretend it had never happened.

Ben called several days later saying he needed some additional information. Helen agreed only if he would commit to stay for dinner.

"Helen, you don't have to do that."

"Oh I'm sorry, I didn't mean to …I just thought maybe …," she ended feebly.

"Helen," he interrupted, "dinner with you sounds wonderful. I'd like that."

Helen felt like a school girl as she prepared dinner, the house, and herself for the handsome police captain. The part of her that believed that she was misinterpreting the captain's intentions struggled with the part of her that was falling in love with the man. It had been a long time since a man had treated her nicely, and Ben was being so very nice to her. He seemed genuinely interested in her thoughts and feelings. Helen after much debate finally chose a dress. It was a pale green with yellow accents. Helen, unbeknownst to Helen, was still a very fetching woman. After being told repeatedly that she was fat and ugly by her abusive husband, she had quit seeing herself as attractive years ago. Trying it on, she examined herself in the mirror. She was disappointed in the reflection. Her shoulders slumped, and she felt like a fool. No man could possibly be interested in her. She thought about calling the captain and giving him the chance to back out of the dinner. Instead, she continued to get ready. She fixed her hair, and for the first time in a long time, she applied make-up for a reason other than to hide a bruise.

Ben thought about flowers but was concerned about the message that might send. He opted instead for a box of candy. He could pass the candy off as dessert. He couldn't remember ever being this nervous around a woman. Some of his trepidation came from courting a woman who had so recently lost her husband. He felt guilty.

Ben Rush audibly gasped when Helen opened the door. She looked beautiful. When he saw her response, he knew she had taken his reaction the wrong way. This poor woman had been treated so badly.

Ben Rush surprised himself by saying, "Helen, you look lovely."

The deep blush that rose in her cheeks only made her prettier. She started to object to his comment, but he stopped her.

"Helen, I wish you could see yourself the way I see you. Saying you're beautiful doesn't do you justice."

Before she could voice another objection, Ben stepped towards her. He placed the candy on a small entryway table and used his heel to close the door behind him. He took each of her hands and looked deeply into her eyes. This felt so right after all the furtive glances he had snuck up to this point. He leaned into her and tenderly kissed her on the lips. It was a soft, whisper of a kiss but still so exciting for both of them. Ben cradled her face in his hands as they lost themselves in each other's eyes.

"I'm sorry, I shouldn't have...," he started, but before he could finish, Helen wrapped her arms around him and held him tightly. She laid her head against his chest and felt his warm embrace as Ben folded his arms around her.

It had been so long for both of them.

Helen could not remember the last time a man had caressed her so tenderly. The passion they felt for each other ushered them down the hall and into the bedroom quickly. Once there, their pace slowed. Sitting next to one another on the bed they held hands, content with this for the moment. He told her again how beautiful she was, and he truly believed this. Seeing her blush yet again, he smiled. Ben touched her cheek gently where the final remnants of her bruise could barely be seen.

"I'll never let anyone hurt you ever again."

Helen leaned into Ben as he slipped his arm around her.

They both hungered for more. Their tender kisses became more ardent, more eager.

"Helen, if this isn't right, I'll understand. If you want me to, I'll stop." As he said this, he prayed she wouldn't pull away. He felt the need to apologize for being there as a part of him felt like a villain for courting a woman so recently widowed. Helen answered his doubts with a series of soft kisses.

Standing now, they melted into one another. Each could feel every contour of the other's body. Ben was embarrassed by his own excitement as there was no disguising his readiness. Helen boldly pressed against him, and now it was Ben's turn to blush. Helen's impish smile added to Ben's embarrassment and his excitement. Their hands explored one another; slowly at first but soon more quickly, more passionately. Mysteriously, Helen's dress ended up in a pool at her ankles. She used Ben for a support as she stepped out of the garment. Ben retrieved the dress and laid it across a chair in the room, saying it was too pretty to see it wrinkled. Helen was touched by his thoughtfulness. It was difficult for the two to disentangle for even those few seconds. They found one another again and, impossibly, held one another even tighter.

As is so often the case, the two lovers fought the urge to move too quickly while not being able to move hurriedly enough. Their passion, white hot and unbridled, sated itself mere moments later. Breathing heavily, they lay next to one another. Ben put his arm around her as she snuggled against him, resting her head against his chest. Both are content to let this moment last as long as possible. Ben breaths in her scent.

He senses she is crying. He doesn't fully understand why. He wants to say something, but no words seem right.

"I forgot it was supposed to be like that," whispers Helen.

Ben answers by pulling her even closer. He wonders, not for the first time, about the indignities this woman has suffered. It hurts his heart to think about these things.

Suddenly, Helen bolts upright. "Oh my God!" she says as she ran naked from the room.

Ben is still getting dressed as Helen returns. She is holding a roasting pan. In the pan is what might have been a chicken at one time. It is burned so badly it is hard to tell for sure.

She starts to quake. "I'm sorry," she says as tears roll down her cheek. For a moment she is back with her husband. In her mind's eye, she sees him approach. She can feel the back of his hand across her jaw. The bird goes flying, grease splatters the wall. She cries harder. Helen braces herself for whatever might come next.

Ben, still pulling on his trousers, looks at the burnt disaster she is holding. He starts to laugh. He sits back down on the edge of the bed, buries his face In his hands, and laughs even harder. "I'm sorry," he starts, but the moment gets the best of him, and he can't finish.

Helen cautiously looks up. Of all the reactions that ran through her head, she never expected this. "You're not mad?" she asks.

"Mad? That may be the funniest thing I ever saw," and erupts into another fit of laughter.

His laughter becomes contagious, and in spite of herself, she begins giggling. Soon they are both lost in raucous laughter.

Finally, they get control of themselves.

Ben looks at Helen. She is quite a sight as she stands there, bare-chested, with big oven mitts, holding the remains of dinner. "Helen, you're the only woman I know that could look absolutely beautiful while holding a burnt chicken."

They hold each other's gaze for a moment.

"Are you hungry?" she asks.

He answers her with suggestive smile.

It was late when Ben left the apartment and made his way home. The evening had been magical. Neither had been bold enough to speak the words aloud, but they were in love. Of that, there was little doubt. Helen took his collar as he lingered at the door. She pulled him close for one final kiss. It was as soft and tender as their first kiss of the evening had been.

Helen smiled when Ben said, "I don't know when I've ever enjoyed a chicken dinner that much."

Now, out on the street, Ben was once again a police officer. A conflicted cop as he thought about Helen ...and her son.

Rush had orchestrated ingenious ways to secure bullets from both Agent Wojick and Donofrio. The Donofrio part was easy as he simply mandated target practice for the station. It had been a bit more challenging to procure a bullet from the agent. In the end, he set up a meeting with the agents at the range, claiming he was running out of time to be recertified with his service revolver. He asked if they would mind meeting him there to discuss a case he was working on. "Feel free to shoot while you're there," he casually mentioned to them, knowing most cops liked to shoot and would probably take him up on the offer.

Ben had sent both bullets in for analysis. The results might be on his desk as early as the next day.

Two days later, Benjamin Rush sat at his desk studying the ballistics results. He hadn't expected to be surprised by the findings, but he was.

# Chapter Forty-Eight

Word got out, and when it did, the news of the fight spread like a proverbial wildfire. Octaviano, considering he was forced to clandestinely promote the fight, did a masterful job of generating interest in the event. At every prior bout at the makeshift arena leading up to the fight, announcements were made. Bruiser did his part. Before and after every bout, he would stomp around the ring screaming threats against Thorn to the crowd. His fury was unquestionable. His passion was genuine.

"Finally, I get my justice! At last, the coward comes forward. You come, you all come and I promise you this. I will beat this man to death!"

The crowd would erupt.

Octaviano, with several weeks to go before the big night, realized that he had better print tickets up and sell them beforehand. The warehouse was huge. So big in fact, that they had never come close to filling the place. That being the case, fans were accustomed to just showing up and paying at the gate. Sensing the interest in this fight, the gangster hurriedly had thousands of tickets printed. He was concerned that his typical clientele would balk at pre-purchasing tickets. He needn't have worried as it had the opposite effect. The tickets, along with the warning that if you didn't have a ticket you might not get in, spurred even more interest in the fight. They sold like hotcakes.

Thanks to the poster that had appeared at *Al's Gym*, there was no possibility of keeping the event from the other boxers. One afternoon when Reilly was not in attendance, Andre held an impromptu meeting with his members. He talked about Reilly's situation. Most of the men at the gym knew that the Thorns were going through some very difficult times. Hope had stopped in at the gym with her daddy several times, and those who had a chance to meet her were enchanted by the little girl. Andre reminded the men that he was Hope's Godfather. "I love that child more than anything else in this world," he told the assemblage. His voice quivered as he spoke the words. "You know me, and you know what I think about this kind of boxing. I know many of you feel the same way. I tried to discourage Reilly from doing this, but he is a man on a mission. I can't stop him, and I can't get in his way. All I can do is try to help him."

One of the men, big, strong, and tough as nails, said with a slight falter in his own voice, "Andre, if I was Reilly and that was my little girl, I'd be doing the same thing." Several others voiced their agreement. One of the men offered, "What can we do to help?" Others chimed in, also offering their support. Montero told them how much he appreciated the offers, adding that he might call on several of them to help get Reilly ready. As the group broke up, a somberness stole over the gym. Andre had known most of these men for years. Some of them had carried heavy baggage with them when they had first walked into this modest training center. Many were already fighting. Some fighting their way out of gangs they had foolishly found their way into. Others were fighting to stay out of prison. Andre had been one of these broken young men. Uppercut had seen something in him that he had not seen in himself; something worth saving. Andre could point to several in the room who UC had done the same thing for. Today, he thought of them all as good, honest, and upright people. Boxing had built their stamina and their physiques, but it hadn't stopped there. It had built their character.

Donofrio had gotten into the habit of stopping at *Augie's Tavern*. He wasn't exactly welcome, but Johnnie tolerated him being there. On his first visit, Octaviano had a conversation with the cop. He told him he didn't want any trouble. He made it clear the broads were off limits. This didn't seem to bother Donofrio. He said he wasn't interested in any of the hookers anyway. Octaviano always knew this cop was pazzo. The boy just wasn't right in the head. Johnnie was more convinced of that than ever after talking to him. Octaviano, if asked, would describe the cop as having a haunted look. He didn't realize how close to the truth his assessment was. Poetically, eyes have been called the windows to the soul. When Johnnie looked into Donofrio's eyes, he saw dark and forbidding places.

Mary had asked Johnnie why he even allowed him to come into the place. The gangster's response was simple, "He's still a cop."

The days when the arrogant cop would strut in like he owned the place were over. There were no more fat envelopes passed across the bar top. Donofrio wasn't there to collect. He was there because it was the only place he felt remotely comfortable. So far, there had been no incidents. The opposite was true. Donofrio would sit in the dark recesses of the bar and nurse a beer. He drank little while there. Sometimes, at slow times, he would sit at the bar. He said little, which made Augie happy as he still held a strong dislike for the cop after what he had done to Mary. Several times, Donofrio had been seen by Augie and others whispering to someone only he could see. Augie would touch the cross he wore around his neck and say a silent prayer at these moments.

"Johnnie, he talks to himself but it's not to himself. It's like there's someone else with him. Someone only he can see," Augie reported.

Octaviano laughed it off but was concerned about this as well. Johnnie had grown up in a Sicilian home; an environment rich in spirit folklore. He had witnessed these phantom conversations and thought they were disturbing. He asked his bouncer to keep an extra close eye on the cop.

Posters for the fight were displayed in prominent places throughout the tavern. Donofrio, upon first seeing one, stood transfixed in front of the notice. Augie and the bouncer both watched the cop to see what he would do; to see what his reaction might be. The cop did nothing. He simply stood there gazing at the poster.

"Johnnie, it was weird. He walked in, saw the poster, and just stared at it. Ten minutes later, he walked out. He just stared at it for ten minutes," said Augie.

The hulking figure of the bouncer stood behind Augie as he told Octaviano about the strange behavior they had both witnessed. "That guy gives me the creeps, boss," is all he offered to the conversation.

Octaviano thanked Augie for letting him know. The gangster correctly assumed that Donofrio and Thorn, both being cops, knew one another. Beyond that, he knew nothing about what their relationship might be like. He wondered what it was about the fight notice that had fascinated the cop.

There were hushed whispers at the station house. Reilly's coworkers knew. They were cops. Cops are supposed to know things. Several of the men approached Reilly and wished him luck. None publically admitted that they would be attending, but many had plans on going. Dominic Augustino was a bit more candid with his old friend and fellow police academy graduate. The two were no longer rookies. They had been on the street long enough to see plenty. Dominic admitted to himself that he had never seen anything like this. Everyone seemed to know about the fight. It was the talk of the town, and Augustino couldn't imagine what the mob scene would be like the night of the fight. There seemed to be a virtual army of urchins out on the street hawking tickets. Augustino had been approached while being shaved at his neighborhood barber shop. The same was true when stopping for a shoe shine. The fact that he was in uniform when getting his shoes shined did not deter the pint-sized ticket hawker from approaching him.

Dominic Augustino felt guilty, he felt responsible. After all, it was he who went to the mob with word of the Thorns problems. Dominic had heard from an insider that Reilly was a doomed man. His opponent, a Russian giant, was unbeatable. Not only that but, according to Dominic's source, this Russian had a personal score to settle with Thorn. He told Dominic about the death threats and about how the Russian promised to treat his fans to something they had never seen before. He promised to beat Reilly Thorn to death in the ring that night. Dominic gasped at the man's description of Petrova; seven-feet tall and 350 pounds of solid muscle. Augustino hoped that these might be exaggerations.

"Reilly, I need to talk to you," he said timidly to his friend while out on patrol.

Reilly said little as they drove. This was becoming more typical of Reilly as of late. Most, but not all of the fellow patrolmen, understood the pressure the young cop was under and gave him a pass on his behavior.

Officer Augustino had something to say. He had lived with the guilt of sacrificing his friend for his uncle's safe passage long enough.

"Reilly, I'm sorry I got you into this mess."

The statement seemed to get Reilly's attention, which was good as there were times when Thorn seemed barely there. He asked Dominic to explain the curious comment.

Augustino as briefly as he could, told Reilly about his Uncle Augie. He described his uncle and his involvement with the mob. He confided how the mob had set his uncle up to be the fall guy if the bar should get busted.

"Reilly, I went to the bar. I met with this Johnnie Octaviano character, and I made a deal with him. I told him about your troubles. I knew he wanted you in the ring. I told him that in exchange for the information, I wanted his guarantee that he would protect my uncle. I'm sorry Reilly. It was me that got you into this mess."

"You didn't do anything," was Reilly's simple reply.

Augustino hoped he would say more, but he didn't. Even when Dominic told him how afraid he was for his friend, Reilly just sat there stoically, silently. Reilly actually chuckled a bit when Augustino repeated the description of Petrova's size that he had gotten from his informant.

"Don't worry about any of that," said Thorn. "None of that means anything."

*Il Uomo* let the question hang in the air. He waited patiently for a reply before repeating, "Johnnie, why do you say you don't know who's going to win?"

Normally, *Il Uomo* gave Johnnie a free reign. The fight had gotten so big that it had caught the boss' attention. Johnnie had given a lot of thought to the outcome of the event. He had fixed many fights in his day but didn't see that as an option. He explained that to *Il Uomo now*. "The Russian's getting huge odds. The smart play would be to bet heavy on the shine and have Petrova take a dive, but *patron*, there is no way he'd do it."

"Tell him Johnnie. You tell him to take the dive, and he takes the dive."

"He fights for honor. Men who fight for honor, even a *bastardo* like this Petrova, don't sacrifice that honor for money."

*Il Uomo* thought about this. He understood honor and let the subject drop.

He reminisced, "Johnnie, you used to like to fight as a boy. Fighting, fighting, fighting all the time."

Octaviano smiled at the memory. He thought back to the day his mentor took his face in his hands and told him he was too pretty to fight. "Johnnie, you're a nice looking kid. I don't want to see that face get messed up. I got a lot of muscle. You're a smart kid. I need you for your brains."

The two may not have been related by blood, but they were family. One had watched the other grow up. The other had watched the closest thing he ever had to a father, grow old. It was a good relationship as the two shared a love for one another. Johnnie's brains had served the family well as the inner circle had grown rich.

Octaviano had learned to never be surprised by the old man's intuitiveness, "You care about this *Africano*. Tell me, why should you care?"

Johnnie told the boss about the night Thorn had climbed into the ring to save his friend. "That took balls," he said. "Now he fights for his little girl. She's sick. She ain't going to make it, but he fights because that's what he knows how to do."

"The *Africano*, can he win?"

"I don't know. I've never seen him fight," confessed Johnnie, "but I'm going to bet a bundle on him"

The old man threw back his head and laughed. He knew that beyond brains, Johnnie had a good heart. He had seen him bring in one stray after another as a child. Not all the strays were four-legged. Johnnie had brought men into the family and befriended them. He showed them respect, and they returned that kindness by becoming some of the family's best soldiers.

"OK *figlio*, what do you say we both bet on this guy and see what happens?" said the boss. He could afford to laugh, the same way he could afford to lose a wager. Johnnie was smart. He had set it up to own the lion's share of the gate along with the concessions. The family would make money that night regardless of what happened to Reilly Thorn.

Time flew. In what seemed to be an impossibly short time the month to prepare was disappearing. Reilly trained; he trained hard, and he trained smart. Andre Montero had done everything he could to prepare Reilly. Collectively, the other boxers in the gym helped anyway they could. When Reilly did his road work, there were usually one or two men to accompany him. Reilly was touched as these men were sacrificing their own training time to help. One man offered him more than advice when he secretively handed Reilly a set of brass knuckles and told him to at least think about it. Reilly thanked him and handed the hideous devices back. There were several times Andre asked the support group to do things they found distasteful. During one of Reilly's sparring sessions, a boxing glove whizzed past his head. He made the mistake of reacting to it, giving his opponent the opportunity to land a solid right to the jaw.

The biggest surprise was the day Johnnie Octaviano showed up. He wasn't in his usual dapper attire. He wore baggy sweat pants and a tee-shirt. The gangster asked if he could have a training session with Reilly. Andre answered that it was his funeral.

"I'm not talking about sparring. I'm not that crazy. I'm here to help."

Andre watched as Octaviano warmed up. He had a good physique. He jumped rope, stretched, and worked the speed bag. Montero grudgingly admitted from the little he saw that he could probably make this guy into a boxer.

Several men watched with rapt attention as Reilly and Johnnie climbed into the ring. "I've watched this guy fight a dozen times. He makes a lot of mistakes that you need to know about."

"I'm listening."

"For starters, he loves the left hook, but he'll drop his right every time." Octaviano took a boxer's stance. "Here, I'll show you." Stepping in, he threw a slow-motion left hook. When he did, he dropped his right hand.

Reilly smiled as he saw the gangster expose his right jaw.

"I thought you'd like that, but there are a couple of other things that might help." Octaviano walked Reilly through other boxing mistakes the Russian made. He exposed his chin when throwing the jab, and he telegraphed the right hand. Johnnie showed him when and how Petrova would expose his body. "You have the reach to make him pay for that," claimed Octaviano.

The audience of other boxers around the ring pounded the canvas while shouting encouragement. They would love to step into the ring with an opponent that did so many things wrong.

The two men, one a crook, the other a cop, stood in Andre's tiny office. Andre asked how he was able to pick out Petrova's issues. Johnny just smiled and said that he always liked the science of boxing. It was an interesting choice of words as Andre had often described it as a science to his trainees. "Well, if you ever get tired of being a gangster, you'd probably make a good trainer."

Reilly thanked him for his help. Octaviano could feel his sincerity.

"The gate's going to be huge," said Octaviano. "Andre cut you a good deal. I have some dough for both of you today. We'll square up the rest after the fight."

Before he left, he had more advice for Thorn. "What I showed you today will help, but keep in mind that it's hard to hurt the Russian. He has a head like a cinderblock and a jaw made of steel. I've seen him take a punch that would knock most fighters out cold. He hates you, Thorn. When that bell rings, he's going to charge you like a pissed-off bull. You could lose this thing in the first minute of the first round. His first punch will be a wild right. He'll want to deliver the knock-out blow right at the start. Be ready to move to the right and come back with your own right hand as you move. Keep moving and stay in the middle of the ring. If he gets you in a corner, he's too strong to move."

Reilly thought about his sparring session with Angel and the tough time he had getting out of the corner against the bigger man.

Octaviano continued, "We told Petrova that this would be a fair fight. We told him that we'll be checking his gloves before the fight and we will. Keep this in mind, the Russian's a cheater. Cheaters cheat. Believe me, we can check his gloves, but he'll try to figure out a way to tip the scales in his favor."

"Why are you helping me?" asked Thorn.

"I'm not, I'm helping me. I'm betting a bundle on you."

Octaviano handed Reilly an envelope. It was thick with twenty-dollar bills.

"Reilly, the odds are all in the Russian's favor. There aren't a lot of people out there that are giving you much of a chance. I believe in you, and that's why I'm putting my money on you. The question is, do you believe in you?"

Reilly nodded tentatively.

"You can do what you want with that money, but if you truly believe in your ability and believe in your heart that you can win this fight, you may want to place a bet on Reilly Thorn."

Montero brought a fighter in from another gym to spar with Thorn. It was a good training practice that many fighters used. He also brought in a lefty even though the Russian was right-handed. Reilly thought that helped as well. Andre knew his protégé was ready on the day a pack of fire-crackers went off at Reilly's heels. Reilly never even flinched as his sparring partner moved in, only to have his jab blocked. As the smoke cleared, Reilly looked at his old friend and trainer and smiled. Andre realized it had been a long time since he had seen Reilly smile.

The time for training was over.

They had done what they could to prepare.

They both hoped it was enough.

# Chapter Forty-Nine

It was his father who first put the worry in his head. At first, he gave it little credence. Donofrio sat in his sad apartment; with him is his recently departed father. The two, who shared no love for one another in their former lives, now got along swimmingly. Mulling it over, Donofrio prepared to ask a clarifying question to his father. Too late, as when he looked again, his father was gone. He was neither surprised nor sad to see him go as he knew he'd be back.

Dad had been around a lot lately.

It hadn't been easy as it was after all a police station. It took some careful planning, but he was finally able to find the opportunity he needed. He thought he had his bases covered the night he put his father down but realized now that he had made some stupid mistakes. His hand shook as he looked over the ballistics report. Rush was a shrewd one all right. He had figured out a way to get bullets from his gun as well as Wojick's. He understood that getting his was easy and smiled at the thought of the compulsory target practice the captain had mandated recently. That Rush was a sly bastard all right. Donofrio wondered at the deceit it must have taken to secure a bullet from the Special Agent.

A note, with several scribbled comments clipped to the manila folder, told the cop what he wanted to know. Rush had written, *58 caliber-Wojick*. Next to the note was a checkmark that dominated the small piece of paper. Donofrio pictured Rush at his desk placing the symbol and then, for emphasis, going over the mark repeatedly.

Below that was a second note reading, *38 caliber-_____ ???*. Donofrio next pictured the Captain with his pencil poised above the paper ready to add a name to the blank line. He allowed himself the slightest of smirks as he suspected that the good captain wanted to write the name *'Donofrio'* on that blank line. Donofrio knew what the problem was. The bullets they had dug out of his father did not match the target practice bullet. Donofrio whispered to the empty room, "Of course it doesn't you dumb bastard. It wasn't the same gun."

Donofrio had savored every moment leading up to his father's execution. He luxuriated in the planning of every detail. He spared no effort as he prepared for the big night. He thought back to the anticipation and the almost giddy feelings he would get as he went over every minute element. He felt like a kid who knew he was going to get everything on his Christmas wish list. He thought about the importance of the gun as he felt his police issued 38-caliber Super Automatic pistol on his hip. While planning, he almost ignored the nagging little voice in his head that told him not to use his service revolver. In the end, after remembering all the good advice that nagging voice had given him in the past, he gave in. He was able to secure a 'clean' weapon; a weapon that couldn't be traced back to him. After seeing the report on Rush's desk, he said a silent prayer to the higher power that had given him that suggestion.

From over his shoulder, he heard, "Don't dawdle, boy." He didn't need to turn to know who was there. He could smell the decaying odor of his father's breath. It was gagging. He wondered how long he had been standing there. Lately, time would go missing on him. He might get home from work in the late afternoon and sit in a chair for a few minutes. The next thing he knew, it was full dark outside. He looked at the clock on Rush's desk. Good, he had only been here for a matter of minutes. Putting everything back exactly as he found it, he left the office.

The next morning, Special Agent Stanley Wojick was dead. Ben Rush had come in to find the report sitting on his desk. In what he considered a curious illustration of irony, his secretary had placed the report directly on top of the Donofrio murder folder.

# Chapter Fifty

As he feared, the training forced him to spend more time away from Hope than he wanted. What he wanted was to spend all-day, every-day at his daughter's side. Every moment Reilly was not training or working, he was with Hope.

Now, on the eve of the fight, Reilly sat at his daughter's bedside.

"Tell me a story, daddy," she husked out.

*'Once upon a time...'* Reilly started.

Hope stopped him.

"No daddy, we have to play our game."

When her father didn't reply, Hope began the ritual by saying, "I promise I won't fall asleep."

Fighting tears, he touched her hand, "That's OK baby if you fall asleep."

"But what about our game?" Starting over, she asked again, "Please tell me a story, daddy."

Struggling to form the words, he said, "No, they'll be no story tonight."

"And?" prodded Hope.

"You always fall asleep during my stories."

"I won't. I promise I won't fall asleep."

Reilly sat like a stage actor who had forgotten his lines.

Hope prompted him by asking, "Will I be in BIG trouble if I fall asleep?"

"Yes honey, you'll be in big trouble if you fall asleep." Reilly is powerless to stop the flow of tears.

"Don't cry, daddy," Hope pleaded. "That's not part of our game."

It was heartbreaking to look upon the gaunt face and emaciated body of his only child. Her breathing was labored. She bruised at the slightest touch. She could barely keep her eyes open.

Tonight's story started like so many in the past, *'Once upon a time there was a beautiful princess who lived in a magical place far beyond the sea'.*

Hope was already sleeping.

Reilly continued the story, this time for himself, *'Everyone in the kingdom loved the little princess. She was so kind, and everyone in her kingdom was happy'.*

Reilly paused to control his tears before continuing, *'Her father loved her more than anyone. He would hold her and protect her and never let anything bad happen to his little princess'.*

And finally, *'No one would ever get sick in this magical place'.*

"You don't have to do this," said Sissy even though they both knew the time for this conversation had passed. Reilly had accepted the money. The money had gotten them out of financial trouble at least for the moment. The two sat at the kitchen table. The rest of the household had been asleep for a while.

Reilly did not reply to the comment, instead saying. "She looks bad, Sissy."

Now it was Sissy's turn to say nothing. There did not seem to be anything to say.

They had each other. They had their love. That had always been enough.

A short time later, "Are you ready?"

"I think so. I hope so."

What else could he say? In twenty-four hours, the fight would be over. In twenty-four hours, Hope would still be sick. He only had control over one of those eventualities. He had the power to influence one outcome but not the other.

Reilly thought ahead to the fight. He looked forward to being in the one place where he could escape thoughts of Hope for a few moments. He felt guilty about this but recognized it as the truth; a truth that he shared with no one.

A second, darker truth, were the threats that Petrova had made. He had promised to *'beat a man to death'* in the ring. Boxing was a dangerous sport. Men had died in the ring. Reilly had never heard of anyone going into a fight with the goal of killing his opponent. Beating him senseless, yes; killing them, no. Reilly had thought a lot about that. It didn't frighten him. What scared him was the comfort the thought gave him.

Hope was dying.

When he thought of being in a world without his daughter, it took his will to live away.

He felt like a coward; a quitter seeking an easy way out. He looked across the small table at Sissy. She was lost in her own thoughts. She was so beautiful even now. He knew full well what she was going through. She was so smart but had always been wrong about one thing. She believed Reilly was the stronger of the two. She didn't realize it, but she was so much stronger than he.

Their eyes met. Reilly reached across the table and took her hand. It was cold. She was always cold as of late.

"I'll be OK," he said, referring to the fight.

"I don't know if any of us will ever be all right again," replied Sissy, referring to everything.

# Chapter Fifty-One

He knew that Stan wouldn't agree to meet him no matter what kind of ruse Donofrio came up with. It wasn't important. He had spent enough time with the big man to know his habits and his movements. He would have liked more time to plan but time just wasn't available. Rush knew Wojick's gun was used in the murder of his father. There was no ballistic evidence tying Donofrio's service revolver to the crime, but that meant little. They had more than enough to arrest the Special Agent, and when they did, Donofrio knew the agent wouldn't take the fall on his own. Oh no, his one-time good friend would sing like a canary. Donofrio had always had good survival instincts. He could probably thank his old man for that as he was forced to survive from an early age.

Donofrio thought of the unfairness of it all. He was the victim in this whole mess. It had all started with his goddamned mother. She was the one that wanted this. And when he went to Stan looking for the sage advice of his best friend, he got just the opposite. Donofrio closed his eyes and thought back to the moment. In his mind's eye, he recalled how excited the big man had gotten at the prospect of offing the old man. He clearly remembered Stan telling him if he was going to be a good son, he would have to do this for his mother.

He could be so weak at times. He should have told both of them, *NO*. Instead, seeing how much it meant to them, he went along with their plan. If they thought that he was going to take the rap on this, they were crazy. The thought of them being the crazy ones brought an insane smile to his face. Oh, they were crazy all right, and Donofrio knew how to fix crazy.

He knew Wojick was stupid. In truth, it was one of the things he liked most about the big man. There was another truth Donofrio bought into; out on the streets, stupid could get you killed.

He told himself to get rid of the gun that he had used on his father. He should have casually dropped it into the Chicago River but he didn't. Instead, he worked a floorboard loose under the sink in his apartment, wrapped the pistol in an oily cloth, and slipped it into the small cubby-hole he had created. Now, once again he held the unregistered gun in his hand. By the end of the day it would rest at the bottom of the river, but it needed to fulfill one more function before dropping it into its watery grave.

Benjamin Rush looked at the report lying on his desk. Wojick was dead. There was little doubt of who the murderer was. There were some similarities between the two killings. Wojick, like the senior Donofrio, was found in an alley. Wojick's wallet had been discarded nearby; the money gone. The senior Donofrio didn't have the option of an open casket at his wake. Wojick's casket would also remain closed. There was one-dissimilarity. The killer, presumably Michael Angelo Donofrio, had been much thriftier with his ammunition this time. There was none of the carnage of multiple bullet wounds as in the first murder.

As was typical, the captain was in the office before the day shift reported. He made his way to the locker room. Upon opening Donofrio's locker, he found it empty. This was bad. He had a rogue cop on the lam. Worse yet, the renegade was not only a murderer but very likely insane.

Donofrio had waited for Wojick to appear. Christ, he was nervous. Stan was massive. If he got his hands on the much smaller man, he probably could *'snap his neck like a chicken bone'* as he had once promised. It had been a while since he had associated with Wojick, so he had no guarantee that the agent wouldn't alter his pattern today. Finally, the man came into view. It was dusk. Donofrio would have preferred it to be full-on dark, but he didn't have the luxury to wait for a better opportunity. From his hiding place across the street, he let the agent pass. Before Wojick got to an alleyway entrance, Donofrio ran up behind him, snatched the fedora off his head, and disappeared into the alley. After a brief second of surprise, Wojick was in pursuit. Donofrio would always savor the look of shock on his one-time friend's face as he suddenly spun to confront the agent. The last sentence he would ever utter in this lifetime would be a short one, "Doni?" Donofrio had his pistol ready. The .38 caliber revolver suddenly seemed very small when compared to the bulk of the agent. This was the frightening part because it put him in such close proximity to the much bigger man. The agent slid to a stop as Donofrio placed the barrel of the gun to his face and pulled the trigger. Wojick had literally run into his own demise. Donofrio by luck had discharged the single shot directly into Wojick's left eye. The bullet as it was designed to do, broke into fragments. The hot shards ricocheted around within Wojick's skull. Stanley Wojick, who was never thought to be particularly bright, had a much lower IQ after the bullet was done with its work. It was over in a second as the giant agent toppled. He was dead before he hit the ground.

Donofrio emptied the wallet and dropped the fedora onto the inert heap at his feet. Before leaving, he whispered, "Goodbye Stan, we'll always be friends."

Captain Rush next went to dispatch. He put out an all-points bulletin with the warning that Officer Donofrio was armed and dangerous. He sent two squad cars to watch the fugitive's apartment. He was worried about Helen to such a degree that he assigned a car to watch her place in case her son should show up.

Back in his office, he closed the door and dialed Helen's number. It sounded like he had woken her up. He loved the sound of her voice in the morning. His intention in calling was to tell her the truth about her son and to warn her. He was afraid that Donofrio would show up for one of two reasons. He would either be seeking sanctuary, or his intention would be to harm Helen. Now hearing her voice, he couldn't bring himself to do it. Instead, he said that he just wanted to call to say good morning. He apologized for the earliness of the hour, saying he had started work so early that he didn't realize the time.

"I can't think of a better way to be woken up," she said. She used the opportunity to invite him to dinner.

He agreed on the condition that he would bring dinner with him that evening. If she was to cook, she might need to go to the market, and he didn't want her out on the streets. Not while her son was on the loose.

Donofrio may not have had a lot of time to plan, but he planned well enough. He had taken what he needed from the apartment assuming that he might never return. Luck is on his side as he is only several houses away when he sees two squad cars slowly cruise down his street. Hiding in shadows at the end of his block, he sees the two-squads come to a stop in front of his building. One uniform stations himself out on the street. A second uniform heads down the gangway. His assignment is to watch the alley. Two other cops climb the stairs heading for his abandoned apartment. That's OK, there's nothing of value or anything incriminating left in the apartment.

"Are you trying to get caught?" asks a spectral voice from over his shoulder.

Donofrio is rarely alone anymore. He is OK with this arrangement as his father has given him good advice. He takes that advice now as he slips around the corner and puts distance between himself and his compromised apartment.

He knows it's not smart. His father tells him he's a fool for even thinking about it, but he wants to see for himself. Keeping to the alleys, he slowly makes his way to his mothers. He has a score to settle there as well. If it wasn't for her, things would not be this screwed up now. Donofrio waited and watched. Maybe it was safe. Maybe they wouldn't send a squad to watch his mother's place.

Just as he was convinced that it was OK, here came the police cruiser. He watched as it glided to a stop several houses down from his mother's. There were two uniforms in the car. Neither of the men exited the vehicle. Donofrio watched them as they watched the house. He found it strange that they had parked down the street. He also found it strange that they stayed in the car. He thought about sneaking around the back. He weighed the odds. Too risky. In his ear he hears, 'Go. Now'.

Reports started to filter in and by mid-morning there was little doubt in Rush's mind as to what he was up against. The empty locker and hastily vacated apartment told him he had a fugitive cop loose in the city. He knew there would be no reason for him to go back to his apartment. Going to his mother's place wasn't an option as Rush would make sure Helen had round-the-clock surveillance. There were a thousand places for the cop to hole-up in Chicago. Rush asked himself if he thought Donofrio would remain in the city. He had little to go on besides a hunch but was convinced the cop wouldn't leave Chicago. He knew the city, which would give him an advantage over being in unfamiliar territory. He now had an idea of where Donofrio wouldn't go or couldn't go, but none of that helped to answer the prevailing question of where he would go. Friends? His fellow officers had been questioned, and none claimed to be friends with the strange and often moody cop. None could recall a time when they heard Donofrio talk about friends that he had outside of the job. Girlfriends? One of the cops mentioned that Donofrio had spoken about a girl named Mary. It was little to go on as Donofrio had mentioned one day that his girlfriend Mary was angry at him. Donofrio had gone on to tell the cop an odd story that resulted in this Mary *accidently* ending up with a black eye. The cop recalled also how Donofrio had finished by saying, "She better watch that attitude, or next time it's going to be a lot more than just a black-eye." Just having the name Mary wasn't much to go on.

That night at dinner, Ben would dance around the question of friends and girlfriends with Helen. No, Michael Angelo was a quiet and introverted boy who hadn't made friends easily. Even if he had friends, it would not have been a good idea to bring them home as his father was unpredictable and volatile.

Helen had hopes that her son would meet a nice girl. She had always felt that would help to ease some of the pain the boy had been exposed to growing up. "If he treated a girl as nicely as he treats his mother, he would have made a wonderful husband," claimed Helen.

"He's a nice looking boy. You would think he might have had at least one girlfriend," mentioned Rush.

No, he hadn't, replied Helen regrettably. There was no mention of anyone named Mary.

# Chapter Fifty-Two

It was time to go. Reilly bent and kissed Hope's forehead. It felt warm. She never stirred; such was the depth of her sleep.

"I love you," he whispered.

Next, he found Sissy in the kitchen. They held each other as tightly as they could. She had made a plea that morning asking him to just not show up. She said nothing now. She cradled his face and kissed him gently on the lips.

Repeating his words to Hope from a moment ago, he said, "I love you."

His father sat on the steps. He knew where his son was headed as he had seen the poster displayed in his barber shop. He had told Reilly that he was going with him. His reason was, *'In case there's trouble, I'll be there to help'*. Reilly looked at his father and smiled. He was struck, not for the first time, of the resemblances between his father and grandfather. The two had been cut from the same cloth; cast from the same die. Reilly thanked him but declined the offer as having him there would mean there was one more thing to worry about.

"Dad, I got plenty to worry about already without having you there."

His father understood. The two men embraced, gently at first but then with more intensity.

"You best come back in one piece, son. That little girl in there needs her daddy." With a slight quiver in his voice, he finished with, "We all need you."

"You worry like an old woman," said the big Russian. "You watch. You gonna see what I do to that black bastard. I'm gonna kill the sonofabitch."

"Vladimir, you don't want to listen to me this whole time. Please listen to me now. That man, he can fight," said Pietir. This was not the first time he had tried to have this conversation. A trainer walked a fine line with his boxer. He needs his fighter to be confident. Confidence could be gained in a variety of ways. Training hard and being prepared for your opponent built confidence. Petrova resolutely refused to make that commitment to train over the last month. Pietir knew his mindset. If he trained, it would be giving the Negro a credibility he did not deserve. The Russian had reinvented the events of that night to suit his own ego. The black man had cowardly snuck into the ring and ambushed him.

Winning begets confidence, and Petrova won all the time. The Russian believed this was due to his superior skill. The truth was that his opponents were inferior. On the rare occasion that a legitimate opponent should appear, Petrova had no compunction to either fight dirty or to cheat.

A mirror leaned up against the wall of the small room where the men prepared for battle. Pietir disgustedly watched his fighter as Petrova looked at himself in the mirror. Pietir did not know the story of Narcissus, but if he did, he would have seen the connection between the ancient Greek and the vain fighter before him. Petrova loved that mirror and the image it reflected. Pietir would tell him that if he spent as much time training as he did looking at himself, he would be better off. Petrova would laugh, too distracted by his own beauty to hear much of what his trainer had to say.

Reilly arrived at the gym mid-afternoon, which was never the busiest of times. Today, it was deserted and strangely quiet when he walked in as Andre had closed the gym at noon. It was still several hours before the fight was scheduled to begin, but Montero was going to use every moment available to get his fighter ready. They began with a weigh-in. Reilly had gained seven-pounds, which was shy of the goal of ten pounds, but Andre was more than pleased with the extra weight. Not only that, it looked like all muscle. Andre had a light workout scheduled for this final day. The two friends spent most of their time in the ring. Together, they went over strategies one more time. Andre, playing the role of Petrova, would come at Reilly in slow motion offering commentary the entire time. Montero had gone back to the arena one night with Angel to watch Petrova. As neither one trusted the gangster, they wanted to make sure the flaws in Petrova's technique that Octaviano shared with them were true. They were. There was little doubt, in a fair fight, a boxer of Angel's size and ability could pick the Russian apart. Reilly's skills were on a par with Angel's, maybe even a little better. That would help. The real concern was the size difference. Thirty or Twenty-five pounds was a lot of weight to give up to an opponent. The night they went to watch Petrova, he was paired against a decent fighter. Andre and Angel watched this fighter land several solid punches to the Russian's head and midsection. The blows had little effect on Petrova. Octaviano had warned them that the, *'Russian had a head like a cinder block'*, and that seemed to be the case. The fight that night ended when Petrova landed a decent punch to the side of his opponent's head. The man crumpled, and Montero suspected it was the brass knuckles that had done the man in.

The time to leave was upon them. Montero had even planned this out precisely with what time to leave, when to arrive, pre-fight rub down, and last minute instructions all scheduled. They killed the lights from the back of the gym and made their way to the front door. As they approached the main gym area, they could see multiple silhouettes backlit against the gym's front window. Reilly dropped his gym bag in order to have both hands free. Andre grabbed a ten-pound dumbbell; the closest thing at hand that might substitute as a weapon. The two approached cautiously.

"What do you want?" demanded Montero.

"We're here for Thorn," came the response.

The voice, Andre knew the voice.

"Angel?" he asked.

Angel Vasquez replied, "And a host of others."

From the group came other comments.

"Hey Reilly, did you think I was gonna miss this?" said Frankie Zucco, a middle weight who had trained at *Al's* for years.

A big eastern European with an unpronounceable name, chimed in. "We going to help you keep an eye on that Russian. You can't never trust no Russian." His name looked like an eyechart. There were few vowels in his first or last name. They called him 'Larry', which he seemed OK with. He was Angel's regular sparring partner.

Sean Barry was amongst them. Sean had come to the gym years ago. He was a drunk who had let the booze ruin his life. His wife had left him. He lost his job. Sean would have two beers and then want to fight everyone in the place. *Al's* had given him a place to vent that anger. Uppercut had introduced him to the True Cross. "You got Jesus in your corner tonight," Sean told Reilly.

Several of the men gave an Amen.

Sam 'Skinny-Boy' Wade, an ex-con turned welterweight, was also there to show his support. Wade credited Uppercut and Andre for putting him on the path to righteousness.

Jake Jacobs, a WWI veteran, said nothing. Jacobs had said little in over ten years at the gym. He was one of many who had come back badly damaged from the trenches in France. *Al's* was the closest thing Jake had to a family. He never explained, and no one ever asked about the jagged scars that ran across both wrists.

And then there was Leo Frankowicz. It took Reilly a moment to recognize why the overweight fighter looked different. He realized it was because it was one of the few times, outside of the ring, that Leo wasn't eating something. "Hey Reilly, I hope you give that stupid Pollack what he has coming."

"He's Russian," said Larry, sounding a bit put off.

"Russian, Pollack, it's all the same thing."

"Leo, you're an idiot."

Several, including Reilly and Andre, laughed at the exchange. Even Leo and 'Larry' chuckled along.

Angel spoke for the group. "We're getting there early, and we're sitting ringside. Larry's right, you can't trust the Russian. Hopefully, if anything goes haywire, we'll be able to help."

The men came up one at a time and pumped Reilly's hand. Each offered a word of encouragement. Before heading out onto the street, Leo managed to lighten the mood by asking, "Do you believe we might have time to stop for something to eat on the way?"

A second contingent was also gathering and making preparations to attend. Dominic Augustino, still feeling he was responsible for getting Reilly into this mess, wanted to do something proactive to help his fellow police officer. Not knowing who to turn to, he contacted Tommy McMahon. McMahon, Reilly's mentor from his academy days, listened as Augustino told of the events leading up to the fight. McMahon then surprised the young officer by saying that he already had plans on being in attendance that night.

Gregory Maloney had seen the notices advertising the fight early on. There was a good reason for this. Maloney was a fight fan. He was often in attendance on a weekend at the warehouse turned arena. He had seen Petrova fight numerous times. Maloney had heard the rants of the big man as he stomped around the ring demanding satisfaction from the black man that had attacked him. Maloney hadn't been there on the night Thorn stepped into the ring, so he never made the connection between this mystery interloper and his one-time academy cadet. When he saw the placard advertising the fight, he recognized the name, *Reilly Thorn*. Maloney remembered Thorn very well. He remembered the afternoon that the class had coerced him into a fight with the young black man. He had thought often over the years of how Reilly had taken a dive.

Maloney, examining the notice, couldn't imagine the circumstances that had delivered Thorn to this fate. Maloney was still close friends with Tommy McMahon, and there were times over the years when McMahon would mention Reilly. He always had good things to say about his one-time protégé. McMahon believed that Thorn would have climbed the police ranks if not for being a black man in a white dominated world. Tommy McMahon had sponsored many young men, and Maloney had oftentimes been their instructor. Tommy had a 'good-eye' for finding young men who would excel in the academy and go on to be exceptional police officers. In Maloney's opinion, this was never more true than with Reilly Thorn.

Upon learning of the fight, Gregory Maloney immediately went to McMahon. McMahon spoke of the medical problems in the Thorn household. His assumption was Reilly needed the money. Both men had donated to the cause when the department had 'passed-the-hat' to help Hope.

"I get that part," Maloney told his old friend, "but there's more to it than that." He went on to tell McMahon of the death threats Petrova was making. "He promises to beat Thorn to death." Maloney considered the Russian unbeatable. He had seen him destroy each of his opponents. He told McMahon of Petrova's size and strength. When McMahon questioned him as to why, Maloney told him of how Thorn had ambushed Petrova one night in the ring.

McMahon had sought out Reilly the week before the fight. As Reilly left the station house, Tommy fell into step next to him. "So tell me Officer Thorn, do you have anything of interest planned for this weekend?" Reilly stopped and looked at his friend and mentor. Tommy was smiling, but there was no doubt as to the concern he saw behind his smile. Reilly took the time to tell Tommy the whole story. He felt he owed it to the man who had done so much to help him and his family.

"The story I heard was you ambushed this man. I knew that couldn't be true." Tommy ended by saying, "I'll pray for your deliverance, and I'll pray for your safety. We all pray this will help to cure Hope." Reilly didn't reply, and Tommy didn't fully understand the aggrieved look that crossed the young man's face.

Johnnie Octaviano as promised visited Petrova before the fight. He was there to check his gloves. Again, he took the sage precaution of bringing his henchmen with him. The gloves were clean. No brass knuckles; no buckshot sewn into the lining. The glove's padding had not been removed. The Russian's size always took Octaviano by surprise. The man was one incredible physical presence. He had walked in confident that Thorn could carry the day, but now, looking at the massive neck and chest and arms, he wondered if he had placed his bet on the wrong guy. The more over-confident Petrova was, the better the chance Thorn had.

Octaviano fed the big man's already inflated ego, "I spoke to Thorn. He wants you to know he has a wife and child at home."

"He's going to have a widow and an orphan at home when I get done with him."

"I'm just the messenger here," said Octaviano. "He asked if you might take it easy on him, so I'm asking. What you do next is your business."

"He's scared, huh? That's good, he should be scared."

Johnnie, satisfied that the gloves hadn't been tampered with, took the precaution of waiting while Petrova's hands were taped and the gloves affixed. He wasn't a fool. He left one of his two associates with the Russian and the trainer. "Don't let this guy out of your sight," he told the man. "Those gloves don't come off again for any reason. He don't even go to the bathroom by himself. You got that?"

Petrova sat on the table and looked at his hands. He would have liked to feel the weight of the buckshot and the security of the brass knuckles, but that wasn't going to happen tonight. He looked at the gangster and thought about offering the man money to turn his back while he doctored his gloves. He chose against this for two reasons. His ego wouldn't allow him to do it, and secondly, he correctly assumed the man would not be foolish enough to disobey Octaviano's orders.

Pietir, sensing the turmoil his man was feeling, spoke to his fighter. "You don't need any of that stuff. You are strong. You go out there and be smart, and you'll be fine." The two men spoke in their native Russian. Pietir's words became more passionate. His fighter, who had always been too overconfident, now needed his confidence bolstered.

"Maybe I should have listened to you. You told me the shine could fight. I wouldn't listen. Tell me the truth; do you think Thorn is scared like the Costa Nostra said?"

The slight pause answered the question for the fighter. Seeing this, Pietir simply said, "No, he is not afraid."

Pietir had spent time over the last month finding out more about their opponent. Thorn had learned boxing as a youngster. He was a cop who had stayed with the sport as a way to stay in shape. The family was now in some kind of financial mess, and the cop was using this match to save the family from financial ruin. Octaviano had told a partial truth when he said the Thorns had money problems. The issues had nothing to with drinking and gambling as the Russian pair had been told. Thorn's daughter was sick. A man who is fighting to save his daughter fears only one thing; losing his loved one.

"No, he is not afraid," Pietir repeated, "but he should be. You are Vladimir Petrova, the strongest man in the world." He took the big man by the shoulders and stared intently into his eyes.

"Who are you?" asked the trainer.

"What?"

"Who are you?" repeated the trainer as he shook his shoulders.

"I am Vladimir Petrova."

"NO! You are the Bruiser. The man who crushes his opponents!" he shouted.

Petrova smiled broadly.

"And what does Bruiser want?" came the follow-up question.

"The shine, I want that goddamn shine."

"Who do you want?"

"I WANT THE SHINE!"

"And what does the Bruiser do to him when he gets him?"

"I will kill the man. I will beat him to death!" Saying this, he jumped off the table and slammed a fist into the lone locker in the room. The metal crumpled like tin foil as he unleashed a series of blows. When he was done he stepped back, breathing heavily, and looked at the destruction he had created. A sick smile crept across his face.

This was the look Pietir was waiting for. His fighter was ready.

The soldier Octaviano had stationed in the room was a big man who prided himself in his fearlessness. Petrova's outburst had unnerved him. He slowly took his hand away from the gun that hung at his side. He took in the Russian monster before him and the ruined remains of the locker. Like his boss, he had bet on Thorn. Also like his boss, he was now questioning the wisdom of that bet.

Reilly in his staging area had stood mere feet away from Petrova and listened to the carnage coming through the thin wall. It sounded like the Russian had gone berserk and took out his insanity on a locker.

"He must have really hated that locker," said Andre as he continued to rub petroleum jelly onto Reilly's temples and face. Montero was pleased to see Reilly smile slightly at the quip.

The walk to the ring seemed long. The place was packed, and Montero and Thorn had to shoulder their way through the masses. Octaviano had the foresight to station several men around the trainer and his boxer. They helped clear a path. One over excited fan was treated to a blackjack to the side of his head when he tried to lay his hands on Reilly. The man crumpled to the floor as the peculiar procession passed by. The noise is deafening as taunts and jeers rain down upon the duo. The first part of the journey is over, and the two men are now climbing into the ring.

# Chapter Fifty-Three

From the police captain's tone on the phone he anticipated bad news. This premonition seemed even more likely when Wojick hadn't shown up for work that morning. A short time later, Rush is sitting across the desk from Agent Wroblonski. The captain gave him the news that his longtime partner was dead. Wroblonski knew that Donofrio was involved as soon as he heard. Rush went on to validate what the federal agent already suspected. He told the agent of Donofrio's visit to his mother and how her son had placed the blame for his father's death solely on Wojick.

Wroblonski knew the senior Donofrio had died violently. Everything else he was hearing was a revelation.

"According to the widow, her son tried to stop Wojick from committing the crime. I don't believe that. I believe Donofrio orchestrated the whole thing," Rush claimed. He went on to say that there was no doubt that Wojick was in the alley the night the senior Donofrio had been murdered. He told him of the results of the ballistics test. Wroblonski was about to ask how they managed to test for Wojick's gun but recalled the afternoon they had ended up at the gun range with the captain. Rush was smart, there was little doubt of that.

Wroblonski thought about his partner. He knew Wojick wasn't too bright but never realized he could be this stupid. The agent thought about the date of the Donofrio murder and realized it was around the same time that Wojick returned to the fold, with hat in hand, promising to behave himself. He had been a real Boy Scout ever since.

"It appears Donofrio managed to get his hands on the ballistics report. He knew we had a positive match on Wojick's gun. He also knew that his service revolver had been eliminated as a crime weapon. He figured that we would bring Stan in and that Stan would talk."

Wroblonski nodded his agreement. He wondered at the planning Donofrio had put into the execution of his father. He had underestimated the little weasel.

"He's gone underground. He's cleaned out his locker at work, and his apartment has been vacated. We have his mother's place under 24-hour surveillance. Beyond that, we know little else beside the belief that he is seriously delusional. We have an armed, dangerous, and insane cop loose in the city and have no idea where he is or where he's headed."

"Friends?" asked the agent.

"None that we know of, it seems Wojick might have been his only friend ever," answered Rush. "The only name that surfaced was a woman named Mary. Donofrio mentioned her to a fellow officer. If she was a girlfriend, he never told his mother about her."

Mary? Why did that name sound so familiar? Wroblonski believed he knew.

"Anything that you might add would help," said Rush.

Wroblonski answered that he knew Wojick and Donofrio had become friends for a short time. "It was just the two of them as far as I knew. That relationship was never going to be good for a guy like Stan. He was too easily influenced; too easy to lead astray. I knew those two were getting into some wild times out there but never thought it would end like this."

Rush, before leaving offered his condolences for the loss of the man's partner. "If you think of anything, anything at all, please let us know."

Mary. He knew Mary. The pieces had fallen into place before Rush left, but he chose to say nothing. He not only knew Mary, he knew where to find her. Girlfriend? Wroblonski didn't think so. Was Donofrio so crazy as to believe the hooker he had once beaten so badly was his one-time girlfriend? Rising, he checked his sidearm, a 58 caliber Police Positive Special Revolver with a four-inch barrel, just like the gun Wojick carried. He was armed and ready when he left the small office. The difference between his departure and the police captains from a moment ago was that Wroblonski had a destination in mind. It might be a long shot, but that's what a cop did; chase down all leads.

On the way, he thought about Mary. He had a vague recollection of meeting her one afternoon at *Augie's*. The memories of what occurred after her beating at the hands of Donofrio were much more vivid. Octaviano had dragged Wroblonski into it as Stan had played a role in Donofrio's plan to get the girl alone. He knew that Wojick eventually made an apology to Mary. There were several mornings that Stan had mentioned that he spent the night with Mary.

Donofrio hid at the entrance to the alley. It is late afternoon, perhaps early evening. He watched as the long shadows blended with the dusk before finally giving way to the night. He missed Mary. She was the one girl who seemed to understand him. He couldn't quite remember where things had gone wrong. He nodded as a spectral voice whispered, *'Your mother'*. They had seemed so perfect together. He knew Mary still loved him. After making things right with Mary, he'd square the books with the old lady. He knew that Rush had been sniffing around the poor grieving widow.  He added his captain to the list of those who would feel his wrath.

*'You have miles to go before you sleep',* came a subsequent thought. Where had he heard that line before? He wasn't sure if this was his inner-voice or some other. He was having more and more trouble distinguishing his thoughts from others.

Sleep? He hadn't had much in what seemed like a long time. He was exhausted and had actually nodded off several times in his little hidey-hole amongst the trash barrels. He woke from his last nap and nearly cried out as a rat walked up his arm towards his face. *'Has the entire universe conspired against me?'* he thought.

He had been hunkered down in the alley for hours. People poured into the bar through most of the afternoon. Donofrio would hear a cacophony of noise spill down the alleyway each time the door opened to admit a patron. *Augie's* seemed to be doing a great business. That wasn't going to work well with his plans. Suddenly, there was a huge commotion as the door opened and a multitude of people spilled into the alley. A caravan of cars and cabs pulled up as people got in and drove off. Many of the patrons, heading for the street, walked past his hiding place. Laughing, they started a chant of *fight-fight-fight.*

What could this all mean? Through the fog, Donofrio slowly puzzled together the pieces. The fight, of course, this was the night of the big fight. He remembered seeing the notice. Thorn was going to get what was coming to him tonight. He would have loved to see that happen. He hated Thorn for the way the other cops treated him. They were nicer to some black cop than they were to him. He actually thought of abandoning his plan and instead head to the boxing arena. He remembered seeing the poster for the first time. He was excited by the idea of going to Stan with plans to fix the fight. They'd make a fortune, but more importantly, it would square things between the two of them. They'd be friends again. He recalled buying a ticket for the event. He wondered if he still had it.

No, no, no, he had a plan, and he had to stick to it. He wondered if anyone was still in the bar as the activity from a moment ago had ended as quickly as it had started. All was quiet now.

He had just made his decision to approach the door when a familiar form appeared in the alley. Special Agent Wroblonski, what was he doing here? He almost expected to see Stan with him. He shook that thought away. Stan was dead. He did remember that even though he couldn't quite recall the circumstances. It made him sad. Stan was his friend.

Donofrio didn't have much of a plan. He would trust his instincts. As the agent passed, he moved quickly behind him and placed the barrel of the gun against the man's back. He ordered him to stop.

"What do you want?" he asked the deranged cop.

"Mary, I'm here to see Mary." Saying this, he demanded the agent's gun.

Wroblonski knew to choose his words carefully. Rush had told him that his rogue cop was insane. Wroblonski didn't need to be told. He had figured that out on his own a while ago. "I'm just stopping in for a beer. What do you say I buy one for you, too?"

Donofrio hadn't expected this. He knew Wroblonski didn't like him. He resented the fact that he and Stan were such good friends. He almost asked him where Stan was and then remembered; Stan was dead. Did Wroblonski know Wojick was dead? "You're going to tap on the door. No funny business. I'll be right behind you."

The doorman was surprised to hear the knock at the door. The entire bar was empty with the exception of Augie and Mary. Octaviano had rounded up all of the girls except Mary to work the fight tonight. Johnnie knew that much testosterone would give rise to other cravings. That's what Johnnie did. He figured out what people demanded and then supplied it to them. Johnnie was going for the trifecta tonight; booze, broads and boxing.

The small window slid open. The gangster manning the door recognized the Special Agent. He threw the bolt and turned the knob. The door burst inward, throwing the man against the wall. The last earthly thought he had was that it was a raid. Donofrio thrust his gun into the man's throat and squeezed off two quick shots. Like his predecessor Guido Santori, he slid down the wall. Guido had died almost immediately upon being blasted with a shot gun. This man was still gurgling and clutching his throat as he came to rest against the floor.

Donofrio ignored the dying man as he jammed the gun again into Wroblonski's back. He slammed the door shut, throwing the bolt. He shoved the agent roughly towards the bar. Augie and Mary stood in shocked silence.

It had all happened so fast. They looked at Donofrio as if seeing him for the first time. He looked ...deranged.

"Hi Mary," Donofrio said. He attempted a smile. "I've missed you, baby."

# Chapter Fifty-Four

Reilly Thorn, standing in the corner of the ring, is bathed in noise and light. The scene is overpowering. Reilly cannot see to the distant recesses of the arena as the lights over the ring only illuminate the venue to a certain depth. He doesn't need to see the far corners as he senses correctly that every square inch of the place is packed. He is able to make out individual random comments from the crowd. There doesn't seem to be a lot of Reilly Thorn fans in attendance this evening as the comments he can hear all contain the word *nigger*. Reilly breathes deeply and evenly, in and out, as he tries to calm himself. He is struggling to stay focused. He is seeking his center.

One overzealous fan tries to climb into Reilly's corner. Before Octaviano's men can make a move to stop him, Angel Vasquez slams a giant paw into his back. He pushes him forward so his face is smashed into the corner post. The man comes away bloody. Vasquez throws him back into the masses.

The crowd roars.

Andre had anticipated that this might be overwhelming for his boxer. He only has a moment to say what needs to be said before Petrova arrives. The only way to be heard over the din of the crowd is to shout directly into Reilly's ear. He begins, "Use it Reilly. You use every taunt and every slur. You hear me. Each time you hear the word 'nigger' tonight, you use that. Every time you hear them chant Bruiser, you use that. Do you understand what I'm saying? You know what they want. They want to see some nigger nobody be beaten senseless tonight. They want to see you beaten and beaten bad, but you ain't going to give them that. You're going to give them something they didn't expect. You're going to give them Reilly Thorn, and when they get a little Reilly Thorn, they're going to want more, a whole lot more."

Reilly remembered the night of his first Golden Gloves bout. The words Andre spoke were similar to what Uppercut had said to him so many years ago. The thought of Uppercut was comforting to him.

Montero and Thorn, without looking, correctly assumed that Petrova was entering the arena as the noise, already loud, gained in amplitude.

"He's here," shouted Andre into his fighter's ear. "Are you ready?"
"Yes."
"Are you ready?" he shouted again.

"Yes!" Reilly shouted back.

Montero stepped back from his fighter and looked at him. He liked what he saw in Reilly's face. He had sparred with his friend enough times over the years to know when Reilly was ready. Reilly was ready. He knew he would never be heard so he simply mouthed the words, "You can do this."

Reilly uses these seconds to shadow box in his corner. He looks at the faces in his corner. It is comforting to see Angel and Leo and the others sitting ringside. He has a second surprise when he sees Tommy McMahon in the row behind his gym mates. With Tommy are Greg Maloney and Dominic Augustino. Reilly is surprised but glad to see them there. He smiles and gives a slight nod at this modest entourage. They are so few amongst so many.

Petrova is now in his corner. This is his moment, the moment he loves the best. He struts around the ring and poses. He flexes his massive muscles. The crowd eats it up. A spontaneous chant of 'Bruiser-Bruiser-Bruiser' threatens to bring down the warehouse. He grabs the turnbuckle and jumps onto the first rope giving his fans a better view of the man they have come to adore.

Reilly stoically waits in his corner. He looks over Andre's shoulder at his opponent as his trainer works the last of the petroleum jelly onto his face. Andre has drilled one important lesson into Reilly over and over again for the past month. *Never take your eyes off the Russian.*

Petrova now looks at Reilly's corner as if surprised to see his opponent standing there. He points a gloved fist at Thorn and stares. The crowd takes up the 'Bruiser' chant again. It's even louder this time. Bruiser now looks back to the crowd. He thrusts both fists to the heavens and unleashes a roar.

The ring announcer tried vainly to be heard over the crowd. That was OK. The crowd knew who was fighting. When he gestured towards Reilly, the entire arena erupted into boos and heckles. Petrova's introduction is met with raucous cheering. The two men are now at the center of the ring. The referee is giving instructions. When he gestures for both men to touch gloves, neither man responds. Reilly remembered all too well how the Russian had used that opportunity to cold-cock Leo.

The ref points them to their respective corners telling them to wait for the bell. As Reilly turns towards his corner, Petrova spins and approaches Reilly's unprotected back...

# Chapter Fifty-Five

After turning off the lights in the bar, Donofrio corralled the three into the back rooms. This had worked out better than he expected. Now, anyone who came by would think that *Augie's*, because of the big fight, was closed for the night and move on. He kept the gun trained on the Special Agent the entire time with the warning to both Augustino and Mary to not make any sudden movements. The warning was really for Augie alone as he had no doubt that his Mary could be trusted.

The look of love and longing on her face told him that she had missed him as well.

The cop patted down the agent and found his handcuffs. In the warehouse, he used these along with his own cuffs to secure both men to a corner of a large storage rack. Donofrio examined his work. The men had their backs to one another with limited movement.

The same voice that had advised him for months, now quietly suggested, "Kill 'em all."

Donofrio, replying to something that only he heard, mumbled out a reply to someone only he could see, "No, not my Mary."

A question only he can hear is asked, and to this he replies, "These two? Yes, OK." And with that, he pulls out his revolver and presses it into Wroblonski's temple.

"No, wait," begs Mary.

Donofrio turns his attention and the gun towards Mary. He looks at her as if seeing her standing there for the first time.

She chokes back a gasp. Donofrio, if it's even possible, looks even more unstable than he did a moment ago. Mary knows she needs to choose her words carefully or today could end very badly for the three of them. "It's been a while. The least you could do is buy a girl a drink." Mustering every bit of courage she has, she turns and begins walking back towards the bar. "Ain't ya coming?" she asks teasingly over her shoulder.

There's his old Mary. He gives the cuffs a quick check. "You boys help yourself to a drink, too," he says with a laugh. "Don't worry, I'll be back."

"Can you move at all?" whispers Wroblonski.

"A little. We have to get out of here. He's going to hurt Mary."

"I keep my handcuff key at the end of my watch fob."

Pocket watches went out of style after World War I with the introduction of the wrist watch. Wroblonski wore a wrist watch but still liked the look of the gold chain against his vest. He no longer kept a pocket watch at the end of the fob, opting instead to attach several keys, including his handcuff keys, to the end of the chain.

"I'm going to turn towards you as much as I can. OK, how far can you move your hands?" Augustino reached as far as he could but was still short of reaching the chain. "C'mon Augie, reach."

Still too far. Both men rearrange themselves and try again.

"I touched the chain," whispers Augie excitedly.

"OK, we go again."

This time Augie is able to pinch the chain and tug it slightly before it slips out of his fingers.

"Again," says Wroblonski, trying to steady his own voice.

This time it is easier to get to the chain. Augie is able to give it a good tug, but it is lodged in the small vest pocket. Wroblonski is powerless to help. He can only encourage Augie to keep trying. Augie, now with a better grip, pulls hard. "I'm afraid I may tear the fabric if I pull too hard," says Augie.

"Be my guest, but just get that key."

On the next pull, they hear a slight tearing sound before the keys fly out of the small pocket. If not attached to the chain, they would have flown across the room. The keys rattle, making more noise than they hoped. Each man holds his breath praying the sound won't bring Donofrio. After a second, they continue.

"You're doing great, Augie," encourages the agent. Wroblonski could barely reach the keyhole on the cuffs Augie's wearing. The same was true for Augie's limited reach. The Special Agent is not sure which set of cuffs he's wearing. He begins by reeling in the watch fob. A second later, he is holding the cuff key. "Augie, I've got the key."

"Great, let's get out of here."

Wroblonski bends his fingers and wrist well past the point of pain in an effort to get the key to engage. It was frustrating as he wasn't even sure if he was working on the right set of cuffs. He could only work on Augie's shackles. He would never be able to contort enough to unlock the cuffs that were holding him.

"What's the problem?" asked Augustino. Wroblonski ignored him. He was close. With an effort, he managed to engage the key in the lock. He took a moment. He said a silent prayer. He turned the key.

Nothing.

It wouldn't budge. He was ready to remove the key, but before doing so, he reseated the key and tried one more time.

CLICK!

Augie was free.

# Chapter Fifty-Six

...Reilly Thorn turns towards his corner. He watches Andre's face. When Andre signals ...

One afternoon at the gym, Andre told Reilly that he needed him to be the best cop that he could be for that day's training. He enlisted the aid of Angel Vasquez, and explained, "We are going to go through a dry-run of the fight from the time we enter the ring. We are going to look for any moments where you might be vulnerable."

They walked through Reilly climbing into the ring and waiting for his opponent. "Petrova might charge you as soon as he gets in the ring," Andre observed. Next, Angel climbs through the ropes. "Don't take your eyes off him for a moment," Andre told him for the hundredth time. He followed this up with, "You saw what happened to Leo when he went to touch gloves with the Russian. When the ref signals you to touch gloves, you take a step backwards and be ready to fight."

Andre, playing the role of the ref, went through mock introductions of each fighter. Next, he tells each man to go to his corner and wait for the bell. As soon as Reilly turned his back, they all understood that this could be a golden opportunity for the Russian.

"How about if you just back your way into your corner," asked Montero. They rehearsed this tactic. It would work OK as Reilly would be able to keep his eyes on Petrova.

"It shows weakness," Reilly said, "I don't like it."

The three men pondered this for a moment when Reilly suggested, "Let's bait him."

He stood Andre in position and said, "I'll offer up my back to him, and you'll be my eyes for those few seconds. If he makes a move towards me, you give me a signal."

They decided on a wink. Andre wasn't too keen on the idea, but they practiced it several times, and it started to feel right. There was little doubt that Petrova would unleash his favorite punch; a wild right roundhouse.

... Reilly spins according to the script. Turning, Reilly sees Petrova already in the process of throwing his big right. It was almost as if the Russian had rehearsed along with them. In one fluid motion, Reilly blocks, ducks, and launches a powerful right into the Russian's mid-section. The crowd roars its disapproval. Reilly would have liked to think the boos were for the Russian's cheap-shot but knew their disdain was for him. In the background, the ding of the bell can scarcely be heard.

The battle is on.

The punch Petrova took to the gut hurt the big man. He wasn't used to that. He was Vladimir Petrova, the man who dished out punishment. Petrova straightens up. He examines Reilly from a safe distance. The Russian didn't have much of a plan tonight besides throwing the sucker punch, and now that that failed, he needed to reassess his situation. Petrova wants to charge at this interloper. He wants to fly across the ring and deliver a message written in powerful fists that no one can hurt the Bruiser. Instead, he waits and watches; suddenly very wary.

Reilly too waits. He has found the place he was looking for, the place where everything except his opponent disappeared into the background. Time and movement slowed. Reilly is keenly aware of every infinitesimal detail. It is an eerily quiet place; it is a strangely comforting place.

All of Reilly's preparation has been reaction based. Let Petrova make his move and then counter that move. Reilly is patient, and he is disciplined. He waits, and then waits longer, for Petrova to come to him. The masses are getting impatient. Pietir screams at his fighter to attack even though he doesn't believe it is the best advice to give. Jeers and boos rain down upon the ring along with some debris. Petrova knows that these taunts are for both men. The encouragement from his corner, along with the scorn from the crowd, is enough to stir Petrova into limited action. Bruiser stomps one of his massive feet onto the mat and growls at Thorn. The ring shakes. The crowd cheers. In the past, this was often all it took to take the fight out of an opponent. Those men were not Reilly Thorn, who shows no visible reaction to this ploy. Petrova now appeals to the crowd. He turns away from his opponent and makes gestures towards Thorn. He expects cheers, but his antics bring more contempt. Reilly considers attacking the Russian's prone back. He is embarrassed to have even thought it. Petrova's actions are all calculated to get his opponent to let his guard down. He has slowly closed the distance between himself and Reilly. Suddenly, the big man spins and is ready to attack. He finds that Reilly, anticipating the tactic, is already dancing away from the Russian. His foot work dazzles the crowd. Some cheer while other fans voice their disapproval at the lack of action in the ring. Petrova attempts a boxing stance, but he's not a boxer. Looking at Thorn, that reality comes crashing in on him. He has had enough. He moves cautiously towards Thorn. Reilly backs away, the entire time warily watching Petrova. Petrova, believing Thorn may be moving away out of cowardice, continues to move towards his opponent. Reilly back-pedals. Emboldened, Bruiser makes his move. He unleashes a right, which finds only air. Reilly counters with a solid right jab to the man's face. It's a good, well-delivered punch. Almost immediately blood begins to stream from Petrova's nose. The Russian becomes incensed at the taste of his own blood. Throwing caution to the wind, he charges Reilly.

This was the moment Andre had trained Reilly the hardest on. "Reilly, you know how to box, but he doesn't. You need to be ready to fight, not just box."

Petrova begins throwing wild punches as he bull-rushes Thorn. Reilly covers, moves, and counters. Christ, Petrova is strong as Reilly can feel even the deflected punches and glancing blows. None of the Russian's punches do any real damage. Reilly has countered with several jabs delivered with surgical precision. The two separate. There is now more blood flowing from the Russian's nose. Petrova is surprised and frustrated to see his assault has had little effect. Reilly has been waiting for the next moment. Petrova telegraphs the left hook he is about to throw. Thorn thinks back to what Octaviano had told him during their training session, 'He loves the left hook, but he'll drop his right every time'. Here comes the hook, and just as he was told, the Russian dropped his right hand. It was a punishing mistake as Reilly unloaded his best punch of the round into the side of the Russian's face. It's a shot to the temple, or what some fighters call, 'the on-off switch'. His head snaps to the side as his mouthpiece flies across the ring.

The bell sounds. Round one is in the books.

Another lesson Andre had drilled into Thorn is to not turn towards his corner at the end of a round. Fighters are conditioned to stop fighting at the sound of a bell. It is a Pavlovian response, and as such, it is a difficult habit to break. They both knew Petrova didn't hold himself to any such constraints. Reilly maintains his position, fists at the ready. It's not necessary as Petrova is still shaking off the effect of the last blow. Reilly has never hit anyone that hard in his life. He's surprised, disappointed, and a little impressed that the Russian is still standing. Reilly goes to his corner, but before he does, Angel Vasquez steps into the ring and positions himself between the Russian's corner and Reilly. Another rehearsed move. If the Russian wanted to get to Thorn between rounds, he'd have to go through Angel. There was a big part of Vasquez that hoped Petrova would try it.

Instead, Pietir has to go and get his stunned fighter and lead him back to his corner.

There is a lot of movement between rounds as food and beer vendors descend upon the crowd. Instructor Maloney, who has seen the Russian fight many times, tells Tommy McMahon to follow him as they make their way to Petrova's corner. They discreetly showed their badges to the hood Octaviano had stationed there between rounds. Maloney watches as Pietir removes a small bottle from between the folds of a towel. Maloney knows those ain't smelling salts. Pietir shows Petrova the small vial, and through a haze, the fighter sees and recognizes the bottle. He excitedly nods his approval and offers Pietir his right glove. A powerful hand reaches out and grasps the trainer's wrist as he starts to unscrew the top from the bottle. The men turn. Maloney can feel the bone in the trainer's wrist break as Pietir drops the bottle into the cop's waiting hand. Maloney shows them his badge as he pockets the bottle. Maloney looks around for anything else the Russian may have smuggled in. Satisfied, they make their way back to their seat. Before walking away, Maloney tells the trainer, "You better check on your boy. He don't look too good." Maloney recognizes a concussion when he sees one. Pietir will have a broken wrist as a souvenir of this night. Petrova, who still doesn't have his wits about him, understands enough of what had just happened. He looks crestfallen. There is still a confused, vacant look to his eyes.

The second round is about to begin. Tommy McMahon will find out later that the substance in the bottle is an irritant. A fighter will smear it on his gloves. The idea is to get your opponent into a clutch, and then rub your glove anywhere around the other man's eyes. Just a little was enough to blur your opponent's vision. Maloney was in the stands one night when Petrova had applied so much to the other fighter's eyes that he had almost completely blinded his opponent. That didn't stop the Russian from delivering a brutal beating to the defenseless man. Gregory Maloney had owed Reilly Thorn a debt of gratitude for a long time. Tonight, he repaid that debt. It was a costly sacrifice as he had placed his money on the Russian, and at this point he doubted if he'd made a wise wager.

Reilly, oblivious to Maloney's intervention, listens intently to Andre's instruction. Montero's advice is to stick to the plan as the plan seemed to be working. Montero rubbed jelly around Thorn's face as he spoke. The time between rounds went fast, usually too fast to cover everything that you wanted to do or say.

Andre had said little about Hope during training or before the fight. Now, Andre looked at his old friend and said, "Let's finish this. We have to get you home. Hope's waiting."

Before the bell, Angel leaves the ring, but before he did, he made sure Reilly was standing and ready. It was the changing of the guard. When Reilly stood, the entire venue cheered as one. Montero thought back to what the gangster had told him, 'they only think they love the Russian'.

Petrova, still seated in his corner, heard the cheers. He looked to Pietir for support. "They cheer for the nigger?" he asked.

His trainer told him, "You are Vladimir Petrova, the strongest man in the world." The words had an empty sound to them. "You are the Bruiser, the man who crushes his opponents." What had worked so well in the locker room now had little of the same effect. Petrova unsteadily rises, and when he does, he is greeted by jeers and catcalls. He looked at Reilly Thorn. Both men are privy to a secret that they alone know but others are starting to suspect. This fight is over. Reilly can see it in the Russian's face. He can see it in his bearing. The unbeatable Russian from moments ago, the man who stomped and posed and pandered to the crowd, is now gone. He had seemed a god, a titan; one of the immortals. Now, there was just a man with slumping shoulders. How had he had looked so much bigger a moment ago? He retreats to his corner as Pietir throws a towel into the center of the ring.

The bell tolled, but it went unanswered.

# Chapter Fifty-Seven

Augustino is free. He takes the key and removes his cuffs completely. He tries the key on Wroblonski's cuffs. No luck. The agent figured they wouldn't work but didn't stop the bartender from trying. They had been lucky so far. It would have been luckier if the agent was free instead of Augie. The two men assess their positions. It didn't take long. Augie was free. The agent was not and wasn't going to get free anytime soon.

Having left the agent and Augie in the warehouse, Mary walks to the bar. She prays Donofrio will follow her. She prays he won't. She prays that she does not hear the sound of two gunshots. In the bar, Mary goes behind the bar on the pretext of fixing both of them a drink. She really wants to have the bar as a buffer between her and the cop. It is a small comfort but still a comfort.

Prostitutes arguably know men better than anyone. Their entire livelihood is dependent on understanding what a man wants and then providing it. Mary prides herself in being good at her trade. Within seconds, Mary could predict if a client wanted someone submissive or passive or assertive. Mary knew when to be the lion and when to be the lamb. She understood whether her client wanted the schoolgirl or the schoolmarm.

She looks across the bar at Donofrio and is struck by the knowledge that she has no idea as how to handle this man. She knows he is crazy, crazy enough to think she'd be happy to see him. She senses that he doesn't remember the pain and anguish he has caused her. If he does remember the events, he has reinvented them in gentler terms. She knows how high the stakes are on this night. One wrong word, one misstep and she could be one of three people lying dead in a deserted bar.

"So, what will it be, Officer?" she says with a smile. She hopes her voice doesn't betray the terror she is feeling.

"You know what I like."

She hasn't a clue, but this gives her the opportunity to look around behind the bar. The sawed-off shotgun is still perched under the counter. She knows little about weapons. She suspects that it's loaded, but she also knows weapons have safeties on them. She would have no idea how to disengage the safety. She plays the scenario out in her head. Too many variables, so Mary dismisses it.

What else is there? There are plenty of glasses and whiskey bottles. There is a hefty wrench that she has seen Augie use to open new beer kegs. There is a small paring knife used to cut up garnishes for the drinks.

"How you doing on that drink, sweetheart?"

"Sorry, I'm never back here," she lies, "and Augie doesn't have anything in order."

Donofrio mulls over the statement. He whispers 'Augie' to himself. Suddenly, a look of concern crosses his face. "I better go check on those two," he says as he begins to climb off the barstool.

"Oh, here it is," she says as she grabs a bottle of the best whiskey the bar has to offer. Mary, pretending to have not heard the cop's last statement, continues, "The good stuff. You always did have good taste." Mary fills two tumblers with ice and pours each a generous helping. She wonders about getting Donofrio drunk but doubts if that plan has much of a chance.

"You always understood me, Mary," he says as they clink their glasses together. He stops with the glass halfway to his lips. He looks pained. He shakes his head trying to get his thought straight. He looks directly into Mary's eyes.

What she sees in his eyes terrifies her.

"You don't know what we done," he begins. "Me and Stan. You got no idea. Stan's dead. Don't ask me how I know that, but I know for a fact that he is."

Mary fights the urge to ask more about Stan. The two had spent many wonderful evenings together. It hurt to hear he was gone. She let him continue.

"Sometimes, when you try to help other people, things get all screwed up. Stan and me tried to help my old man, and we did. We helped him a lot but no good came from it. I swear to God things got even more screwed up. How could that be? The funny thing is my father's dead but you know something?" He pauses to look at Mary to see if she knows the answer. "We get along better now than we ever did when he was alive. Isn't that crazy?" he asks with a crazed smile on his face. "He was never there for me before. Like when I was a kid, he was never there for me. I swear he didn't even seem to like me. But now, now that he's gone things are better. It's been good to have him there to talk to these past few months. I think we finally understand one another, maybe for the first time in our lives."

He takes a sip of his whiskey. "Ahh, that's smooth."

"I miss Stan. I'm hoping someday he ...you know like my father, he ...well, you know what I mean ...I'd like that. It would give us a chance to square things between us. The truth is things didn't end on the best terms. That was a shame. It didn't have to be like that."

Mary could only wonder at the odd statements.

And then he sat. He said nothing. His drink went untouched. A moment passed and then another. Mary stood in frozen fear. She dare say nothing. She asked no question nor did she move. She sensed something was building inside Donofrio; something that would make everything up to this point seem somewhat normal. She thought about Augie. She prayed he'd somehow be spared at the end of all this. Mary thought again about what Donofrio had said this evening. She knew his father was dead as Stan had mentioned it. So what did Donofrio mean when he claimed that he and his father still spoke to one another? She shuddered at the depth of his insanity.

He looks directly at Mary. He studies her intently. "Ma?" he says in a voice barely above a whisper. "What? How'd you get...?" He lets the question go unfinished. "It was you, ma." He starts to rise. "Don't try to look all innocent. It was you," and then louder, "Don't pretend that you don't know what the hell I'm talking about. None of this shit needed to happen, but no, that wasn't good enough for you." Donofrio, standing now, raises his weapon. Mary closes her eyes awaiting her fate when from behind, a sound, the sound of a door opening.

"Leave her alone!" screams Augie.

As Donofrio turns, Mary grabs the wrench and slams it with all of her might into the back of the deranged policeman's skull. The sound of the skull fracturing will haunt Mary the rest of her life. He manages to squeeze off one errant shot. It splinters the door frame next to where Augie is standing. The cop collapses into a heap. Augie and Mary approach cautiously. They jump as Donofrio quivers once more. He is now still. Augie kicks the revolver across the floor. They stand over the body. Neither of them breathes. Augie is comforted to see that Mary still has the wrench poised and ready for another strike if needed. It won't be necessary.

Donofrio is dead.

Augie and Mary rifle through his pockets. They find his handcuff keys. Wroblonski is now extricated and examining the scene before him.

"This is Rush."

"I've got Donofrio," said Wroblonski. He told the captain to come alone.

Now on the scene, Rush takes inventory of the situation. He is standing in an illegal drinking establishment with a corrupt Federal Agent and a dead cop. A dead cop who was not only insane but guilty of two murders. Rush had an embarrassing mess on his hands.

"Listen up, all of you," he began.

The banner headline on the Sun-Herald read...

# CITY MOURNS HERO

By B. Rhodes, City Desk Editor

Officer Michael Angelo Donofrio was laid to rest today at Resurrection Cemetery on the outskirts of the city. The funeral procession, which included squad cars, vehicles, and mourners crippled traffic on Archer Avenue as a multitude turned out to say a final farewell to a true Chicago hero.

As reported in yesterday's paper, Donofrio had been assigned to work with federal agents led by Special Agent Theodore Wroblonski. This federal agency was in Chicago to investigate violations of the Volstead Act. They were tightening the net on a major bootlegging operation the night that Donofrio lost his life. Wroblonski, in an interview, reported that they had requested a brave and trustworthy officer from the local police department to help with their investigations. Captain Benjamin Rush immediately volunteered Officer Donofrio, describing him as 'our best man'.

In a possibly related story, Agent Stanley Wojick, who was part of this federal task force, was recently shot to death in an apparent robbery gone wrong. Now, in light of these new circumstances, that investigation is being reopened.

Special Agent Wroblonski has been assigned to investigate the deaths of both Officer Donofrio and Agent Wojick. No one is in custody at this time, and according to Wroblonski, there is little to go on.

*Augie's* closed after the tragic events on the night of the fight, but that was OK as shortly thereafter Prohibition ended with the ratification of the 21st amendment. Prohibition had cost the country billions in a futile effort to enforce these restrictive laws. At the same time, it helped to build a criminal empire that made billions of dollars by breaking these same laws. Augustino went back to owning a small shot and a beer joint where Rose would put out a small buffet at lunchtime. Johnnie, who had a lot of connections in Chicago, helped Augie get one of the first liquor licenses issued in the post-Prohibition world. Augie, who was getting on in years, asked Mary to come work for him. "Give up that life, Mary," he told her. He understood when she thanked him for the offer but said she had chosen her path. Augie was proud of himself for remembering the name of his favorite poem, 'The Road Not Taken', and the poet, Robert Frost. He knew he would not forget it this time, but if he did, that was OK as he knew the gist of it.

Ben Rush was there for Helen through the mourning process. He held her and comforted her as she lamented the death of her only child. She would forever be the 'poor widow', having lost both her husband and son in such violent ways.

For Rush, sacrificing his integrity was a small price to pay when compared to what this woman had endured. After what they both considered an appropriate time, they married. They were happy. Helen had set up a small shrine in their home to honor her hero son. They never spoke of her first husband and rarely spoke of Michael Angelo. There were times Ben would find Helen staring at a picture of her son. She wore the look of a person who is debating whether or not she wanted to ask a question. One question might lead to others. To Rush's relief, the questions went unasked.

# Chapter Fifty-Eight

The crowd sits in stunned silence. Many had lost money tonight, but it was more than just that. They had been promised that the price of their ticket would include carnage and destruction. They had been promised blood. Where was death on this night?

If their fallen hero couldn't deliver on that promise, perhaps their new champion could. Reilly does move towards the Russian's corner. The throng hopes for an assault. From the crowd a new chant begins as they repeat, 'Kill him!' They are disappointed. Petrova stands with his hands on his knees. His mind has been delivered a knockout punch, but his body hasn't received the message yet. Reilly helps Pietir maneuver the hulking figure into his corner and onto the chair. It is an act of kindness that Petrova does not deserve. The few boos from the mob are quickly drowned out by cheers. The chant of Thorn, Thorn, Thorn, started softly but quickly grew in intensity. Soon, the entire venue reverberated with the sound.

The ring announcer intercepts Reilly on his way back to his corner. He takes his wrist and raises it high in the air. The entire venue echoes with the chant of Thorn. Reilly steps over the towel that Pietir had thrown into the middle of the ring. He gives a brief thought to all that the towel represents. He has a fleeting image of standing at Hope's bedside with a towel in hand.

Reilly exits the ring surrounded by gym mates, fellow officers, and the same mob guys who had escorted him in. His exodus is vastly different than his arrival as the crowd now *'Hails their Conquering Hero'*, until such time as a new hero should appear.

Octaviano waits in the changing area for Thorn. He is full of smiles and congratulations for the winner, but Reilly doesn't look like a victor. He looks defeated. There is a melancholia about him that infect the other revelers in the small area. Johnnie is anxious to set up Thorn's next fight. He pictures it being even bigger than this event. Who knows, perhaps a rematch with the Russian? Looking at Thorn at this moment, he can't imagine any scenario where he might get Reilly to climb back through the ropes. He doesn't need to bring up the topic tonight. He will however bring it up, and with no surprise, Reilly will turn him down. He will continue to approach the fighter but in time realizes that Thorn's fighting days are over.

Angel and the rest of the gym members ask if Rellly wants them to hang around. He tells them no, that he'll be fine. He thanks them as each man offers their congratulations. They move on to the betting windows. They had all watched Reilly train and knew his resolve. It was an easy decision to put their money on their friend to win tonight. That was true for all except Leo Frankowicz. He had bet on the Russian.

Tommy McMahon feels the pain of his protégé. A mentor might take too much pleasure in his apprentice's accomplishments and too much responsibility for their failures. Tommy is not sure why this doesn't feel like a victory, but it does not. He looks at Reilly and remembers the brave little boy from decades ago. There is now grey in that boy's hair and the start of wrinkles on his handsome face. He tells him he is proud of him. He doesn't need to as they both know this already. Tommy leaves with Greg Maloney and Dominic Augustino. Dominic, before leaving, says, "Thanks Reilly, from my entire family." He gives Octaviano a knowing look on his way out.

Johnnie tells Reilly he'll square up with him tomorrow. He doesn't think it's such a good idea to have him on the street with that much money. Between the cut of the gate that Andre had negotiated and the sizeable wager Reilly had placed on himself to win the fight, money would not be an issue for the Thorn family for a long time.

Now, it is just Reilly and Andre. The two men say little to one another. Montero wants to congratulate Reilly, but he senses that isn't what his friend wants to hear. Reilly showers and changes, and by the time the two leave the arena, it is all but empty. They say nothing to one another as they walk until it is time for each man to head in a different direction.

As Reilly moves on, Andre calls to him, "You did a good thing tonight, Reilly. Good for the family. Good for Hope."

Reilly makes no reply. He doesn't turn towards his friend as he doesn't want him to see the tears streaming down his face. Instead, he runs.

He runs home.

He wants Sissy.

He needs Hope.

# Afterword

Time helped because time heals. There would never be enough time in a thousand millennia to completely close the wound and fade the scar.

Hope fought. Coursing through her veins was the blood of fierce warriors and fearless hunters from a dark continent. She fought until there was no more fight in her, but in the end, it wasn't a fair fight.

In the end, the disease was too big and too strong and too heartless, and she was but a little girl.

When asked why, their minister answered, "Because sometimes God needs his angels by his side." He could see that the family took little comfort in his words. He asked them to pray and to put their trust in the Lord. The same God who had turned his back on this devout family when they needed him the most.

Life somehow went on for the family. Grandmother continued to work at the laundry even though Reilly told her she didn't need to. Sissy continued to teach and take classes. Both women held onto anything that might help them forget if only for a moment.

Reilly never did climb back through the ropes. While on duty with Dominic Augustino, they were fired upon. A cop needs to be 100% engaged in their work 100% of the time. Reilly wasn't. Still grieving from his loss, he shouldn't have been back on patrol. He made a foolish decision and took a bullet in the hip as a result. It wasn't life threatening, but it left him with a pronounced limp. His days as a cop on the street were over. He took a desk job but wasn't suited for it. Ben Rush helped him get hired on as a security guard in one of the downtown buildings. At dark times, Reilly regretted that the bullet hadn't torn through him. He cursed the Lord for not sending a barrage of bullets that would release him from this world's torment.

He was embarrassed by these thoughts. Sissy still needed him and he needed her. They held onto one another fiercely. They cried until they could cry no more. They mourned until their entire beings ached. Reilly had always been considered the strong one in the family, but he had always known the truth. The real source of the family's strength was to be found in his wife.

Reilly settled into his new role as a security guard. He worked in downtown high-rises for the rest of his life. One day decades later, when Reilly was well into his senior years, he met a little girl by the name of Sharisse. Her mother worked as a cleaning lady in Reilly's building, and she would bring Sharisse with her on days she couldn't find a sitter. The little girl was so reminiscent of Hope. Reilly would eat his dinner with the child as they watched cartoons. She would color him pictures, and he would tell her stories of princesses and magical places. The two formed a strong love for one-another until the day the building hired a new cleaning service. Reilly never even had the chance to say goodbye. Fate brought the two back together when Sharisse was a teenager. Reilly was able to do for Sharisse what he was unable to do for Hope, and he did it gladly.

Grandfather, Hope's Papa, was too old to work. He was never even sought as a day-laborer anymore. He took care of the house. He let the dandelions grow in the yard because Hope had thought they were pretty. He was home every day surrounded by a thousand things to remind him of his little ray of Sunshine. He took on the toughest assignment. No one in the family had stepped foot into Hope's tiny room. On the day she left them, the door had been closed and had remained closed ever since. Days became weeks, and weeks became months and still the room went untouched. Finally, there came a day when Papa quietly and reverently entered the room. He was the only one home. He went in with the intention of gathering up Hope's clothes and donating them to a local charity. Instead, he sat in the rocking chair that he had so lovingly sanded and painted, and he wept. It took time, but little by little he was able to find the strength to carry on. Her few clothes went to a charity with the exception of her frilly pink dress. She had worn it on the train the first time Sissy took her to the clinic. It was her favorite. Papa held the dress to his chest and pictured Hope parading around the house asking everyone if she looked beautiful. She did. The memory brought a smile to his face and tears to his eyes. The dress, along with several other keepsakes that he could not bring himself to part with, was placed to the side. Her tiny bed went to a family in need. They offered Grandfather some money, but he refused. Taking it would have dishonored Hope's memory. When they came for the bed, they asked about the rocking chair. He couldn't bring himself to part with it. Knowing what the family had just endured they understood. The few toys Hope owned were well worn. Papa boxed them up and took them to Provident hospital. He brought them to the nurse's station in the children's section. They knew the Thorn family well as Hope had spent time in their care. Mrs. Fish was not amongst the donated toys. She, above all else, held too many precious memories. Grandfather's work included painting the room as it aggrieved him to look at the soft lilac color. He removed the curtain his wife had sewn for the single small window and replaced it with a shade. No matter what he did, this would always and forever remain Hope's room. Before he finished, he took Mrs. Fish along with the pink dress and arranged them lovingly on the rocking chair in the corner of the tiny room. With a last look, the aged grandfather turned off the light and closed the door.

C. Drnaso 2017

# *Acknowledgements*

If I was to draw a picture or take a photograph or write a poem, it is relatively painless to ask for and receive feedback. Those creations can be absorbed and critiqued quickly. Asking someone to read and comment on a manuscript is an entirely different matter. THORN weighed in at roughly 114,000 words. It took special friends and family to take on this daunting challenge. THANK YOU ALL...

To my sister **Pat Koche**, who has been so enthused and encouraging about my writing right from the beginning. THORN is dedicated to you. It is still not a big enough thank you for all your help and support.

**Dave Karpowicz**, my oldest friend in the world. Thank you for staying by my side through CLEARING and again through this latest effort. Dave is the author of the self-help book, *'Dying Beautifully'*

For my nephew **Richard Koche,** for your help in researching the diagnosis, care, and treatment of childhood leukemia during the 1930s. Richard works tirelessly to find cancer cures at Sloan Kettering in NY. What, it would kill you to call your uncle once in a while?

To my cousins, the avid readers **Jim Chessare** and **Pat Bidinger** who read an early draft. Your feedback greatly influenced the direction of the final product.

Thank you **Ruth Richter,** for your encouragement and feedback. You did double duty by reading both an early version as well as the pre-final version. (Not to mention your gifted proof-reading skills)

To my dear friends, **Lourdes Aguirre** the artist and cellist and **Mike Hock** the writer and artist. I know how much you both have going on in your own life and yet you took the time to read and comment. Thank you for the gifts of art, music, friendship, and licorice.

**Ean Adams**, my friend, the modern day Renaissance man. Your haikus, music, artwork, and photography are so inspirational. Thank you for the tremendous help with both CLEARING and THORN.

To **Bob Morsut**, head of The Kenny Agency. Thank you for your support and your commitment to the disenfranchised writers of the world

**Dave Fedro,** my cousin, the retired cop and golfer. Thank you for helping me understand weaponry and ballistics.

To my enigmatic friend **Mark Grochocinski**. Thank you for your feedback. We never seem to have a bad conversation. That's both precious and rare.

For **Carol Racic**, the water color artist and animal lover. Thank you for the review and encouragement. If everyone was as generous and kind hearted as you, this world would be a utopia.

To **Dave Nies**, acrylic artist, high school friend, and easily the most voracious reader I've ever known. Thank you Dave for your in-depth analysis of CLEARING and again for the well thought out feedback of THORN.

A very special thank you for my cousins **Dan** and **Gloria Yakes** for reading my words, offering your feedback, securing my documents, being so encouraging, and keeping my computer running. (That last one's a biggie)

To the music makers who keep me company as I write. Joni Mitchell, James Taylor, Carly Simon, Cat Stevens, Crosby, Stills, Nash and Young, Miles Davis, Frank and the rest of the crooners, Chet Baker, the Beatles and all those Classical Baroque masters. Your brilliance humbles me.

And finally, to **Marilyn,** my beautiful wife and best friend. Thank you for understanding the commitment I take on when writing a novel. Hopefully this isn't too cliché but you really do complete me.

Made in the USA
Lexington, KY
15 May 2017